Torrens McCullagh Torrens

The Life and Times of the Right Honourable Sir James R. G. Graham

Vol. I

SALZWASSER
VERLAG

Torrens McCullagh Torrens

The Life and Times of the Right Honourable Sir James R. G. Graham

Vol. I

Reprint of the original, first published in 1863.

1st Edition 2022 | ISBN: 978-3-37500-235-0

Verlag (Publisher): Salzwasser Verlag GmbH, Zeilweg 44, 60439 Frankfurt, Deutschland
Vertretungsberechtigt (Authorized to represent): E. Roepke, Zeilweg 44, 60439 Frankfurt, Deutschland
Druck (Print): Books on Demand GmbH, In de Tarpen 42, 22848 Norderstedt, Deutschland

THE LIFE AND TIMES

OF

THE RIGHT HONOURABLE

SIR JAMES R. G. GRAHAM,

BART., G.C.B., M.P.

BY

TORRENS M^{c}CULLAGH TORRENS

IN TWO VOLUMES.

VOL. I.

LONDON

1863.

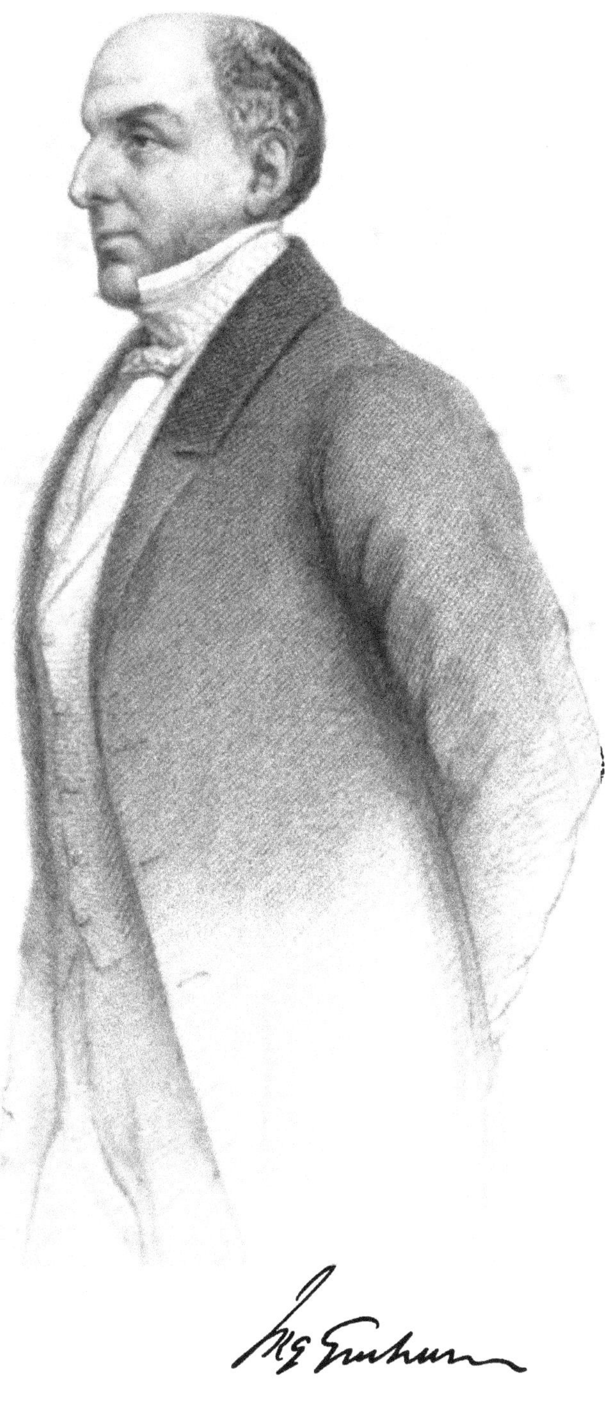

PREFACE.

I HAVE undertaken to write the Life of Sir James Graham, because I think a tribute of respect is due to his great qualities and eminent services as a public man. For this I believe one must trace the story of his life without party fear, favour, or affection, and before the remembrance of the man as he was passes away from the popular mind. If no attempt be made to mark the lingering shadow ere it flies, it will soon have faded, never to be recalled. Twenty or thirty years hence the anatomy of his inmost thoughts and motives may be given to the curious; and historic analysts will no doubt prize the minute details and subordinate considerations, that his official and confidential papers may disclose. Till then such documents are a sealed book,—necessarily and fitly so. But biography is not history, and the effigy in the market-place, whose attitude and features the many are to recognize, must be formed of other stuff than that of which retrospective delineations of statesmanship are made, when the interest of its life-battle is passed, and the generation that witnessed it can recall the accents of its voice no more.

I have long felt that justice was not done, in his life-time, to Sir James Graham. He had been identified in turn with both of the great political parties in the State; and when he broke from each, sooner than surrender his personal convictions, he came in for the usual amount of reproach and denunciation. No man in political life can expect anything else; and, whatever he felt, he was the last man to complain of it. Neither ought we.

But there is a time for all things; and when the grave has closed over the illustrious dead, it is time to brush away the blinding dust of popularity, and the dark mire of odium through which, in the course of a chequered life, it was his fate to pass. The impressions of his character, which many opportunities of close observation have left upon my mind, I shall not pretend to disguise. Neither can I forget that on more than one important subject I found myself, when in Parliament, voting differently from him. But while disclaiming identity of opinions, I look back, I own, with great satisfaction to the more frequent occasions on which I was fortunate enough to be reckoned with him, in support of measures tending to ameliorate the condition of the people, and to extend their constitutional rights. Had I the power, I should not try to hide from myself or others the faults and foibles of such a man. That does not seem to me a wise or worthy way of dealing with a great reputation. Its best chance of true vindication is, when full and fair opportunity is afforded it for vindicating itself. Is it not better than any praise or criticism of ours, to make a man who in life thought, spoke, and acted much, tell his own tale and plead his own cause?

So far as with propriety we may, let us hear what he said himself, rather than what has been said of him by enemies, or for him by friends. The best days of his life, as he once observed, were spent in the House of Commons; his best efforts were devoted to extend the power and to sustain the influence of that assembly; and in its records the best proofs of his great and varied ability are to be found. Personal recollections furnish many important materials for illustrating other portions of his life; and occasional reference to correspondence not falling within the line of reservation for a future day will hardly be deemed unacceptable. But in the use of such materials I have scrupulously had regard to the feelings and susceptibilities of others. The exercise of such forbearance may seem to some a fault; but I shall be content to bear the blame of being but an indifferent gossip if I escape the censure of being an unfaithful friend.

CONTENTS OF VOL. I.

CHAPTER I.

THE GRAHAMS.

1410—1782.

CHAPTER II.

PARENTAGE AND EDUCATION.

1782—1812.

CHAPTER III.

FOREIGN TRAVEL.

1812—1815.

CHAPTER IV.

A MEMBER OF PARLIAMENT.

1818—1819.

CHAPTER V.

POLITICS AND FARMING IN CUMBERLAND.

1820—1824.

CHAPTER VI.

CORN AND CURRENCY.

1824—1826.

CHAPTER VII.

MEMBER FOR CARLISLE.

1826—1828.

CHAPTER VIII.

RELIGIOUS FREEDOM AND RETRENCHMENT.

1829—1830.

CHAPTER IX.

THE ADMINISTRATION OF EARL GREY.

1830.

CHAPTER X.

THE FIRST REFORM BILL.

1831.

CHAPTER XI.

THE SECOND AND THIRD REFORM BILLS.

1831—1832.

CHAPTER XII.

ADMINISTRATION OF THE NAVY.

1832—1833.

CHAPTER XIII.

BREAK UP OF THE GREY GOVERNMENT.

1834.

LIFE AND TIMES

OF THE RIGHT HONOURABLE

SIR J. R. G. GRAHAM, BART.,

G.C.B., M.P.

CHAPTER I.

THE GRAHAMS.

1410—1782.

THE home of the Grahmes has been at Netherby for many generations. Local tradition loved to tell how in the troubled days of Henry of Lancaster a gallant knight, son of Malise, Lord of Monteith, hurt by the ingratitude of the Scottish king, for whom he had risked life in many a field, withdrew with several of his clan to the English Border, and took up his abode in the Debatable Land.* It was a wild and barren region, whose inhabitants knew no other law than that of force. Possessions there "John with the Bright Sword" had none; but he contrived to make himself a name as a protector of the weak, and as a terror to ruthless men. His skill and prowess

The debatable land. *1410.* *John with the Bright Sword.*

* Playfair, Antiq. Baronetage, vol. vii. p. 296.

1530. in defending the frontier land he had often harried became the favourite theme of fire-side tale; and long after he had passed away from scenes of feud and foray the child of the moss-trooper dreamed of his fleet horse and sable plume.

The Clan Grahme. His descendants grew and multiplied in the neighbourhood of the old tower, built on a rising ground that overlooks the valley of the Esk, where once a Roman camp had been. Gradually they obtained possession of many a fertile croft and patch of upland on either side of the stream, till Arthuret and Nicoll Forest were full of them. The rulers of both realms claimed their allegiance, and they impartially paid it to neither. In Wolsey's time Lord Dacre, then Warden of the Cumberland Marches, advised that as Canonby seemed rather disposed to belong to Scotland, it should be wholly laid waste. "As for the rest of the debatable land, he had caused much of it to be burnt and destroyed, and should not fail, God willing, so to proceed from time to time until it was clearly waste, without one house or hold standing within it." *

He was scarcely, perhaps, as bad as his word; the Grames were hard to exterminate.

Partition Treaty. Partition by treaty was made in 1552 of the district so long the source of disquietude and disorder, that portion being allotted to England which lay between a line drawn from the Sark to the Esk

* Cotton MSS., in Lysson, Magna Brit., vol. iv. p. 22.

and the sea.* No great improvement seems to have followed therefrom; and in the latter years of Elizabeth complaints were frequently made of misdeeds and maraudings by the men of the Border. 1552.

The spirit of chivalry was dying out, and homage to the authority of law was still unknown. Justice itself rode girt with a weapon amid the crowd, and smote too often on chance the nearest seeming delinquent. Blind severity begot lawless stratagem, and cruelty was frequently baffled by daring or craft. A story is told of one Jock Grahme, of the pear tree, whose brother lay for execution in the castle of Carlisle, being, as was said, unjustly accused of participation in some recent foray. As Jock rode by Corby Castle he saw the heir of the Salkelds, then a child, playing near the gate. "Would master like to ride?" he said, and on the boy consenting, lifted him to the saddle-bow, and ere he could be overtaken he had borne away his little hostage beyond the Border. Mr Salkeld was sheriff that year, and the child was not restored until the condemned moss-trooper had got his reprieve.†

Jock of the Pear Tree.

A statute was passed making it capital felony to levy *black mail.* The Act set forth, "That whereas many persons residing in Cumberland, Northumberland, Westmoreland, and the bishopric of Durham, had been taken, some forth of their own houses and

Black mail made felony, 43 *Eliz.* c. 13.

* Hutchinson, History of Cumberland, vol. ii. p. 531.

† Playfair, Antiq. Baronetage, vol. vii. p. 296.

1600. some when travelling by the highway, and carried away as prisoners, and kept until redeemed by great ransoms; and whereas of late time there had been many incursions, raids, and spoiling of towns, villages, and houses within the said counties, so that many had been forced to pay a certain rate of money, corn, or cattle, commonly called black mail, to divers inhabiting near the Borders, being men of name, friended and allied with those who, in those parts, were known to be great spoil-takers, to be by them freed, protected, and kept in safety."* All persons who should thenceforth in any way take part in the same, or who having cognizance should not make discovery thereof, should be adjudged to be felons and suffer death without benefit of clergy. Rigorous provisions were likewise made by the same statute against the harbouring of outlaws from both kingdoms, who still continued to infest the Borders.

Decree of Extirpation. But Parliamentary interdicts were of little effect in those days; and James I., upon his accession, resolved to extirpate the clan of the "Græmes," who bore the repute of being at the bottom of the mischief. Four hundred persons, with Walter, the chief of
1606. their name, were driven from the debatable land and shipped from Workington, some to Ireland, and the

* Entitled an Act for the more peaceable Government of the parts of Cumberland, Westmoreland, Northumberland, and the Bishopric of Durham. Repealed by 7 & 8 Geo. IV.

rest to the Low Countries. The more peaceably-disposed of their kindred were spared; amongst them Fergus "Grame," of Plumpe, in Kirkandrews, with whose son the better fortunes of the family were destined to begin.* From olden time, the Border shires were divided into wards, of which Cumberland had five. That which lay nearest the frontier takes its name from the Esk, which rises in the Cheviot hills. At Canonby it becomes for a short distance the boundary between England and Scotland; entering Cumberland it passes by Kirkandrews, Netherby, by the edge of Solway Moss, and, being joined by the Leven, falls into the sea near Rockliffe marsh, its course through Cumberland being about six miles.† 1606.

Belted Will.

Lord William Howard, who had married the heiress of the last Lord Dacre, and had succeeded thereby to the neighbouring estates of Gilsland, was made the Warden of Eskdale, wherein they lay. The new Lord of Naworth ruled the Marches with an iron hand, maintaining a little garrison‡ for the repression of violence and his own defence in case of need. The influence of his probity and vigour was not bounded by his own broad lands, but far and near the unruly Borderers learnt to reverence the name of "Belted Will."

The debatable land recently cleared of so many of its former inhabitants was granted by James I.,

* Lysson, vol. iv. p. 22. † Ibid. iv. p. 103.
‡ Ibid. p. 31.

1624. Grant to the Earl of Cumberland. to Francis, Earl of Cumberland, at a fee-farm rent of one hundred and fifty pounds a year. In the letters patent, it is described as lying between the rivers Sark* and Esk, the Scotch Dyke and Solway Sands, and containing 2895 acres of meadow and arable, called "known grounds," 2635 of pasture, beside marsh land and moss, in all 8400 acres.

Sir Richard Graham. They were destined however to revert ere long to one of the ineradicable race which had till lately occupied them. Richard, son of Fergus Graham, of Plumpe, had early made his way to Court. His winning manners and good parts found acceptance there. He became master of the horse to the Duke of Buckingham, and accompanied Prince Charles into Spain. Not long afterwards fortune threw in his way the opportunity of becoming the possessor of the still wild and but half-reclaimed region where he had been born, and wherein above all other lands his ambition longed to strike its roots.

Purchase of Arthuret and Kirkandrews. By successive purchases he obtained from George, second Earl of Cumberland, Netherby Hall, and the manors of Arthuret, Lyddell, Randillington, and Nicoll Forest, comprising the whole of the parishes of Kirkandrews and Arthuret, with a portion of that of Bewcastle,† the rent payable to the Crown for the

* The Sark is the boundary between Cumberland and Scotland for about five miles, near Solway Moss.—Lysson, vol. iv. p. 107.

† Lysson, vol. iv. Par. Hist. p. 28.

entire being two hundred pounds a year. Upon his subsequent recognition in 1629 as tenant *in capite* by Charles I., this amount was reduced one-fourth, and he was created a baronet in the same year. Appendant to the manor of Arthuret was the advowson to the parish of the same name, which prior to the Reformation had belonged to the Abbots of Jeddburgh, in Dumfries. That of Kirkandrews and the chapelry of Nicoll Forest likewise went with the estate.* 1629. Baronetcy.

A follower of Sir Richard, Archie Armstrong,† became court fool to Charles I., and made a little fortune by his place. Unluckily for him he chanced one day to make merry at the expense of Laud. The news had lately come of the uprising of the Scots against the attempt to introduce the English liturgy, and Archie, as the Archbishop passed on his way to the council, cried,—"Wha's feule now? Doth not your Grace hear the news from Stirling about the liturgy?" with more to the like effect. Laud complained to the King, and an order was forthwith made, dismissing the jester, and banishing him from Court.‡ Stripped of his gay Archie Armstrong. 11 March, 1639.

* Lysson, vol. iv. Par. Hist. p. 12.

† "Archie, by kings and princes graced of late,
Jested himself into a fair estate."
Prefix to his Book of Jests.

‡ Rushworth's Historical Collections, vol. ii. pp. 470, 471.

1648. coat and cap, Archie went back to spend the evening of his days among the folk who knew him when a boy, and in Arthuret church-yard the jester sleeps —a wiser and a happier man than his ill-fated master.

Sir Richard at Edgehill.

Sir Richard took the Royalist side in the civil war, was left for dead at the battle of Edgehill, and having recovered of his wounds, remained near the person of the King until compelled to take his final
1648. leave of him in the Isle of Wight. He thenceforth
1653. lived in retirement until his death. He left two sons, George and Richard. Of George, the second baronet, no particular mention is made. Attached like the rest of his family to the House of Stuart, whence they claimed to have originally sprung, he was content to remain quiet during the Commonwealth, and to pay without too audible murmuring the exactions of Cromwell. With the Restoration, gratitude for past benefits budded into fresh hopes of royal favour, and in due season fruits were not wanting. Another baronetcy was conferred upon his brother, who settled at Norton Conyers, in Yorkshire. Sir George lived unambitiously at Netherby; but his eldest son Richard, by Mary, daughter of the Earl of Annandale, was destined to play a more conspicuous part.

Sir George of Esk.

Second Baronetcy, 1662.

The first politician of the family.

Educated at Westminster and Christchurch, Richard early showed the possession of qualities that fitted him for public life. He married Ann, daughter of the first Lord Carlisle, was chosen member

for Cockermouth, and made one of the most notable 1682.
speeches against the Exclusion Bill, which, as it could 1778.
not bind Scotland or Ireland, and would set aside 2nd Nov., 1680.
the lineal heir without naming who should succeed to the Crown, would leave all to the dark chances of the future, and sow broadcast the seeds of civil war.* These were, in fact, the grounds on which Danby and Halifax, agreeing in nothing else, concurred in opposing the bill. The young politician became an object of consideration. His grandfather's half-forgotten services were recalled by the thought of those he might render in a different field; and his connections being high, and his possessions large, the King offered to make him a peer of Scotland. He was
created Viscount Preston, of Haddington, and took Viscount Preston. 1682.
his seat in the Upper House of the Scottish Parliament, retaining, however, his rights as an English commoner; he was subsequently chosen knight of the shire for Cumberland.† His politics were Tory; but, like Ormond and Godolphin, he distrusted and disliked French influence, and had no mind to aid in
subverting the Protestant faith. Charles II. sent May, 1682.
him ambassador to Paris. His brother Fergus accompanied him and acted as his private secretary.‡

* Parl. Hist., vol. ii. p. 1186.

† Before the union with Ireland, Lord Mornington (afterwards Marquis Wellesley) in like manner sat as a peer in one kingdom and as a commoner in the other.

‡ MS. Letter of apology to Mr Secretary Jenkins, Preston being ill of the gout. 9th Dec., 1683. In State Paper Office.

1682. Embassy to Paris. The outfit of an ambassador and his first expenditure on his establishment in a foreign capital was in those days a costly affair. Preston was neither extravagant or exacting, and we find him asking beforehand, when extra expenses were to be incurred, how far he should go. But the rate at which money was squandered at Whitehall too often left the Exchequer low, and his own private resources were not great. When accounting to Mr Secretary Jenkins for what he had spent at the end of his first year, Preston says of the sum allowed him for his voyage and outfit, "he had not yet received one farthing, for that he paid interest for £700, which he was forced to take up for that purpose."* His confidential letters expose the corrupt dealings of Louis with too many English statesmen of the time. He was re-
Oct. 1685. called by James II. to take part in the administration at home, made a Commissioner of Excise and Chancellor to the Dowager Queen; and was entrusted, along with Middleton, with the management of the government business in the House of Commons. When the King first began to quarrel with the Church, he counselled moderation and forbearance. His advice, with that of every other honest friend of the infatuated monarch, was over-ruled, and James stumbled onwards blindly to his ruin.

Secretary of State. When Sunderland was dismissed for intriguing

* MS. Letter to Secretary Jenkins, 30th Oct., 1683. State Paper Office.

with the partizans of the Prince of Orange, the Secretaryship of State was conferred on Preston, whom the King knew that in his extremity he could trust, though he dare not confide to him all the mad designs of the cabal who secretly advised him.* Amidst almost universal defection, Preston remained true. He saw the King at Whitehall the evening before his flight, of which he knew nothing till the following day, when, feeling that the constitutional authority of James had been subverted by his own hand, he resigned his office to the Lords of the Council assembled at Guildhall, who had undertaken to act as a Provisional Government. Unlike many of his late colleagues, he declined to pay his court to William, or to seek any share in the newly-established order of things. He became in consequence an object of suspicion, and was thrown into the Tower, where he lay some time.

1688. 27th Oct., 1688. Dec., 1688. 30th May, 1689.

Some days after James had quitted the kingdom he created Preston an English peer by the style and title of Baron Esk, in Cumberland; and Lord Mountague having commenced a suit at law against him, he asserted his right to be sued as a peer. Mountague complained to the Lords, and Preston was summoned before them. On the letters patent being produced, they appeared to have been executed by the fugitive King at St Germain, on the 21st January, 1689,

Claim to Peerage. 11th Nov., 1689.

* See Preston's letter to Dartmouth, 11th Nov., 1688.—Dalrymple, Appendix.

1690. three weeks after his abdication had been declared by Parliament. The judges on being consulted declared the patent void, and Preston was committed to the custody of Black Rod for having wrongfully claimed the privilege of a peer. But having thus shown their determination to draw a rigorous line against all acts of the deposed monarch involving rights of sovereignty, the House appears to have had no desire further to harass Preston, and upon his petition, a few days later, disclaiming any intentional disrespect, but in no way renouncing his claim, an order was made for his release.*

June, 1690. Lord Mountague proceeded for the profits of the office of Master of the Wardrobe, which he claimed under a patent for life from Charles II., but which James had bestowed on Lord Preston; and the jury gave a verdict for the plaintiff for £13,000.†

Conspiracy to recall James. The popularity of the new government soon seemed to wane. Taxation grew apace, jobbing of all descriptions throve. Men who, like Montgomery and Argyle, had helped to bring in William, sulked at his preference for his own countrymen, and he in his turn refused to send back his Dutch Guards. The Council Chamber, as he suspected then, and as we know now, was full of treachery. Of Whigs as well as Tories who had concurred in James's deposi-

* Lords' Journals, 11, 12, and 27 November, 1689.

† N. Luttrell's Diary, 28th June, 1690.

tion, not a few already wished him back. "It was 1690.
time for the nation to recover from the delusion into which his ill-conduct had plunged it:" yet he had respected the right of Habeas Corpus, which now was wholly suspended.* They willingly persuaded themselves he had had a lesson which would henceforth keep him within the bounds of law and liberty. Lord Clarendon, William Penn, Lord Dartmouth, and Turner, Bishop of Ely, were of the number, and they got Preston to come to town to confer with them.† Mr Elliot and Mr Ashton were also in their confidence. In December the three last-named undertook to visit St Germain for the purpose, it would seem, of informing James of the real state of opinion in England concerning him, and of endeavouring to lead him to abjure the despotic courses which had caused his overthrow. "The Protestants were the natural weight and power of these kingdoms by having the heads, hands, and wealth of their side, to the odds of at least 200 Protestants to one Catholic,—the King might think of nothing short of a Protestant administration, and of nothing more for the Catholics than a legal liberty. He might reign a Catholic in devotion, but he must reign a Protestant in government; and he must give them a model of this at St Germain, to tell the nation what

* Dalrymple, Book vi. p. 460.

† Burnett, Hist. Own Times, vol. iv. p. 22.

1691. they might hope for when he came."* William was sickly and childless, and none could tell how soon the exiled sovereign might return, as his brother had done thirty years before, without stipulation of any kind. Now, if ever, was the time to make terms. "No great force," Burnett admits,† "was to be brought over with King James, but a few resolute men as a guard to his person would serve the turn, now that the nation was so incensed at £4,000,000 of taxes. If he managed his coming over with such secrecy that he should bring over with himself the first news of it, they believed that this revolution would be more easy and sudden than the last." Perilous as the experiment was, Preston and his friends resolved to try. A vessel was secretly hired to take them to France. They went on board at midnight upon New Year's eve, and had got down the river as far as Tilbury, when the smack was boarded by an officer named Billop, their papers seized, and they themselves brought back in custody. Their design had been in fact betrayed, though its exact nature was probably unknown, and Caermarthen, with characteristic promptitude and vigour, had sent for Billop a few hours before, and ordered him to search all vessels clearing outwards from the Thames.

* Result of a Conference between many Whigs and Tories, among the papers found on Ashton when arrested, and proved at Preston's trial.—State Trials, vol. xii. p. 711.

† Hist. Own Times, vol. iv. p. 122.

Preston was indicted with Ashton and Elliot for high treason, and forthwith brought to trial before Chief Justices Holt and Pollexfen, the Chief Baron, and two of the puisne judges. On being arraigned, he objected that he was described as Sir Richard Graham Viscount Preston of the kingdom of Scotland, whereas he was entitled under the letters patent of King James to the privilege of peerage, and consequently he demanded to be tried as an English peer. He could not produce the letters patent, because they were in the custody of the clerk of the House of Lords, without an order to that functionary to give them up. The Chief Justice replied that, being a court of inferior jurisdiction to that of Parliament, it was impossible for the judges there to make such an order. The prisoner then asked for a copy of the indictment, in accordance with the provisions of 46 Edward III., which declares that a prisoner may have a copy of any record that would serve him for his defence. He argued the point with much ingenuity, blending a dignified firmness in the assertion of his constitutional claim with courteous deference to the bench. But he was told there was no precedent, and that the thing could not be allowed. Holt declared they must interpret the law when doubtful as their predecessors had done. Pollexfen said that if all prisoners had time to consult their counsel how to pick flaws in indictments, the days of the year would not be

1691. Trial of Preston.

Refused copy of Indictment.

1691. enough for jail delivery. Somers, with more candour and learning, admitted that the statute insisted on was set forth at length in Coke's Reports, although he had never seen it elsewhere. The judges then called upon Preston to prove its existence by producing a copy from the rolls. He was prepared for this, and proceeded to do so, calling a witness who produced an attested copy from the Parliamentary archives. The statute was read, but the Court ruled that it referred only to records which might be pleaded or used as evidence by a prisoner in his defence, and in this sense the indictment was not a record, "because an indictment for treason could help no man." Repeatedly he prayed that his counsel might be heard in support of the objections he made, but from beginning to end they were not suffered to open their lips.

Preston then demanded time to prepare for his trial, which involved all that was dear to him and his posterity. He had had seven days' notice indeed; but during the first three he had not been allowed to communicate with his solicitor or any of his friends.* He wished for a day or two's further delay to examine the names in the jury panel, and to send for witnesses. By this time, however, the judges had grown weary of his dexterous fencing, and would hear no more. Holt assured him that what had been over-ruled should do him no harm

* State Trials, vol. xii. p. 671.

with them, but they would sit at eight o'clock on the following morning, and his trial must then proceed. 1691.

Evidence against him.

The principal evidence against him consisted of papers found upon Ashton, some of which were written in cant terms, others in cipher, but all of which had alleged reference to the design of a counter-revolution. Three of them were sworn to be in Preston's writing. It was a smaller hand than he usually wrote; and the witnesses were not cross-examined. Some of the papers were in the handwriting of Clarendon, some in that of Dartmouth, and others in that of the Bishop of Ely.* Three of the Cabinet Council, Caermarthen, Sydney, and Nottingham, were called to prove in whose custody the papers had been between the arrest and the trial. Holt and Pollexfen told the jury that, in default of any reasonable suggestion to the contrary, they must presume the accused was privy to the contents of all the papers, that those in his handwriting were enough in themselves to convict him of treason, and that his attempt to make his way to France in time of war betrayed a guilty purpose.† Preston called no witnesses; and, worn out by the length of the trial, or despairing of making any effectual resistance to the array of influence, authority, and evidence against him, he declined to

* Dalrymple, Book vi. p. 465.

† State Trials, vol. xii. p. 742.

1691. enter into any protracted controversy as to the proofs made by the Crown, and briefly left his case to the jury. He was pronounced guilty. Ashton was tried and condemned the following day, and sentence was passed on both. Ashton was an enthusiastic Jacobite, and knowing that he was obnoxious to Government on other grounds,* resigned himself composedly to his fate.

Preston had few enemies and many friends. His wife prayed the Queen for his reprieve, but Mary, as she was advised, replied that it was in her lord's power to save himself by making a full discovery.† This Preston would not do, and he was told to prepare for execution.

Preston's daughter.

His daughter, then very young, was loved by many in Mary's train, and one day, while her father still lay in the tower, was surprised by the Queen gazing at a picture of James, which had not been removed from the walls of Kensington. Mary asked why she wept. "I am thinking," she said, "how hard it is that my father should suffer death because he loved yours." ‡ The logic of despair was irresistible. Preston's execution was postponed; Caermarthen privately recommended the sparing of his life as a means of holding in check Clarendon, Sey-

* Dying Declaration of Ashton, State Trials, vol. xii. p. 819.

† Narcissus Luttrell's Diary, 19th Jan., 1691.

‡ Dalrymple, Book vi. p. 466.

mour, and others, "whereas by his execution these ends would be baffled." * 1691.

Upon his return from Holland the King desired that the unhappy statesman should be brought before the Council. The Lord President questioned him at length concerning the extent of the disaffection on which he and his friends had reckoned. Preston boldly averred its prevalence, and cited numerous facts of notoriety to justify his assertion. He declared that many of the proudest nobles in England and Scotland had avowed their discontent and disappointment with the new order of things, and he intimated plainly that if pressed he could prove that this was so among Whigs as well as Tories. Caermarthen had his own wrongs to avenge, and he grasped at the supposed opportunity of ruining with the new sovereign the men who had pitilessly persecuted him a few years before. He was about to proceed with his interrogatories, when William, who stood behind his chair, touched his arm, saying, "My Lord, there is enough of this," and abruptly brought the sitting to a close. The curtain falls upon the pretended disclosures of Preston, and rises not again. The prisoner was sent back to his cell, there to remain for some time longer. But his discerning eye had marked William's look and ges- Scene at the Council.

* Letter of Caermarthen to William, 3rd Feb., 1691. Dalrymple, Appendix.

1691. ture, and if he persuaded himself that the bitterness of death was past he did not err.

Conduct of William. The new sovereign had no sympathy with the sanguinary rancour of the factions that surrounded him. He saw that he had no interest in becoming their mutual executioner. He wished for no further proofs of the little reliance he could place on the constancy of many who had shown him the way to the throne, expecting to find in him a nominal chief, and who already resented his claim to be real master. Godolphin and Marlborough were daily corresponding with James about bringing back the army to his cause.* William suspected, knew not whom not to suspect,† when his wife's sister and uncle were plotting against him, and his deadliest foes were they of his own household. Conspiracy was everywhere, from the Secretary's office to the home of the Highland chief, and its whisperings were but too audible in the anterooms of Kensington, as well as under the piazzas of Covent Garden. The honourable men who had never betrayed his father-in-law while they ate his bread, and who had never abjured his cause, even when they thought it lost, appeared to the King well

Preston pardoned. worth conciliating. Preston was one of these; and William cheerfully granted him a free pardon under

June 4. the sign manual. Some days after his liberation he presented himself at Court, and was permitted to

* Macpherson, vol. i. p. 680.

† See Letter of Queen Mary, 26th Aug., 1690.

kiss the Queen's hand on his restoration to freedom. He subsequently produced the letters patent of pardon in the King's Bench, which the Court thereupon allowed.* 1691.

Meanwhile many about Government gave out that he had made a full confession. Burnett, whose intrigues at Paris Preston had exposed eight years before, ridiculed the "weak part" he was said to have played; and Narcissus Luttrell, careful to note all the scandal and gossip picked up in Westminster Hall of a morning, or the coffee-house where he dined, "heard somebody say that he had made an ample discovery, which, it was believed, would lead to a pardon." † The Jacobites only knew that he was free, and knew not what he had told. Credulous in their fears, as they had been in their hopes, they avoided rather than sought his company, and their conduct seemed to furnish proof of the imputations against him. How differently he was regarded by those who knew the truth is demonstrated by the fact that before many months he was again committed to the Tower. About the same time the house of his brother in Norfolk Street was searched, and large quantities of plate seized, which had been packed in cases ready to be sent to St Germain. Colonel Graham narrowly escaped arrest, and did not return to England for some time. Preston was at length

* Patent Rolls, Will. and Mary, Part ii. No. 9.

† N. Luttrell's Diary, 1st May, 1691.

1691. finally set at liberty, but the elasticity of his spirit was broken. With his convictions and feelings it was impossible for him to be reconciled to the Revolution; but the new sovereigns had given him his life, had given back his children their patrimony, and he would henceforth meddle no more in dynastic plots or schemes. His obligations, however, were greater than he could bear. For one who had played so prominent a part, to remain in the world observing a merely negative course was impossible. He resolved to quit it for ever, and to betake himself to a country life and the pursuit of letters for the rest of his days. At Nunnington, not far from his brother's seat at Norton Conyers in Yorkshire, he possessed an old-fashioned mansion, pleasantly situated on the banks of the Rye; and there, surrounded by his family and a small circle of friends, he occupied himself in translating Boethius' Book of Comfort, part in prose and part in verse. The rendering of the original is sufficiently close; but Preston was a politician, not a poet, and the work as a whole is calculated to add but little to his fame.* He had evidently been led in the choice of his subject by the supposed coincidence of fate between himself and his original; and in his account of the great patrician's life he touchingly expresses his sympathy and admiration for the constancy in suffering Boethius

* The first edition was published in 1695, and the second, with some corrections, appeared in 1712.

showed. "He had so much strength of soul and thought, and he showed so much judgment in all his managements, that even a most knowing prince feared his parts; and his virtues and integrity became his crime and wrought his ruin; for with these he sought to curb and restrain ill men. It being dangerous for him to refuse office, he was called often to advise his prince on the weightiest affairs of state, which he did with inviolable equity."* But it is in the preface that the pent-up stream of his own bitterness breaks forth without control. "Heaven thought fit to permit him to fall into the hands of his tormentors, whose persecutions only ended with his life, and those who gave a cruel liberty to their tongues to traduce and vilify his afflicted virtue, to debase and decry his sufferings, and who by stabbing his fame and reputation became more criminal than those partial judges who condemned him to death. Hence he was the subject of reflection and discourse among pretenders to policy, the inquirers after and tellers of news, who were generally the knaves and fools of their country, and of those mean-spirited men who, being at a distance from the dangers and misfortunes with which he was oppressed, thought they might safely pass a censure upon his actions and carriage, pretending that their demeanour should have been with more firmness if they had been in his circumstances,

1695.

* Life of Boethius, prefixed to translation, p. 25.

1695. when most of them had not souls calmly to think upon what he with constancy and bravery did endure." *

His death, 22nd Dec., 1695. Preston did not long survive the completion of his task, and in the church of Nunnington, beneath a monument of black marble, with no other inscription than his name and age, his remains repose.

1703. His son Edward was but 17 years of age when he succeeded his father. His wife was the daughter, and one of the co-heiresses, of Sir Marmaduke Dalton, of Hawkswell in Yorkshire,† by whom he had an only son. Charles, the third Viscount, died at an
1739. early age without issue, leaving his estates to his father's sisters Catherine (the wife of Lord Widdrington) and the Hon. Mary Graham; the latter died unmarried, and the whole of the property vested in the former. Lord Widdrington had been a partizan of the Stuarts, and was, in 1715, attainted of treason. His life was spared, but his honours and estates were forfeited. Netherby, being the inheritance of his wife, escaped the consequences of his attainder. His death took place in 1743 at Nunnington, where his remains were laid beside those of Preston.

6th Nov., 1745. When the Pretender crossed the Border, he passed on his way to Carlisle close to Netherby. Lady Widdrington was fortunately absent, the

* Preface, p. 8.

† Whitaker's Hist. Richomondshire, vol. i. p. 329.

care of the place having been confided to a gentleman named Nicholson. 1757.

By her will in 1757, she bequeathed the whole of her property to her cousin, the Rev. Robert Graham, D.D., second son of William, Dean of Carlisle and Wells, who had been Clerk of the Closet to Queen Anne.

Dr Graham had early entered the Church, and held for some time the small living of Kirkandrews. Upon his succession to the family estates, he relinquished the incumbency, and devoted himself wholly to the discharge of his temporal duties. These in his estimation were neither light nor few. The inheritance to which he had succeeded, though extensive and valuable, was morally and socially in the worst possible condition. Few hedges were to be seen; the use of coal and lime were almost unknown. The people, slothful and inert, "retained a smack of the old habits" of the Border; and produce enough for their own subsistence was all they tried to raise.

Dr Graham.

Condition of the estate.

The tenantry by desultory efforts at reclamation from time to time had extended their farms. But between and around them lay a wilderness of moss and moor. This waste Dr Graham set himself to have surveyed and enclosed. He first drained 1000 acres; and built villages of eight or ten houses, and let them for two or three years rent free.* The labour was necessarily one of years and the cost

Extensive reclamations.

* Playfair, vol. vii. p. 298.

1760. enormous. The undertaking was, in fact, little less than the creation of another estate hardly inferior to the one bequeathed to him. He was obliged to borrow large sums of money at high interest, to be expended in wages amongst the people around him. The benefit to the district and to the population was probably clearer even to his sanguine view than that likely to accrue to himself. He could not reasonably hope that the liabilities he contracted would be liquidated in his day; and he was too quick-witted to place implicit faith in the calculations of surveyors and contractors, or to doubt that they looked on his enterprise as an unlimited source of profit. Nevertheless he entered with enthusiasm upon the business of experimental improvement, and lived to see much of what he had designed carried into execution. By manifesting a personal interest in the welfare of those around him, he gradually infused something of his own spirit into their way of life. He was all for making things better, whatever their actual plight might be. If a man would not try to improve his farm, and make his house more cleanly, and show a desire to get better crops out of the land, he would not employ or help him. But for all who would work there was wages; and for all who would mend their by-roads, plant new hedges, or lime their fields, there was ready help to be had from the laird. He himself planted much, and encouraged others to do so.

Treatment of his tenants.

Before his time there was but little timber of any value near the family dwelling, and still fewer trees serving for ornament. He sought the advice in laying out gardens and pleasure-grounds of Mr Howard of Corby, with whom he lived on intimate terms, and whose taste and judgment he appreciated as they deserved.* With his assistance the pleasure-grounds were laid out and the plantations formed, which now lend beauty and shelter to a spot then cold and bare. While the slow work of clearing and planting was going on he commenced the building of a mansion on the old site, more suitable to the property than any which had previously existed. Camden spoke of the place as a hamlet on the right bank of the Esk, consisting of an old feudal keep and two or three cottages, near to which lived the Grahams of ancient Border fame. "There hath been marvelus buildings, as appeer by ruinus walls; and men alive have seen rynges and staples in the walls as it had been stayes or holds for ships. On the one side of it is The 'batable Ground, so that it is a *limes Angliæ et Scotiæ*. The ruins be now three miles at least from the flowing water of the Sulway Sands. The grass groweth now on the ruins

1760.

Netherby.

Rebuilding of the Hall.

Camden's account of Netherby.

* Mr Howard was the grandfather of the present proprietor of that beautiful seat which originally belonged to the Salkelds, and which was purchased of them for his second son by "Belted Will." Mr Ph. Howard sat for many years in Parliament for Carlisle, and was warmly attached to the late Sir James Graham.

1761. of the walls."* The ancient border house at Kirkandrews, opposite to Netherby, is a square tower of three storeys, the windows small, the door of iron; the cattle lodged below, the owners above.† There is a gradual descent from the principal and oblong fort, on the north-west angle towards the Esk, in which several streets are very visible. In one, running north and south, on the west side towards the river, by digging among the ruins for stones, were discovered two rooms parallel to the street. The southernmost plainly a cold bath, from the cement and large thin flags laid at the bottom. At Netherby has been found everything that denotes it a fixed Roman station. A fine hypocaust was discovered in 1745, contiguous to the old bath opened in 1732, and the present shrubbery was the burial-place, in which a statue was discovered. The hypocaust was supported by fifty-four pillars of solid stone, thirty-six of which were covered with flags and cement.‡ During the excavations of 1760 many additional remains of classic interest were discovered, indicating the extent and permanency of the Roman settlement there. Amongst the rest was a tablet bearing a votive inscription by the Second Legion to the Emperor Adrian. The antiquities of the place were collected and arranged by Dr Graham, who devoted

* Lett. in Gough's Camden, Brit., vol. iii. p. 449.

† Pennant, *Ibid.*

‡ Camden, Britannia, vol. iii. p. 451.

a room in his new mansion to the purposes of a museum. 1764.

While the building was in progress Dr Graham and his wife spent some time at Naworth, which had been placed at their disposal by the Earl of Carlisle, and it was there in April, 1761, their second son James was born.* Dr Graham may be said to have altogether built Longtown, about three miles distant, which had previously been no more than an obscure village. He likewise, at his own expense, improved the little harbour at the mouth of the Sark, so as to facilitate the export of agricultural produce. The effect of works so numerous and extensive, carried on probably in many cases with more of generous zeal for improvement than circumspect economy, was the increase of population generally on the estate. None could say whether the improved productiveness of the soil would not keep pace therewith; and with so liberal a paymaster, those who lived by labour feared no lack. But towards the close of his beneficent life Dr Graham probably became aware how hazardous a thing it is factitiously to create permanent wants and expectations, and how difficult it is to stimu-

Visit to Naworth.

Longtown.

* A curious misapprehension seems to have arisen respecting the fact above-mentioned, and it has been supposed that it was the grandson of Dr Graham, not his son, who was born at Naworth. The origin of the mistake will be hereafter explained.

1771. late safely the progress of local improvement, where all without a circumscribed limit remains stationary and stagnant as before. The Netherby estate under his management became a marvel rather than a model. He had done wonders, and rich and poor were equally loud in his praise. But he had not counted beforehand the cost of doing so much so fast, with so lavish a hand. A great portion of his reclaimed lands looked well to the eye, but never yielded him anything like a remunerative rent.* He increased the number of schools, and it was not his fault if education was not diffused. But grammars and copy-books, though he had made them plenty as cranberries in the market of Longtown,† could do little to render the old generation far-sighted enough to provide for the time when his exceptional shower of gold should cease, or practically to realize the fact that it would and must do so. His aim was excellent, and his speculation splendid: he loved much, and his reward was with him. The canker showed itself not in his time that was begotten with the good he had done, and it was reserved for another day and generation to see the noble work which he began firmly and effectually solidified.

* Hutchinson, vol. ii. p. 550.

† "The sale of cranberries at Longtown is so extensive that they may be deemed an important article of commerce." —Lysson, vol. iv. p. 117.

Early in the winter of 1771, a portion of the parish of Kirkandrews, in which his improvements had been most successfully carried on, was visited by a strange calamity. Without any phenomena having being observed calculated to give warning of the impending catastrophe, a vast tract of Solom or Solway moss began to move slowly but steadily, the dark and ponderous mass descended from the higher level, on which for ages it had seemed to be fast moored, and ceased not its onward course till field after field and cottage after cottage were absolutely submerged beneath it. Day after day the devastating flow moved on. Some hasty efforts were made to arrest its progress where inequalities of the ground suggested the possibility of success; and when these failed attempts were made, but equally in vain, to alter its direction. Alarm and consternation spread as the unhoused inhabitants told the tale of their mysterious ruin wherever they sought shelter. People flocked from all the country round to see the "travelling moss;" but the destruction wrought by it was so complete that strangers could with difficulty be persuaded that where nothing but a black and sterile bog now stretched, over a space of five or six hundred acres, stubbled fields, cattle-garths, and gardens, newly-made byers, and snug though humble human dwellings, recently had been. The rental of the region thus laid waste did not, it

1771.

Travelling moss.

15th Nov.

1780. is said, exceed £400 a year,* but the loss and misery entailed upon its former occupants it was hardly possible to estimate. The unlooked-for burthen of their support and replacement fell upon the humane and generous laird, and he accepted it without a murmur. As soon as the aggressive flood was stayed, means were adopted to hasten its solidification; and in the course of the ensuing summer portions of it were found sufficiently consolidated to be removed. The expense of clearing the desolated tract was necessarily great, and several years elapsed before the traces of this singular calamity had wholly disappeared.

Political opinions.

Dr Graham was the first of his family who was a Whig. His genial temper preserved to him the friendship of those from whom he most widely and warmly differed in politics; and his genuine liberality in matters of belief won him the confidence and affection of men of all persuasions. If ever man acted up to the distinctive rule of Christian morals, it was he. Gentle to his children, considerate to his servants, forbearing with the obstinate, ever ready to forgive a poor man's debt or a rich man's wrong, a kind landlord, a lenient magistrate, and a fast friend, he was the joy of his own household, and the most welcome guest at every neighbour's board. The adhesion of such a man to the "Blues" in the county, apart from his large territorial influence,

* Playfair, vol. vii. p. 298.

would have been counted a great gain, and heading as he did a numerous body of freeholders, it went far towards counterbalancing the previously preponderating power of the house of Lowther. In the long memorable contest of 1768 he took a part, to which, as we shall presently see, his grandson, after the lapse of 60 years, felt proud in being able to refer. The chief cost of the struggle was borne by the family of Bentinck, who then possessed considerable property in Cumberland, but who have ceased since then to be connected with the county. 1782.

Dr. Graham succeeded by his second son.

As the extensive property of the Grahams was now possessed by the younger branch, it seemed not unreasonable that they should have the same rank as their progenitors. Dr Graham did not care to ask such a distinction for himself, but he looked forward to its being borne some day by his eldest son. Charles was not destined, however, to enjoy either patrimony or title. At an early age he had married the daughter of Mr Gorges, M.P. for Eye, in Suffolk; he seemed to have the promise of long life and happiness before him when summoned to the deathbed of his father, but hardly had the obsequies of Dr Graham closed when death again visited their house, and the youthful heir was carried to the tomb. 2nd Feb. 14th Feb.

Charles Graham left an only daughter, and the estate being settled in the male line, its possession was allowed to remain in abeyance until the close

1782. of the year, when, in default of any claim on behalf of a posthumous son, it devolved to James the next brother, then in his twenty-second year. Thus Netherby eventually fell to the second son of the fourth son of the second son of Sir George of Esk. Not many weeks after Dr Graham's death his po-
March. litical friends, among whom was the Duke of Portland, came into power; and the baronetcy which they
Creation of baronetage. would have gladly offered him was conferred upon his successor. In the course of the same year, Mr Fox having seceded from the administration, Mr
July. Pitt was named Chancellor of the Exchequer; and in the break-up and reconstruction of parties which soon afterwards occurred, Sir James espoused the sentiments and opinions of which that minister was the foremost chief and champion.

CHAPTER II.

PARENTAGE AND EDUCATION.

1782—1812.

The new baronet.

THE newly-created baronet had not completed his twenty-second year when he came into possession of Netherby. Men of stronger understanding have been dazzled at a maturer age by fewer gifts of fortune than had fallen unexpectedly to his lot. He had not been trained to the business of estate management, then less carefully followed by the hereditary owners of the soil than it is in our day; and it would have been strange, perhaps, if surrounded, as he was sure to be, by gay companions and flatterers of all sorts, he had not made the mistake of counting rent as synonymous with available income. Every young man of his class and pretensions, who aspired to the character of possessing spirit, did the same. A world of interminable enjoyment lay before him. He was young, gay, and rich; for the encumbrances left by his father, he was told and believed, were nothing compared to those of many a finer gentle-

1783. man. His property was just then beginning to show the beneficial results of Dr Graham's improvements; and had it been wisely treated there is little doubt that its progress would have been one of steady and rapid advance in permanent value. But Sir James was devoted to pleasure, and readily yielded to the suggestions of those about him, who assured him his lands were very much under-let. The depressing influence of the war with America was passing away; industrial enterprise was re-

Prosperity of the country.

covering its elasticity; Mr Pitt was entering upon that course of wise frugality in finance, and a free development for the energies of trade, which form the truest basis of his claim to remembrance as a great statesman; and the country at large believed that there was in store for it a long period of peace and prosperity. The cost of living was reduced, but not so much as habits of luxury were increased. Those who lived by farming and trade were said to be making more money than they had ever done before; and those who had no experience of the labour and care by which it was made, but who deemed their occupation in life to be the spending pleasantly what had come to them without trouble,

Raising of rents.

soon found that they wanted more to spend. The Netherby rents, which had hitherto been for croft and holm land about 25*s*. per acre, and the improved moor 6*s*. or 7*s*. an acre * (some as low as half-a-

* Hutchinson, vol. ii. p. 548.

crown), were now raised considerably. A check was probably given thereby to the accumulation of farming capital on the estate. But prices were good; new markets were opening for produce in Ireland and Lancashire. Sir James gave fifteen years' leases, and we are told by one who visited the district a few years later that no tenant had thrown up his farm in consequence of the advance in rent.* 1784.

Further enclosures.

The recollection of what Dr Graham had done, and the example of what was doing in every county of England at the period in question, stimulated the owner of Netherby to further enclosure. Large tracts were after a certain fashion brought into cultivation, and occupiers were never wanting. But without scientific knowledge or practical experience to direct and advise, the exertions of the tenant and the expectations of the landlord were often doomed to disappointment.

Abuse of lime.

Lime was applied to the newly enclosed lands, they gave for a year or two abundant crops, and what seemed to have proved so easy a specific for ensuring fertility was adopted without discrimination. There were scarcely any soils which on breaking up did not seem benefitted by the application of lime. But when to replenish the declining yield the heavy doses of this stimulant were repeated on light land, or that which had been recently re-

* Hutchinson, vol. ii. p. 552.

1785. claimed from moss, they not only failed of producing the good effect anticipated, but infinite harm was done. "The wet clays were *mortarized*, the light soils worked and disintegrated, till their texture was destroyed, and both were rendered almost sterile, until drained and re-cultivated with manure and no lime." *

Marriage, 9th June. In 1785, Sir James married Lady Catherine Stewart, eldest daughter of John, seventh Earl of Galloway, by Anne, daughter of Sir J. Dashwood, of Kirklington, Oxfordshire.† The Earl had been a
1764. friend of Lord Bute, and was made a Lord of the Bedchamber to George III.‡

Lady Graham. Lady Catherine was in many respects a very remarkable person. She was above the ordinary height, and at her marriage, which took place in her twentieth year, she was the object of much admiration. Her expressive and dignified features are preserved in the family portraits; and from her the future statesman inherited the lofty and commanding presence by which he was distinguished. Her husband on the

* Dickinson's Report, p. 33.

† Gentleman's Magazine, 1785, p. 488. In Annual Register of the same year the marriage is stated to have taken place on May 10th.

‡ Lord Galloway's second daughter, Susan, was married to the fifth Duke of Marlborough; the younger sisters married Lord S. Chichester, the Hon. William Bligh, Sir Edward Crofton, the Hon. George Rushout, and Mr Phillips Inge of Thorpe Constantine, in Staffordshire.

contrary was of slight frame, and rather diminutive in stature. He is spoken of as having been a genial, lively, hospitable man, unequal intellectually to either his father or his son, but affable and generous, kind to his dependants, and esteemed by all who knew him. Many children were the fruit of their union, but it was not until the seventh year that their eldest son was born. The event, long wished for, was the signal of much rejoicing in and around the Hall, and there are those still living who recollect the feastings in the park, and bonfires on the hill-side, which marked the occasion. He was named James after his father, Robert after his paternal grandfather, and George, after Sir George of Esk. 1792.

Birth of eldest son, 1st June, 1792.

The little Sir James, as he sometimes was called, took life easily. He had a happy, unambitious temperament. His expenditure was lavish, and his encumbrances great. But his possessions lay around him on every side as far as he could see. His rents were often irregularly paid, and arrears were allowed to accumulate, but there seemed to be no lack, and with cheerful faces about him he was content. The more Lady Catherine gave to the poor the better he was pleased, but he probably set more value on the warm clothing and fuel she dispensed than on her pious admonitions.

Parental characteristics.

Lady Catherine's natural energy of character showed itself in her works of benevolence. "She would see for herself—she would, in winter time, see

Active benevolence.

1793. if the poor had blankets enough for covering. A couple of miles was nought to her. She would walk it and back, and did na care for weather, to see after them that were sick. She was verra religious, partic'lar so, and gave away small books they called tracts: and she was verra charitable. I mind her once when she was overtaken in a storm, and got fairly fixed in the moss; she had tried to get across a burn, where the rain had made it too deep. It chanced of great luck I heard her cry, and with help of my father carried her right over the brook, wading up to our hips. We got her to a house near hand, and I ran for the carriage to Netherby to bring her home. Ah, there was never the like of her in this country. A fine, bold, good-hearted woman, aye. She went away to London, when Sir James died, and we never saw her no more."* The affection and regard in which Lady Catherine was held by all who knew her, and especially by her own family and dependants, is still a fresh and fragrant memory in the place where the chief part of a long life of usefulness was passed. Her devotion to her family was tender and unceasing, and her image was indelibly impressed upon their minds. From earliest childhood it was her anxious care to impart to them the truths and principles which governed her own life, and on which she set a higher value

Maternal influences.

* Recollections of an old dependant of the family still living.

than any gifts of worldly fortune. She would not admit that she was very proud, but she confessed that she was very fond of her eldest son, who early gave promise of mental and bodily vigour, and after he had passed out of a state of tutelage she exercised over him a gentle ascendency which he never affected to disown. 1794.

Archdeacon Paley.

Among those who, next to his mother, exercised intellectually most influence perhaps over the circle wherein his boyish days were spent, were two persons of no ordinary eminence in the same profession, but who were singularly contrasted in their ways of thought and life and conversation. William Paley had for many years been Archdeacon of the diocese, and Isaac Milner had more recently become the Dean. Both were frequent visitors at Netherby, but of the two the laird no doubt considered Dr Paley the more agreeable companion. The Archdeacon loved to vary his studies in utilitarian theology with the recreation of angling. When vicar of Dalston, he spent many a summer day on the banks of the Esk, whose current widens and deepens as it winds through the park of Netherby; and after his subsequent promotion in the diocese, in 1782, he was not less frequently a visitor there.

Sir James was full of anecdotes of the sociable divine, and loved to tell how he disenchanted Mr Howard, when fishing one day at Corby, who had asked him if the quiet of the wooded glen through

1794. which the Eden flows was not propitious to high philosophic thoughts, by replying, "Nay, nay, with rod in hand I think of nothing but the salmon." Another story never failed in its recital to excite the merry little baronet's laughter. Some one, praising the conjugal peace enjoyed by a gentleman in the neighbourhood, who had not had even an argument with his wife for more than thirty years, appealed to Paley whether it were not admirable as a domestic example. "No doubt," said the doctor, "it was verra praiseworthy, but it must have been verra *dool.*"

Though not a Borderer by birth, Paley had from his boyhood lived so much in the North that he spoke habitually with the accent peculiar to that region. His host at Netherby was himself not wholly free from provincial pronunciation, and it may be that he relished the humour of his friend all the better for its local hue and texture. The Archdeacon's wit, like his wisdom, was essentially worldly and matter-of-fact. He had too much good sense and good nature not to respect the earnest spiritualism of his Very Reverend brother; but sympathy in it he had none. An Established Religion with him was an indispensable saddle and bridle, without which society could not be made to subserve its highest uses; and the Church as an institution was maintainable not upon any ground of divine origin or claim to possess the inherent light of transcendental truth, but specifically, and indeed solely, as the best practical means of national education.* He wished as sincerely, no doubt, as the Dean to see the influence of the clergy raised, and he understood human nature too well not to agree with him, that if it were done it must be done by themselves. But beyond proofs of more exemplary habits of self-control, more thrift in household economy, more punctuality in every-day dealing, and more careful attention to parish duties, he would seem to have had but limited views of clerical improvement.† Nevertheless, Paley's personal and social influence was eminently good. He did not trouble himself indeed about matters of controversy or doctrine, and enthusiasm was an ingredient forgotten when his mind was made. But, on the other hand, he was tolerant, forbearing, charitable, and true, acting up to his own convictions of what was right, and willing to believe that those of others were as genuine, and might be as saving and as pure. 1794.

In 1790 he obtained the rich preferment of Bishop Wearmouth, in the diocese of Durham, and he spent there a portion of each ensuing year. He retained, however, his archdeaconry. The Rev. Fergus Graham, brother of Sir James, who held the

* Moral Philosophy, book vi. chap. 10.

† One of his most remarkable exhortations to his diocesan brethren was to keep out of public-houses, because they could not avoid hearing from those they were likely to meet there profane and unseemly talk.

1795. living of Arthuret, married his daughter; and his many ties of intimacy and friendship remained unbroken in and around Carlisle.

Dean Milner.

Dr Milner was a man of a wholly different stamp. Distinguished at Cambridge for his attainments in physical science, he owed his promotion rather to his experimental success in the laboratory than to his reputation as a divine. But from the period of his promotion to the Deanery he seems to have become animated by religious fervour in a degree then rare among dignitaries of the Church. He laboured to redeem his office from the reproach of being a sinecure, preaching constantly in the white-washed ruin, which in his day had few traces left of a cathedral, and busying himself with religious undertakings of various sorts. Over the minds of those who knew the intensity of his self-devotion he exercised no common influence. His visits to Netherby were frequent, and he became Lady Catherine's first of friends; she shared his strong evangelical opinions, and the tenets he inculcated were earnestly impressed by her upon the minds of her children. As a staunch churchman, Sir James attended all the usual ordinances of religion, but his convictions were probably less profound than those of his wife. He took little interest in her pious conferences with the Dean, and never could be brought to comprehend the harm of dancing, or the sinfulness of short whist.

The Archdeacon's views of "things lawful and things not convenient," comported better with the notions inculcated by his father, who had in truth known Paley well, and had esteemed him highly. He looked on "cards and dice as the harmless occupation of a vacant hour," but though he refrained from their enjoyment on Sunday out of respect for the day, he thought "conversation often not more edifying nor always so inoffensive." * He respected the Dean as a good man, and liked much of his cheerful talk about practical science and many other concerns. But Milner, though he tried hard, could never thoroughly satisfy him that every race-course must be a sink of iniquity, and that going to the play was the first step on the road to perdition. In September, 1808, the Dean lifted up his voice in the Cathedral against the "races," and a project having been set on foot about the same time to build a theatre by subscription in Carlisle, Milner did his best to defeat it, exhorting all his friends in private to refuse their aid.†

1798. Play-houses.

Points of belief, or questions that directly involved contrariety of opinion as to morals, seldom formed the theme of argument between them. But the host was less reserved where the great principle

* Paley's Moral Philosophy. Book V. chap. viii.

† Letter from Borough Bridge to one of the supporters of the scheme, who had attended his discourses against play-houses.—28th Sept. Life of Milner, p. 262.

1797. of sectarian freedom seemed to be compromised by the political dicta of his guest. Enough of the Jacobite lurked about him to make him a staunch defender of Church and Crown; but enough also to make him look with toleration on Catholic tenets and to sympathize with Catholic wrongs. Both agreed that the Establishment must be maintained, the one because he deemed it essential to the maintenance of the existing monarchic and aristocratic order of things, the other because he believed it to be the especial depositary of Scriptural truth.

The Baronet would have relaxed the restrictions imposed upon the Catholics, because he thought, with Mr Pitt, Lord Grenville, and Mr Canning, that the constitution would be all the firmer if relieved from the odium of exclusion, and the Dean would have perpetuated that exclusion, not because he was indifferent to the danger of their discontent, but because he feared to give encouragement to what he deemed soul-destroying error. Sir James was no match for Milner in tongue combat, but he stoutly defended his own position, and could never be driven into abandoning it. Lady Catherine was not always a silent witness of their lively but good-humoured differences, and her womanly wit knew how and when to interpose so as to give another turn to the conversation ere either grew too warm. Opinion was indeed more curiously divided on this question than on any other. While the great body of the clergy throughout the kingdom were vehemently opposed to the concession of Catholic claims, Mr Wilberforce was among its warmest advocates. If Lady Catherine had any literary pride it lay in being one of his correspondents, and when writing to a mutual friend, we find him alluding with admiration to her tone of calm and elevated confidence in the overruling care of Heaven, and in the eventual preservation of the country when dangers seemed gathering around it during the darkest period of the war.* But even the persuasive expostulations of Mr Wilberforce failed to shake Milner's dislike and dread of concession to the Catholics, and he continued throughout a resolute opponent of the measure.† 1800.

Sir James was a decided Tory. He adhered closely to the principles of Mr Pitt, in whom to the end he reposed unwavering faith. Mr Addington he regarded as an unworthy supplanter of his illustrious chief. He was one of the many who refused, even at the bidding of Mr Pitt in 1801, to give "the Doctor's" administration an unqualified support. When the distinguished object of his admiration returned to power his delight knew no bounds. On every point where Mr Pitt dissented from the views then prevalent among the friends of Court and Church, Sir James cordially agreed with him. Politics of Sir James.

* Letter to Lord Muncaster: Wilberforce's Diary, 16th March, 1800. Vol. ii. p. 359.

† Life of Milner, p. 457.

1802. He looked on war with France as a sad necessity, regarded negro slavery with detestation, and wished to see religious disabilities removed.

Member for Ripon. On the decease of Mr Lawrence, with whose family he had long been intimate, Sir James Graham
Sep., 1798. was returned for Ripon. In 1802 he was re-elected; and in 1806 was once more returned for the borough; but at the general election of 1807 he gave way to the Hon. F. J. Robinson, afterwards Lord Goderich.

Bishop Vernon. The see of Carlisle was, during many years, filled by Dr Vernon, who subsequently took the name of Harcourt. The Bishop took little part in religious or political discussion, satisfied himself with performing the stated duties of his office, maintaining as much of discipline as the laxity of the time allowed, and keeping at Rose Castle a better table, and dispensing a more liberal hospitality, than his predecessors had done. He liked coming to Netherby, and the lady and the laird liked him; and one of the earliest recollections of the subject of these memoirs was of the good-natured prelate in his white whig and purple coat receiving young and old, clergy and laity, at the
Archbishop of York. palace on "public days." When the archiepiscopal see of York fell vacant, the baronet, with many other persons of distinction in the county, sought by every allowable means to secure their diocesan's promotion. Sir James made no secret of the interest he took in the affair, and talked about it so frequently at home,

that when intelligence of the appointment having been made reached Carlisle, an old groom who had heard it in the town rode hard to Netherby to bring his master the tidings, and making his way into the dining-room, he exclaimed, "Sir Jams, Sir Jams, the Bishop has got the place!" Lady Catherine was also glad, but felt much more concern as to what manner of man was destined to be Dr Vernon's successor. 1802.

Her friend, the dean, would, she was persuaded, be the worthiest and best that could be found; but she knew that Calvinistic tenets were not in fashion, and she could only pray that she might live to see the time when they would be no longer a bar to high preferment. Milner told her that the idea of his having a mitre was utterly vain, and that he was well content with what he had, which seems to have been most true.

School days at Dalston.

Such were the principal persons within the sphere of whose intermingling influence young James grew from infancy to boyhood. At Dalston, a village some six or seven miles distant, the Rev. Walter Fletcher, then Chancellor of the Diocese, kept a private school, where the sons of several of the neighbouring gentry received their first lessons in Greek and Latin. James and his brother William became his pupils, as did also at the same time the young Lord Glamorgan, afterwards Duke of Beaufort.

1803. What progress they made in their studies does not very distinctly appear. Mr Fletcher was a good scholar and an amiable man, who enjoyed the esteem in after life of most of those entrusted to his charge. His wife, for some forgotten cause, seems to have been less popular with them. In resentment at some real or imaginary wrong, which they ascribed to the influence of the lady, the heir of Netherby is said to have suggested to his companions a singular method of vengeance, namely, that they should sow her flower-garden with thistles; and this piece of mischief he undertook to execute accordingly. As might be expected, he had his share in whatever boyish scrapes the little confraternity at Dalston got into; and he was doomed to bear the penalties of their detection. But in after life he looked back with pleasure on his first school days, and always spoke of his old preceptor with kindness and respect. Mrs Fletcher still survives, and forgets only the mischievous pranks of the early inmate of her dwelling.

Rose Castle. Rose Castle, the episcopal palace of Carlisle, is situated not far from Dalston, and Bishop Vernon frequently included the Chancellor's pupils among his numerous guests. A gentleman who lived in the neighbourhood, loved to recall in after days in what different trim the boys used to turn out on such occasions. Lord Glamorgan seldom cared what he wore, or how he looked; young Graham had

even then about him something of the future dandy, 1804.
his dress being scrupulously neat and well put on. Besides a pleasant day now and then at the Bishop's, he was allowed to visit sometimes at the Oaks, the residence of Mr Blamire, whose son was nearly the same age. The boys became good friends; and the companionship of boyhood proved the forecast of their association during a brief but notable interval in their public lives, in a manner as little dreamed of by them as by any friend of either.

A lady who was intimate with the family of Dr Fletcher recollects the period of young Graham's residence at Dalston, from 1802 to 1804, but is not certain how long he remained there. "He was then a very handsome boy, tall for his age, and intelligent-looking. I particularly remember his being at Naworth with the Fletchers one day to meet my father and mother, and their remarking the interest he took in the place, his father having been born there while Dr Graham was rebuilding Netherby." *

John of the Gate.

There were till very lately some few persons living who remembered the freaks and pastimes of his holidays at home. One of them, John Routledge, better known by the epithet of "John of the Gate," was often heard to tell how young James and he used to seek opportunity for sallying out to fight

* Memorandum by Miss Mouncey, Carlisle, June 26th, 1862.

1805. the boys of the village of Longtown; and how on one occasion, when they had got the worst of it, he had to take his youthful master to the river-side, "wash his face, and make him all tidy," before he could venture home. They had no real quarrel with the Longtown lads; but there was no one else at hand to have a tussle with; so whenever they might without observation they fought them.

Westminster. From Dalston he was sent to Westminster, then a favourite place of education with many of the great families whose sons were expected to take part in public life. Among his school-fellows were Lord Charles Lennox (afterwards Duke of Richmond), to whom he was fag during his first year, Lord John Russell, and Thomas Vowler Short, the present Bishop of St Asaph. The latter was two years his senior, and as they did not board in the same house, they were not companions. Lord John was just his own age, and during a portion of his stay at Westminster had a place in the same form, and there began that intimacy, which, with many interruptions, caused by the diversity of their political views, lasted during their lives.

On his return to the country for vacation he would sometimes stay at the house of Mr Mouncey, in Carlisle.

1806. "I recollect his coming in 1806," says the daughter of that gentleman, "to my father's house, to remain for the night on his way to Netherby; for the mail in those days left at six in the morning, and did not arrive from London till very late in the evening. He had perfectly at the time the appearance and manners of a man, though still very young."* The worthy baronet marked, with more of pride than he sometimes cared to own, the early promise of distinction in his eldest son. A friend who had been warm in his expression of admiration, ventured once to say to him, "The lad is full of life, good looks, and talent, and as for height, he would put you in his pocket." "You are quite mistaken, my dear sir," was the reply, "for I can assure you he is never out of mine." 1806. Personal appearance.

His progress under Dr William Carey,† then master of Westminster, does not seem to have been in any way remarkable. He construed Latin fluently, and found it easy to commit long passages to memory. He also showed an early fondness for Greek, for the sake of the noble images and ideas it disclosed, and the impressive music of the language. His tastes even then were greatly governed by his ear for rhythm. In Homer he took particular delight, and early grew familiar with the finest thoughts and accents of the father of heroic song. But the book which he knew best at school, and which in after years was perhaps his chief favourite, was Horace, with every line of which he came to be as Classical studies.

* Memoradum of Miss Mouncey, before quoted.

† Subsequently raised to the See of Exeter.

1807. familiar as the elder Pitt is said to have been with the Eclogues of Virgil.

StStephen's Chapel. When not above fifteen he began to take a lively interest in the debates in Parliament, which the students at Westminster have always enjoyed the privilege of hearing. He heard the last words of Pitt and Fox ere they passed away from the scene of their long and glorious rivalry, and continued to listen with hardly less pleasure to the exciting harangues of Windham and Canning, and the earnest expostulations of Sheridan and Grattan against the continuance of the Penal Laws. It was a time of perplexity and peril. Napoleon was at the summit of his power. Austria lay bleeding and broken; Italy and Holland and Switzerland were reduced to the condition of tributaries; and men waited breathlessly to learn where the blight of conquest next should fall. Antagonism to Imperial France had come to be nationally a passion and a principle; and though everywhere upon the continent England had hitherto failed to check the tide of aggression, the splendour of her success at sea made up for her defeats, and hardly any one thought of proposing an abandonment of the war. All that the leaders of opposition in either House ventured upon was the endeavour to circumscribe its desolating range, and to urge incessantly on Government the wisdom of conciliating Ireland by the removal of religious disabilities, and of extinguishing discontent in England by timely reform.

Under the gallery of old St Stephen's Chapel, with 1808. its dark oak panels and brazen chandeliers, young Graham listened with thoughtful sympathy to the earnest accents of the minority on the left of Speaker Abbott's chair, and marvelled how it came to pass that, with the exception of the gay and versatile Secretary for Foreign Affairs, the majority on the opposite side seemed to have so few amongst them who could speak as well. He heard Mr Whitbread inveighing against the folly of quarrelling with America, and Mr Grattan, in low and quivering tones, with imagery quaint and picturesque, and argumentation full of antithetic pomp, pleading for a people whom he had striven to make independent, and still wished to make free. There too he heard his kinsman, Lord Archibald Hamilton, denouncing unconstitutional tamperings with the representation; and a representative from his own county, Mr Curwen, in simple but vigorous language, trying hard to get efficient penalties imposed on the sale of seats in Parliament, and on the buying of voters at elections. There he heard Mr Wilberforce, his mother's friend, pleading for the liberation of the negro, and Sir S. Romilly gently, but firmly, remonstrating against the cruelties of the Criminal Code. And as he sat there in his school-boy's gown and watched the wordy fray, there woke within him the first stirrings of ambition, and that desire to make for himself a name, that eventually became the

1809. chief animating motive of his life. He often called to mind in after years his boyish evenings in the House of Commons, and always viewed with dissatisfaction the projects entertained for the removal of the school, from a remembrance of the advantages he felt he had derived from its proximity in his time to the ancient home of Parliament.*

Rev. G. Richards. On quitting Westminster, in 1809, he was placed for some time with the Rev. G. Richards, as a private tutor to prepare him for the University. His new preceptor was Vicar of Bampton near Farringdon, in Berkshire, where he then resided. Mr Richards had been a Fellow of Oriel, and enjoyed no little distinction for his taste and skill in composition. He had in his day obtained the prizes for both English and Latin verse, as well as that for the best Essay in English prose. He was devoted to the pursuit of literature, and rather plumed himself upon the grace and purity of his style. How far his pupil may have imbibed from him any of that precision in the choice of words, or the tendency to measured pomp of expression, which characterized some of his earlier efforts as a speaker, it is impossible now to tell. There are few, perhaps, who have obtained great excellence in composition who cannot trace back through the twilight of early impressions the first tendencies and predilections for particular

* Speech at a meeting of Old Westminsters, respecting the project for removing the school, 16th May, 1860.

authors, and who cannot refer many of their own habits of thought and phrase to the influence of the first teacher who took the trouble to unfold to them the origin and comparative value of words. The Vicar of Bampton discerned in his pupil a readiness to appreciate nice distinctions in the use of epithets, and in the choice of expressions, highly characteristic of the precocity of his mind. Perhaps he sympathized too readily with the prematurity it ought to have been his aim to check rather than encourage: but without the means of accurately estimating his method of instruction we are not at liberty to turn the telescope of conjecture the wrong way, or to judge by the result. 1809.

Sir John Throckmorton.

While at Bampton young Graham frequently visited the neighbouring seat of Sir John Throckmorton, one of the most eminent agriculturalists of his day, and one of the early friends of Mr Coke of Holkham. At Buckland he heard of the many improvements in husbandry and estate management, which then possessed an engrossing interest for the more thoughtful and enlightened owners of the soil. It was then and there he once told a friend who questioned him on the subject, "that he took the infection of experimentalizing in agriculture," and became imbued with that desire for the application of science and capital to the cultivation of the soil, which constituted one of the most active and pleasurable impulses of his subsequent life.

1810. Christchurch. In June, 1810, he entered as a Gentleman Commoner Christchurch College, Oxford; his tutor was Dr Goodenough, afterwards Dean of Wells.

Recollections of Oxford. "My own impressions of him," writes one who had preceded him from Westminster, but who was in the same class during the next two years at Oxford, "were of a man who wished to work, but who was not forward in his general education. I think I remember him attending a lecture on Aristotle's Rhetoric. There was no great *éclat* about it, but I recollect that he exerted himself, and was one of those who were occasionally called on to construe, Bishop of St Asaph. which marked that the lecturer esteemed him as taking pains with the subject. It was considered a voluntary lecture, in which no idle man would have taken an interest. The age at which he entered Christchurch was what was then considered young, and this, perhaps, prevented him from taking that interest in academical studies which he might otherwise have done. I do not recollect him in any mathematical class, and I know not whether he made any progress in that department. He did not take a degree, because, as far as I remember, he would not have been likely to have obtained honours; and gentlemen commoners in those days rarely took degrees, except in the hope of doing so."*

Lord Middleton. The late Lord Middleton, who was also his class-fellow, and who read with the same private tutor

* Letter from the Bishop of St Asaph, 16th July, 1862.

at Oxford, used to say that there was little indication about him at that time of the qualities for which he was afterwards distinguished. He was best in some of those portions of exact science which were then taught at the University, being well up in algebra and arithmetical calculations of all sorts, of which he seemed especially fond. In other respects he did not bear the character of being either particularly clever or studious; and nobody ever thought he would turn out a great parliamentary debater. Nevertheless, it was here that he completed his acquaintance with classic literature. For the Latin poets and historians he seems to have imbibed an early admiration. He took a peculiar pleasure in apt quotation; was sure to be down on a blunder with sharp and ready jeer, whenever committed by another, and was punctiliously accurate himself in his way of giving any line or fragment which his fastidious taste permitted him to cite. His speeches in after life attest his familiarity with the least as well as with the best-read Roman writers; and those who had the opportunity of hearing them are not likely to forget how daintily and with what seeming delight he would deliver a sarcastic warning from Horace, or a ringing verse of Virgil. 1810.

In manner, at this time, he is said to have been rather reserved, and indisposed to make new acquaintances. His vacations were chiefly spent at home. He was already an expert angler and good

1811. shot, and he looked forward enthusiastically to the period of the year when many of his father's sporting friends assembled at Netherby for the grouse-shooting.

Mr Starkey was an old friend of his father, and used to visit Netherby. Sir James valued highly the opportunities of sport his own property afforded, and wished to secure and extend them. The moors, which lay between the northernmost verge of the estate and that of Mr Charlton, of Hesselside, in Northumberland, were prized above all others on the Western Border for their grouse and black game. They formed part of a manor, the title to which was disputed; and the question was at last settled by a suit at law; and the decision having gone in favour of Mr Charlton, Sir James agreed to take the moors at a yearly rent, an arrangement which continued undisturbed during his own and his son's life-time.

Fox-hunting. Of the autumnal visitors to Netherby, few came oftener and none had a heartier welcome than Mr Starkey, a gentleman connected by birth and property with Lancashire, but who resided chiefly at Goldsborough Hall, a fine old manor-house of James I.'s time, belonging to the Lascelles family, in the West Riding of Yorkshire. It stood in the centre of the well-known district which was hunted by the Bramham Moor hounds, and it was chiefly on this account that Mr Starkey had chosen it for his residence. He was a man greatly esteemed for his genial manners, unaffected hospitality, and his consideration for the comfort of all around him. The capacious stabling of the Hall was always full during the hunting season, and his delight was to make welcome men for the most part younger than himself. His likeness, on a grey pony, which he rode for many years, is still to be seen in several of the farm-houses of the neighbourhood; and his memory, as well as that of his amiable and accomplished wife, have not yet faded from local recollection. The young Oxonian was one of his hunting guests in the winter of 1811. He soon became an especial favourite with him, and often subsequently visited the Hall. 1811.

Allerton Park, the residence of Lord Stourton, lay at a short distance, and in the companionship of his sons, who were of congenial tastes and years, Mr Starkey's new visitor spent many happy days. An intimacy, which afterwards ripened into enduring friendship, sprang up between him and the Hon. Edward Stourton, better known afterwards as Sir Edward Vavasour. They were nearly of an age, both keen sportsmen, and forward riders in the hunt. The second brother, Charles, who some years later took the name of Langdale, shared in their amusements, but, like his new acquaintance, he was desirous of foreign travel, and in the course of the ensuing summer both quitted England to visit the Mediterranean. Family of Stourton.

1812. Last term at Oxford. Meanwhile, he returned to keep his last term at Oxford; but the hope of academic distinction, if it had ever existed, being gone, pleasure had more attraction for him than study for its own sake. The discipline of the University at the time was in all respects of the least rigorous sort. Looking back after a long interval on the practical indifferentism as to morals and religion which then prevailed, he could not help regarding it as somewhat strange, considering the high pretensions of the place to peculiar zeal for orthodoxy.

"When I was matriculated, I was not compelled to state what I knew in matters of religion; but I was called upon to subscribe and to swear to what I believed. During the two years of my residence at college I was never, with the exception of the required attendance at chapel, once called upon to attend any lectures, either upon theology or divinity. During the whole of that time I never received any religious instruction whatever, apart from that which I derived from the enforced attendance at chapel, and I am ashamed to say that whilst I was at Oxford I never, during the whole period of my residence, heard a single sermon." *

He quitted Christchurch in 1812, the last payment entered in his name in the college books being for the quarter ending Lady Day.

* Hansard: Debates on Provincial Colleges in Ireland, 30th May, 1845.

CHAPTER III.

FOREIGN TRAVEL.

1812—1815.

State of Politics.

The spring and summer of 1812 he spent for the most part in London. Amid the pleasures and frivolities of the time there ran a deep and bitter current of political feeling. The Prince Regent had deliberately broken with the party in whose principles and leaders he had once affected to place unbounded confidence, and thrown himself into the arms of their rivals. Society was divided between those who exulted in the renunciation by Carlton House of its old predilections and those who reviled the faithlessness of the Prince, and ridiculed his attempts to cast the blame of his secession upon his former friends. Moore, then at the zenith of his fame as a satirist, never wrote so wittily or so well as when the Regent was the subject of his verse. Every drawing-room and coffee-house laughed at his too faithful rendering in rhyme of the celebrated letter * to the Duke

The Regent

* "I am proud to declare I have no predilections,
My heart is a sieve, where some scattered affections

1812. of York, in which the Prince declared that the re-

breaks with the Whigs. strictions on his regency being about to expire, he meant to show that he had no predilections, and that he would be glad of a coalition, in order to be rid of government by party. Lords Grenville and Grey rejected haughtily every attempt to lure them into combination with Mr Percival and his colleagues; and their resolution was approved, with few exceptions, by the whole of their party. The personal conduct of the Prince had long tended to lower him in popular estimation; and his desertion of the too faithful friends of his youth from the moment he attained power was regarded as an evil omèn by many whose sympathies were not with them.

In such a condition of the social and political atmosphere young Graham first began to feel sympathy with the practical strife of party. Some of his relatives, like Lord A. Hamilton, and not a few of his father's personal friends, belonged to the opposition. The new Court and the old Ministry had about them nothing to countervail in an ardent and enthusiastic nature, the natural attraction towards great and generous principles, like those of religious freedom, abolition of slavery, and popular progress. Some of the best men of the Tories refused to

Are just danced about for a moment or two,
And the finer they are the more sure to run through."

A parody on the celebrated letter from the Prince Regent to the Duke of York, 13th Feb. 1812.

belong to the administration, the weakness of which was shown by the success of Mr Canning's motion in the House of Commons for the adjustment of Catholic claims,* and the defeat of a similar proposition of the Marquis Wellesley in the House of Lords by a majority of only one. After the death of Mr Percival the defence of the costly, and, as it then seemed to the most sanguine, doubtful policy of the war, devolved mainly on Lord Castlereagh, for Mr Peel was only entering upon his apprenticeship to office as Secretary for Ireland, and Mr Huskisson's abilities and resources were not generally known. There was but one man on the Treasury Bench who possessed the strength of intellect and gift of speech that fitted him to contend with any hope of mastery with the many critics and opponents of the Government. Mr Plunkett had entered public life as a Whig, and he still professed to adhere to the leading principles of his early friends. But having taken office with the coalition in 1806, he continued to retain it under subsequent administrations. With the exception of Mr Canning, he had now no equal in debate; but, indolently proud, self-tormentingly fastidious, and unaffectedly averse to dealing with great questions of which he did not feel himself to be thoroughly a master, he could rarely be induced to take part in the desultory and distracted conflicts of the day. The fortunes of the

1812. Liverpool Administration. 22nd June. 1st July. 11th May. Mr Plunkett.

* The Resolution was carried by a majority of 235 to 106.

1812. great European struggle had of late gone in favour of France, and no one dreamed that Imperial ambition was soon to "o'erleap its sell, and fall on t'other side." The Duke of Wellington, after fighting his way to Madrid, had been driven back to the frontiers of Portugal; and the continent seemed more abjectly than ever at Napoleon's feet. Ministers had nothing to propose but new loans and taxes, and the old determination to concede nothing for the sake of peace abroad or contentment at home. There was little in their conservatism to win the confidence or fix the imagination of youth: much to repel the one and disenchant the other. Mr. Graham was bent on being a politician, and was resolved to be a Whig; and being proposed by Lord Morpeth, he was admitted a member of Brookes's Club.

21st June, Brookes's Club.

Foreign Travel.

At the end of the summer he went abroad. The greater portion of the continent was still closed against English travellers; but he visited the chief sea-ports of Portugal and Spain, which had been delivered from the presence of French troops.

The Cortes of Spain.

Cadiz had many charms for him, and he lingered there for some time. The Cortes held their deliberations within its walls, and he was a constant listener to their debates. It was the first outflow of national intellect and feeling, long pent up in silence and darkness under the decrepit rule of the Bourbons, and all was fresh, sanguine, and generous, in the prevalent tone. The aim of the leaders was direct,

and for the most part disinterested. They earnestly 1812.
sought the domestic regeneration of their country, simultaneously with its deliverance from a foreign yoke. Many of them had studied profoundly the institutions beneath whose shade other nations were prosperous, independent, and free; and they could not be persuaded that cuttings stuck down in the ruined pleasure-grounds of the palace, or the untilled, uncultivated sierra, where a languid and laughing peasantry looked lazily after their flocks, would take long to grow strong—strong enough to resist the treacherous blast of reaction. They believed in themselves and their book-learned principles, both of which were excellent in their way; but they made the mistake of ascribing to their fellow-countrymen in general, and to their expectant king, the capacity to appreciate the benefits they could confer. It is hard to say which was the least to be relied on, or whether the sequel is most calculated to awaken detestation of the perfidy of Ferdinand, or pity for the degradation of the populace who passively acquiesced in his cruelty and baseness.

But in 1812 the disenchantment and destruction that was in store for the Spanish parliamentarians was hidden from their eyes. Foreign armies still struggled for ascendency in their fields, and but a few towns and a small portion of the country recognized the authority of the Constitution. They had little aid to offer the liberating armies sent by England,

1812. and little pay to offer the guerilla bands, whom hatred of the stranger and love of adventure inspired, rather than anything deserving the name of political spirit. Votes of thanks were easily given, but votes of money the Cortes had not the means to make good. There was nothing for it but to ask subsidies from England, and keep talking at Cadiz, which they did well. In time patriotic eloquence and the enactment of a first-rate code of enlightened laws must have their effect. So they went on, legislating against the inquisition and the slave trade, pronouncing in favour of first principles, and recording unalterable convictions in a stately and sonorous style, just as if Joseph were not at Madrid, or as if they could trust Ferdinand for a national chief whenever he should get there;—as if by creating a pretentious show of constitutionalism beneath the glances of dark-eyed beauty, and amid the laudatory tappings of its fan, they were really establishing a free government in Spain. But if the unforeseen result was sad, the rhetoric was at least delightful. The young traveller never tired of listening to the debates in the Cortes. It was not to be expected that he should discern cause for misgiving and doubt where all around him was radiant with
Arguelles. patriotic enthusiasm and joy. Arguelles was his favourite orator, and many years after he would dwell with melancholy pleasure on his recollection of the speeches of this gifted and accomplished man. He saw a good deal of him in private, and marvelled at

the accuracy of his knowledge of English life, and the force and originality of his comments upon men and things. Though full of business at the time, Arguelles not unfrequently found leisure to expound to him his views of Spanish politics with less reserve than he would have ventured probably to use in talking to some of his own countrymen. And thus for the first time his youthful English confidant caught a glimpse of the dark and grim realities that lurked in the statesman's mind, amid the gaudy show of a sudden improvization of liberty. Though he spoke cautiously, and as a man bound at all hazards to act up to the part he had undertaken, whatever fears he might have that others would fail, he left on his hearer the impression of a man sincerely sorry to believe that he was honester and wiser than those about him. The confidence he was able to inspire by his glorious declamations in the permanent freedom of his country, he was unable to create in himself. It was the first chill experienced by the would-be politician, and it never wholly passed away. 1812.

The Duke of Wellington at Cadiz.

During his stay at Cadiz he was the guest of Sir Henry Wellesley, to whom he had been introduced by letters from influential friends in England, and it was at the house of the hospitable Minister he first met the Duke of Wellington. The great soldier held the command of the Spanish as well as the English armies. His personal pre-eminence no one ventured to question, and the advantage of

1812. concentrating authority in such hands no civilian was prepared to dispute. But faction for its own purposes secretly worked upon the national susceptibility of the Spanish officers, and more than one of the generals, on whose co-operation the chief of the allied armies had relied, doggedly refused to obey orders coming from him.* The Duke remonstrated, and complained to the executive government, but in vain. The Regency would willingly have enforced all he required, had they known how. But they were too conscious of the frailty of their tenure of power to take decisive steps in the right direction, and impunity served to render the prospect for the future more lamentable than even the experience of the past. As soon as the campaign of 1812 was over, the Duke resolved to bring matters to a point in his own way. He came to Cadiz, and proceeded forthwith to explain to the Council of Regency on what conditions alone he could retain the double command. He told them plainly that it was impossible for him to do so "unless he possessed sufficient power, and that if they did not feel authorized to trust him therewith he must beg leave to relinquish the command of the Spanish armies." His requirments were, "That the officers should be appointed and promoted solely at his recommendation; that he should have the power of

* Napier, Hist. Peninsular War, vol. iv. p. 290.

dismissing those whom he thought deserving of that punishment; that the resources of the State applicable to the equipment and payment of the troops should be applied as he recommended; that the chief of the Spanish staff should be sent to his head-quarters; that all reports should be made to him; and that he himself should report direct to the Spanish Government." He begged an early answer on all these points, as he must return to his head-quarters in a very few days.* The position he was compelled to assume was sufficiently difficult and invidious, but the moral courage he displayed in telling the Spaniards what it was necessary they should hear had its reward. They yielded all that he required, voted him thanks and compliments, and he was admitted to make his acknowledgments in person to the assembled Cortes.†

1812.

Dec. 30.

He earnestly recommended the leading men of all parties to adjourn their political differences, and to concentrate their thoughts on the prosecution of the war. He advised them not to meddle with the Holy Office, lest the powerful party of the Church should be alienated,‡ and though upon this and other points his advice was not followed, he was listened to with the utmost deference and respect.

* Letter to Don J. de Carvajal, Minister of War, Cadiz, 25th Dec., 1812. Wellington Despatches, vol. x. p. 1.

† Napier, Hist. vol. v. p. 400. ‡ Ibid.

1812. A Christmas dinner at the Embassy.

During his stay at Cadiz many Spaniards of distinction were invited by his brother to meet him at the Embassy. It was Christmas time, and the dinners were served partly in English fashion. Mr Graham and Mr C. Stourton, who had more recently arrived from England, were present at one of them, when the renowned chief, on whom all eyes and thoughts were fixed, suddenly caused much amusement and surprise by setting fire to some brandy which he had poured over a mince pie just as he would have done if he had been at home.

Sails for Sicily.

At the end of a protracted sojourn at Cadiz Mr Graham was desirous of visiting Sicily, (then garrisoned by British troops,) and whose people were occupied with similar political changes to those in progress in Spain. The *Furieuse*, one of the finely-built frigates taken from the French during the war, lay in the roadstead; and he gladly availed himself of the offer of her commander, his old acquaintance, Capt. Mouncey, to give him a passage to Palermo, where Lord Montgomery discharged confidentially certain political functions, as well as the duties of a military command under Lord William Bentinck. Letters from home commended the young tourist to the notice of the Major-general, who seems from the first to have formed a high opinion of him, and who thought he discerned the qualities calculated to fit him in an eminent degree for official service. He offered to make him his private secretary. The proposal was promptly accepted; and at twenty-one Mr Graham became for the first time initiated in the details and mysteries of diplomatic life. He had not been long thus occupied when there appeared reason to believe that it might not be impossible to detach Murat from his alliance with Napoleon. The "first cavalry officer in Europe" had quitted the Imperial army after the retreat from Moscow, in deep ill-humour, and on his return to Naples, found his people anxious only to be disengaged from the obligations of an alliance, which, always burthensome, was no longer gilded by the light of victory. A few of his old comrades in arms, incapable of comprehending how one who owed his crown to Napoleon could ever entertain the notion of deserting him, clung to the idea that Joachim might remain in a less active position during the next campaign, without absolutely breaking with his brother-in-law or incurring the reproach of unfaithfulness to his cause. But the majority of those admitted to the royal council were more dependent on the maintenance of his ephemeral power, and less concerned about the honour and interest of France. They saw the star of conquest waning, and read the omen with reference to their personal fortunes. If Naples continued in the wake of the falling Empire it must share its fate: Murat and his family would be treated as mere intruders, without a claim to consideration; and all who adhered to them would be driven into poverty and

1813.

Alienation of Murat.

1813. exile. If France were about to be brought within limits more compatible with the independence of the neighbouring countries, Murat could do nothing to prevent it: and for the sake of Italy he ought not to attempt to do so. With the name of king he had hitherto been a vassal; though he ceased to be a vassal he might still remain a king. It was not his fault if Napoleon had over-reached himself, and seemed to be on the brink of losing the conquests of many years. Murat had led for him the cavalry of the Grand Army throughout the Russian invasion and retreat, as no one but himself, in Napoleon's judgment, could have led them, and instead of thanks he had been snubbed and spurned for his pains. And now what was he to do? "Act with dignity and reserve, but with loyalty to his benefactor," muttered his French adherents: "communicate secretly with the English, and come to an understanding with the Austrians," whispered his Italian prompters. He wavered long; listened by turns to every suggestion; resolved and recanted his resolves repeatedly; one hour cursed his fate that ever he had been a king, and the next resumed his naturally joyous mood, embraced his children, laughed with his attendants, called for his favourite horse, and amid the greetings of the populace and the golden serenity of all around him, felt that the kingdom he had governed with a light and lenient hand could not depart from him. Something would happen to bring the war to an end before it was necessary for him to make the terrible choice between political prudence and personal honour. But day after day rolled by, and no tidings came of a nature qualified to allay his disquietude and trouble. It grew more and more clear that Napoleon would never yield until it was too late. The unhappy Joachim at length consented to send a secret message to the English Embassy at Palermo, the result of which was the opening of negotiations, having for their object his secession from the cause of the Emperor, and in certain contingencies his open junction with the allies, upon condition that in any event the kingdom of Naples should be guaranteed to him and to his descendants for ever.* 1813.

Secret negotiations.

It was in the conduct of the negotiations arising out of this state of things that the young official found his first opportunity of distinction. They had not proceeded far when Lord Montgomery fell ill and was compelled to leave Palermo. The entire management of the affair devolved, in consequence, at a most critical juncture, on his private secretary. His assiduity was untiring, and his instinctive caution supplied the want of diplomatic training and experience. Mr C. Stourton had followed him from Cadiz, and their leisure hours were spent very much together; but Mr Graham soon became thoroughly absorbed in his work, not a day passing for a considerable time in which he did not devote nine or ten hours to

* Colletta, Hist. Naples, vol. ii. chap. 4.

1813. business. Upon Lord W. Bentinck's return, after his 26th Sept. unsuccessful expedition to the south coast of Spain, to resume his political functions at Palermo, he found Mr Graham at his post, and fully recognized the services he had rendered. Military co-operation with the Austrians in Italy being soon anticipated, he accepted a staff appointment under Lord William, who then held the command-in-chief of the British forces in the Mediterranean. Meanwhile the negotiations with the King of Naples continued, and Mr Graham was sent to Murat, with whom he concluded the preliminary armistice that separated him from Napoleon.

Convention with Murat.

The next step was to secure the assent of Austria. Communications were difficult, and time pressed. The French still held Rome and Central Italy, while Eugene Beauharnois governed as Viceroy at Milan. No one, at the disposal of the King of Naples, seemed to possess the qualities fitting him to undertake so venturous a mission. For opposite reasons the unhappy Joachim distrusted equally his French and Italian advisers; and at last the young English secretary undertook to act as envoy to the Austrian General. He had to pass through the whole extent of territory then occupied by French troops on his way to the head-quarters of Marshal Bellegarde, where he remained several days. Though provided with a Neapolitan passport, the journey was one of no inconsiderable hazard; and

Perilous adventure.

on his return through Rome he narrowly escaped 1812. being arrested. When they met afterwards at Naples he told Mr Stourton "that he owed his safety to his Swiss servant, as he not only had official despatches but an English uniform in his trunk." *

The person whose presence of mind and adroit- Bodinet. ness lent him such important aid in his perilous adventure was Bodinet, a valet whom he had brought with him from England, and who had lived with his father for some years. Bodinet had a singular facility for acquiring and speaking foreign languages, and it was by this means that he succeeded in baffling the vigilance of the French at Rome. He used to say that he could speak any European dialect, and to boast that when he once met a fellow-servant as well up in strange tongues as himself, they perplexed their uneducated brethren, who only understood French, German, or Italian, by talking to each other in Russian in the servants' hall. Lady Catherine placed great confidence in this man, and felt less solicitude about her son because the faithful attendant was with him. She gave him many injunctions ere setting out, one of them being that he should be careful every night to place a copy of the Scriptures on his master's dressing-table. A friend who happened to enter his room earlier than usual one day at Palermo saw the volume, and asked

* Letter from the Hon. C. Langdale, 18th Sept., 1862.

1814. how it happened to be there. "Oh, that is Bodinet's doing," was the reply; "he never forgets that my mother desired him to place the book so that I should see it the first thing when I rise in the morning."

Captain Napier.

Among the ships composing Lord Exmouth's fleet, then cruising off the coast of Italy, was the *Euryalus*, commanded by Captain Charles Napier, whose originality and energy of character already fixed attention upon him wherever he came. The Admiral entertained a high opinion of him, for he possessed, as he once told Mr Graham, "both dash and craft." An acquaintance then began, which was renewed at various periods of their subsequent lives; and in their widely different careers they were brought more than once into contact, resulting for a time in relations of confidence, and eventually in memorable personal collision. But the first impression left by the enterprising though eccentric sailor on the mind of the politician was never effaced; and we shall find him recurring to it in a moment of great national emergency, after an interval of forty years.

Mr Graham accompanied Lord W. Bentinck throughout the campaign in Northern Italy, was sent on various missions to the Austrian head-quarters, and was fortunate enough to obtain the praise and thanks of his chief and of the Government. He witnessed the surrender of Genoa to the allies, and always spoke feelingly of the manner in which the hopes of Italian independence had been raised only to be dashed by English and Austrian diplomacy at that period; and he sympathized ardently in the mortification felt by his generous and high-minded chief, when the expectations he had sincerely, but perhaps unwarily, held out to the Lombards and Tuscans were falsified. Charmed by the novelty and excitement of the scenes he visited, he gave himself up to the enjoyments of the hour. His taste for dress made him dwell with curiosity and pleasure on the picturesque costumes around him; and, in the gaiety of youthful companionship, he sometimes indulged in the pardonable foppery of trying how some of the Southern garbs became him. A gentleman lately mentioned to a mutual friend that he had seen him in a Greek costume enter the opera-box of the English General at Genoa, where his handsome face and figure, thus set off to singular advantage, attracted no little observation. He brought home with him a curious variety of dress, chiefly of Sicilian manufacture; and his intimates used to say when he appeared in a waistcoat of a colour and pattern they had not seen before that his valet "had been to the Palermo box." 1814.

Return to England.

On his return to England, after an absence of more than two years, he could not help observing the important changes that had taken place in things around him. The Government which had brought the war to a successful termination was supposed now

1815. to hold power by a lease of lives renewable for ever. There was no longer any pretence made of conciliating the Whigs; and the Radicals were thenceforth to be put down with a high hand.

1816. He soon began to enter eagerly into the discussion of the many exciting questions to which the circumstances of the time were giving rise, especially those connected with social and financial policy. The fall of agricultural prices induced the Legislature to adopt prohibitory duties on the import of corn, whereby the landed interest hoped to save their own revenues from the diminution inevitable on the cessation of war expenditure. The holders of office whose incomes had been raised to meet the enhanced cost of living during the war were influential enough to dissuade the Government from making any proportionate reduction of salaries, though fixed incomes were worth much more than they had previously been. Great numbers of persons were necessarily thrown out of employment; and profits and wages fell so low that wide-spread suffering and discontent speedily began to appear. Ministers attempted to continue the Income Tax during 1816, but were driven to abandon it by an outburst of angry feeling on the part of the commercial and professional classes. Its remission lulled for a season their ill humour, but mitigated in no perceptible degree the privations of the labourer and artizan. Distress deepened on all sides, and disaffection to the existing order of things was rife. Specifics of all kinds abounded. Some were partial, some general, but none commanded national assent. Every man had his nostrum, in whose efficacy he confidently believed. The writings of Cobbett, then in the prime of his vituperative vigour, made a deep impression on the minds of men the most dissimilar in their ways of life and thought. Our young politician was, amongst others, struck by their racy and pungent originality; and he read with more of interest than pleasure the fierce diatribes of the then popular and powerful *Register*. His mind was not one, however, that would long hang dependently on any other, and least of all upon one so wayward, capricious, and inconsistent as that of Cobbett. His own method of thinking and of speaking was instinctively logical. He turned, therefore, to the pages of Hume, Adam Smith, and Ricardo, for the solution of the evils that perplexed those around him; and to the leading principles they proclaimed he soon became a proselyte. The Catholic question was then almost the only one on which all shades of liberals were agreed. Free trade was still in obscure infancy; and many of the Whigs, and nearly the entire of the Tory party, were opposed to Parliamentary reform. At popular meetings in most of the great towns resolutions were passed in favour of annual Parliaments and universal suffrage; and the language in which these changes were advocated

1816.

Parliamentary Reform.

1816. on the platform and in the press was violent in the extreme. The prodigality of the Court and the conservatism of the clergy were the subjects of unceasing attack, and the principles of monarchy and an established church were assailed in various quarters. Lord Grenville, Lord Wellesley, and the section of the Tories which for many years had acted in concert with the Whig opposition, became alarmed, and gave their support to the Government, which called

1817. Measures of repression. for new measures of repression.* Lords Grey and Holland in the Upper House, and Mr Brougham, Lord Althorpe, and Sir J. Macintosh in the Lower, while disclaiming extreme opinions, strongly opposed the suspension of the Habeas Corpus Act; and denounced with warmth the unconstitutional power asserted in Lord Sidmouth's celebrated circu-

27th March. lar to Lords-Lieutenant of counties, wherein any Justice of the Peace was declared to have the right of issuing a warrant at his sole discretion for the apprehension of any person publishing opinions he might deem seditious, and detaining him in custody until he should find sufficient bail. Many of the Whigs sided openly with ministers, or refused to take any part against them. While thus opposition in Parliament was rendered numerically powerless, discontent grew wider and deeper out of doors. In the world of fashion, or amid the amusements of a country life, there was little to remind a young

* Speech of the Regent, opening session of 1817.

man of four-and-twenty of these things; and his family and local connections were not likely to foster ideas of personal ambition if he espoused the side of popular progress. Lord W. Bentinck had given him a letter of introduction to Lord Lansdowne, which he had not failed to present. But though the impression he made was favourable, no particular intimacy arose in consequence of the introduction: and to the majority of the Whigs of distinction he was hardly known. 1817.

His kinsman, Lord Archibald Hamilton, was one of the few representatives of Scotland in the House of Commons at that time, who professed himself a Whig, and something more. His manly beauty and high but gentle bearing, his known earnestness of purpose, and punctilious care that every public act and word of his should be in keeping with the most elevated standard of self-denying patriotism,—the consistency of his political life, and the charm of his manner in society, all contributed to win the admiration and attachment of his youthful friend. Lord Archibald was indeed a remarkable man. Through the influence of his brother, the Duke of Hamilton, he had early obtained a seat in Parliament for Lanarkshire. From the outset he evinced a decided predilection for the views advocated by Sir S. Romilly and Mr Whitbread, rather than for those entertained by the party leaders of his own order. After the fall of the Grey and Grenville adminis- Lord A. Hamilton.

1817. tration he acted generally in concert with Lord Folkestone, Sir F. Burdett, Lord Althorpe, and the eminent persons above named. They were "the impracticables" of their day in the estimation of all the temporizers and trimmers of party, and though valued for their spirit and ability by its older chiefs, they often incurred from them the reproach of being too outspoken and thorough-going. The confidence of the people, and the amelioration of their social condition, seemed to them better worth working for than any scheme, however subtle, for the conciliation of the Court. When the Duke of York was accused of complicity in the sale of commissions by his mistress, few of those who had held high office, and who dreamed of holding it again, were disposed to inquire into the scandal; and, had it not been for the uncompromising section whom Mr Whitbread led, it is certain that no censure would have been passed upon the flagrant misdeeds of the Horse Guards. On many subsequent occasions they seceded openly from the aristocratic majority of the opposition. Questions of administrative abuses, of taxation, and of trade engaged their constant attention. After the close of the war they saw with apprehension and dismay the state of physical privation to which the working classes were reduced, and though sometimes differing among themselves as to specific measures of relief, they were bound together by the deep conviction that unless the industry of the people was relieved of its fetters, and their share in the representative system increased, the great institutions of the country could not long be maintained, or its credit and independence preserved. The death of Mr Whitbread left them without any acknowledged head, and for several years their numbers were too inconsiderable to have much weight in the balance of parties. But upon society, upon literature, and, finally, upon the growth of opinion among the mass of the community, their influence was every year more and more perceptible, and few amongst them contributed more worthily to the general result than Lord A. Hamilton. He had never been much of a debater, and the premature infirmity of deafness rendered him averse to taking part in public discussion. In private, however, he retained all his zest for politics; his time and money were ever ready to aid in promoting the cause he loved, and his counsel was continually sought by the associates who had long known its value. He liked Mr Graham, and was looked up to and loved by him. At Brookes's and elsewhere they were constantly together, and it was with Lord Archibald that the first projects were discussed for obtaining a seat in Parliament. 1817.

A seat in Parliament.

Mr Graham longed to take the place which he felt he was qualified to fill in political life; and had his opinions been of a less decided stamp, or had they been in private expressed less warmly, his father would in all likelihood have furthered his ambition.

1818. But the old country gentleman had been too long accustomed to regard the maxims of Church and State propounded in the Eldon and Castlereagh school as those of irrefragable wisdom, to encourage the new-fangled doctrines of reformers and liberals, and his son knew that he could not expect from him the means of obtaining a seat in the House of Commons.

Maternal sympathy.

His mother had more sympathy with his parliamentary aspirations. Intellectually there was more in common between them, and although Lady Catherine never liked his Radical associates, she believed that they were much safer company for him than mere men about town. A life of politics, however unprofitable or ungenteel (for Liberalism in those days was regarded as a decidedly shabby creed,) was in her eyes infinitely better than a life of pleasure. She was glad, indeed, when Mr Starkey induced her son to pay him a long visit once more at Goldsborough, and she was happy when fishing and shooting and the society of old friends in the county occupied his attention at home. But she had too true an insight into a nature like his to suppose that with these he would long be content. He had seen just enough of the world to wish to see more of it. With good looks, and good spirits, and great expectations, and, above all, with a most winning way, when he chose, he had found it easy to make himself acceptable to women as well as to men. Amongst the latter indeed he was less generally popular. He was often self-absorbed, and his manner was already complained of as uncertain,—a fault which grew upon him as he grew older, and did him more harm throughout life than all other foibles and errors taken together. Young men forgive inattention, and old men are tolerant of the caprices and follies of youth, but neither will bear without resentment apparently deliberate slight. The acquaintance with whom you laughed and made free yesternight cannot understand why he is passed in the morning with a ceremonious bow, looked at with half-closed eye, or listened to with a half-unconscious stare. The unintended offence is never forgotten, and seldom forgiven, because from its very nature it is a thing unfit to be complained of, and incapable of being explained away. In female society Mr Graham fared better, for there he never seemed to give himself airs. Clever women declared he was most intelligent, and fine ladies vowed he was charming. Lady Catherine, happening to pay a visit at Lowther soon after he had been there, found Lady Lonsdale and her daughters full of praises of her son; and rumour, which spares no one, busied itself with the possible consequences that might arise from the old intimacy between the families having been thus renewed. But as these surmises came to nothing, and there appeared no immediate likelihood of his settling down in the country as the idle heir of one

1818. who was but in his fifty-seventh year, his mother was easily reconciled to his projects for getting into Parliament, where, as she thought, he might one day do much good, and could hardly do any harm.

Proposal to stand for Hull.

It was not until the General Election of 1818 that the opening he so anxiously longed for presented itself. Through the intervention of some of the friends he had made at Brookes's, he was recommended to the constituency of Hull, whom he offered to represent as the champion of Religious Liberty, Slavery Abolition, Non-intervention in Continental feuds, and in home policy Retrenchment and Reform. Such was his creed at starting in public life. Many were the aberrations from it in after times laid to his charge; many the accusations made by party rancour of total recusancy. Yet, before we have done with the story of this strong man's life, it will, we think, be shown that in the main he was not wanting in continuity of purpose, or indifferent to that law of consistency with himself, whereby a man of action must after all be judged.

After some negotiations with those who undertook to act for the popular party in the borough, he agreed to stand. Lord Milton promised that the influence of his family should not be wanting; and although Mr Wilberforce could not be expected to interfere on his behalf, the fact that he was a personal friend of the new candidate's family would tell, it was hoped, with many in his favour; for the great assailant of the slave-trade had himself for many years sat for Hull, and his name had never ceased to be a watch-word with a numerous section there. He was told by experienced electioneerers, that the fact of his being a stranger to the people and the locality would do him no harm; yet his heart somewhat misgave him when he contemplated the enterprise on which he was about to enter. The chance, however, he had so long desired was come; he was committed to the venture, and resolved to go through with it. Quitting London, he wrote to his friend Mr C. Langdale, who lived at Houghton some fifteen miles distant, announcing his candidature, and begging him to come over and help him. 1818.

CHAPTER IV.

A MEMBER OF PARLIAMENT.

1818—1819.

1818.
Election for Hull.

MR STANIFORTH had sat for Kingston-upon-Hull during the four preceding Parliaments. Though a silent member, he was a useful man of business, and looked diligently to the personal interests of his supporters. He had materially aided in opening the trade with the East by adding more than one large vessel to the mercantile marine of the port; and it was the boast of his friends that during the period of his connection with the town he had in one way or other spent half a million of money amongst its inhabitants. With the leading merchants and principal members of the then close corporation he was still a favourite; but his devotion to the Liverpool ministry had always been a subject of reproach with many; and his recent support of the suspension of the Habeas Corpus Act, and his omission to oppose the hated Corn Bill of 1815, had rendered him very unpopular. His colleague, Lord Mahon, it was understood, did not mean to stand again; and in his stead Mr Mitchell, a wealthy West India proprietor, had agreed early in March to become a candidate on similar principles to those of Mr Staniforth, though not in coalition with him. On the other hand, many hundred names were subscribed to a resolution that at least one seat should be contested. The difficulty was to find "a third man" able to rally sufficient popular support around him, and willing to incur the expense. Several individuals who were asked, declined; and it was not until the end of May that Mr Graham was induced to come forward. Personally he was wholly unknown, and politically he could only offer earnest protestations of zeal for public liberty and of a desire to promote the good of the town. He was indeed commended as a young man of promise to certain of the electors, by influential friends in London and elsewhere; Dean Milner, amongst others, writing from Carlisle to vouch that "having been acquainted with him from childhood, he knew him to be a person of talents and attainments and of an excellent character, that he had been educated in the very best of principles, both moral and religious, and that he was convinced the electors of Hull would do well to make choice of one who was so well qualified, and so likely to support and defend the established constitution of his country, both in Church

1818. and State," *—a certificate of character for the publication of which he was not a little bantered.

On the 9th of June a hand-bill announced Mr Graham's expected arrival on the following day, and requested his supporters to assemble at some

Entry into Hull.

distance from the town on the Beverley road. At the hour appointed, a considerable number of persons were ready to receive him at the place of rendezvous. He was accompanied by the Hon. C. Langdale, Mr (afterwards Sir Edward) Haggerston, and the Rev. R. Sykes, all of them well known in the town. It did not escape notice that the two former were Roman Catholics; the latter gentleman was a clergyman of the Established Church. When the roadside greetings and introductions were over, a cavalcade was formed, which gathered strength as it approached the town; and thus escorted, the new candidate was drawn through the principal streets, amid a scene of much excitement, to his committee rooms in Lowgate. There, for the first time, not without much misgiving and emotion, he addressed a vast and varied multitude.

June 10, First speech in public.

Mr Graham said, "As a perfect stranger to most of you, it is my duty to give you some explanation why I appear on this occasion as a candidate to represent this ancient borough in the House of Com-

* Kingston; Wit, Humour, and Satire. An impartial record of the spirit of party as evinced at the General Election of 1818, &c. Hull, Tate, 1818, p. 24.

mons. Difference in political sentiment with intimate connections in my native county has prevented me from seeking the object of my ambition, a seat in Parliament, in that quarter. I was, of course, obliged to turn my attention elsewhere, and having often heard that in Hull there was a large body of electors whose sentiments were consonant with my own, the desire became irresistible to represent a place which has so often and so much distinguished itself in the cause of liberty, a desire, I flatter myself, neither illegitimate nor presumptuous. I would not, however, rashly enter upon the means for the accomplishment of my wishes, supposing that some gentleman, more competent, might prefer his claim to your support; but up to this hour, no one having appeared, I offer myself to you as a 'third man,' to give you an opportunity to exercise your rights as Englishmen and your privileges as burgesses, assuring you, that if I have the honour to be returned to Parliament by you, it will be my pride, as it will be my duty, to devote myself to your service. It is due to you as well as to myself to deal with you with perfect sincerity; I therefore declare frankly that my principles are genuine Whig principles. Ministerial extravagance and undue influence are objects of my unfeigned abhorrence, and all my efforts will be used in restraining them, whether in the shape of places, sinecures, or pensions. It will hardly be imputed to me as a crime, that I love 1818.

1818. peace rather than war. If it be, I plead guilty to the charge. I consider war as a curse to human nature, and peace as an inestimable blessing, which it will be my constant endeavour to preserve. I am a friend to religious as well as civil liberty, and I see no reason why men should be placed at a disadvantage, or debarred from promotion, on account of their religious opinions. Pains and penalties or civil disabilities of any kind are, in my opinion, persecution, when suffered by men on account of their faith, whether they be Dissenters or Roman Catholics." [Some of those who stood behind him here intimated that he was treading on dangerous ground, and urged him to avoid the subject. His reverend friend, Mr Sykes, however, rebuked the interruption, exclaiming, "Let him alone, he is saying the right thing, and it will tell best in the end." Mr Graham continued],—

"No man ought to be made to suffer privation or disfranchisement on account of his belief, because religion is a matter not betwixt him and his fellow-man, but betwixt him and his God. I am a friend to reform in Parliament; not that wild enthusiastic reform, which instead of improving the constitution would, by producing anarchy and confusion, undermine and destroy it, but a moderate reform, which would infuse new life into the constitution, and restore it to its former health and vigour. Such

are my principles, and I should not have been 1818.
justified to myself if I had not plainly stated them. I conclude with thanking you for the consideration you have shown me, assuring you that nothing will be of equal value to me save the approving testimony of my own heart that I have done my duty to you and to my country. Should I be so fortunate as to be the object of your choice, and should I live to appear before you at a future election, I feel no doubt that my countenance will be as free from shame as on the present occasion, and for the best of reasons, because my conduct will be found to have accorded with the principles I have avowed. It was to be expected that, unknown as I am to nearly all of you, and unaccustomed to address so large an assembly, I should feel no little embarrassment; but I throw myself upon your candour to excuse the imperfections which you have perceived, and of which I am deeply conscious."

Brief and unpretending as was this address, its distinctive tone and purport fully satisfied his supporters. The old electioneerers about him interchanged with one another looks and hints expressive of their conviction that "he would do," and the crowd, taken by his appearance and manner, were only curious to know when he was to speak again.

On the same afternoon all parties were surprised

1818. by the formal announcement that Mr Staniforth had withdrawn. At first it was regarded as a feint; but upon inquiry the fact was ascertained that having been called upon to pay certain claims for travelling charges to non-resident freemen, and other demands outstanding from the previous election, he had in disgust resigned. There was talk of setting up some one in his room; but as no substitute could suddenly be found, his chief adherents resolved to raise amongst them a sufficient fund to carry their old champion free of expense. Considerable sums were said to have been subscribed, and Mr Staniforth eventually resumed his former position. Meanwhile, the canvass under the yellow flag (the Whig colour of Yorkshire) was prosecuted with vigour. From hour to hour its success was attested by the heightened vehemence of party anger, the augmented scale of seductive offers to secure wavering aid, and the increased profusion wherewith squibs and pasquinades were showered from the printing press. In some of those that have been preserved we find the young Laird of Netherby caricatured as a "Bond Street Lounger," —"Cock of the North,"—"Yorkshire Dandy,"— and "Catholic Emancipator;" while his antagonists in their turn are reproached the one with being a slave-owner, and the other as being the docile hack of Lords Liverpool and Castlereagh.

Success in canvassing.

In one election squib the old member is thus made to plead for re-election:—

"I admire the present ministers and all their favoured race; 1818.
By swelling their majorities I've procured you many a place.
Beneath the wings of ministers (the truth I now must tell)
I buy you very cheap, and I sell you very well.
Certain places, as vacated, are held at my command
For those who vote for me, and for me make a stand;
In Customs or Post-office I apply to have it done,
I've obtain'd good situations for a father and a son,
In comfort now they live, and with happiness are fraught,
Before they got their places they were not worth a groat."

Expensive contest.

It was evident that the contest would prove a severe one. The City of the Humber has ever been noted for the costliness of its political struggles. Head-money, day fees to staves-men, and travelling charges of non-resident freemen, have oftener emptied purses of aspiring candidates than secured the services for the great sea-port of Yorkshire of eminent men. As is common in such cases, "the probable expense" was generally set down in the first instance at a moderate figure. Our would-be senator was gradually, but vaguely, apprized of the real nature of his liabilities as the exciting struggle went on. Once in the *melée*, he could hardly be expected to give much heed to muttered warnings from home, or from confidential friends on the spot. The political atmosphere was charged with fervid heat. Great principles of social change and intellectual progress were at stake. Everywhere men's passions were aroused against a profligate Court and a prodigal Administration. Wise men were angry, and the multitude were hungry.

1818. Kingston-upon Hull, long used to protracted battles between blue and buff, kept holiday, and revelled in the enjoyment of its septennial carnival. The Tory candidates, Messrs Mitchell and Staniforth, gave out that they were resolved to stop at nothing to secure the seats: how could the young Whig from Cumberland draw rein when once in mid career? For the first time he had heard the intoxicating sound of popular applause. After his first speech he was the darling of the mob,—very handsome, very winning, very bold, full of fun, and six-and-twenty,—on he went from day to day, canvassing electors in their homes, haranguing them by torch-light in the open air, joining in their noisy feasts, and ready with a biting jest or merry laugh whenever his opponents came in his way.

The "Young Adventurer." To repel the imputation of his being an untried man, and one unused to deal with the practical concerns of a busy and varied community, a statement headed "The Young Adventurer" was circulated by his committee, respecting his employment in 1813 in affairs of importance abroad.

"It had confidently been asserted that Mr Graham was unaccustomed to business, and that if elected they would probably never hear of him again. In truth, Mr Graham had already been employed, and actively, in the public service. It did so happen that, seeking only amusement abroad, he found a

situation of real business, and preferred it;" (a 1818.
succinct narrative then followed of the part he had taken in Sicily, as already mentioned;) "for which he had received the thanks of the Government, while at no time had he either sought or received pay, promise, or reward. Could it in candour, then, be said that Mr Graham was not a man fitted for and fond of business? He was essentially formed to be a man of business; and the electors of Hull might depend upon it they would hear of him again, and in a way of which they would not be ashamed.

"FAIR PLAY IS A JEWEL."*

Against other taunts he defended himself with spirit and judgment. "He had been accused of being an enemy of the Established Church. He had been most rigidly educated in its principles, and he loved it from the bottom of his heart. But because he loved the Church, was that a reason why he should not be a friend to toleration? Was it for him to say, because he lived in the bosom of the Establishment, that the numerous religious parties into which the country was divided, amongst whom he saw many adherents of the highest talents and strictest integrity, were absolutely wrong? They laboured in their calling according to their knowledge, and would have their reward in the other world. Why should they be persecuted in this? He was a friend to

A liberal Churchman.

* Spirit of Party, p. 34.

1818. liberty in every legitimate sense of the word. He neither wished the consciences of his countrymen to be shackled, nor the limbs of his fellow-creatures, in any part of the world, to be bound at the will, and for the profit, of their brother men. He was accused of not being rich, while his opponents boasted of their wealth. He pleaded guilty to the charge. But though he derived no emolument, either from the stripes of the wretched negro or the conversion of paper into money, he would undertake to pay all the *necessary* expenses of the election as far as he was concerned. He had been called a man of straw. He thought, however, that the 'man of straw' would take as much pulling to pieces as either the man of flesh or the man of paper." * West India slavery was as inexhaustible a theme of sarcasm as the system of private banking just then in especial discredit. As no quarter was shown him by his antagonists in their printed lampoons, he replied without reserve in his speeches; and the effect produced by them, addressed as they were, night after night, to a vast concourse of people unused to such excitement, no little perplexed his opponents. Since the time when Mr Wilberforce, then likewise a young man, had stirred by his thrilling words the matter-of-fact minds of the constituency, nothing half so vigorous or telling had been heard on Humber's side. Neither Mr Mitchell nor

* Speech, 15th June, 1818.

Mr Staniforth could vie with their youthful antagonist in force of declamation, and they learned with vexation that his power in this respect appeared to increase daily. Their sanguine friends assured them this could not be true, and that it was ascribable solely to the exaggerating medium through which popular objects are proverbially seen. But it was quite true for all that. Mr Graham would not have been what he was, a susceptible, elastic, versatile, and ambitious man, had it not been so. The first sentence of his first speech from the window of his committee room nearly stuck in his throat. He was not free from embarrassment, though somewhat more assured when he tried again next evening. Elate with his success in canvassing, he did better the following day, and so on. But after a week's stimulating exercise in the art, his self-possession and facility had grown apace. The painful self-consciousness which blurs the mirror of the memory when it needs to be most clear had passed away. He was able without misgiving to think aloud, and without confusion to endure interruption and the ill-timed suggestions of those about him. He could venture to deal more calmly and deeply with topics he had at first but tentatively skimmed; and when at length he came to speak from the hustings, friends and foes were equally charmed by the ease and dignity of his manner, and the high-minded yet practical tone of all

1818. he said. The pervading impression may perhaps be best conveyed by a snatch or two from the ephemeral rhymes of the day:—

Election squibs.

"The Mayor, who's a man not much given to *banter*,
Declared that his party would win in a canter.

* * * * * *

Blue Mitchell spoke next, he was hardly a minute,
It was all very well, but there wasn't much in it;
I hope he will mind all he says to perform,
And vote for economy, peace, and reform.
Our Graham spoke next, and he spoke like a Briton;
When he spoke of taxation the right nail he hit on;
By taxes tea, sugar, and malt are made dear,
They lessen our bread-loaf, they spoil our strong beer;
And Graham has told us again and again,
That it is the duty of Parliament men
To see that the money is properly spent
Which up from the country in taxes is sent.
But the far greatest part of them get all they can:
To *share* public money, not *spare*, is their plan.
These are Graham's own words, and I really believe
He is all truth and daylight, and would not deceive." *

* * * * * *

"Whereupon there arose such thund'ring cheers,
I expected to lose both the drums of my ears,
Wedged up in the midst of a mass of live lumber,
That lifted and heaved like the waves of the Humber.
But when Graham stood up, silence enter'd the throng,
And listen'd like love to the mountain lark's song." †

Mr Graham was nominated by the Rev. Richard Sykes of West Ella, and seconded by Mr Thomp-

* Spirit of Party, &c., p. 78. † Ibid. p. 71.

son, who had himself been for many years in Parliament an earnest advocate of retrenchment and reform. After the other candidates and their respective friends had spoken, his turn came. 1818.

"It was difficult," he said, "at all times for a man to speak of himself as he ought, and especially where he was a stranger and untried. But such in some measure must be the situation of every one who, like himself, was about to request a favour at the hands of persons that had no opportunity of trying his qualifications, and who must of necessity be compelled in addressing them to speak of the future, and not of the past. It had been said that this large commercial town ought to be represented by some man of tried assiduity, and long acquaintance with public business. These no doubt were valuable qualities; but he believed it would be found by an examination into our Parliamentary history that the youngest men were not always the most inefficient. Mr Fox commenced his brilliant career at the age of nineteen; and his famous India bill was brought forward when he was only thirty-two years of age. His celebrated rival, Mr Pitt, was a member of Parliament at the age of twenty-one; and Chancellor of the Exchequer when he had scarcely completed his twenty-third year. Even those well-known patriots, Marvel and Wilberforce, men whose names conferred celebrity on this their native town, were both returned to Parliament in early

Speech on the Hustings, June 17.

1818. life; and both were distinguished for their talents and their industry. For his own part, he should say that he detested an idle life. Brought up to no profession, he was anxious to employ his time and abilities, such as they were, in the service of his country. He might have obtained a quiet seat for some insignificant borough in his own neighbourhood, and have slept undisturbed in conservative obscurity. But he wished to represent a liberal borough like Hull, where there was a fair opportunity of rendering himself useful. As to his principles, he begged leave to enter upon a short exposition of them; he wished to give the burgesses a touchstone to which recourse might be had in future should he falsify his professions. He was anxious for the country's prosperity—a prosperity which was the result of their industry and commercial enterprise, and of the constitution under which they lived. In theory the constitution was nearly perfect, and he firmly believed that in practice a greater degree of liberty and happiness was enjoyed under it than ever had been enjoyed under any other. To the existence of every government the preservation of order was essentially necessary: between absolute liberty and anarchy there was but a step. It was the duty of the Legislature to adjust the balance. It was its duty particularly to correct that tendency in perhaps all governments to render themselves absolute. The state of things during the last Parliament, in his opinion, proved the existence of such a tendency at present amongst us. The power of the Crown had astonishingly increased with the increase of the army, the navy, and the public revenue. There was scarcely a family in the kingdom, one or more of the members or dependents of which were not in some measure under the influence of the Crown from one or other of these causes. Let them examine the conduct of the last Parliament. Was any act passed therein favourable to the liberty of the subject? On the contrary, was there not one in particular passed for suspending the personal freedom of every man? Was any measure adopted for the promotion of truly British objects? Not one! But they had enabled ministers to continue a standing army of 140,000 men. 1818.

"There was one subject on which he wished to dwell more particularly, the suspension of the Habeas Corpus Act. On all hands it had been allowed that the great body of the people were loyal. Disturbances indeed had existed in certain quarters, but they were fomented by hired emissaries, and suffered to ripen into maturity by those whose office and duty it was to prevent them. Notwithstanding this, the last Parliament was influenced to pass an act of indemnity, by which all hope of redress was at once cut off from those who had been dragged from their families and buried within the walls of a prison, to the injury of their health and fortunes. The situation of the Continental States might render

1818. great standing armies necessary, but the good old British principle was to encourage our navy. It was the navy which ensured our triumphs in Europe, in Asia, and in every quarter of the globe. If the electors now returned as members a majority of men disposed to vote at the nod of the minister, he would not say that all was lost, but that assuredly all was in danger. But if they were determined to send men disposed to support the principles of toleration, the freedom of commerce, a strict economy, in fact, men more anxious to serve the nation than themselves, then the country might be saved. This was in the power of the nation: it was in the power of the electors of Hull, and upon these principles he stood there to solicit their suffrages."

The polling. Mr Mitchell headed the poll, and kept his precedency throughout. The struggle lay between Mr Staniforth and Mr Graham. At the end of the second day the latter was in a majority of 33; and extraordinary efforts were made to turn the preponderance on the following day. Many doubtful votes were tendered, and in the existing state of the law, little discrimination as to their acceptance or rejection was deemed allowable. At the close of the poll, on the 19th June, the numbers stood, for Mitchell 1323, Graham 1074, Staniforth 1036. But the rising cheer of exultation was unexpectedly hushed by a new incident; and the bewildered

crowd were told that the election was not yet won. 1818.
A scrutiny had been demanded by the friends of the ex-representative; and the sheriff, as returning officer, had, without hesitation, complied with the request. The confidence of the elected but unreturned member seems for a moment to have been staggered by the check he had thus met with in the midst of apparent victory. In his speech to his supporters at the close of the poll he was unable to restrain his feelings of disappointment and chagrin. He had always, he said, endeavoured to maintain a due proportion between the object of his hopes and the vehemence of his desires. But those who heard him would make allowance for the difficulty he felt in preserving conventional forms of equanimity, when after so hard a fight the cup of triumph seemed to be suddenly stolen from their lips. The exclamation of Mr Burke in the hour of defeat recurred to him,—"What shadows we are, and what shadows we pursue! I should have felt proud and happy if I had been returned as one of your representatives, but God only knows what is best for me; he only knows whether it is best for me to be in Parliament, or even whether it is best for me to live." * But his spirit soon rallied, and he applied himself with renewed energy to the difficult task before him. It was, indeed, no easy matter to

A scrutiny demanded.

* Speech of Mr Burke on declining the poll at Bristol, 1780.

1818. reconcile the people to the strange species of tantalization to which they had thus been subjected. None could tell how long the scrutiny might last; and unless vigilance and enthusiasm could be kept up without flagging, it was clear that the silent but sure influence of money would prevail after all. The battle had to be fought over again with varied odds. How was victory so narrowly won to be maintained? Mr Graham exerted himself to the utmost, and showed no little tact and skill in keeping his party organization unrelaxed during the anxious period that ensued. The court of scrutiny had no power to compel the attendance of witnesses, or to enforce testimony upon oath; yet the discretion it assumed as to what were and were not adequate grounds of disqualification, was of the largest and loosest description. Many persons of the humbler sort were deterred by promises of advantage, or fears of losing work or custom, from defending the votes they had given; and many more, whom no such motives swayed, shrank from the ordeal of personal interrogation to which they were liable. The expense incurred by all parties was great. The scrutiny did not terminate till the 11th July, when it appeared that 168 votes had been struck off which had been given for Mr Mitchell, 143 which had been given for Mr Graham, and 109 which had been given for Mr Staniforth. A majority of 14 still remained unassailable for the popular candidate, and thus, after a contest

Declared duly elected.

which had lasted for more than a month, and which had cost upwards of £6000, he obtained the privilege of sitting in Parliament as one of the members for Kingston-upon-Hull. 1818.

Netherby. The tidings of the triumph at Hull were received with mingled feelings of pleasure and of pride at Netherby. Lady Catherine rejoiced with a mother's joy in the success of her son; but her husband was too stout a Church and King's man to admit that he was glad, and when told of the expense, he declared that such amusements were too costly for him. The necessary amount was raised at interest through the instrumentality of a professional friend, and the baronet was not asked to contribute in any way. The lesson in electioneering however thus learned was never forgotten; and throughout his after life Mr Graham was scrupulously careful to avoid wasteful expenditure, though on one or two occasions he did not shrink from incurring the liabilities incidental to severe contests.

Lord Althorpe. By an entry in the Journals of the House of Commons it appears that a petition was presented against his return early in the ensuing session, by certain electors belonging to the defeated party. No further steps however were taken in the matter, and he was allowed without interruption to enter upon his parliamentary career. He took his seat on the third Opposition bench, beside his friend Lord A. Hamilton. Near them sat Mr E. Ellis, Mr T. F.

1819. Kennedy, and Sir R. Wilson; and below them Sir F. Burdett, Mr Hume, and Lord Althorpe. His Lordship, recently a widower, at this period seldom mingled in society, but he was a constant attendant in the House, worked hard in Committee, and entered with freedom and affability into communication with all who knew him, upon the subjects of legislative discussion. Mr Graham had been early impressed with a sense of his high qualities as a public man; and soon learned to share the sentiments of personal loyalty, with which he gradually came to be regarded by many of the best men of his time. He had recently broken up his establishment in Pall Mall, and resumed his former chambers in the Albany, where he continued to reside for many years. His time and attention, while in Town, were almost wholly devoted to political study, and attendance in the House of Commons.* In debate he took comparatively little part at this time, possessing few of the qualifications for distinction as a speaker, and being wholly devoid of the ambition to shine. In habits and characteristics no two men could be more dissimilar than the grave, plodding, and sorrow-stricken heir of the house of Spencer, and the foppish, gay, and ambitious member for Hull. Yet there was between them enough in common to render the growth of intimacy easy and mutually agreeable.

* Unpublished Memoirs of John Charles, third Earl Spencer: by Sir Dennis Le Marchant, Bart.

Besides the general identity of their opinions on all 1819.
leading questions of interest, both were zealous students of political economy, a science which in those days had few votaries in the sphere wherein they moved. Of statistical inquiry, Lord Althorpe was especially fond; and it was possibly from him that Mr Graham, his junior by several years, imbibed many of the opinions by whose advocacy he was subsequently known. It cannot be doubted that from the same source he acquired many useful impressions and ideas, with reference to agriculture and the management of landed property. On these subjects his Lordship rarely spoke without animation bordering on enthusiasm. He had acquired by his marriage a considerable estate in Nottinghamshire, where he usually resided during the autumn and winter, and where he occupied himself with the varied practical details of experimental farming. Here, too, his talent for arithmetic, which had first showed itself by his attainment of distinction at Cambridge, enabled him, with little effort, to keep exact accounts of all his outgoings in wages, purchase of stock, &c., and of his incomings when the produce of his farms was sent to market. He subsequently convinced himself thereby that he had lost money by his experiments in tillage,* but it was his delight to tell how successful he had been as a cattle farmer, and to the latest period of his life

Study of political economy.

* Memoirs of Lord Spencer, &c.

1819. he continued to derive the greatest enjoyment from the breeding and rearing of stock. A friend whom he had not seen for some years visited him on one occasion at Wiseton. They had long sat together in Parliament, and their first talk naturally fell upon the public topics of the day. But after a short time his Lordship exclaimed, "You are anxious, I am sure, to see my new stock; let us go and look at them." And so saying, he led the way to the grazing fields, which were to him no fabulous Asphodel. Nor was it until every yearling of quality and high-bred bull had been viewed and criticized, that he thought of reverting to public affairs. The genuineness and simplicity of character of such a man, his freedom from all prejudice of sect or class, and his unaffected zeal for the welfare of his country, rendered him the best of guides and counsellors for a youthful politician. Though shy and reserved in what called itself *par excellence* "Society," he was peculiarly accessible to all whom he believed really anxious to gain information or seek advice. His mind moved slowly, and because he was conscientious he was often cautious in expression. But those who consulted him felt that in his greatest reserve there was no *arrière pensée;* and in all the complications of political life he never was suspected of insincerity or mystification. He knew not how to flatter, for he knew not what it was to be false, and he disdained to hector even when he con-

demned, because he thoroughly respected in others 1819.
the right to differ, and because he was willing to believe them as exempt from selfishness or cowardice as he was himself. He did not at this period aspire in any degree to lead; but all who knew, loved and trusted him, and gradually his personal influence became very great.

Motion to reduce Lords of Admiralty.

It was after consultation with Lord Althorpe and other influential members of Opposition that Sir M. W. Ridley gave notice early in the session of an address to the Regent to reduce the number of the Lords of the Admiralty. The motion was one of several which had for their object the retrenchment of useless expenditure, and the diminution of the overgrown power of Government through the exercise of political patronage. It was opposed by Sir George Cockburn, who represented the department in the Commons, by Mr Long Wellesley, and Mr 18th March.
Canning; its chief supporters were Lord John Russell and Mr Graham. The speeches of both on the occasion are curious in their way, but for opposite reasons; that of the former has in it all the characteristics with which the political world has since become familiar. A more signal illustration of an early fixed and subsequently unchanging style can hardly perhaps be found. Just the reverse is remarkable with respect to the first essay of his equally ambitious but less practised associate. Mr Graham's speech, delivered in the dialect and with the gesture of an ex- Maiden speech.

1819. quisite, savoured too much of anxiety for out-of-door applause, to win the respect of the House of Commons. Most of his assertions were true, indeed, as to the excess of patronage and the political corruption it engendered. But his generalities were too violent and too vague, and his indignation seemed too vehement to be sincere. His apprehension that the power of the Crown was increasing and ought to be diminished, sounded too like a reading out of date from the pages of Burke; and the inartistic mode in which he intimated his belief that venal motives were chiefly potential in keeping up supernumerary offices and undeserved pensions made his hearers stare and smile, rather than listen or reflect. In a collegiate debating club the speech would have gone well; for the chapel of St Stephen it was certainly a mistake; and the best that can be said of it is, that its author had the good sense to recognize it as such, and that he studiously took care in his subesquent efforts to efface its unfavourable impression.

But it is not so easy to get rid of a bad manner as those may imagine who have never tried; the first may indeed be repudiated as faulty, and another adopted in its stead; but however well chosen the new garb of thought may be, it is a good while before the easy unconsciousness comes that was the best charm of the old one. Mr Graham does not appear to have spoken frequently, but he voted up to the mark with his party; the outsiders swore that he would one day go as far as Burdett; and at Brookes's he was thought a promising fellow. 1819.

Mr Tierney.

Some indeed of the more temporizing and timid from the first disliked him. He was not, they said, the style of man that was wanted; he was too saucy for his years, too confident on his legs, and too sarcastic across the dinner table. He had no scruple about rallying them on their too frequent attacks of the gout on the eve of trying votes in the House of Commons, and it was probably in pique at some caustic remark of his upon the want of efficient leadership, that Mr Tierney is said to have called him "a manly puppy."*

Sir M. Ridley's motion was lost by 245 to 164; Mr Wilberforce, Lord Althorpe, Mr Brougham, Mr Fowell Buxton, Mr Coke, Mr Grattan, Mr Tierney, Sir J. Mackintosh, and Sir J. Newport, voting in the minority.

Marriage.

Other thoughts occupied his mind for some time. In common with a numerous crowd of admirers he had been much attracted by the beauty and accomplishments of the youngest daughter of Colonel Callander of Craigforth, in Stirlingshire, who subsequently took the name of Campbell on succeed-

* MS. Diary of the late Mr John Lewis Mallet. Mr Mallet was the son of the well-known M. Mallet du Pan, but was himself an Englishman. He was connected by marriage with Sir Thomas Baring, and lived on terms of intimacy with many of the political men of his day.

1819. ing to the baronetcy of Ardkinglas. Her mother was Lady Elizabeth MacDonnell, the daughter of the fourth Earl of Antrim. Caroline, an elder sister, was the wife of Thomas, the only son of Richard Brinsley Sheridan, whose premature decease in the life-time of his distinguished father had been so much deplored. Fanny, the youngest of the family, then reigned at Almack's, queen of beauty, and all the world of fashion was at her feet. Mr Graham had many rivals for her hand, but his suit was accepted, and their marriage took place on the 8th July, 1819.

Croft Head. This union proved one of singular happiness, and was always spoken of as the most fortunate event of his life by the subject of these memoirs. Croft Head, a small country-house, the grounds of which adjoin those of Netherby, was given him by his father for a residence, and there he spent the greater part of the five ensuing years.

At the first drawing-room Mr and Mrs Graham attended after their marriage, George IV. asked one of those who stood near him who they were, and on being told, exclaimed, "They are the handsomest couple I ever clapped my eyes on."

Meeting at Peterloo. During the autumn political discontent began to manifest itself throughout the manufacturing districts in forms expressive of new ideas of organization. Birmingham, denied parliamentary representatives, proceeded to elect delegates in its own way.

In the neighbourhood of Manchester, a great open-air meeting was convoked for a similar purpose. Between 40,000 and 50,000 people assembled to hear a speech of Mr Henry Hunt, then at the zenith of his fame as a demagogue, and to pass resolutions of co-operation with the unenfranchized elsewhere, by which it was hoped that the Legislature might be overawed into concession of their claims. Violent language was indulged in on the occasion, but no breach of the peace had occurred, when the yeomanry drawn up in the immediate neighbourhood were ordered by certain county magistrates to disperse the assemblage. The scene which ensued has often been described, and its memory is one of the most painful of our time. Many of the unarmed populace met their death by sabre wounds, and many more were maimed or killed in the tumult and terror of the hour. Wherever the tidings of the catastrophe were borne, shouts of execration rose from the operative classes, and fierce vows of retribution were publicly exchanged. Alarm spread among the higher orders. A vast democratic conspiracy was said to be on foot for the overthrow of the established order of things. Circumstantial revelations were pretended to be made of strategic plans of insurrection. Large bodies of rebel artisans were ready, it was said, on a given day to march on London, overthrow Church and Throne, rob the Bank, and establish universal suffrage. Ministers participated in the general

1819.

1819. panic, and called Parliament together before Christmas to consider the expediency of adopting an additional code of coercive laws. The nature of these enactments was forthshadowed in the speech from the Throne. To save time, some of them were introduced by Lord Sidmouth in the Peers, others by Lord Castlereagh in the Commons. In the former, they encountered little resistance; Earl Grey denounced their inexpediency in one of his ablest speeches, and thereby severed finally his party connection with Lord Grenville, with whom he had so long acted. Lords Holland and Erskine took a similar course, but their protests were in vain, and the bills restraining the right of assembling in public meetings, and the liberty of political discussion in the press, received the almost unanimous sanction of the Lords. Nor was the case very different in the Commons, where the apprehensions of class overbore generally the animosities of party. A minority led by Lord Althorpe and Sir F. Burdett, stoutly resisted, indeed, many of the more obnoxious provisions of the new bills; it included Mr Brougham, Lord Milton, Mr Coke, and others, amongst the rest the member for Hull.

One of the Bills which was directed against organized agitation by means of the interchange of delegates between different localities, prohibited any person from taking part in the proceedings of a town meeting who was not an inhabitant or freeman of the place. Lord Althorpe and his friends resolved to fight the measure clause by clause; but they found it hard to keep together a sufficient number to make a respectable show of strength either in debate or division; and every man who was willing, whether able or not, was pressed into the service. Mr Graham was in this way induced to rise in Committee without preparation, and try what he could do in making off-hand objections. He wished to know if a member who sat for a borough of which he was neither inhabitant nor freeman would come within the mischief of the act? He paused to listen for the report of his shot; but few were attending, and nobody cried "hear." He looked to see if it had hit; but the Under-Secretaries were talking to one another on the Treasury Bench, and Lord Castlereagh was occupied in smelling the hot-house flower in his button-hole. Mr Graham repeated his question in other words, but with no better effect. He felt half vexed with himself at having got up, but he was up and must go on; so he thought he would argue the point. The case was not an imaginary one, he said, for it was his own, as he happened to sit for a borough of which he was neither a freeman nor an inhabitant, and of which he was not likely to become either, having no connection with the place. At this unlucky proffer of irrelevant information he heard, or thought he heard, something like a suppressed laugh. He felt himself getting confused, a 1819.

1819. little at first, and then very much so. For a few minutes he rambled on through common-place and reiteration, but no timely cheer came to his rescue, and he sat down without any distinct recollection of what he had said or what he had intended to say. Mr Henry Lascelles, who sat opposite, whispered to a mutual friend, "Well, there is an end of Graham; we shall hear no more of him." The premature epitaph was perhaps luckily repeated to him next day, and it had the effect of stimulating him into making an effort which should efface the memory of this break-down. For once he doubted the wisdom of his favourite Hooker, that "Voluntary and extemporal far exceedeth premeditated speech." This time he would prepare every sentence, every phrase, and when all was fashioned to his mind, he knew that he could trust his memory for the rest.

Seditious publications bill.

On going into Committee on the seditious publications bill, he spoke at some length, addressing himself especially to the danger of surrendering in a moment of panic the necessary outworks of constitutional freedom.

"At a season like the present, everything should be done which was calculated to increase the public confidence in the House; but so far from this having been done, in his humble opinion, they had either altogether lost that confidence or it was greatly on the decline. It was not for him to say that the present measures were inapplicable to the state of things which existed; it was enough that he should remind the House of the irritation that prevailed, and ask them whether there ever was a period in which they were called upon to exercise a more calm, deliberate, and sober judgment? What else could make any measures which were proposed effectual; what else could justify the House in making a permanent alteration in the law of England, affecting one of the noblest institutions and best safeguards of the constitution? No man could detest more heartily than he did the blasphemous and seditious libels which of late had issued from the press; they were loathsome as they were noxious, and he regretted the evil effect which they were calculated to have upon the public mind. He detested them for the wickedness of their purpose, and he detested them the more, because he well knew that a flagrant abuse of a right on the part of the people was too frequently the first occasion of tyranny in rulers, and the best pretext for the introduction of coercive measures. Those men were the worst friends of the people, who for the sake of unworthy lucre would rob them of the consolations of religion, who would subvert all order, and wade through bloodshed to the enjoyment of precarious power: and who at the same time furnished the enemies of a free constitution with an excuse for its violation. But, on the other hand, it was the paramount duty of that House, as the constituted guardian of the public weal, not to permit itself to be hurried away by the influence of alarm or temporary irritation, to the adoption of permanent measures of coercion, hostile to the spirit and practice of the constitution which it professed to uphold. He confessed he could not help revolting at the practice which he had repeatedly observed on the part of Government of exaggerating alarm and enhancing the character of difficulties, merely for the purpose of creating a pretext for undermining those institutions which our ancestors had raised, and for 1819.

1819. abridging those liberties which were due to the labours of good men in earlier times. He was not disposed to attribute bad motives to the ministers of the Crown, but he could not help observing, what the circumstances fully justified, that it looked as if it were their object by showing impunity for a season to flagitious libellers, to produce an ill feeling towards the freedom of the press, in order to secure its permanent abridgment,—permanent he would say, for privileges taken from the people were neither easily nor quickly recovered. He had ever been taught to consider that in times of domestic irritation, moderation in the deliberations of the Legislature was its true duty, and its safest course. He had the sanction of Mr David Hume for that opinion, when he stated that nothing but its own violence could overturn established authority, as overacted zeal was certain to produce a similar feeling on its opponents. Though he deeply deplored the recent turbulence of the people in different parts of England, on the other hand, he was not exclusively jealous of the danger proceeding from that source. He viewed with equal suspicion the conduct of the Government, and the steps which they were taking, by the adoption of coercive measures, to suppress those liberties to the enjoyment of which the people were justly entitled. Upon these general grounds he was led to express his alarm at the system which they were pursuing, and to state how unwilling he was to consent to any alteration in the law of the land which tended to abridge the liberty of the subject. He would now explain the particular reasons which rendered him hostile to the bills immediately before the House. He thought it unnecessary to make any observations as to the known advantages of the liberty of the press, or as to its being the palladium of freedom, and a tower of strength to resist military force or despotic ambition. The force of these truths time had, it might be supposed, already brought home with conviction to the mind of every man. But it was not when the enemy was before the gate, and ready to possess himself of the stronghold, that such a general declaration ought to be relied on. He solemnly believed that the present measures went directly to violate that hitherto sacred privilege, the freedom of the press. By that privilege every man possessed the right to publish what he pleased, without any restraint previous to publication. After publication, he possessed the right, if charged with a libel, of having that question, both as to the law and the fact, ascertained by a jury. These might be considered the fundamental rights of a publisher. In the best times of our history a disposition prevailed to interpose strong preventives of their abuse, without an infringement of the principle of the privilege. At various times, no small degree of ingenuity had been exercised for the purpose of making that abuse the ground of depriving the people of the right altogether. The law of England was on this point sufficiently severe; for it not only imposed, in cases of conviction, fine and imprisonment without limitation, but it also left in the discretion of the judges the power of calling for recognizances, as had been seen in a recent case, during the life of the offender. A criminal prosecution was not held as a justification, nor admitted as evidence in extenuation; and until of late the Attorney-General had the power of holding a prosecution over the head of a publisher, *in terrorem*, for an indefinite period. These powers he thought quite adequate to the suppression of every offence which might be committed. Various new powers had, however, been required. The first of these was an increase of punishment after the second conviction; the second, that after the conviction a power should exist of 1819.

1819. searching for libels; then there was a stamp-duty upon all small publications; and above all, it was required, prior to publication, that persons intending to publish should enter into personal recognizances, and find sureties for the payment of any fine which might be imposed upon them. With regard to the first point, he should only repeat the observation that the law as it existed was sufficiently severe in itself without any addition whatever. In fact, it never had been exercised to the extent of which it was capable. It appeared to him that the additional punishment for the second offence would only tend to create a difficulty in obtaining a verdict for the first; and though banishment might have been very good in the time of the Star-chamber and the Stuarts, he did not think it applicable to the present day, and he trusted they would never live to see its re-establishment. It was a punishment which in Scotland had been brought into use; and during an unhappy period, it had also been known in Ireland; but since the Revolution, it had been unknown to the law of England. They had heard banishment spoken of as being more mild than transportation. To rich offenders it might be so, but to a poor man he thought it would be the reverse; because, if transported, his expenses would be paid to the place of his destination by Government, and when he arrived there he would be sustained by the same means; whereas if he were banished to a foreign shore, he must either continue a libel to his country to obtain bread, or die a disgrace to his country for the want of bread. The experiment of enacting transportation for three years for such offences, he was told, had been tried; but not a single individual had been condemned to that penalty. With regard to the right of searching for libels, he thought this involved a power pregnant with the greatest hardship. The search was not to be confined to the libeller alone, but by an order of the court it might be extended to any other person, whose drawers and papers might be ransacked in search of a squib, or a newspaper, or a pamphlet, which might have been pronounced a libel: that was to say, every printer and publisher in England was liable to an arbitrary order of a court of justice, and to an inquisitorial power to search his premises and papers upon the most trifling grounds. It was impossible to view this clause without feelings of the strongest disgust. Upon the subject of the third point, he saw nothing against the principle of imposing a stamp duty upon the sort of publications which had been described; but he did think such a measure would be found to have a disadvantageous effect; for while, as he admitted, it would lessen the circulation of pernicious works, it would also suppress many publications of the most beneficial character. The most obnoxious of all these powers, however, and that to which he had the strongest objection, was that which called upon the publisher to enter into recognizances, and to find sureties, for his ability to pay any fine to which he might become liable. He did conceive that this power was subversive of every principle of the constitution, because it amounted to nothing less than a restriction before the printing took place. It was, in fact, a species of censorship, which, if adopted, must tend to undermine the liberty of the press, the preservation of which had hitherto been considered the great bulwark of our liberties. It was a dangerous precedent, against which it was impossible too forcibly to contend. The principal defence which had been set up in favour of these measures was their necessity. Necessity, he thought, was a very doubtful plea, which ought not to be allowed, at least without the most serious deliberation. Why, he would ask, had not the existing laws been acted upon? Why were not the powers which those laws gave applied to the evils which

1819.

1819. had been stated to prevail to an alarming extent? Before any new powers were granted, he thought it was the duty of the House to see that the old ones were insufficient for the purposes of public justice. In 1818 not a single prosecution had been instituted by his Majesty's Attorney-general; and in 1819 only one person had been brought to trial, and that individual who had been so brought to trial had been severely punished. During the whole of this period blasphemous libels upon blasphemous libels, seditious libels upon seditious libels, had been published in rapid succession, and yet no step had been taken to suppress them. To what was this want of apparent energy to be ascribed? It was not difficult to trace it to its new source. It was thought convenient to bring the liberty of the press into disrepute, in order that by its frequent abuse it might be put down altogether. He had heard also of improper prejudices being excited against these measures. He denied that any such improper prejudice had influenced his mind; he was decidedly against any permanent alteration in the law of England in the most trivial particular, and above all against an alteration in one of the most essential parts of our constitution. For these reasons, so imperfectly stated, he should feel it his duty to vote against the further progress of these bills."

But reasonings of this description were ineffectual; and the Six Acts, with hardly any modification, became law.

The substance of his speech was approved of by those who voted as he did; but the prevailing sentiment was the other way; there was nothing in it of originality to command reluctant attention, or of practical experience to arrest the impatient desire of rigour. He had devoted much care to its preparation, and its delivery was unspoilt by the defects observable in his previous efforts. In a thin House the absence of conversational buzz passes, sometimes, with the self-love of a young speaker, for the silence of attention. But when he has sat down without a cheer, and listened in vain throughout the rest of the debate for an answer, either quizzical or complimentary, the vexatious fact breaks slowly but irresistibly upon him that he has failed, and as ineffective speeches are seldom reported, he feels as he walks home that, even with his constituents, what has cost him so much trouble will do him but little good. In this mood he is rarely disposed to comfort himself with the reflection that it is something to have spoken for half an hour on the absorbing question of the day, in the first assembly in the world, without faltering or making any obvious mistake. Yet this too is something,—nay, a great indispensable thing for all who are not born with the transcendent gifts of genius. Mr Graham returned when the Session closed to his new and pleasant home, and as he gazed upon the Christmas hearth resolved to forget his feelings of disappointment and to try again. 1819.

CHAPTER V.

POLITICS AND FARMING IN CUMBERLAND

1820—1824.

1820. WHEN Parliament re-assembled after the holidays, men's thoughts were occupied with the sudden death of the Duke of Kent, and with that of his father George III. The demise of the Crown had been for some time anticipated, and preparations were already so far advanced for the dissolution that must ensue that the same newspaper which announced the death of the king contained an address from Mr Brougham to the electors of Westmoreland.*

Accession of George IV.

February.

An expiring House of Commons is proverbially unmanageable; and in the then existing state of public feeling Government naturally apprehended the effects likely to be produced by a prolonged canvass of all the great constituencies. In his first mes-

* Annual Register, vol. lxii. part i. p. 19.

sage announcing his accession, George IV. was consequently advised to recommend the adoption of such measures as would facilitate an early dissolution. No precedent could be cited for such an intimation from the Throne, the true constitutional doctrine, as stated by the Opposition, being that Parliament ought not to be asked to contemplate, still less to further, the extinction of its own existence. But no practical hindrance was thrown in the way, and votes *ad interim* were agreed to without a division, providing for the immediate necessities of the public service. Lord J. Russell brought in a bill to defer the writs for Grampound, Penrhyn, Barnstaple, and Camelford, until the assembling of the new Parliament, gross corruption having been found to be habitual in all of them. Mr Graham was among its supporters; it was carried in the Lower House, but lost in the Upper through the instrumentality of ministers.* 1820.

Many members quitted town to look after their elections, and those who had no contests before them gladly left the gloomy Metropolis soon after the late king's funeral. On the 28th February Parliament was dissolved, having lasted little more than a year and a half, to the no small disappointment of those whose seats had cost them dear, and to none more so than the junior member for Hull. He felt that he had done nothing to insure his re-election without incurring Dissolution of Parliament.

* Hansard—1820, vol. i. p. 156.

1820. the hazard of another expensive contest, for which he was not prepared; and he anxiously looked round in quest of another and less costly seat. But politics are a selfish game, and as there are never comfortable seats in Parliament for all who want them, the eve of a general election is just the time when professions of friendship are apt to be most severely tried; and when a man who has not made himself indispensable to his party, and who does not happen to possess irresistible local influence, is almost certain to be

Looking out for a seat.

jostled out of the race. Every one at such a juncture is thinking of himself or his immediate connections. He would be delighted to be of use if the quarter where he has the power of doing so were only pointed out to him. Failing this, he is ready to write a letter of inquiry and recommendation to an excellent friend of his in another shire, whom he has not seen for some time, but who can do much in the borough near which he lives, *if* the thing be still open. Of course the borough turns out to be long since provided with candidates, and so the affair comes to nothing. The regular brokers are ever ready to hear all that the aspirant has to say for himself, and full of professions of their belief that he is "just the sort of man who ought to be in Parliament." Their willingness to undertake the matter admits of no doubt; but the question again and again turns up, "How far is he willing to go?" If he is prudent and names a moderate figure, the professional trafficker in seats applauds the prudent resolvé not to do anything foolish, warms, rather than cools, in his tone of sympathy and service, and within five minutes remembers that he has another engagement which he must keep: and so vanishes with hurried expressions of hope that his would-be client will let him see him again. Or if the candidate in his eagerness is tempted to talk loosely about possible expenditure he finds out by degrees that he has been quietly put into the weighing-house, and that his value is determined there, by considerations and calculations regarding which he is carefully kept in the dark. 1820.

County politics.

Mr Graham consulted the few political friends on whom he thought he could safely rely, but to small purpose; and in the general ejection of troublesome Liberals threatened by the organs of Government, he began to think that he was to form one of the unnoticed and unregretted victims. Meanwhile letters from Cumberland kept him advised of all that the "Blues" were talking of doing in county and town. The Popular Party had long been dissatisfied with the state of the representation, monopolized as it had almost become by the powerful house of Lowther. Mr Brougham's bold stand in Westmoreland stimulated no doubt the hope that they might, by a vigorous effort, assert their local freedom simultaneously with their neighbours. In both counties the battle was simply for independence. At that time Lord Lonsdale vir-

1820. tually returned four out of the six members for Cumberland, namely, Sir James Graham, of Kirkstall, for Carlisle, Sir John Lowther for the county, and Mr J. H. Lowther and the Right Hon. J. Beckett for Cockermouth. Lord Morpeth had occupied for some time the other county seat, and Mr Curwen represented the popular interest in Carlisle. Why not send in two Reformers for the county, and as many for the town? Mr Curwen was ready to stand for the former, if Mr Graham and Mr James of Barrack Lodge would undertake to contest the latter. The decision regarding the double contest, in both city and shire, seems to have been come to before the intentions were ascertained of some of the persons whose co-operation was most essential to success. The first announcement was made in the *Carlisle Journal* of Feb. 5, when it was briefly stated that an opportunity would be given to the freeholders of Cumberland to declare their sentiments on nearly the same question as that which agitated Westmoreland. "Two Blue (or *anti*-Lowther) candidates would offer themselves for the county, and likewise two for Carlisle." Mr Graham had been fully apprised from the outset of what was in contemplation; and he was now invited to stand for the Border city.

Invited to stand for Carlisle.

The gentleman whom Mr Graham was thus asked to oppose was a younger son of Mr Thomas Graham, of Edmond Castle, whose branch of the family was

remotely connected with that of Netherby. He had 1820.
been early bred to the profession of the law, became a partner in the firm of Graham, Kinderley, and Domville, practising as solicitors in Lincoln's Inn, and was for many years Auditor to Lord Lonsdale. He acquired in right of his wife considerable estates in Yorkshire; was subsequently created a baronet, and in 1812 was returned for Carlisle, which he continued to represent in several successive Parliaments. Strong in the support of the Tory interest then ascendant in the corporation, he sought re-election; and there being, as was understood, no tie of confidence or intimacy between them, his youthful namesake was expected to become his opponent. But though Mr Graham did not contemplate standing again for Hull, and could not regard exclusion from Parliament as other than a deep mortification, he prudently determined to decline. An angry contest so near home during his father's life-time would under any circumstances have been a source of painful embarrassment to him, considering how widely their political sentiments differed. The struggle would moreover be a costly one; the interest of the money borrowed to defray his previous election expenses formed a serious deduction from his limited income, and he felt that he ought not to encroach upon it much further. He made up his mind therefore to wait for another opportunity. Mr James had not the same motives for declining, and it was

1820. ultimately resolved that he should stand along with Mr Curwen. It was not yet generally known that the last-named gentleman was about to be put in nomination for the county likewise. Urgent appeals, however, were made to the yeomanry and 'statesmen to reserve their votes, form committees, and raise subscriptions for the coming contest* about to be fought on behalf of a resident country gentleman in the Independent interest. Lord Morpeth, to whom a design had been imputed of coalescing with Sir John Lowther, declared "that he had formed no coalition, and that he would stand alone."† This only served to widen the schism between the two sections of Liberals; and when it was announced that Mr Curwen was the forthcoming candidate, the friends of each prepared to secure his return regardless of what might become of the other. Mr Graham had promised whatever influence he possessed to Mr Curwen, and though he sincerely desired Lord Morpeth's election likewise, the peculiar nature of the contest exposed him to misapprehension, and he believed, though erroneously, as we shall presently see, that the part he took would be remembered to his disadvantage by the family of Howard.

The election for the city took place first. Mr James was objected to by the Carlisle Whigs as

* Carlisle Journal, February, 1820.

† Address, 19 Feb., 1820.

going too far, and though personally popular he was defeated at the poll, both the old members being returned. Mr Curwen was the following week put in nomination for the county. His wife's father had been the champion of the Independent interest in 1768, and his name was still had in popular remembrance. Mrs Curwen bid her husband tell the constituency that she was ready to sell her jewels if necessary to secure his return; and at the close of the first day, Lord Morpeth's friends advised him to withdraw. Upon his double return, Mr Curwen elected to sit for the county; and Mr James came in for the city without opposition. 1820.

Westminster election.

A struggle, not wholly dissimilar, took place at the same time for Westminster, which Mr John Cam Hobhouse* contested on Reform principles with Mr George Lamb. The conflict was a severe one, most of the Whigs and many of the Tories supporting the latter, while the former, who advocated household suffrage and triennial Parliaments, was backed by the friends of Sir Francis Burdett, and generally by the younger men of the Liberal party. Mr Graham then lived in Montague Square, and took no little interest in Metropolitan politics. He took the side of Mr Hobhouse, and canvassed for him during several days.† In Westminster as in Cum-

* The present Lord Broughton de Gifford.

† Hansard—Speech of Sir J. Graham in Debate on Church Rates, 23 May, 1837.

1820. berland "advanced opinions" triumphed, although in other places of importance their relative strength does not appear to have been materially changed.

Returned for St Ives.

In the mean while, a friend who knew his desire to be in Parliament undertook to secure for him a favourable introduction to the constituency of St Ives. The representation of the little Cornish borough had frequently been divided, each party being strong enough to return a member of its own. He was fortunate in being on friendly terms with Mr Lindon Evelyn, who was the favourite candidate of the ministerialists; and his own canvass was so successful that before the day of election came he had made himself as popular with the Liberals. The seats, however, were sharply contested by Sir Walter Stirling, who had sat for the borough in the preceding Parliament, and Mr Meade; but at the close of the poll the numbers were,—for Mr Graham, 205; Mr Evelyn, 160; Sir W. Stirling, 146; Mr Meade, 98. Had this majority been less, the seat which it gave would probably have been more secure. The boroughs of which St Ives served as a specimen were at the time treated by politicians of all kinds as incapable of exercising any really independent choice. They were distinguishable from the close boroughs chiefly in this, that instead of returning avowedly the direct nominees of their respective owners, they were each divided among some two or three potential individuals, who sometimes agreed and sometimes differed among

themselves as to the persons who should be elected. 1820.
The semblance of popular election was kept up by occasional contests; but the stranger who ventured to present himself as a candidate was seldom admitted to a knowledge of the hidden mechanism by which the machinery of a make-believe representation was worked. A certain number of respectable inhabitants of the place were really independent, and voted according to their liking; so that canvassing was not altogether useless, or the oratory addressed to public meetings wholly unmeaning. The more judicious dealers in such matters rather encouraged an undergrowth of independence than otherwise; for they felt that it covered the roots of the sinister influence which it was not desirable should lie too bare. Owing to circumstances which are long since in great part forgotten, and which from their exclusively local character it would now be difficult to explain, Mr Graham's appearance as candidate, and his rapid success during the brief period he had spent in the borough, excited an amount of jealousy and enmity of which he was then hardly aware; and no sooner was his return declared than certain parties set about the work of undoing it, with what result we shall presently see.

Birth of his son.

A few weeks after his election for St Ives his wife presented him with a son.* His happiness

* Frederick Ulric, the present baronet, born in Montague Square, 7th April, 1820.

1820. seemed to be complete. The way which so lately he feared that he had missed seemed to have again opened for him to public life; and no domestic hope remained unrealized. He did not as yet indeed possess the advantages of a large income; but when he married he had made up his mind to relinquish the indulgence of more than one expensive taste; and the self-denial cost him but little effort. The habits of his subsequent life appear to have been formed at this period, and they were never departed from. His sole ambition lay in the House of Commons; his only thought of happiness was centred in his home; and few men have had more of affectionate respect and devotion than it was his good fortune in the circle of his own fireside to enjoy. There all the haughtiness and cynicism of manner which was too frequently complained of by strangers seemed to be utterly forgotten; and those who only saw him in the unreserve of family intercourse have never been able to comprehend how one so lovable and so loved could have become the object of so much dislike with those whose means of observation were but casual and rare.

Civil List. When the new House of Commons were asked to agree to a large Civil List for George IV., several attempts were ineffectually made to put a bridle in the mouth of palace prodigality. Mr Hume moved on the 4th May for accounts of detailed expenditure during the last five years of the Regency, in order that the Commons might the better understand what were the real needs to be provided for. Among the sixty votes recorded in his favour was that of Mr Graham. We likewise find him voting for Mr Brougham's motion the following day, to take into account the droits of the Crown and Admiralty and other funds not usually deemed to be within the immediate control of Parliament, before settling the Civil List; and likewise for that of Lord J. Russell, to defer the Report on the Civil List until the estimates for the year should have been fully examined. 1820. 8th May.

Many animated discussions took place on the subject of agricultural distress, which Mr Brougham and Mr Curwen ascribed to the burthens peculiarly affecting land, and Mr Sumner and Mr Western to the failure of the law of 1815 to secure a protection of 80*s.* a quarter to home-grown wheat. Mr Huskisson and Mr F. Robinson denied, indeed, that such was the intention of the act, but the speakers on all sides of the House professed to be earnestly in favour of protection to agriculture, and Mr Ricardo himself only ventured to ask that it should be limited to an amount sufficient to countervail the peculiar imposts on land. The doctrines of free trade were the favourite targets at which the rhetorical shafts of Whigs and Tories were competitively aimed, and the only politicians who in the Parliament of 1820 seemed to have had the foresight to perceive the eventual triumph of those principles, or the courage to promote their gradual adoption, were The Corn Laws.

1820. certain members of the unpopular Government of the day. Lord Liverpool and Mr Canning entertained opinions far more liberal on these and other subjects than it was possible for them fully to avow without breaking up the administration. But they sanctioned and defended the progressive development of a policy founded thereon by Mr Huskisson and Mr Robinson; and we now know that in the Cabinet their views were in the main supported by Mr Peel. Mr Graham voted generally with Mr Brougham and Mr Curwen, and placed great faith in the economic wisdom of Mr Ricardo. But he does not seem to have ventured to meddle as yet with financial or fiscal topics in debate; and his name hardly occurs in any of the discussions of the year.

Reform of Parliament. Various attempts were made to raise in a practical shape the question of Parliamentary Reform. Lord A. Hamilton moved for a return of all the registered voters in counties in Scotland, in order to show by how few the representatives of that part of the united kingdom were nominated; and Lord J. Russell re-introduced his Bill for disfranchising Grampound, and transferring its members to Leeds, whose rising population, wealth, and intelligence entitled it to direct representation. But ministers refused to recognize the principle that a place had any specific claim on account of its size or condition to send members to Parliament; and nothing was done to abate the injustice of which the rising commercial and manufacturing towns complained. The Radicals, while they supported each abortive effort at piece-meal reform, exulted in its defeat, while the Whigs lamented in vain the obstinacy of their aristocratic rivals, who, as they said, were digging a political grave for them both. Under this date Mr Mallet writes :—"The result of all this will be that Brougham will adopt a line of his own in Parliament, and that he will set up for himself upon some broad principle of Parliamentary reform, disregarding the opinion of the aristocracy, and placing his lever on a strong popular feeling. He will have the regular support of Sir R. Wilson, Alderman Wood, Whitbread, Lushington, Moore, Bennett, Lambton, Graham, Curwen, and some others, and Burdett, Hobhouse, Ricardo, and Denman will generally vote with him. Brougham is seriously engaged in the formation of his little party." * But other work awaited Mr Brougham. 1820.

Mr Graham voted with Sir Robert Wilson against the renewal of the Alien Bill. In the minority were also Lord Althorpe, Mr A. Baring, Lord Duncannon, Lord Folkestone, Mr Hume, the Hon. W. Lamb, Mr Lambton, Dr Lushington, Sir J. Mackintosh, Lord Milton, Lord J. Russell, Mr James Scarlett, and Mr Tierney. Mr Graham's name again occurs in a minority of 63 against 113 opposing Renewal of Alien Act. 2nd June. 7th July.

* MS. Journal, June, 1820.

1820. the second reading of the bill. Again on the third 12th July. reading we find him voting in a minority of 23 against the measure.

The estimates for the civil and military establishments of 1820 rather exceeded than fell short of those for 1819; and the revenue being deficient, recourse was once more had to temporary loans. No serious opposition, however, was offered to the measures of Mr Vansittart; and the friends of retrenchment contented themselves with two or three motions of a subordinate kind. To all of these Mr Graham 15th May. gave his support. We find him voting with Lord A. Hamilton to reduce the number of Barons of the Exchequer in Scotland from five to four; and with Mr 4th July. Hume for resolutions setting forth the unequal cost of collecting the revenue in the three kingdoms,*—the grievous losses which continually took place by the defalcation of Receivers-general, and the saving which would be effected by the suppression of their offices.†

Conduct of the Queen. All other topics of interest, however, were forgotten during the summer and autumn, in the unfortunate proceedings against the Queen. Soon after the King's accession her Majesty had signified her intention of returning to England, whence she had

* It appeared that the cost of collection in England was £5 17*s*. 10*d*.; in Scotland £9 6*s*. 11*d*.; and in Ireland £15 8*s*. 11¼*d*. per cent.

† In the course of a few years £117,115 had been lost by malversations of this description.

been absent many years; and of asserting the rights 1820.
and privileges which appertained to her as sovereign consort. An attempt made on the part of the Government to dissuade her from her purpose failed, and her name was by order in Council omitted from the Liturgy. A short time after her arrival in London ministers informed both Houses that they had in their possession proofs of her Majesty's conjugal infidelity, and that the King was resolved to seek for a divorce by Act of Parliament. To avert the scandal of such a proceeding, Mr Wilberforce moved and carried an address to the Queen praying her to waive certain pretensions for the sake of the public good; but she was advised to adhere throughout to her declaration of innocence, and to the maintenance of her right to be recognized as Queen of England. She would have consented to live abroad during the remainder of her life, had her regal rank and state been secured to her; but this her advisers declared could not be done unless her name were restored to the Liturgy, or a guarantee were given for her reception with sovereign honours at foreign courts. George IV. refused to concede either of these points, and the divorce bill, which was in fact in the nature of a criminal prosecution, was proceeded with in the House of Lords. The Commons adjourned from time to time, until the third reading was carried in the Peers by a majority of only nine; whereupon Lord 10th Nov.
Liverpool abandoned the bill, and Parliament was

1820. prorogued, without any speech from the throne, on the following day.

From the outset the Opposition had vehemently espoused the side of Queen Caroline; and during the period that intervened between the commencement and the close of the proceedings against her, frequent motions were made in the Commons on particular incidents or questions connected therewith. Mr Brougham, Lord A. Hamilton, Sir F. Burdett, and Mr Wetherell took the leading part in the discussions that consequently arose; and in all the divisions that took place upon the subject the name of Mr Graham is found among their supporters. At the commencement of the following session a yearly income of £50,000 was settled upon the Queen; and the excitement which her case had created was fast subsiding when her death put an end to the deplorable controversy concerning her.

1821. Early in 1821 a petition was presented from certain electors at St Ives against the return of Mr Graham. That of Mr Evelyn was likewise challenged; and both were informed that an inquiry would be pressed for before a committee, and a scrutiny of votes demanded. Election committees were then as now bound by no legal precedents, and were liable to have their decisions modified or reversed by no Court of Appeal. They were more numerous in their composition, but their judgments were generally believed to indicate rather the predominance of political feeling than any unlearned anxiety to decide in conformity with evidence, or according to any established interpretation of the law. Not being Courts of Record, no uniformity of practice has ever been rendered possible in them; and each question being determined with closed doors by a majority of votes, without any obligation to state either to the parties concerned or to the House the grounds of decision, eager partizanship has seldom been restrained from betraying its leanings in the Committee Room. It is not very long since one of the most eminent men who in our day has occupied the woolsack pronounced an election committee to be an "abominable tribunal." It has ever been at best a species of lottery, in which friendly prejudices have been the prizes and hostile prejudices the blanks; and in which no man has ever been able to calculate the result. But when, in addition to this, opportunity is afforded of provoking a contest in the Committee Room more costly than that which has already taken place at the poll, the anomaly and injustice of the system is rendered complete. In the last-named respect, things were, if possible, worse forty years ago than they are now; and when an opulent borough-monger wished to drive an intruder from his political preserve, he commonly resorted to the expedient of offering him wager of purse. Mr Graham was known to have the command at the period in question of but very moderate resources, and he made no

1821.

Election Committees.

1821. secret of his resolution not to involve himself in extravagant parliamentary outlay. He was therefore looked on as fair game, and threatened with a protracted and expensive investigation. The result none could foresee; but the odds were decidedly against any man who professed the opinions which he did, and who voted, as we have seen, so steadily in support of them. What then was he to do? To engage in an unequal struggle with total uncertainty as to the event, and with the certainty only of being compelled to load himself with a new and heavy burthen of debt, or to relinquish the seat he had occupied for a twelvemonth, and take his chance of finding another? It was for him a hard choice to have to make, and it cost him many an anxious hour ere he came to a determination. Some considerations connected with the position and prospects of his family had no little weight with him. He took a gloomy view of the state of the country, believed that the old landed interest was on the brink of ruin, and knew too much of the neglected and exhausted condition of the Netherby estate not to feel grave misgivings as to his father's and his own position, if something were not speedily done to retrieve it. On the other hand there was little to dazzle or mislead him in the aspect of political affairs. The Liberals seemed to have less chance than ever of obtaining power; and even if they should,

Hesitation as to defence of seat.

what right had he to expect any advancement from them? He could not help voting frequently against the Whig leaders; and no wheedling of self-love could delude him into the belief that he was anybody in the House. As the unexpected winning of a cup by an only horse is said to have been the ruin of many a young man on the turf, it is possible that if he had happened to have made one decided hit in debate, he would have been unable to abandon even for a time the seductive arena: and placed in the circumstances he then was, an hour's rhetorical success might have cost him dear. As it turned out, his failure as a debater from 1818 to 1821 was one of the luckiest things that ever happened to him. He had gone into Parliament without the training which most men have found indispensable for the attainment of distinction there; and though his indomitable perseverance might have surmounted this, as it did other obstacles, he would hardly have had as fair a chance of rising ultimately to eminence or position had he retained his seat, as he found in temporarily relinquishing it. Much of this no doubt was hidden from his eyes at the time: and it was not without a severe mental struggle between prudence and ambition that he made up his mind to decline the defence of the St Ives' petition. Mr Evelyn, to whom money was less an object, refused to give way, and succeeded in keeping his seat; but

1821.

Takes the Chiltern Hundreds.

1821. on the 16th May a new writ was ordered for the borough of St Ives, in the room of Mr Graham, who had accepted the Chiltern Hundreds.*

Residence at Croft Head. Withdrawn from political life, he now resolved to settle down quietly at Croft Head, and to devote himself to country pursuits, and the care of the estate which was eventually to be his. He looked around him, and endeavoured to compare other properties with that in which he was so deeply interested. Farming in Cumberland. Cumberland was still to a great extent one of the worst cultivated counties in the kingdom. The high price of corn during the war had stimulated enclosure, and the breaking up of the lighter pasture lands for tillage. But comparatively little had been done in the way of drainage, which alone could have mitigated the hazards of such a system of agriculture. With an average rain-fall of from forty to upwards of fifty inches in the year, profitable husbandry without drainage was, save in the most favoured districts, a matter of extreme difficulty, and generally a thing impossible. The hope of a gambling price for wheat or barley, one year out of seven, continued still to lure the farmers into repeating the same precarious culture; and it was not until advancing rates and falling markets seemed to render the experiment desperate, that rude efforts were made here and there at surface drainage by means of sods and stones.

* Commons Journals, 1821, p. 347.

A few tenants held what in that region were looked on as large takes, and paid as much as £300 or £400 a year. But in Eskdale, as elsewhere, "the generality of farms were from £15 to £30 per annum; some few extended to £100 or a little more." * 1821. Size of farms.

The condition of the agricultural population at this period was one of perplexity and gloom. The power of legislation had been strained to the uttermost to secure a steady and remunerative price for corn; but it had failed to do so. Wages continued to fall, and rates to rise. Emigration on a scale sufficiently large to influence the labour market was still in the nebulous state of speculation, whence little light of hope, and no warmth of comfort came, to mitigate the embarrassments of the landlord and the difficulties of the tenant. Parliament had decreed a return to a metallic currency, whereby it was believed the prices of all agricultural produce must be still further depressed. Many occupiers of the soil in Cumberland turned from profitless tillage to cattle-farming. But distress had fallen on the commercial towns and cities likewise; and the selling price of stock and dairy produce in Liverpool and Manchester was no longer such as to repay their cost, and provide for unabated rents and increased local charges.

Small farms prevailed almost universally at

* Cully's Report on Agriculture of Cumberland in 1805.

1821. the time; and the application of capital to improvements, whether of house or land, was a thing comparatively unknown. Far from being an unfavourable specimen of the period, the Netherby estate was regarded as one where a man was fortunate to possess a holding. The old laird lived for the most part at home, spent his income amongst his tenantry, was considerate for their wants, and seldom peremptory on rent day. Yet the appearance of homesteads, offices, cattle-sheds, fences, roads, and implements of husbandry as they then existed, could we recall it accurately now, would present a curious contrast to that which is to be found at the present day. To say that the difference is altogether due to the life-labour and care of one man would be indeed untrue; but who shall say how far the early and rapid change for the better which has taken place throughout the western region of the Border is not fairly attributable to his energy and perseverance.

The Netherby estate. Contrasted with what it afterwards became, the Netherby estate has been truly described as being "in 1821 in a most ruinous condition. The good land which had been exhausted by repeated corn crops was chiefly divided into small farms of from 40 to 100 acres in extent. The estate was overburdened by an excessive population; a great portion of it was unenclosed; the farm-buildings, with few exceptions, were very bad; three-fourths of the land was completely saturated with water, and a great extent of moss and cold pasture on that account alone remained uncultivated." * 1821.

There were few farm-houses to be seen with slated roofs. The rooms, though not destitute of comfort, were small, incommodious, and ill-ventilated. The farm-yard was badly enclosed, and hardly ever drained; the byre formed of the roughest materials afforded but imperfect shelter from the weather, and the barns were of the worst and scantiest description. The fences, unequal and broken, served but little purpose, save that of defining the boundaries of adjoining farms; and the roads, ill-formed and unrepaired, were almost impassable in winter-time. The chief part of the manure of the farm was suffered to go to waste, and no efficient substitute was employed.

Necessity for a change of system.

Left undisturbed by politics or pleasure to listen to the complaints and perplexities of those around him, Mr Graham became seriously alarmed for the consequences that must ensue from such a state of things, and with characteristic energy he endeavoured to excite in the mind of his father the same apprehensions that disturbed his own. The whole landed interest seemed to him to be sinking daily deeper into a slough of despond, from which there would by-and-by be no extrication. Something effectual

* Report of Mr Browne, steward of the Netherby estate, revised by his predecessor, Mr Yule.

1821. ought promptly to be done, or all would go to ruin. But his father, to whom the details of business had always been irksome, was every year less and less inclined to make any serious effort to extricate his possessions and his dependents from their embarrassed condition. The management of the estate had been committed for some time, almost without control, to a Mr Ellis, in whose hands the tenantry and work-people deposited their earnings, and by whom a running account was kept of these deposits as against rent. Sir James drew upon the steward as he wanted money, without regard to half-yearly or annual balances; interest was charged or allowed as the case might be on the various sums that passed through Mr Ellis's hands; and the result was that while he became virtually master of all around him, neither laird nor tenants could tell, or wished perhaps to inquire, exactly how they stood with regard to each other. But the general results of the system were but too certain. Every year the sum of arrears grew larger, and the pressure of interest payable on encumbrances became more burthensome. Mr Graham naturally looked with anxiety at the existing state of things, and with apprehension at the prospect before him. He sought ineffectually to get some satisfactory explanation from Mr Ellis of the system he pursued, and tried in vain to arouse his father to somewhat more of active superintendence over his affairs. At last, through the intervention of

Payments on account.

Lady Catherine, he succeeded in obtaining power himself to undertake the management of the estate. His aptitude for accounts was now for the first time put to the proof. He had a real love of the thing for its own sake, and he embarked in the laborious and ungrateful work with energy and confidence. But the difficulties were greater than he had anticipated. In his impatience to disentangle the complications of the self-willed steward's mode of rent banking, he was not unfrequently imperious and arbitrary; and the old manager, who saw that his reign was drawing to a close, grew sulky and supercilious at what he considered the ignorance of his inexperienced inquisitor. They had more than one hard tussle for it before the question of financial supremacy was solved, and the Baronet was more than once appealed to in defence of the old-fashioned methods of dealing. But Sir James would not interfere; his son persisted in having his own way, and the controversy ended in Mr Ellis resigning his charge, and removing to Liverpool, where he resided for many years. 1821.

Taking the direction of affairs into his own hands, Mr Graham set about his work of thorough reformation. He overhauled the rent roll, and sifted each account minutely. He found three hundred tenants whose rents, though not excessive, had fallen so much into arrear that it was thought better to wipe out the greater part of them.* Six thousand

Assumes management of estate.

* Dickenson's Prize Report on Farming of Cumberland, p. 18.

1821. pounds, which could not have been enforced without resort to great severity, were thus relinquished. But while lenient in this respect he insisted upon changes calculated to prevent the recurrence of a similar state of things. Whenever leases fell in, or the smaller tenants proved insolvent, he increased the size of the farms. But this was done with so little of the blind love of uniformity, that thirty years after there still remained about one hundred and

Drainage. fifty holders of this class.* He "drained much of the inferior land, without charging the tenants any interest on the outlay; and in no case was more than three shillings and sixpence per acre added for the cost of drainage."†

By assisting the occupiers to remodel the farm-houses and offices where he did not rebuild them himself, and everywhere insisting on the application to the soil of the mode of tillage then most approved, he accomplished much. A substantial alteration for the better was commenced. Its progress was at first slow and sometimes not unattended with difficulty. But by degrees his energy and perseverance began to tell upon the productive condition of the property, and upon the social welfare of its inhabitants. He got rid of useless trees and fences, and of the weedy fallow, till then so often to be seen. The old thatched hovel of the labourer disappeared. The narrow and filthy cattle-fold gave place to the well-

* Dickenson's Report, p. 18. † Ibid.

paved and commodious farm-yard, sheltered by outhouses as durably built as the dwellings to which they belonged. A better breed of sheep and black cattle were fed on pastures that no longer recalled the days when almost all the Border country was moor or moss; and pigs and poultry came to be of less account in the eyes of the tenantry, and to be kept within closer range. The improved systems of manuring and of cropping which he had first heard of with curiosity at Buckland, and afterwards discussed with men of his own county at Workington, were introduced as rapidly as the prejudices of the old occupiers permitted. But the obstinacy with which men inhabiting a secluded district, and all engaged in like pursuits, adhere to the way of life in which they have been brought up, needs not to be told. To have suddenly interdicted all the inveterate habits of bad husbandry by an arbitrary exercise of will, would have probably dislocated the whole industrial machine, and placed serious obstacles in the way of practical success in the experiment he had undertaken. He preferred to proceed tentatively. With the aid of Mr Yule, a skilful Scotch agriculturist whom he engaged as steward, he gradually changed the face of affairs. Many of the poorer occupiers were obliged to give up their holdings; but this was done (to use the words of one who recollects everything that took place at the period referred to) "with every kindness and consideration for the feelings and

1821.

Farming improvement.

1821. necessities of the people, and without injustice being inflicted on any." A large proportion of the tenants were in circumstances hardly removed from the rank of labourers, though keeping farm servants; and for want of skill not realizing half the amount that might have been secured had their labour been better directed. Those who were found most worthy were made tenants on a larger scale, supplied with capital on easy terms, and advised and instructed as to the proper use of it. Of those who were displaced, some obtained occupations elsewhere, others sought employment as waged labourers, in many respects thereby bettering their condition, and some emigrated. The eye-witness already cited, says "he never heard any complaint beyond what might have fallen from thoughtless people who disliked being put out of their old jog-trot course." He mentions one instance of a tenant who, by slovenly farming and intemperate habits, had made himself a nuisance to all around him; but as his father and grandfather, men of good character, had held the same land, he was treated with indulgence, and repeated efforts were made to reclaim him by advice and aid. But it was to no purpose; he made no progress towards liquidating his heavy arrears of rent, and his mode of life was dissolute as ever. Under these circumstances he had at length notice to quit; and, finding that he could no longer trifle with the forbearance of his landlord, he expressed a wish to go to America. Not

Considerate treatment of tenants.

only was the debt due by him to the estate cancelled, 1822.
but means were afforded him of removing his family across the Atlantic, and many articles of considerable value were given him which were likely to be useful to a man in his new position. Other cases of a similar description might be mentioned. On the other hand, no man was permitted to undertake the cultivation of more land than he could show that he possessed the means of cultivating properly. It was sometimes hard to refuse the son of an old occupier who was willing to work and ready to out-bid some neighbour or stranger in future rent. "My man, you are not able," Mr Graham would say, "you have not capital enough, and as things now go, you will only beggar yourself or help to beggar me." Where land had been thoroughly run out, he would sometimes take it for a time into his own hands, in order that he might superintend more closely the process for its restoration. He had less faith in tillage than stock farming, for the soil and climate of Cumberland; and never subsequently deviated from his early predilection in this respect. He soon became an expert farmer, and was regarded as a first-rate judge of the qualities of horses, cattle, and sheep.

"At the commencement of the present century Galloway cattle.
Galloway cattle began to obtain a footing along the border of Scotland, where the long-horned breed had kept tolerably pure. Some few might have ex-

1822. isted in the northern confines of the county for a long time before. Some enterprising occupiers in the Abbey Holme selected and introduced a few well-bred Galloway cattle into their district, for the purpose of rearing a distinct breed, approved for hardiness and milking qualities. The kind soon began to predominate there and in the neighbouring parishes, and finally to nearly displace the long-horns. Mr Graham, for the greater encouragement of his tenants (along with distributing about £60 in premiums for superior management, &c., annually till 1840), every year gave three or four bull calves and stirks of the Galloway breed in prizes from his own herd, which had been carefully selected from the best stocks in Galloway. This was a sure method of extending and improving the breed in the district, and was most successful on the inferior farms, the short-horns being generally preferred on the good land." *

Roads. At first he found great difficulty in convincing the tenant farmers of the need of better roads. The old system by which their repair was left to be done when and how it might by the occupiers of the land through which they passed, suited the desultory habits and short-sighted views of agricultural life theretofore prevalent; and for a time he remonstrated in vain against the blind unthrift that caused so much time and labour to be wasted in every process

* Dickenson's Farming of Cumberland, p. 49.

requiring the transport of produce to market or of manure to the field. The circumstance, however, that the boundaries of the estate were coincident with those of the parishes of Arthuret and Kirkandrews facilitated his obtaining the imposition of a special rate for the making and repair of highways in the district. A portion of this was applied in the payment of a person who acted as surveyor and inspector; and the good effects of the change became visible in due time. 1823.

Working-ton.

Workington, the residence of Mr J. C. Curwen, member for the county, was at this time the local centre of agricultural improvement. Its hospitable owner loved to gather round him there proprietors and farmers, squires and 'states-men, men of every degree; and hardly any of those who took an interest in the rearing of stock or the culture of the soil with better intelligence than had been done by those who went before them, were missing on such occasions. Thither came Mr Saul of Green Row, and Mr Rigg of Abbey Holme, and Mr Rook of Akehead, and Mr Blamire of Thackwood, the friend and confidant of all the men of his class in the county. The expectant master of Netherby came with the rest, and was not the least welcome visitor at the Hall. At these joyous and instructive meetings he learnt much of the practical application to the circumstances and capacities of his native county, of those experimental improvements which had elsewhere been so success-

1823. ful. But he learned something more, which in due time he likewise turned to account. In familiar talk with men of various classes and characters, he got a true insight into the wants and feelings of the community amongst which he lived, and whom it was his ambition one day to serve.

Encumbrances on Estate.

The encumbrances on the estate at this period amounted to about £120,000. Loans were negotiated on better terms with Insurance Companies, the financial effect of which was to reduce the annual interest payable by nearly one-third. His father was content to draw a stated income of £8000 a year; and when the necessary out-goings for the improvement of the property were provided for, little remained for their indefatigable and laborious author. He denied himself the gratification of possessing a permanent residence in town, believing that he could not afford it if Netherby were kept up as it ought to be. In the enjoyment of rural life he passed the next two years, discharging the duties of a country gentleman, and attending closely to every branch of county business. He was the cause of many retrenchments and reforms in local taxation and expenditure. The rates had been suffered to increase year by year, until their burthen became exceedingly oppressive, and the grievance was felt the more because a system of gross jobbing was known to prevail in every branch of the outlay, while the public asked in vain for any satisfactory account. With the co-operation of men like Mr Curwen and Major Aglionby, he applied himself to the reformation of these abuses, incurring not unfrequently the personal hostility of those who had long found their profit in them; he had the satisfaction of seeing the public charges reduced, the salaries of public officers cut down, the highways materially improved, and a strict account of local monies annually made public. 1823.

CHAPTER VI.

CORN AND CURRENCY.

1824—1826.

1824. Succeeds his father.

At his father's death in 1824, new claims and responsibilities devolved on Sir James Graham. The settlement made on Lady Catherine was ample, but the provision made for his sisters he felt to be inadequate, and he voluntarily undertook the payment to each of them of several hundreds a year during their lives.

His desire for reclamation, planting, building, drainage, and agricultural improvement of all descriptions, grew with the hope of augmented means for gratifying it; and an estate of eighteen thousand acres afforded him practically unbounded scope for his wise and beneficent ambition. He believed that he could not substantially improve the condition of those around him without permanently benefiting himself, and he sought no higher gratification or advantage than that which was to be obtained through the social and economical elevation of those amidst whom he dwelt. But progress, to be safe and lasting, must be suffered to move slowly. When he first began he expected to see his dreams of amelioration quickly realized. As obstacles arose which he had not foreseen, he endeavoured to moderate his expectations, and to reconcile himself to delay. But as further ramifications of the work he had undertaken spread themselves out before him, in whatever direction he turned, his spirit misgave him, and the question daily pressed for an answer more and more importunately,—Had he sufficient means at his disposal for the completion of his task? A farm, however fertile or well situated, could not have justice done it by the most hard-working occupier without capital; how then could an estate? He had laid down the rule as indispensable for his tenants; did it not apply equally to himself as a landlord? A rich man might in his position convert the old Debatable Land into a garden; but he was not a rich man. With a large rent-roll he found himself encumbered by a weight of obligations which left him no superfluous income to spend; and his sense of what was just and generous to others had prompted him to add very considerably thereto. If there were any immediate prospect of better times for land-owners, he felt that with frugality and care he might maintain his social position without foregoing the large outlay he thought necessary for agricultural improvement. But he looked

1824.

1824. in vain for any signs of such a change. Trade had indeed revived; the manufacturers were said to be busy; foreign speculation was beginning to try the strength of its wing, preparatory to its memorable flight round the world; and the new Chancellor of the Exchequer was collecting the materials of the glowing financial statements of giant-stride prosperity which were to be long associated with his name. But the landed interest still remained depressed almost as much as ever. The benefit of protecting duties remitted on silks and ribbons was infinitesimal, while the depreciation consequent upon a return to cash payments was palpable; and the pressure of taxes and rates remained as before. Encumbered proprietors were everywhere forced to exact more rigorously than ever the payment of unabated rents. Produce and stock were consequently brought to market sooner than they would have otherwise been; and thus prices, in spite of the conjuring promises of legislative interposition, were kept in a state of constant and ruinous fluctuation. The young fruit of improvement and the ripe fruit of economy were alike eaten up by the caterpillar and the canker-worm of misrule; and the more far-sighted an owner or occupier of land might be, the further he saw into the gloom that overspread the horizon.

Thinks of disposing of Netherby.

It was under the influence of feelings like these, that, soon after his father's death, Sir James seems to have first entertained the idea of disposing of his

patrimonial inheritance, and of devoting himself for 1824.
the rest of his life to wholly different pursuits. Netherby would have doubtless fetched a great price in the market; it was seldom perhaps that a property at once so extensive, attractive, and capable of remunerative development was offered for sale. Several good estates might indeed be carved out of it; and after liquidating all existing charges, the balance of the purchase-money would place him in a position of ease and independence highly favourable to the pursuit of business or politics, or both. A life of mere indolence or pleasure he probably never thought of. His brain was ever busy, and his bosom swelled with high and noble aspirations. He had as yet done nothing, it was true, to convince others that he had in him the qualities of a great administrator or parliamentary chief, but the conviction was early implanted in his own mind: and though it had been for a time almost smothered by a tangled overgrowth temporary in its nature, it was fast rooted there and ready to shoot upwards on the first opportunity. He knew that towards the acquisition of influence in public life, nothing so commended a man as his claim to be regarded as the representative of some great interest, or the exponent of the wishes of some important class. If he was not therefore to be the spokesman of that from which he sprung, he would identify himself with some other leading section of the community, and take his stand as a banker

1824. instead of a land-owner. Full of this idea he went the length of inquiry as to the openings that might be available for one who could bring to a London house of established character a considerable accession of capital. The firm of Pole, Thornton, Downe, andC o., desired just then to extend its resources, and to obtain the strength of new connections: and the matter at first sight wore to him an appearance highly attractive. Fortunately the negotiation had not proceeded very far, when he was induced by a friend to whom he had confided his wishes, to consult Mr James Evan Bailey of Bristol. "Tell him," said the wise and experienced banker, "to hold fast by Netherby, and keep clear of banking. Nothing he can say on the subject can change my opinion." Within twelve months Messrs Pole, Thornton, Downe, and Co., failed; and thus, narrowly saved from ruin, Sir James put away all further thoughts of commercial enterprise, and reverted with zeal and energy to the pursuits in which he was better fitted to excel.

Messrs Pole, Thornton, Downe, and Co.

Agricultural pursuits and country business had never indeed wholly absorbed his attention. His fondness for reading increased every year. At Croft Head he was often found imbedded in books, and in the library at Netherby he spent a still greater portion of his time. On quitting Parliament in 1821 he had resolved not to think of entering it again before he had had an opportunity for much deeper and more diversified study than he had ever pursued before. His course of reading now embraced most of the poets and historians of celebrity,—Shakspeare, Pope, and Dryden being his favourites among the former, as Clarendon and Gibbon were among the latter. Many traces, indeed, are discernible in his own compositions of the spirit of the great chronicler of the Civil War, and of the style of the matchless undertaker of the obsequies of empire. But his studies were varied, and in a certain sense desultory; and, his memory being most retentive, he would frequently quote a long passage which had struck him in the perusal of a book, without having any especial admiration for the work as a whole. It is not easy, therefore, to name his favourite authors; but the writings of Burke beyond a doubt were those that left the deepest impress on his mind. The magically translucent gloom through which the greatest mind of its time surveyed the present and foretold the future was singularly congenial to his own. Few, save those who shared his domestic intimacy, could have supposed how early a disposition towards despondency showed itself in his nature. His animal spirits were ordinarily high, and in out-of-door pursuits and recreations, or the cheerful society of friends with whom he was wholly at his ease, he was full of playful humour and was glad to be gay. But the fluctuations of his temperament were sudden, and as unaccountable to himself as to those around him. To the world without he haughtily maintained

1824.

General reading.

1824. the equanimity of reserve, and seemed to repel its sympathy. But from an early period he appears to have been troubled with misgivings and perplexities. In the social condition of the country, in the inappeasible war of creeds, in the blind rancour of toil-worn discontent, and the blinder selfishness of privilege and power, he found ever-recurring food for dejection. The touching and solemn sadness of Burke, more especially in his later writings, filled his imagination, and tended to increase, perhaps, his own predisposition to melancholy. The solemn pomp of Burke's warnings and complainings had the fascination of mournful music for his ear, and seemed to haunt his dreams alike in the autumnal quiet of Eskdale and amid the din of public conflict. How often in his long career did those sad words of the rejected candidate at Bristol break unbidden from his lips—"What shadows we are, and what shadows we pursue!" Again and again, at long intervals, we find them recurring, like the fitful wail that runs through the music of Beethoven, or like the tolling of the once familiar college bell, heard intermittently through the ephemeral uproar of busy life. Without the originality or imagination of him who may be called the poet of politics, he had a deep and true sympathy with the greatness and weakness of Burke,—with his unselfish hopes and fears, his scornful defiance of unpopularity, and his feminine sensitiveness to neglect or reproach,—his eager grasp-

Influence of Burke.

ing at power, which he felt he would have used not unworthily, and the painful intensity of his consciousness that in his sunniest hours of triumph, disenchantment dogged his steps, and that his most loved illusions would forsake him ere he reached the grave. To the crowd, and even to ordinary acquaintances, little of all this betrayed itself; but to the few who knew him well, there was always evident a despondent turn of thought and feeling, without a recollection of which many things in the story of his life must seem anomalous and unaccountable. 1824.

Rev. T. Matthews.

Among his neighbours in Cumberland, the person in whose society he took most pleasure at this period was the Rev. T. Matthews of Wigton Hall. His friend had taken orders early in life, but for many years had not held any cure of souls. He was endowed with an excellent understanding, a clear, practical insight into the characters of individuals, and a manly solicitude regarding the social wants and perplexities of the time. Though full of active benevolence towards those in need, and easily kindled into indignation at local-jobbing or injustice, he was not, in the party sense of the term, much of a politician. His ideas of reform were economic rather than organic, for he loved his fellow-men in general better than he trusted them. He wished to see the cost of laborious living lowered, and the price of daily toil increased. His leanings were all towards abated taxation and the liberation of trade. He did not

1825. quarrel about questions of suffrage or voting, but he wished to see the scramble for existence rendered if possible less fierce before the extension of electoral rights. Mr Matthews was a well-read and accomplished man, without intolerance or assumption, willing to listen to any earnest expression of opinion whencesoever it came, and ready to make large allowance for the prejudices of class and the defects of education.

Cumberland 'states-men.

Not very far from Wigton lived Mr John Rooke, with whom Sir James had first become acquainted at the farming shows at Workington. Mr Rooke belonged to the peculiar race of middle-class yeomanry, known in Cumberland by the name of 'states-men. They had been until then very numerous, and generally well-to-do in the world. Cultivating the fee-farms they had often inherited through many more generations than the great lords of the soil could number, they combined with the industry and thrift of yeomen, much of the independent spirit and bearing of those who claim distinctively to be of gentle blood. They were on the whole about the most estimable and useful class in the county,—the fairest dealers, the most independent jurors, the stoutest backers, the best neighbours, and the steadiest friends. Intermarriage sometimes allied those of the wealthier sort with the gentry and clergy; but these were the exception, not the rule. Their younger sons periodically hived off to the towns, and after a time were lost sight of in the mingling swarms of trade and commerce. But when the eldest of the family happened to die childless, or through ill-fortune was compelled to part with what was always spoken of as "the estate," it was the especial pride of some younger branch that had thriven better away from home to redeem the old place, pay off the mortgage, and set up the name anew. As their properties varied greatly in size and value, so their habits differed likewise. Many were too poor to send their children to the grammar school; and, save for a few here and there who showed rare aptitude for learning, collegiate training was unthought of. From boyhood the sons of the 'states-man were more apt to be proud of the well-bred hound, the fast-trotting cob, the prize heifer, and the fowling-piece that never missed fire, than the dozen volumes (not counting the old big Bible) that were kept locked up in the oak press in the parlour. Improved notions of husbandry, requiring as they usually did an outlay of ready money, made but slow way amongst the 'states-men as a class. Stock farming and fruit gardening came easier to them, and were more to their taste. When, as would sometimes occur, the inheritance passed to the widow or only daughter, it was her pride to show that she was worthy of its possession, and able to compete with her neighbours of the sturdier sex in all that was to be fed or grown on the land; and when a prize fell to her lot it was hailed with a hearty cheer. 1826.

1825. No class, however, had suffered more from the trying change of the times than the 'states-men of the Border. Year after year their well-bred and well-cared-for cattle brought prices "that would nothing like pay;" and year after year their faith waxed fainter and fainter in getting the price that Parliament had put upon corn. They had no rent indeed to pay; yet somehow or other they grew daily more short of cash wherewith to replenish their stock, or purchase the little comforts that use had made
Mortgages. necessaries of life. Inhabiting, for the most part, sequestered spots of a region remote from enterprise, and whose industrial atmosphere no thorough draft of quickening intercourse or intelligence served to freshen, their tendency was to become angry and obstinate, and at last reckless and desponding. The tenure by which they held their small properties afforded them fatal facilities for borrowing; and their unacquaintance with any other means of doing so than that which offered in the next market town, made them ready prey for the monopolists of usury in the locality. In 1825 many of the best of the 'statesmen were said to be wading up to the saddle-girths in debt. They were too proud to lay bare their condition to any but those of their own sort; but the terrible truth that they were all sinking together deeper and deeper into the slough of irredeemable mortgage was beginning to force itself upon the minds of the more reflective and thought-

ful amongst them: and one of the most intelligent of these was the owner of Ake-head. 1825.

Mr John Rooke.

Though John Rooke can hardly be said to have been intellectually a type of his class, he was a fair exponent of their wishes and their wants. Bred amongst them and taught from infancy to cherish the deepest sympathy in their manly love of independence, their open-hearted habits of intercourse, and their honest pride in working as early and late as any labourer, while they held their heads as erect as that of any gentleman, he had for some time turned from the hopeless struggle he saw going on around him to the study of books, from which he hoped to draw some light of comfort and encouragement for his own, and the other agricultural classes of the community. He could not resist the conviction that a fundamental change in their condition was, to a great extent, inevitable; and that if they could not adapt themselves promptly to the state of things which analytical and mechanical science were bringing about universally, they must hopelessly sink lower and lower, and at last wholly disappear. He taught himself something more than the rudiments of agricultural chemistry; and then the love of inquiry lured him on into geology, which was still for the weariest tread in a state of unfathomed and unsolidified moss, and in which he very soon lost his way.* He sought with eagerness to understand the

* See his work entitled "Geology as a Science applied to

1826. construction and cost of every new implement of husbandry produced by mechanical skill, and he spent many a summer's day in discussing its specific and comparative worth, and trying whether he could not improve upon it. But all his investigations tended to bring him at last to that of political economy, which, as he used to say, was "the debatable land" between farming and politics. He had read Adam Smith at the instance of his friend Mr Matthews, and some of the writings of Ricardo, by the advice of Sir J. Graham. They debated the many perplexed questions of prices and wages, profits and rent, population and poor laws, by the fireside at Wigton, and renewed their grave and anxious discussions as often as they met elsewhere. Each had his favourite point of attack in the existing system of clumsy and partial legislation which they all condemned. With a very circumscribed knowledge of statistical facts, and a somewhat imperfect method of expounding his ideas, Mr Rooke's intuitive good sense and entire freedom from class prejudices led him to the conclusion that absolute liberty of corn importation would be the safest and best basis of national policy. Sir James did not go so far, because, as his custom was, he went wider a field, and insisted on looking not only

the Reclamation of Land from the Sea, the Construction of Harbours, the Formation of Railroads, and the Discovery of Coal, with an assumed outline Map of the Granite Formation of the Earth."—London: Ridgway, 1828.

ahead but around, and backwards as well as onwards. 1826.
In his view, monetary and mercantile questions were intimately associated,—so intimately that without shutting one eye and peering with the other alone, he did not understand how it was possible to look at the practical interest connected with corn apart from those connected with currency. Intermingling with both, in his mind, were those of party and class, and those of taxation and empire. He would not if he could have severed them, and he certainly could not if he would have done so.

Ministerial policy.

He was not so engrossed by agricultural pursuits as to be indifferent to national and party politics. He had watched with interest the gradual disintegration of the old party of Resistance, which still held together under the Premiership of Lord Liverpool, but whose power of cohesion was passing away under the influence of Mr Huskisson in commercial matters, and of Mr Canning in foreign affairs. He placed no unqualified confidence in either; but, like many of the Whigs, he was ready to co-operate with their adherents in advancing the cause of Religious Liberty and Freedom of Trade. Their principal short-comings in his eyes were their irresolute, and as he thought mischievous policy, with regard to the currency, and their maintenance of places and sinecures at the high rate of pay fixed during the period of war prices. Looking at these matters from a country gentleman's point

1826. of view, he probably exaggerated the danger and mischief of the course which he condemned. We look back without emotion at the troubles of a time whose perils and perturbation have long since passed away, and find it hard to catch the echoes of the complaints and reproaches then loudly heard throughout the land. It is difficult to put ourselves back into the condition of monetary affairs as they were in 1826. The storm of the preceding year had subsided, but every shore and creek of credit was strewn with wrecks. The spirit of industry seemed to be crushed by the fearful suddenness of the calamity that had recently befallen it, and ministers in their terror lest credit should too rapidly revive and speculation be stimulated, as they said, by the use of paper money not capable of immediate and universal conversion into gold, resolved to suppress finally and summarily the small-note circulation by Act of Parliament. With a similar hope of checking speculation on the part of the merchant, and at the same time steadying prices of corn in the home market, a new sliding-scale was enacted, whereby plenty to the consumer and a remunerative profit to the grower were to be infallibly secured. Sir James believed that these elaborate attempts—the one to regulate the price of money, and the other to regulate the price of food by means of statute law—were alike detrimental and vain, and being convinced that his class were being once more fooled into leaning on a staff, that sooner or later would inevitably pierce their hand, he set about the task of disenchanting them of their reliance on a Corn Law, and of leading them to head the over-taxed community at large in a demand for a sweeping reduction of expenditure, and for freedom of banking as well as freedom of trade. Such was the theme of his celebrated pamphlet on "Corn and Currency," published in 1826, addressed to the land-owners of England. 1826.

His mind was instinctively disposed to look at all sides of a question; and the deliberate statement of a case of which he was fond, was marked by a provoking candour, that purblind partizanship never could bear. It was the very wantonness of a love of mischief, in the eyes of the hacks, whose rule of political discussion is to admit nothing that seems detrimental at the moment. But for this mode of argument he had a supreme contempt. There was for him no pleasure in a controversy where there was not much to be said on the other side. He delighted to poise difficulties in his mental hand; and to wring the tribute of reluctant admiration from opponents by the judicial amplitude and fairness of the way in which he recapitulated and condensed their arguments before he stated those to which he himself inclined. "Upon the whole," was his favourite phrase when about to cast the balance of conflicting considerations; and until he passed that point, he did not give

His mode of argument.

1826. rein to the passionate and crushing eloquence for which he was so remarkable.

Pamphlet on Corn and Currency. An early illustration of this tendency to repudiate the errors of his friends as well as those of his antagonists, is to be found in the prefatory remarks on the divided condition of the agricultural interest, with which the Address to Land-owners regarding "Corn and Currency" opens.

In a tone of mingled remonstrance against past divisions, and concern for the dangers he supposed to be impending over his class, he rebuked the blindness of the land-owners in general, who, "while their estates were melting away, while their encumbrances were increasing, and their means diminishing, did not seek to discover the real causes of the evil, or unite to obtain the proper remedy, but wasted their strength in a fruitless struggle of parties. One faction clinging to the Government of the day, blindly supported its prodigal expenditure, in the hope of sharing its patronage and of making a provision out of the public purse, for dependants which the family estates could no longer bear; while the opposite faction, irritated by disappointment and long exclusion from all participation in Government, were tempted almost to triumph in the ills which their antagonists had created." He reminded them of the great advantages they possessed by reason of their predominant power in Parliament, and their influence over every other order in the State. "Were there then no limits to the power of the landed proprietors, constituting as they did a vast majority of both Houses of Parliament, and backed as they ultimately must be by all the power of the Crown? He freely answered that he knew no bound but public opinion, and this was a barrier which they could not pass. The seat of public opinion was in the middle ranks of life, in that numerous class removed alike from the wants of labour and the cravings of ambition, enjoying the advantages of leisure, and possessing intelligence sufficient for the formation of a sound judgment, neither warped by interest nor obscured by passion. Public opinion thus established could not be outraged with impunity, and hence the established check which they possessed over the legislature itself. For there were measures which King, Lords, and Commons, though united, could not carry. It behoved, therefore, the land-owners not only to act in concert, but so to frame their measures as to combine with their own the interest of the community, and to establish their case upon grounds which they could maintain conjointly with the safety and prosperity of the State."

1826.

Controlling power of opinion.

He disclaims having made any new discoveries, but wishes to urge the need of considering the two questions of the Corn Law and the Currency in their close connection with each other. Since 1815 the object had been to raise the price of corn above that prevalent abroad. The design was to raise wages,

1826. and with them the price of all the necessaries of life; but this could do the labourer no good. Rents were raised by high prices, which forced inferior soils into cultivation. But it was doubtful whether legislative protection profited the land-owner as much in the long run as he imagined. The home-grown crop was seldom exactly adequate to domestic requirements, and no more. At one time the prohibitory system was unjust to the grower: at another to the consumer. The consumer was injured in the interval between the rise of price and the importation of foreign grain; and thus the alternate evils of redundancy and scarcity, unsteady prices and uncertain rents, were the inevitable consequences of the existing system of Corn Laws. Farming was made a gambling speculation; no caution could guard against ruinous losses, for no prudence could foresee the chances on which they depended. He anticipated the decline of manufacturing industry if the prohibitory duties should become permanent, and this the land-owners ought to deprecate, because the manufacturing population at home was the best customer of the farmer.

Futility of a high duty on corn.

Thus early we have unfolded the essential features of that policy which in after years he contributed so much to impress upon the public mind, and to engrave upon the tablets of permanent legislation. By feeling and habit an aristocrat, he wished for the safety, if not for the ascendency, of his order;

but by reflection and reason convinced that their retention of power was only to be secured by a careful avoidance of all real or supposed antagonism to popular interests, he counselled them to abandon the exclusive claim to pecuniary advantage at the cost of other classes which agricultural protection delusively promised, and to seek a compensatory gain in reduced civil and military estimates, and a re-adjustment of contracts and liabilities, suited to a return to a metallic currency. 1826.

Peculiar burthens on Land.

With Mr Ricardo, he was willing that a moderate fixed duty should be secured to the landed interest to countervail peculiar taxation. In this peculiar taxation he counted tithes, a portion of the poor rates, and one or two other burthens, such as highway rate and county rate. "The amount of the duty was a fit subject for discussion," but at this point, he maintained, the great difficulty arose, in consequence of the factitious variations in the currency caused by legislation,—now in favour of paper, now of gold. "It was impossible to establish a fixed protecting duty with fairness when the standard of value was itself unfair. This was the core of the whole subject."

Standard of value.

A comparison of the various opinions with regard to the true standard of value, entertained by eminent thinkers and writers on the subject, enabled him more perfectly to illustrate his own. We find the latter stated with great earnestness of language, though

1826. rather in the negative and argumentative form than in the condensed shape of definition. He considered the exclusive reference to gold as the test of value, to be a departure from the traditionary policy of the country in such matters,—as likely to cause instability of price by the necessary liability of any single commodity to vary in available amount from time to time, wholly irrespective of the actual wealth or poverty of the nation,—and as tending to create a factitious and arbitrary basis of currency, which in seasons of adversity must always present a temptation to weak or empirical rulers to tamper with the relative value of property and its encumbrances, labour and its wages, produce and its price. He refers to the comparative steadiness of the price of corn during the long period that elapsed between the Revolution of 1688 and the end of the American war, during which a mixed gold and silver standard existed, and no depreciation of the currency took place. The Bank Restriction Act of 1797 he considered the fountain whence all subsequent errors flowed, but the warnings of Mr Pitt ought not to have been neglected as to the manner of its repeal, and Government ought to have told the country that the Bill of 1819 would make a difference of five-and-twenty instead of three per cent. in liabilities and contracts. On this special ground he urged the policy either of accommodating taxation to the enhanced weight of encumbrances, or of continuing the permission to the banks to issue notes on their own responsibility, without statutable check ; and as Parliament seemed averse to the latter alternative, he argued that the land-owners ought earnestly to insist upon the former. High prices for corn they could not keep up for their own benefit with a metallic currency; but all the odium and resentment of limiting the supply of food to the nation would accumulate year after year at their door, so long as the miserable device of a high corn law was maintained. But here they were arrested by the past variations in the value of the currency, and the price which they had first to settle was the price of money.

1826.

Prices of money and corn.

His theory of prices will best be given in his own language :—

"The value of money is in the inverse ratio of its quantity, the supply of commodities remaining the same. Increase the quantity of money, prices rise. Decrease the quantity of money, prices fall. On the other hand, the quantity of money remaining the same, increase the quantity of commodities, prices fall; decrease the quantity of commodities, prices rise. Thus a decrease of the quantity of money produces the same effect on the price of a commodity as an increase of the quantity of the commodity itself. If corn be that commodity, an addition to the value of money, such as the diminution of its quantity occasions, insures as effectually a fall in the price of corn as the opening of the ports and free importation; in which of the two cases prices would fall lowest, is a simple question of proportion between the increased

1826. supply of corn and the decreased quantity of money." (Page 18.)

* * "In 1819, Mr Peel relied implicitly on the wrong datum of three per cent. being the full extent of the depreciation as indicated by the price of bullion, a price which he and his colleagues had, by their own measures, artificially reduced; and having first deceived himself, he succeeding in misleading the Legislature, for by use of examples which were not applicable, and by the oversight of the most important considerations, he carried the restoration of the ancient standard of value without any adjustment of contracts made in a debased currency, or provision for the increased encumbrance of all debts, taxes, and annuities.

France and America.

"It was strange, also, when reliance was placed on historical examples under circumstances totally dissimilar, that the course pursued by other countries, in a state of affairs identically the same, should have been entirely overlooked; for in France, after the abolition of the *assignats* and *mandats*, and re-establishment of a metallic currency, the Government ascertained the value of the louis-d'or, as compared with *assignats* at different periods, and in this simple manner on reference to the given market price of the louis-d'or, at any given time, contracts were reduced to their real value: and more recently, when the French Government altered the value of its money to the extent of five per cent. only, it provided by law for a corresponding adjustment of all debts. The United States of America, also, when in the last extremity of their struggle for independence they resorted to a depreciation of their currency, guarded against the fatal effects of their own measure by enacting that no bargain or contract for land should be valid, if on a credit of longer term than three days. In the example of France we find retributive justice;—in the example of America prospective wisdom; but in vain shall we seek to discover the slightest vestige of either virtue in the British enactments of 1797 and 1819. Here by law we depreciate the currency, and by a solemn resolution of the House of Commons denied the fact of depreciation. Here by law we raised the value of money, and instead of avowing our purpose and preparing for its effects, we mystified the intention and were blind to the result." (Page 44.) 1826.

"For a hundred and fifty years prior to 1797, 50*s*. was rather more than the average price of wheat, and while gold is at £3 17*s*. 10½*d*. an ounce, that wheat on an average in a series of years must be under 50*s*. is as certain as the revolution of the planets round the sun." (Page 50.)

* * * * "With the same standard we must have the same price; there is no escape from the dilemma; and if the land-owners would preserve their estates, either the standard must be adjusted to their encumbrances or their encumbrances to the standard. I have already spoken with perfect freedom of the existing corn laws; their effect on the price of corn is now absolutely nugatory, excepting in years of inadequate supply,—then their burthen becomes intolerable to the consumer, and fatal to the prosperity of the manufacturer. Public opinion is strongly opposed to them; in their present shape, and with the present standard, they may create famine; they certainly estrange the hearts of the people from the ancient possessors of the soil; they are liable to be swept away by force in a year of scarcity; and importation without protection may be established on their ruins; but on an average of years, while Mr Peel's Act remains unaltered, the monopoly which they give must be abortive in raising prices. Let me implore, therefore, the land-owners to abandon the futile attempt of artificially maintaining high prices under the ancient standard; let them

Danger and delusiveness of prohibition.

1826. make a timely compromise with the public, and take an ample, but fair, protecting duty, with open ports, on the admission of foreign corn; a duty equivalent to the burthens imposed on the producers of corn to which the consumers of corn are not equally liable." (Page 68.) "It is impossible to perpetuate in this country any legislative enactment, the tendency of which is to degrade and to impoverish the labouring classes; yet such is the decided effect both of our present corn laws and of Mr Peel's Act of 1819, unaccompanied by an adjustment of contracts or adequate reduction of indirect taxes. The paramount duty of every Government is attention to the interests of the community, of which the labourers must form the great majority; the right of property itself is instituted for the good, not of the few who possess wealth and honours, but of the many who have them not; if the majority be deeply injured, the public peace is in danger; if the majority want food, private property becomes a nuisance." (Page 73.)

Free Trade in Money.

"Since we must then have a free trade in corn, let us have also a free trade in money, and destroy that fatal connection between the Government and a single chartered bank, which facilitates the prodigality of the ministers, and invests an irresponsible body with the most delicate and important function of State,—the control over the circulating medium. * * * But shall the East India Company and the West India proprietors be suffered, for one day, to retain the full enjoyment of their exclusive privileges? Shall the consumer be forced to pay an exorbitant price for his tea and for his sugar, that particular interests may be benefited; and shall the nobility and gentry of these realms, the owners of the native soil, alone be sacrificed? On the contrary, let us adopt the sound principles of free trade; but let us not limit their application to the staple produce of our land. Let us destroy the heavy duties on timber, which at the expense of every man building a ship or a house in the mother country are at best a paltry premium to our colonies; and since we are bent on establishing an open competition with the foreign manufacturer, let us at once reduce largely those taxes which affect both the commerce and manufactures of our country." (Page 98.) * * * "And inasmuch as I have proved that Mr Peel's Bill in full operation will be a bonus to the annuitant of more than 30 per cent., I strenuously and boldly contend both for the equity and the necessity of imposing a direct tax to a considerable amount on all annuities charged on land or payable from the exchequer." (Page 101.) 1826.

Such were the principal features of "Corn and Currency," which in its day made no little stir among political and commercial men of every shade of opinion. The fearless candour of its admissions gave great offence to some: the boldness wherewith vast changes in our fiscal and financial policy were advocated startled many others. But we who can now judge dispassionately of the practical worth of the numerous suggestions it contained, cannot fail to observe how much of what was then deemed by courtiers and officials chimerical and illusory, has since been extorted by the power of that public opinion which the Pamphleteer of 1826 so energetically invoked. The peculiar hardships incident to the period of monetary transition were indeed alleviated only by the slow action of time; and his dream of "free banking" he was not destined to see realized. But as a minister of the Crown he shared

1826. the responsibility and credit of abolishing the monopoly of tea, and ultimately that of corn, neither of which seemed to the hereditary chiefs of party, possible or advisable, when "Corn and Currency" was written.

Debates on the Corn Laws. Parliament was occupied during the session of 1826 with the discussion of the measures referred to in the pamphlet; the tables of both Houses were covered with petitions from the agriculturists against any change in the corn law, and from the inhabitants of towns in favour of its repeal. Motions in the latter sense were made by Lord King and Mr Whitmore, but they obtained no general support. The leaders of Opposition approved in the main the currency measures of Government; and while they admitted the prevalence of distress and the need of reduced taxation, they rejected the idea of anything like an abrogation of differential duties

Earl Grey. on foreign corn. Earl Grey was resolved to stand by what he conceived to be the interests of his order, regarding trade as well as reform; but taking a gloomy view of the country's prospects consequent upon commercial depression and popular distress, his language created an impression that he was not disinclined to entertain certain of the proposals advocated by Sir J. Graham.* "He did not think that, looking at the average price of corn, the distress could

* Hansard, Debate in the Lords on Corn Laws, 1st May, 1826.

be fairly ascribed to protective laws. As long as the value of the currency was doubtful they could not determine what the amount of the protecting duty ought to be. He was friendly to a metallic currency, but he doubted whether the country could go through the distress attending such an alteration. Faith must be kept with the public creditor; but it was a sacred maxim of law, *Nemo tenetur ad impossibilia.* If they were once placed in a situation in which they could not keep the country in a state of decent prosperity, they could not be held to do that which was impossible; and therefore it would be their duty not to throw the whole state into utter confusion. Meanwhile it was necessary that ministers should show the country, not only by their expressions, but their acts, that they were desirous of relieving the people of all unnecessary burthens of any description." 1826.

Conflicting claims of money, land, and labour.

The conflicting emotions which the promulgation of views like these excited it is difficult adequately to recall. Nobody would agree to more than half the bargain offered by anybody else. The monied interest was furious at the notion that dividends or annuities should ever be subjected to taxation, no matter how greatly the value of money was raised, but they concurred in the prayer of the working-classes that the ports should be opened and the establishments cut down. The landed interest for their part considered it monstrous that they should

1826. be held to encumbrances contracted in paper when they must pay in gold; and nearly every peer and 'squire would have backed ministers had they proposed a tax on annuities, and a statutable deduction on mortgages, jointures, and portions for younger children; they only demurred to schemes for reducing the high price of wheat, for which they said Parliament had given them a permanent guarantee. The working classes, indeed, were for all these changes; but as they had representatively no voice in the matter, their sentiments went for nought. In the journal of Mr Mallet the feelings of the monied interest at the time are vehemently expressed. "It was an act of great cowardice on the part of Lord Liverpool not to take any notice of Lord Grey's hint as to passing a sponge over the public debt. He is a man of expedients, and would take to that if he found it necessary."* Under the same date he criticises with great severity Sir James's pamphlet, the popularity of which he considers a perilous sign of the times.

Alarm of monied interest.

"A young Cumberland baronet of very large landed estates and radical opinions has just published a pamphlet on the Currency and the Corn Bill, written with some talent, in which he assumes that all debts, public and private, contracted for during the last war were incurred in a depreciated currency, and

* MS. Journal, May, 1826.

that the landed proprietors have by law a monopoly 1826.
of the corn trade, so that they are as much entitled to the continuance of it as the fund-holders are to their dividends, all settlements and engagements founded on landed property having taken place upon the faith of that monopoly. He does not contend that it ought to continue, but that if it be given up the land-owners have a right to a large remission of taxation, and to a compromise with their creditors, for which purpose all annuities, public and private, ought to be heavily taxed, and the taxes now bearing on the other classes of the community proportionally reduced. After satisfying himself as to the justice of this course of proceeding, he boldly recommends the land-holders to avail themselves of their power, which is subject to no check save that of public opinion, and to lay their hands on the public creditor and on all mortgagees and annuitants, the most helpless class of the community and the least useful; and encourages them by the assurance that the industrious and labouring classes (the mechanical force) will be all on their side. The currency was not depreciated for more than eight or nine years, and for a much shorter period only to the extent assumed by Sir James Graham, and yet he recommends a tax on all debts in the nature of annuities, at whatever time contracted. There is in each act creating stock an express clause that such stock shall never be subject to any deduc-

1826. tion or tax whatsoever peculiar to the annuitant. With regard to the Corn Laws, the principle of them has varied in every possible degree, from bounties and free trade to prohibition: so little is it the law of the land in the sense of an adherence to legal contracts. The only possible plea upon which these could be disturbed would be the inability of the people to pay the public debt, a case of overwhelming and permanent distress, or such a case as the French Revolution, when the safety and independence of the country were in imminent danger. But the fact is that wealth and luxury have been and continue to be progressive in Great Britain. There is hardly a landed proprietor whose income has not doubled in the course of the last thirty years: they owe this entirely to the increased prosperity of the country; to manufacturing industry; and by giving to that industry the stimulus of cheap food the landowners will reap an ample harvest in the course of another generation. On the contrary, the annuitant has suffered from the depreciation of money and from high prices, without any compensating circumstance, and it is in the very nature of their property that it should gradually deteriorate in value; and yet the bare-faced and unprincipled proposal of Sir James Graham is evidently received with great favour by the aristocratical classes, who will not forego any of their present advantages without a fearful

Legislative supremacy of Land.

struggle, in which all public principle will probably be wrecked. They are the masters, and may do what they please; and besides getting all the land, the eldest sons may also, if they think fit, place the burden of the taxes on the shoulder of their mothers and brothers and sisters, and all persons having charges on their estates." * 1826.

How little the writer of "Corn and Currency" merited the suspicion of being actuated by the motives thus sweepingly imputed to him in common with all his class, we need not pause to discuss. But the injustice of class imputations is proverbial, and we might look in vain for a more striking instance of its pervading inveteracy. The pamphlet was abused and extolled for many weeks into a second edition, which went off as rapidly as the first. Among the criticisms of other censors it fell under the lash of Mr Cobbett, who, after he had, in his own characteristic dialect, "sweated and bled young Stanley of Knowsley, and the old Bristol miser's son, Mr Wood,"—his Whig opponents at the election for Preston,—devoted himself to what he called the "exposure and scarification" of the literary descendant of "John with the Bright Sword." Mistaking Sir James the greater for Sir James the less, he made himself merry with the proof of degeneracy betrayed in his diminutive stature, and lavished every epithet

Pamphlet denounced by Cobbett.

* Mallett, MS. Journal, May, 1826.

1826. of ribaldry and abuse upon the "odious aristocrat." By the time, however, his blundering philippics appeared, the public attention had been diverted to other objects, and Sir James had re-entered Parliament as member for Carlisle.

CHAPTER VII.

MEMBER FOR CARLISLE.

1826—1828.

At the dissolution of 1826, Mr James, who for some time had represented Carlisle, retired, and Sir James Graham was called on by requisition to become a candidate in the Liberal interest. He was already well known in the city, having taken an active part in many of its local affairs. He now came forward as the popular champion to resist the overweaning influence of the house of Lowther. The chief topics dwelt on in his address were the Abolition of Slavery, the total removal of Religious Disabilities, Retrenchment in the public Expenditure, and a reduction within moderate limits of the Import Duty on Corn. Mr Canning and some of his colleagues were favourable to the gradual abrogation of slavery, and to the concession of Catholic claims. But they were opposed to the repeal of the Test Act; and respecting retrenchment and a modified

1826. General election.

1826. Corn Law, their real opinions were not yet avowed. They constituted moreover but a minority of the administration, and the influence of Government at elections was given to the supporters of the majority in the Cabinet, headed by Lord Eldon and Sir Robert Peel. Sir Philip Musgrave, the Tory candidate, was taunted by the popular party with supporting a Government that maintained religious disabilities, negro slavery, excessive taxation, and a high price of bread. When canvassing some of the humbler voters in Caldewgate, Sir Philip was betrayed into expressions of ill-humour at the blunt refusals he received, which had well nigh cost him dear. He was loudly reproached with indifference to the many privations which the hand-loom weavers and other artizans were actually suffering; and when he replied impatiently that all the talk about low taxes and cheap bread was a mere delusion which they were fools to be gulled by, he was answered by a storm of hooting, and was bidden to be gone from that quarter of the town. Disdaining to obey this humiliating mandate, his canvassing party was surrounded by an angry mob; blows were given, and stones flung; and for several hours it was impossible to allay the tumult. Some members of the Corporation, endeavouring to interfere, were ducked by the populace in a mill-dam. The city constables fared no better; and Sir Philip was forced to seek refuge in the house of a weaver, whose door stood open, and whose pro-

Sir Philip Musgrave.

tection he was fain to implore. The man assured him of his safety, but told him at the same time that he was glad of an opportunity of making him personally acquainted with the real lot of the people he sought to represent. For this purpose he compelled the terrified candidate to take his seat at the loom, and to the infinite delight of the crowd who assembled to witness the spectacle, he kept Sir Philip plying his shuttle for the space of nearly an hour. Three hundred special constables* had been sworn in, but instead of resorting to their aid, a detachment of the 55th Foot, stationed in the neighbourhood, were ordered to clear the streets, and deliver the unhappy baronet from his imprisonment with hard labour. The people regarding the appearance of the troops as illegal, received them with volleys of stones. Many of the soldiers were but recent recruits, and upon the first provocation, they fired with ball cartridge, without waiting for orders. Two women were killed, and many persons were seriously wounded. 1826.

Sir James was absent from Carlisle during the affray, but arrived the same evening; the horses were taken from his carriage, and he was drawn into the town by the people, whose excitement knew no bounds. Night had fallen, but from a window of "The Grapes," where his committee sat, he delivered a speech, which, after the day's occurrences, went far to decide the election. A word too much of Sir James invited to stand.

* Hansard, Debate on Carlisle Petition, 3rd April, 1827.

1826. sympathy with the popular exasperation might have led to disastrous consequences; yet it was impossible for him to affect insensibility to the painful events of the day. He used the advantages they gave him with forbearance and skill, allaying the alarm of the few without abating the enthusiasm of the many. His subsequent canvass was a prolonged ovation: and no second ministerialist entered the
9th June. field. On the hustings he reiterated his condemnation of the existing Corn Law as equally hurtful to producers and consumers. He was in favour of a moderate differential duty, while he inveighed against the obstinate retention of high imposts on the chief necessaries and comforts of life, in order to keep up salaries, pensions, and sinecures. "But," he added, "he could not flatter his hearers with a hope that this important question would meet with any serious attention while the House of Commons was constituted as it had theretofore been. He would boldly assert that the influence of the Executive had too great a preponderance there. There were too many placemen who were under the patronage of the Crown, and who, for obvious reasons, were resolved to maintain a high rate of expenditure." With regard to Reform, he would sweep away all decayed boroughs, and transfer their representatives to larger constituencies. But such a change would be of little avail if it were not accompanied by a reasonable and just extension of the franchise.

The friends of Mr James insisted that he should be once more put in nomination. The polling had hardly commenced when a cry was raised that an orderly had just ridden into the market-place, and that a detachment of soldiers was at hand. Shouts of "more butchery" rose on every side. The Mayor, Mr Hodgson, vainly strove to restore order by declaring he could not believe that the troops were in the town, as no requisition had been made for their presence. Sir James proposed that two gentlemen should be named at once on his part and that of his opponent to ascertain how the fact really stood. Mr William Brougham was named on the popular side, and with a friend of Sir Philip Musgrave, soon discovered a troop of dragoons posted in one of the suburbs. Captain Wheeler, the officer in command, informed them that he was there by the express desire of the Mayor. It was not without difficulty that Sir James succeeded in tranquillizing the people when this became known; and it was not until his Worship had signed an order for the military to withdraw to a distance of four miles that he ventured to make his way from the town-hall. Mr James had made no preparation for contesting the city, and the struggle, though an excited and angry one, was on the part of his adherents altogether hopeless. He received one hundred and forty unsolicited votes; but Sir Philip Musgrave had two hundred and thirty-eight, and Sir James Graham two hundred and eighty-three.

1826.

Returned for Carlisle.

1826. In his speech on the declaration of the poll, he warned Lord Lonsdale "to beware how he struggled with the noble spirit of independence which was rising from the dormant state in which it had lain so long; and bid the Lord-Lieutenant of the county take care, or the lesson which had been taught him in Carlisle would be taught him elsewhere." These words were received as an intimation that the county representation would not be left undisputed when opportunity served. The flatterers of Lowther Castle scoffed at the menace thus thrown out in the excitement of a borough victory, and the master of Netherby was often asked with a sneer, "When he meant to take the county by storm?" The day came sooner than he or they anticipated, as we shall presently see.

Results of general election.

Elsewhere the results of the general election were less encouraging to the hope of popular progress. In Westmoreland Mr Brougham was again defeated; in Northumberland Lord Howick and Mr Beaumont were beaten; in Yorkshire Lord Milton with difficulty obtained a hearing, and the representation was divided; in Huntingdonshire Lord J. Russell lost his seat; and in Bedfordshire Mr Pym was ousted to make way for Mr M'Queen, a strong opponent of Catholic claims. The No Popery cry was everywhere raised, at the bidding of the Government managers, and though in the principal towns no remarkable change took place, not a few borough elections were lost and won thereby. In England the friends of resistance to emancipation decidedly gained strength; in Ireland things went the opposite way. The family of Beresford was deprived of the representation of Waterford, and that of Foster of the representation of Louth. The country grew daily more and more agitated as the influence of the Catholic Association became more generally felt, and towards the close of the year Government resolved upon initiating ex-officio prosecutions with a view of striking terror into its leaders, a course which the Liberal party in England highly disapproved. Before these proceedings could be brought to issue, Lord Liverpool, who for fifteen years had filled the office of Prime Minister, was struck with paralysis, and for some time the future policy of Government remained in suspense. 1827.

Grant to the Duke of Clarence.

At the opening of the session the King sent a message to the Commons, asking for an additional grant out of the Consolidated Fund for the Duke and Duchess of Clarence. Ministers proposed on the 16th February that £3000 a year should be settled on the Prince, and £6000 a year on the Princess during her life. Lord Althorpe objected, "that with distress and ruin running through every part of the kingdom, and with a revenue deficient £4,000,000 in the course of the year, such an addition should be proposed to the burthens of the people." Mr Brougham, Mr Abercrombie, and others, took a similar view. On 16th Feb.

1827. a division, the grant was carried by 167 to 65, Sir J. Graham voting in the minority.

Presence of the Military at elections. The irritation caused by the conduct of the magistrates at Carlisle during the recent election did not soon subside, and a petition was entrusted to the new member for presentation from Richard Pattison, the brother of one of the victims of the fray. Sir James brought the case before the House in a temperate speech, calling attention to the misuse of his authority on the part of the Mayor, and to the apparent need of re-asserting, in terms that might serve as a warning to others, the standing orders which forbade the presence of a military force at elections. "Badgering" a candidate was a popular pastime, that might no doubt be sometimes carried to excess, and he admitted that his colleague, Sir P. Musgrave, had had some reason to complain of the treatment he had experienced. But he contended that three hundred special constables formed a civic force amply sufficient to quell any disturbance that was likely to have arisen in a place like Carlisle; and what he complained of was, that instead of relying on it, the Mayor, who was known to be a warm partizan, and whose partner was the conducting agent on the unpopular side, had without necessity called in a body of troops, bid them load and fix bayonets, and finally charge an unarmed and defenceless multitude.* With regard to what had occurred on the

* Hansard, Debate on Carlisle petition, 3rd April, 1827.

subsequent day, he could bear witness to the peaceable demeanour of the crowd, until they were exasperated by the ill-advised resort of the Mayor a second time to the illegal expedient of introducing the soldiery. He disclaimed, however, any wish to press for the interposition of the House on the score of its violated privileges, and contented himself with moving that the petition be brought up. 1827.

Delays in Chancery.

Mr D. W. Harvey, in moving for returns of the state of business in the Court of Chancery, drew a vivid picture of the fearful evils of the state of arrear into which suits had fallen, owing to the inveterate habits of procrastination of Lord Eldon. The Attorney-General defended the Chancellor, and opposed the motion; Mr M. A. Taylor and Mr Hobhouse supported, while Mr Peel and Mr Canning resisted, what amounted to a vote of censure on their learned colleague. It was rejected by 132 to 66, Sir James voting with the latter.

Vacillation of the King.

For many weeks the chief power in administration remained in a state of abeyance; George IV. could not make up his mind what to do. He feared to entrust the guidance of affairs to Mr Canning, whose growing popularity out of doors and growing courage in council he had long observed with chagrin. In the affair of the recognition of the revolted Spanish Colonies, he had attempted in vain to trifle with the Foreign Secretary, and to make him renounce the pledge he had permitted him to give in the

1827. name of Great Britain. Mr Canning's peremptory refusal to submit to the sinister demand is a model in its way of courteous resistance on the part of a proud minister to the requirements of an unprincipled sovereign. Unknown and unsuspected at the time by those outside the innermost circle of the royal confidence, it failed to awaken the majority of the Cabinet to the real views of Mr Canning. He was known to be so poor, and remembered to have been so supple, his health was obviously so impaired, and office had become so much more than ever indispensable to him, that they could not persuade themselves he would really abandon it, no matter who was placed over his head as first minister, however warmly he might threaten to do so. The King, whose insight into character was keener than that of those about him, read more clearly the ambitious heart of Canning, and hesitated to make a proposal whose issue, whatever it might be, he feared to learn. Week after week he remained at Windsor in a state of irresolution, the accounts of Lord Liverpool's state confirming daily more and more the hopelessness of his recovery. In Parliament little was said or done. The public suspense grew anxious; and at Holland House, and elsewhere, people began to ask whether the crisis must not end in Canning's making friends with the Whigs. "It was," said Sir James Graham, "the most exciting interval that could be imagined, all parties being at fault, and neither King nor minister making any sign." 1827.

Attitude of the Whigs.

Lord Althorpe had long distrusted and disliked Mr Canning. "If Canning," he used to say, "really thinks with us, why does he not resign? Catholic Emancipation could then be no longer resisted, and other great reforms would inevitably follow. I suspect that he courts us merely for our votes, and as soon as he can do without them he will fall back upon the Tories, and leave us only the shame of having been his dupes." * He viewed with apprehension the symptoms of an approaching coalition, and proposed to Mr Brougham to move an address to the Crown against any ministry founded on a system of compromise. † The proposal being declined, he called a meeting of his friends at his chambers in the Albany, when a resolution was taken adverse to all ideas of administrative fusion. Earl Grey, Lord Tavistock, Lord Milton, Lord George Cavendish, and Sir J. Hobhouse concurred in this view, while the Duke of Devonshire, Lords Holland, Lansdowne, and Carlisle, Messrs Brougham, and Tierney, and Sir F. Burdett leaned the opposite way.

Canning insists on being chief.

Meanwhile, the King had been persuaded to try whether the Foreign Secretary would submit to have

* Unpublished Memoirs of Earl Spencer, page 170.

† Roebuck's History of the Whig Ministry of 1830, vol. i. p. 484.

1827. an anti-liberal colleague named as Premier, while he should retain the office he then held and the leadership of the Commons. Mr Canning had made up his mind. During the suspense that occurred he had warily felt his way. He knew that he could count upon a large amount of support from the Whigs the moment he was known to be in danger; and conscious that he was master of the position, he replied firmly but respectfully, declining the royal offer.

28th March. In a conversation at Windsor the King opened his mind unreservedly to him on the Catholic question. After stating that even "at the time of his closest connection with Mr Fox" his opinions were decidedly adverse to concession, he asked, "what he should be able to say to those who relied on his firmness for the maintenance of the Protestant cause if he were to name what would be called a Catholic Prime Minister?" Mr Canning took the liberty of answering that question by another:—"How should he be able to show his face to those to whom, in and out of Parliament, he had always asserted (because he always believed) that the Catholic question was an open question, on which the members of the Government were free to act according to their own opinions, without entailing any disadvantageous consequences upon themselves, if he should allow it to be proved in his person that those whose sentiments were favourable to the Roman Catholics were to be excluded, solely on account of those sentiments, as much as the Catholics, from the highest elevations in the State, and from the greatest objects of ambition? He could not, therefore, consent that in his person such a principle should be established; and he felt bound honestly to tell his Majesty in plain terms that the substantive power of First Minister he must have, and what was more, must be known to have, or he must beg leave to retire from a situation which he could not longer fill, either with satisfaction to himself or with benefit to the King's service." * Thus foiled, George IV. relapsed into his former irresolution, fearing to part with the minister whom he professed to regard as "one who had placed the country in a position with respect to Europe in which it had never stood before," and ashamed to falsify the pledges he had given to others, never to place any man of his opinions at the head of affairs. The Duke of Newcastle hoped to bring his waverings to an end by seeking an audience, in which he unskilfully intimated his resolve and that of other peers to withdraw their support from Government in case Mr Canning were named First Minister. The King affected to be offended at what he termed unwarrantable dictation, and seized upon the excuse to get out of his difficulty. He went through the form of in-

1827.

* Minute of the Conversation corrected in presence of the King, dictated by Mr Canning; A. G. Stapleton's George Canning and his Times.

1827. ducing Mr Peel to propose to Mr Canning that the Duke of Wellington should be First Lord of the Treasury, all other offices remaining unchanged; and upon the proposal being declined, he at length desired Mr Canning to form an administration. The Duke of Wellington, Lords Eldon, Bathurst, and Westmoreland, Mr Peel, Mr Goulburn, and Sir H. Hardinge refused to retain office, and it speedily became known that the Duke of Devonshire, Lords Lansdowne and Carlisle, Mr Tierney, and Mr Lambe had agreed to join the new Government. Mr Plunkett and Mr Robinson were raised to the peerage; Sir James Scarlett became Attorney-General, and Mr Stanley (now Lord Derby) and Mr Spring Rice Under Secretaries of State; Sir James Mackintosh became Judge Advocate, and various other posts were conferred on persons holding similar opinions. At a numerous meeting of the Whigs held at Brookes's, Mr Brougham, who had taken a prominent part in bringing about these arrangements, succeeded in carrying a resolution, with but few dissentients, in favour of the new Government.* It was upon this occasion that Sir F. Burdett made the speech, long afterwards remembered, in which he pronounced consistency to be the least of political virtues, and declared that, though as a party man he had been hitherto opposed to Mr Canning, he was ready "to stick his knees into his back as long as it was necessary

Canning premier. 11th April.

Meeting at Brookes's.

* Unpublished Memoirs of Earl Spencer, p. 175.

to prevent the return of Lords Eldon and Sidmouth 1827.
to power." Sir J. Graham, not without reluctance at seeming to sever himself for the first time from Lord Althorpe, concurred in the course agreed on by the majority of the party, and with them took his seat on the ministerial side of the House, when it 1st May.
reassembled after the recess.

Combination against Mr Canning.

The members of the new Government on vacating their seats were returned without opposition. The prosecution of the Catholic leaders was abandoned. The meetings of the Association were suspended. Ireland, so long agitated, seemed to have been suddenly tranquillized at the prospect of a tolerant and impartial administration of the laws. It was evident that the business of the much-interrupted session must be speedily brought to a close. But, short as was the allotted interval, it proved long enough for faction to do its deadly work. A systematic opposition was organized among the ex-ministers and their adherents, which had for its unconcealed object the destruction of the man whose genius they envied, and whose popular sympathies they feared. Mr Peel, who had taken his seat on the ministerial side below the gangway, stated that his reason for quitting office was his unchanged opinion on the Catholic question.

When General Gascoigne was about to bring 3rd May.
forward a motion in regard to the Shipping Interest, Mr G. R. Dawson, late Under Secretary, interposed

1827. with a demand that the patents appointing Mr Tierney Master of the Mint, and Sir J. Macintosh Judge Advocate, should be laid on the table. He proceeded in a tone of acrimony to assail the motives and intentions of the new Government and its supporters, accusing the Premier of "trickery and playing out a farce," and the Liberals with "sinking their old principles of reform and religious liberty for the sake of office." Mr Brougham, from behind the ministers, defended the new alliance with great energy. Lord J. Russell stated that some time before he had tried to induce the Whig leaders to make Reform a party question, and that thereupon it had been considered by them, but that their determination was, in the event of their coming into power, not to make it a Cabinet measure. He had himself indeed so little hope of its success, that he had already stated publicly he had no intention of bringing the subject again under discussion. The personal attack on Mr
7th May. Canning was resumed a few days later by Sir H. Hardinge, who said that "the Catholics had been sacrificed to the desire for office, while just enough had been done to alarm the Protestants of
Declaration of Lord Althorpe. the Empire." Lord Althorpe, who until then had retained his old seat on the left of the chair, immediately rose and declared that he could no longer remain acquiescent or silent:—

"When first he had seen the list of the new Government, he confessed it was his wish, if not his expectation, that he might be able generally to support it. That wish and that expectation had been much increased by the discussions that had since taken place. Some doubts might, in the first instance, have suggested themselves to his mind regarding the junction which had been formed between the new head of the Government, and some of the friends with whom he usually acted; but those doubts he was bound to declare were now removed. It was impossible not to see that the time was arrived when they must choose between an administration actuated by liberal and enlightened principles and one of Toryism in its most objectionable form. From the new Prime Minister he differed widely on two most importants points, namely, Parliamentary Reform and the repeal of the Test Act. He was sorry to find that there was a Government with which on these topics he could not agree, but he should be worse than a madman if, upon that account, he should refuse to go along with men with whom on so many other subjects he cordially concurred, and whom it was obvious they could not replace with better. He thought, he must own, that the Catholic question ought to be brought forward as a Cabinet measure, because of its vast importance, and because it could never be raised so effectually as in that shape. But if he voted against gentlemen opposite because they declined to discuss it at present as a Cabinet measure, he should displace them to bring into power those who would make it indeed a Government question, only because they were resolved never to yield it. Upon these grounds he should give the new Government his most decided support." 1827.

So saying, he crossed the floor, and took his seat behind the ministers.

The impression made by this brief but striking

1827. address both in and out of the House may well be imagined. It left Mr Canning without a Liberal adversary in the Commons of any weight or influence, and he had thenceforth to deal only with his former colleagues there. Sir James Graham was beyond measure delighted at finding himself once more side by side with the man to whom he looked up with most respect and affection in public life. The difference between them had been of but a few days duration, and many years elapsed before they disagreed on any material question again.

Vengeance of Earl Grey.

But there was another member of the party on whom Lord Althorpe's speech produced a very different effect. Lord Grey had, in 1807, been driven from the Foreign Office by an opposition which installed Mr Canning in his room; and twenty years had not appeased his resentful egotism. On several questions of domestic and foreign policy he had in the interim been obliged to concur with his early competitor in eloquence and fame; but his personal jealousy and aversion grew only the stronger as the lines of demarcation between them became less distinct; and when the schism came between the progressive and the retrograde sections of Lord Liverpool's Cabinet, he instinctively showed his sympathy with the latter, eliciting their vehement cheers by his defence of the course they had taken, and by the bitterness of his taunts directed against his and their former associates now in coalition. Long exiled from office,

he probably entertained little hope of ever regaining 1827.
power. His sins against George IV. were not to be forgiven; by half the Liberal party in the Commons he was looked on with distrust; but in the Lords he consoled himself with the leadership of a small minority, whom his haughty waywardness did not embarrass, because they had for many years nothing to lose or gain. And had Mr Canning succeeded in forming an administration out of the wreck of the old one, with such aid only as the Tory party might have supplied, Lord Grey would have looked superciliously on, and contented himself with a glittering sarcasm or two at their incorrigibility. But when to man the new ship his detested rival sought to impress his peculiar crew, all his slumbering envy, hatred, and malice wakened, and imperiously he forbade their enlistment under him. There were some whose neglect of his arrogant veto gave him comparatively little concern; perhaps some might be named whom he would have parted with gladly. But the severance of Lords Lansdowne, Carlisle, and Holland wounded him sore; he was vexed that Mr Tierney, Mr Stanley, and Mr William Lamb should have agreed to take office; and Lord Althorpe's defection stung him to the quick. He now stood nearly alone, and if he was to be avenged he must single-handed avenge himself. He had not been asked to take office, because he would certainly have refused, and because Mr Canning, who understood human nature

1827. well, felt that his own position would not be strengthened thereby. But though he hardly expected an invitation, he was mortified beyond measure at seeing the best and the most of the party he had nominally led so long, enlist under the only man of whom he was thoroughly jealous. He could not impugn the motives of those for whom all his life he had professed the greatest esteem; but his utterance was almost choked when he first came to speak of them as "his noble friends opposite," and asked them in language, faultlessly courteous, but implacably bitter, whether they had not agreed to sink the Catholic question upon entering the new Cabinet. It was upon the refusal to do so that he and his colleagues had sacrificed office twenty years before, and from that course he could never depart while he remembered his rights as a citizen, and the obligations of his Privy Councillor's oath to give at all times honest advice to the Crown. Of the new Premier he spoke in terms of mingled insult and scorn; and of his late colleagues as men who had been perfectly justified in refusing to serve under him.*

Replies of Lord Lansdowne and Holland.

Lord Holland, whose devotion to the cause of civil and religious liberty had been quite as unswerving, repudiated with dignity the exclusive tone of virtue assumed by Lord Grey, and calmly rebuked his insolence and injustice by reminding him that when "all the talents" had occupied the Government

* Hansard, Debate in the Lords, 10th May, 1827.

bench, the Catholic question had been postponed, but not retarded or thereby betrayed. Lord Lansdowne repelled the imputation of the coalition being the fruit of intrigue, and added, that "for himself he could only say that he had never been even on such terms of acquaintance with Mr Canning as their respective situations in society might have rendered probable, and that there never had been the slightest approximation towards a junction before the events of the preceding fortnight.* 1827.

Opinion of Sir James.

With all the admiration he was disposed to feel for Lord Grey, Sir James condemned as strongly as any of those around him, this ebullition of blind and selfish rage. Lord Grey condemned agitation in Ireland; and he saw that Mr Canning's elevation to power had, like a spell, lulled the storm. He professed to consider Lords Eldon and Sidmouth as enemies to the constitutional rights of the subject; yet he laboured with all his might, and, as the event proved, not unsuccessfully, to restore the ascendancy of their principles in the administration. He had been made aware from the first of all the negotiations which had led to the junction with Mr Canning, and his most intimate friends and nearest connections had sanctioned the course thus taken. Yet, because his personal leadership was compromised, he not only refused to acquiesce in the judgment of the whole of his party, but lent his aid to a

* Hansard, Debate in the Lords, 10th May, 1827.

1827. factious opposition, who, in the words of Sir James, "Rent the proud heart and shortened the existence of a great minister."* Canning's genius Lord Grey could not deny; his success was but an aggravating circumstance; but his crime, not to be forgiven by the opulent Earl and the great majority of the peers, was that he possessed neither money nor blood; and these were about the only things recognized by Lord Grey as warranting a claim to political power.

Death of Canning.

Night after night Mr Canning was assailed by his late colleagues and their personal connections with every species of vituperation. Sir James remarked with painful interest the progress of the inveterate feud, which nothing could allay; and learned from Lord W. Bentinck and others, at first with incredulity and then with wonder, how a man like Mr Canning could suffer, as he was too truly said to do, from the attacks of those who, till recently, had been his partizans and colleagues. He knew not then what it was to be subjected to such an ordeal; and he never was doomed to pass through it, with physical strength undermined, with private fortune broken, and with the miserable consciousness that amid all the flatteries and blandishments bestowed on him at Court, his tenure of office was not worth an hour's purchase, from the moment his sovereign

* Hansard, Debate on places held by Privy Councillors, May, 1830.

should be shown the way to get rid of him. 1827.
Friends and admirers bid Mr Canning seek repose; but sleep had forsaken his eyelids; the ambitious current of his blood was chilled; the goal of life towards which he had so long strained was won, and yet in winning, lost; the actress's son had been at length made to feel that neither the consent of the Crown nor the acclamation of the people could enable him to be Prime Minister of England. On the 8th August the broken-hearted statesman sunk to rest at the Duke of Devonshire's villa near Chiswick, in the same room where Mr Fox had expired just twenty years before.

Succeeded by Lord Goderich.

On Lord Goderich being named Premier, Lord Carlisle entered the Cabinet, as Privy Seal; and by way of trimming the balance of parties, the King insisted on Mr Herries, one of those who had lately refused to retain office under Mr Canning, being made Chancellor of the Exchequer. Distrusting the purpose with which this was done, Lord Lansdowne waited on his Majesty, and expressed his wish to resign. But George IV. desired to see the coalition die, without incurring the direct responsibility for its death. He therefore disclaimed all sinister intentions, and persuaded the Marquis to remain. Mr Huskisson was abroad when he received the intelligence of Mr Canning's death; and on reaching England he assured his widow that no consideration should ever induce him to act again with those who

1828. had contributed to that event.* He was recognized by the friends of Mr Canning as their new chief; and the leadership of the House of Commons was by general consent conceded to him.

Mr Huskisson and his friends.

Mr Huskisson had long been personally liked and valued by the Liberals, and especially by the more advanced section. He asked Lord Althorpe to be chairman of the Finance Committee, at the beginning of the session of 1828, believing that no abler or more independent person could be found to occupy that position, and because he was at heart anxious for measures of economical reform, such as his Lordship and his friends were accustomed to advocate. Mr Herries entertained very different views, and demurred to a selection made without his privity. Their disagreement upon the subject was made the occasion for the break-up of the administration. But it was generally understood that its doom had previously been sealed, and that had this difference been reconciled, others equally fatal would speedily have been found. Upon the fall of the Goderich administration the Whigs resumed their seats in opposition. The friends of Mr Canning, strange to say, consented to retain office under the Duke of Wellington, one of the inducements held out to them being that Mr Huskisson should continue to lead the House of Commons.

* Biographical Sketch, prefixed to Mr Huskisson's Speeches, p. 147.

But little real unity of feeling existed in the new Cabinet; and when, upon the difference arising out of the discussions on the East Retford Enfranchisement Bill, Mr Huskisson, Lord Dudley, Lord Palmerston, and Mr Grant resigned, it was felt that on questions of general policy they agreed more nearly with those who had been their colleagues in the preceding year than those with whom they had been more recently associated. 1828.

From this time a great deal of intercourse took place between Mr Huskisson and Lord Althorpe. Sir J. Graham shared their intimacy, and became a particular favourite of the ex-minister. In spite of his radical leanings and unorthodox notions with regard to banking, there was much in the young pamphleteer that pleased him. He had read "Corn and Currency" with no ordinary interest, and at heart he approved of many things in it which certain Whig friends of the writer deemed heretical. Mr Huskisson, in his life-long battle against monopoly, was obliged to disclose his views of economical reform one by one. Had he done otherwise, he would have been able to accomplish no practical change whatever, and he was essentially a man desirous of working out in substantial results those portions of theoretical truth which from time to time he found applicable troubling himself little how imperfect the symmetry might be of his transitional system. But though as yet he said nothing about ulterior objects

Intercourse with Mr Huskisson.

1828. of fiscal and financial improvement, they were ever present to his mind, and he noted with pleasure the kindling of congenial hopes in the minds of those not restrained by official responsibility from letting their light shine before men. He hailed with satisfaction the promulgation of opinions favourable to the opening of the China trade, to a modification of the Bank Act, and above all to a revision of national burthens by means of an Income tax.* His time for avowing these sentiments had not come, but he rejoiced to see attention directed towards them by others; and no immaturity of conception or rashness of expression led him to undervalue the worth of such aid. In his new acquaintance there was something more of pretension and of the air of a man of fashion than suited his essentially prosaic temperament. There was, however, infinitely more to be liked and valued. On Reform and the Currency he professed opinions which Mr Huskisson did not approve, and his notion of a fixed duty on corn equivalent to the peculiar burthens on land the great free-trade minister believed to be impracticable. But the object they aimed at was the same, namely, without injuring agricultural industry to secure for the community at large the best supply of the best food, on the best terms, and this Mr Huskis-

* Biographical Memoir of Mr Huskisson, from authentic sources, prefixed to his Speeches, vol. i. p. 212.

son had satisfied himself, and soon satisfied his young friend and admirer, could best be done by a modification of the sliding scale of duties on the import of foreign corn. 1828.

On the introduction of the Corn Bill of 1828, of which Mr Huskisson was avowedly the author, he declared that,— Corn Law Compromise.

"The object, as it seemed to him, of the House should be to pass a measure which men might believe and look upon to be a lasting if not conclusive one; an award, if he might be allowed the expression, between the exaggerated prejudices entertained against all freedom of trade on the one side, and the exaggerated hopes which might have been conceived by the other; a measure, which if it was not the very best which could be introduced, might yet be one which should prove an adjustment of the question, so long agitated with so much inconvenience to society. * * * He believed the measure then proposed was one more likely to abate those angry squabbles which the absence of final measures had given rise to, than any other that in the present condition of the country could be introduced. As for those who objected to it on the score that the interests of agriculture were not sufficiently protected, and who professed themselves pleased with the act of 1815, he could only say that while he lamented, from the bottom of his heart, the mass of evil and misery, and destruction of capital, which that law in the course of its twelve years' operation had produced, he did believe that he could make it distinctly appear, if the moment were a proper one, that its effect as far as regarded the agriculturists themselves, had been to keep the prices of 31st March.

1828. produce lower for those twelve years than they would have been, even if the trade in corn had been entirely open."*

The new bill had the cordial support of Lord Althorpe, Mr Brougham, Sir J. Graham, and all their friends; and the confidence and respect in which Mr Huskisson was held as the chief financial reformer of his day gave to his reasonings, whatever may be thought of them now, a weight and influence not easy to resist. It was not long, indeed, before opinions more advanced began to be proclaimed by some of those who in 1828 had received Mr Huskisson's measure of compromise with satisfaction. But Sir James, whose feelings of personal regard for him were deep and lasting, and who always gratefully confessed how much he owed to his wise and gentle teaching, was slow to renounce the terms of "the award" between conflicting interests carefully and deliberately settled by him.

Representation of Cumberland.

In December, 1827, a vacancy had been caused in the representation of Cumberland by the death of Mr Curwen, and in accordance with the wishes of his Liberal friends, Sir James accepted the Chiltern Hundreds, and presented himself as a candidate for the county. The part he had taken in county politics in 1820 led him to doubt whether he should have the support of Lord Carlisle, and it was

* Corn Importation Bill, March, 1828. Huskisson's Speeches, vol. iii. p. 257.

under this impression that he wrote the following letter:— 1828.

"Netherby, 11th December, 1827.

"MY DEAR LORD,

"Mr Curwen died yesterday; and I have resolved to abandon my seat for Carlisle, and to declare myself a candidate for the county. If family connection, past intimacies, long habits of good neighbourhood, and general coincidence in political opinions could authorize me to rely with confidence on the support of any friend, I should turn to your Lordship without a fear. I am aware, however, that you may fairly be of opinion, that on a similar occasion I acted unkindly towards you, and that the present is not an unfit opportunity of marking your disapprobation. It would be tedious and probably useless to enter now on my vindication. I choose rather, not blinking the recollection of that transaction, to throw myself on your generosity, and to trust to my general character as it may now stand in your Lordship's estimation.

"If on the whole you think me worthy of the high station of representing my native county, no past differences will, I am confident, prevent you from giving me your support on public grounds; if your opinion should be unfavourable, I must ever regret that I have failed to conciliate the individual whose esteem I should most value, and whose support would be my greatest honour.

"I shall be anxious to hear your Lordship's decision; but be it what it may I must ever continue,

"With sincere regard and respect,

"Your faithful and obedient

"J. R. G. GRAHAM."

1828. The circumstance thus alluded to was indeed one sufficiently trying to the temper of the person addressed. As Lord Morpeth he had sat for some years for Cumberland, and so long as the Liberals were content with one representative he was tolerably secure of not being opposed. In the excitement of the public mind, however, at the accession of George IV., the cry, as already stated, was raised that Cumberland ought to return two men of the Blue party; and no one took a more decided part in urging the adoption of this course than Mr Graham. Lord Morpeth did not believe that it would be found possible to carry two Liberals, as the event proved, and not choosing to be forced into an expensive contest, of which the issue was, to say the least of it, extremely doubtful, he withdrew. Mr Curwen took the seat thus vacated, and Sir John Lowther, without difficulty, retained the other. Lord Carlisle did not suffer the recollection of these transactions, however, to weigh with him when asked for his support by Sir James, and his prompt reply contained an assurance of cordial good-will, and the generous recognition of claims founded on personal fitness for the coveted post. In a letter from his son to a mutual friend, about the same time, a similar feeling was expressed. No one could possess, he said, higher claims to represent the county than Sir James Graham, and no better choice could be made.*

* Letter from Lord Morpeth to Mrs Howard of Corby.

Lord Lonsdale viewed with undisguised aversion the candidature of the "Radical Baronet," as he called him. But Sir James was not to be deterred by a political nickname, or the threat of a cry of No Popery, from stoutly maintaining his principles. He everywhere told the 'states-men that he meant to vote for Parliamentary Reform and Catholic Emancipation. He had no desire, indeed, "to swamp the influence of property in the representation;" and if he had his way he would try "to satisfy the Catholics without injuring the Church." As a candidate for Cumberland in 1828, he could not be expected to enter into any detailed discussion of the subject; but he intimated frankly the tendency of his opinions on the question. In 1825 a settlement of the question had been proposed and carried in the House of Commons, but defeated by the interposition of the Duke of York in the Peers, to which he always looked back with regret. It contained a provision for the payment by the State of the Catholic clergy in Ireland, a measure which "had he then been in Parliament, he would have undoubtedly supported," * as the only one that could really secure the Anglican establishment in that country from ultimate subversion. To avert such an event he was ready to make great personal sacrifices. He

1828. Catholic Emancipation.

Established Church in Ireland.

* Hansard, Speech on Mr Ward's motion to inquire into the Temporalities of the Irish Church, 12th January 1844.

1828. now hazarded his return for Cumberland, rather than forego his liberty of voting for what he deemed justice to the Catholics; and six years later we shall find him relinquishing power rather than compromise the principle of a Church establishment. The feeling that animated him on both occasions was the same. He was early convinced, and he died in the conviction, that an Established Church was an essential element of the constitution; and that whatever anomalies or difficulties its preservation might entail, it was the duty of the Legislature to maintain its existence intact in each part of the United Kingdom. But in Ireland, where the Anglican communion had always been but a small minority of the people, he was persuaded that a Protestant establishment could only be securely maintained by compensating the pastors of the majority for the loss of the territorial revenues that had formerly belonged to them. His personal popularity was such that no antagonist could be induced to enter the field; and the Tories thought it best to be content with one seat, and to suffer him without a contest to occupy the other. Throughout the remainder of the struggle for the removal of Catholic Disabilities, no one was found more punctually at his post, and few rejoiced more sincerely in the triumph of religious freedom. But he was deeply penetrated with the conviction that for the sake of personal and party consistency concession had been deferred, until the evils of

Returned for the county.

delay had become almost irreparable, and the opportunities of settling the question in a safe and statesman-like manner had been irredeemably lost. 1828.

Sir James took little part in the debates of this year, and seemed more bent upon acquainting himself minutely with the details of public business, and with the forms of parliamentary procedure, than upon premature display. He felt that he had not yet acquired the secret of success in debate. Though dainty and self-possessed, his manner of speaking was not calculated to produce any great effect on the House. Every phrase was studied, and every cadence measured by his fastidious ear. But it was too palpably so. He was still, as Burdett said of him, "emphatically a dandy." His intonation, occasionally fine, was too often finical, and a morbid fear of the appearance of vulgar excitement restrained him from resorting to those arts of gesture which have helped most orators to produce effect. He early acquired the habit, when speaking in public, of placing one hand behind his back, and limiting his action to an occasional wave or slight uplifting of the other. When he had acquired the weight of experience, and was felt to speak with authority, the gravity of such an attitude harmonized well with his deliberate and didactic utterance. In the pamphleteer baronet, rising from a back bench behind Mr Hume, with a well-dressed head of glossy black hair, a very high shirt collar, a very close-fitting blue

Mannerism in debate.

1828. coat, and a very striking waistcoat, it rather served to heighten the impression of foppery, which the House of Commons never likes, and to provoke the sneer from antagonists that he would be worth more to his friends when he took less account of himself. He was not unconscious of his own deficiency, though he failed to detect its fundamental causes. He fancied at times that he should never attain the mastery he so ardently coveted; "I have tried it every way," he once said, "extempore, from notes, and committing all to memory, and I can't do it. I don't know why it is, but I'm afraid I shall never succeed."*

Debate on Scotch Notes. Towards the close of the Session he could not resist the temptation of moving for a Committee of Inquiry on the first reading of a bill for limiting the circulation of Scotch notes to the portion of the kingdom lying beyond the Border. The opportunity thus presented itself of expounding certain of his opinions on the subject of currency, which neither of his economic friends, Lord Althorpe or Mr Huskisson, could persuade him to forego.

3rd June. "Sir J. Graham said he always rose in that House with embarrassment, and on that occasion he felt greater embarrassment than usual, when he recollected the magnitude and the difficulty of the subject with which he had to deal. He had voted for the Bill of 1819. He had then yielded to a doctrine which experience and subsequent consideration had proved to

* *Ex relatione* Sir Francis Baring.

him to be the most palpable folly that ever had been palmed 1828.
upon that House as sound and wise policy. Misled by Mr Ricardo, who stated that the whole difference of the standard value would be the difference between the value estimated by the mint and the market price of gold—and that the difference would be no more than five per cent.—misled by that authority, he had unhappily voted for the Bill of 1819. The Chancellor of the Exchequer had surprised him by stating that twenty-two millions of sovereigns were then in circulation. But were all that had been issued in actual circulation? The proposed Bill was unnecessary, because Scotch notes, as the Committee of 1826 had reported, did not displace the gold currency of England to any extent. But in the Border districts, one of which he represented, Scotch notes circulated, and men of all opinions concurred in petitioning that they might not be deprived of the advantages they afforded. Seven-eighths of the rent of his own estate had been paid in the paper currency of Scotland, and no loss had been sustained in that district by failures of persons issuing such notes. Mr Goulburn had said that there was a natural antipathy between a pound note and a sovereign; yet on one side of a line which he could jump over they were asked to make gold the only circulating medium below £5, and on the other paper. Was ever anything more anomalous than this proposed by any set of Ministers? Lord Liverpool and Lord Goderich, in their letter to the Bank of England during the pressure of 1826, had favourably contrasted the stability of the Scotch banks contemporaneously with the failure of those in England. It was not then the system of currency that was in fault, but the system of banking. Why not try to amend what was faulty instead of meddling with what worked well? Mr

1828. Locke, in speaking of the evils attendant upon a diminished or diminishing amount of currency, had said, 'The exigencies and uses of money not lessening with its quantity, and it being in the same proportion to be employed and distributed, still, so much as its quantity is lessened, so must the share of every one who has a right to this money be the less, whether he be land-holder for his goods, or labourer for his hire, or merchant for his brokerage. The land-holder usually finds it first, because money failing and falling short, people have not so much money as formerly to lay out, and so less money is brought to market, by which the price of things must necessarily fall. The labourer feels it next, for when the land-holder's rent falls, he must either abate the labourer's wages, or not employ, or not pay him. The merchant feels it last, and will be sure to leave our native commodities unbought on the hands of the farmer or manufacturer. People not perceiving the money to be gone, are apt to be jealous one of another; and each suspecting another's inequality of gain to rob him of his share, every one will be employing his skill and power the best he can to retrieve it again, and to bring money into his pocket in the same plenty as formerly. But this is but scrambling among ourselves, and helps no more against our wants than the putting on a short coverlet will, amongst them that lie together, preserve them all from cold. Some will starve, unless the father of the family provide better and enlarge the scanty covering. This pulling and contest is usually between the landed man and the merchant, with whom I join the monied man. The landed man finds himself aggrieved by the falling of his rents and the straitening of his fortune, while the monied man keeps up his gain, and the merchant thrives and grows rich by trade. These he thinks steal his income into their pockets, build their fortunes on his ruin, and engross more of the riches of the nation than comes to their share. He therefore endeavours by laws to keep up the value of land, which he suspects lessened by the others' excess of profit; but all in vain, the cause is mistaken, and the remedy too. It is not the monied man's gains that makes land fall, but the want of money, and lessening of our treasure, wasted by extravagant expenses and a mismanaged trade, which the land always is the first to feel.' Hume's words were these: 'A nation whose money decreases, is actually weaker and more miserable than another nation which possesses no more money, but is on the increasing hand. The alterations in the quantity of money are not immediately attended with proportionable alterations in the price of commodities; there is always an interval before matters be adjusted to their new situation, and this interval is as pernicious to industry when money is diminishing as it is advantageous when it is increasing. The workman has not the same employment from the manufacturer, though he pays the same price for everything in the market. The farmer cannot dispose of his corn and cattle, though he must pay the same rent to his landlord. The poverty, beggary, and sloth, which must ensue, are easily foreseen. But in every kingdom into which money flows with greater abundance than formerly, everything takes a new face; the merchant becomes more enterprising, the manufacturer more diligent and skilful, and even the farmer follows the plough with more alacrity and attention.'"* 1828.

The foregoing passages as cited from Locke and

* Hansard, 3rd June, 1828.

1828. Hume may serve to illustrate his singular tendency to make quotations of unusual length. He proceeded to review with great minuteness the policy which had been pursued since 1819, and ended by moving for a Committee of Inquiry into the subject before any further steps should be taken. Mr Huskisson and Mr Peel resisted the amendment, as calculated to unsettle men's minds on the subject of the currency, and to create doubts as to the determination of the legislature to adhere to a gold standard. Mr A. Baring and Mr Denison declined to vote for the proposition of a committee, not because they were satisfied with the policy ministers had pursued, but because they were not prepared to undertake the responsibility of initiating a different system and urging its adoption on the House. The former declared his opinion, however, that the great aim should be to keep the currency expanding in proportion to the growth of trade, which could only be done, he thought, by means of paper money, founded on a gold standard. The latter confessed that at one time he and Mr Ellice had together devoted much labour and research to the question of the true value of gold as a foundation for paper circulation; but when at the end of their consultations they found themselves differing widely as to the standard worth of the sovereign, he gave up all idea of stirring the matter further, convinced that every change of value, in whatever direction made, was in itself a source of practical evil that could hardly be exaggerated. Lord Howick, Mr Attwood, Sir F. Burdett, Sir M. W. Ridley, Sir J. Wrottesly, and Mr Liddell, spoke in favour of the amendment, which after two nights' debate was rejected. 1828.

Reports of Parliamentary Debates.

Frequent allusion was made during the debate to the speech of the mover of the amendment, the ability displayed in which was admitted by all. The report in Hansard hardly accounts for such compliments. It is in some parts ingenious, clever, and forcible, but as a whole it gives one the impression of incompleteness in delivery of what the speaker had designed and intended to say. But the report may have been either fragmentary when originally taken, or curtailed unskilfully for republication. Members of the House of Commons were less consulted in those days as to the accuracy of the reports given of their speeches in the daily prints, and we are compelled to believe that what we find set down to the rhetorical account of Mr Fox, Mr Pitt, Mr Canning, and Mr Plunkett, in the volumes of the Parliamentary Debates, affords us but a very inadequate notion of what they actually said. Of the last-named of these illustrious persons, Sir James Mackintosh has said that he would have been superior to any one of his day, had he devoted his rare talents more to politics and less to law. Yet we seek in vain for the sustaining proofs of the influence we know that he exercised over the reason

1828. and feeling of the House of Commons on many remarkable occasions: and when at the close of life a friend, every way qualified for the task, undertook to edit his speeches, and requested him to allow some of them to be read over to him for his correction, his severe taste was so offended by the clumsy rendering of noble thoughts, and his self-complacency so disturbed by the comparative poverty of the language ascribed to him, that he invariably seized the first pretence for creating a diversion in favour of luncheon or a morning walk, and at length the undertaking was abandoned in despair.

Select Committees. It was in the course of this session that Sir James began to take an active part in the important portion of the business of the House which is done in Select Committees. He was probably not considered of sufficient standing to be nominated on that of Finance; but he was chosen a member of those appointed to inquire into Criminal Commitments, Schools of Anatomy, Removal of Irish Paupers, Relief of Able-bodied Poor, and Expense of Printing Votes and Papers,—a tolerably sufficient indication of his readiness to take his share of the more laborious work of the House, and of his supposed fitness to do so. The familiarity he had already acquired with the details of local business at quarter sessions, and in connection with the Poor Law, qualified him for entering upon these investigations in a practical spirit. It was not now for the first time that he made trial of his power of sifting evidence, and riddling the truth out of reluctant or evasive witnesses. But it was in his capacity as a member of Select Committees that he became known for its possession; and it was undoubtedly through its constant exercise in that capacity that he acquired a proficiency therein that may be said to have been almost unrivalled. 1828.

Repeal of Test Act.

Before the secession of the Canningites from the administration, a majority of the House of Commons, of whom the new member for Cumberland was one, had decided that the Test Act should be repealed: and the Duke of Wellington, true to his principle of making the best of his position, whatever it might happen to be, told his colleagues that he thought they had better make a merit of necessity, by admitting the Dissenters to municipal and corporate offices, rather than let fall the reins, and leave the King in the hands of the Whigs. The resolution of the Cabinet to forego its known opinions on this branch of the great question of religious liberty, was naturally hailed as a triumph by the Opposition; and great fear came upon all those who believed the existence of the Church to be in danger, when at the close of the Session certain words of ominous import fell from the Premier in the House of Lords, regarding his desire that some way might be found of accommodating the differences that had so long distracted Ireland.

CHAPTER VIII.

RELIGIOUS FREEDOM AND RETRENCHMENT.

1829—1830.

1829. Representation of Oxford. THE parliamentary year 1829 was occupied with the passing of the Catholic Relief Bill, and the many exciting incidents that preceded and followed it. With one of these only is the name of Sir J. Graham associated in a way which requires notice. Mr Peel had accompanied the avowal of his conviction that emancipation could no longer be resisted with the resignation of his seat for Oxford; and upon an appeal to the electors of the University he was rejected by a large majority. The Home Secretary was compelled to purchase a seat at Westbury; and Sir Robert Inglis entered the House of Commons as representative of Oxford.
4th March. When presenting a petition numerously signed against the Catholic Relief Bill, the new member took occasion to remark upon the many individuals of distinction in science, letters, and art, who were

opposed to the measure; and he expressed his belief 1829. that a decided preponderance of the intelligence, learning, and rising talent of the country, as well as of the population generally, was adverse to concession.

Sir J. Graham said that he thought the newly- Mr Peel. elected member for the University was so intoxicated with his recent triumph that he could not judge dispassionately of the real state of public opinion throughout the kingdom. Without meaning any personal disrespect, he must tell Sir R. Inglis that he, for one, regretted deeply that triumph; and he felt persuaded that "if, as he supposed, perilous times for the Church were at hand, the High Church doctors of the University would soon see cause to regret the choice they had made and the champion whom they had selected.

> Turno tempus erit magno cum optaverit emptum
> Intactum Pallanta; et cum spolia ista diemque
> Oderit.

He had less difficulty in speaking of the Right Hon. Secretary, because he was not then in the House to hear him. He had in private no acquaintance with him. He had been opposed to him on almost every occasion since he had himself entered public life. He had not voted with him, he believed, five times since he had been in Parliament. He thought him, however, a really honest and conscientious man; and considering the great sacrifices he had recently

1829. made, the connections from which he had torn himself, the public attachments which he had broken asunder, the dangers which he might have created by a different course, the difficulties which he might have aggravated by adhering to the old system of exclusion, the civil war which he had averted by departing from it, and the great public services in every way which he had rendered to the State by his manly avowal of his change of opinion,—considering all these circumstances, he thought the right honourable gentleman entitled to the highest praise, and to the hearty support of every friend of the Catholics." * This frank and warm appreciation of the motives which actuated Mr Peel on the occasion of his first memorable act of party renunciation possesses an interest for us of which neither its subject nor its author could then have dreamed.

Attendance on Select Committees.

He was again named upon several of the Committees to which were confided practical inquiries of importance; amongst others may be mentioned those into the practicability of reducing the Estimates for the Militia, into the Law of Entails in Scotland, and into the Constitution of Vestries in England and Wales. To the last in particular he devoted great attention, and from its report eventually emanated the change in the law of local assessment, with which the inhabitants of the metropolis subsequently became familiar under the title of Hobhouse's Act. It

* Hansard, Debate on Catholic Petitions, 4th March, 1829.

has recently been superseded by other enactments; but in whatever particulars it may seem to have been deficient, it is entitled to the credit of having been the first legislative attempt to apply the principle of municipal self-government to the inorganic masses of population and property forming the modern additions to London. 1830.

State of parties.

The state of parties at the beginning of 1830 was anomalous in the extreme. Ministers, enfeebled by the alienation of the Canningites on the question of bit-by-bit reform, and of the followers of Lord Eldon on the Catholic Relief Bill, were confessedly dependent on the forbearance of the Liberals for their retention of power. Among the less prominent members of the Government, several desired to cultivate more intimate relations with the Whigs. Sir George Murray went out of his way to give assurances in private that he meant to act as Colonial Secretary in accordance with their views; and he received cordial expressions of satisfaction from Lord Althorpe. Sir Henry Hardinge was a frequent guest at Spencer House, and professed opinions there which created the impression that he might honourably constitute an element in another coalition.* On the other hand, Lords Rosslyn and Jersey, and Sir James Scarlett, who still belonged to Brookes's, actually held office in the Government; while, as an acknowledgment of Earl Grey's support,

* Unpublished Life of Lord Spencer, p. 175.

1830. a peerage had been conferred on his son-in-law, Mr Lambton. Many of the party professed friendly feelings towards the Government, and were ready, as in 1827, to enter into an alliance if the opportunity were afforded them.* The King's antipathy to Mr Brougham formed an obstacle to every project of fusion; but, in the opinion of some of the most influential members of the Whig party, it was not an insuperable one. Between them and the adherents of Mr Canning there had gradually grown up ties of political sympathy and confidence. Mr Huskisson and Lord Althorpe, though still differing on questions of Parliamentary Reform, were entirely in accord on those of Retrenchment and Taxation. Sir James Graham enjoyed the confidence of both; and it is doubtless to his knowledge of their views respecting the possibility of an administration being reconstructed on a comprehensive basis, that we are to ascribe the expression which he perhaps inconsiderately let fall in debate, and of which he was subsequently often reminded, that with the exception of the currency, he did not know any general question of moment on which there was any essential difference between his friends and those who sat opposite to them. But whatever others may have wished or anticipated, it is certain that the Duke had no thoughts of remodelling his cabinet at this time, on coalition principles. His tactics in

Canningites and Whigs.

* Roebuck's Hist. of the Whigs, vol. i. p. 131.

Parliament, as in the field, were to deal with difficulties and dangers, as they arose, troubling himself comparatively little with those beyond the horizon, and trusting to his capacity and good fortune to encounter them when they came. He had settled the two great questions of the Test Act and Catholic Emancipation; and neither Repeal of the Union nor Parliamentary Reform had assumed the tangible proportions of reality. In a word, he did not see, and nobody could undertake to show him, on what question of magnitude or moment any formidable combination could be formed against Government in the House of Commons. 1830.

Mr Huskisson believed that it was possible to organize an amount of pressure in favour of retrenchment and a general re-adjustment of taxation, in which men of various sections might consistently take part, and which, being certain of general approval out of doors, the Government would be unable to withstand. The germ of this idea may be found, in a speech of great moderation of tone delivered on the Address, in which he depicted the prevalent depression of industry, and pointed out the only quarter in which effectual relief might be sought. Mr Huskisson.

"He did not despair of seeing the country restored to a situation of prosperity; but from all the information which he possessed, he felt satisfied that there now existed that degree of pressure on the productive classes generally, which,

1830. were it to be permanent or long continued, would be incompatible with their continuous existence. * * * It was by studying to benefit to the utmost the industrious classes, that we could alone lay any solid foundation of public happiness, or revive prosperity." *

Great distress indeed prevailed at this time among all classes of the people. Commercial enterprise had not recovered its elasticity since the panic of 1825; and in spite of the amended sliding scale, the price of corn failed to afford the farmer any adequate profit on his outlay. Agricultural labourers and skilled artizans sought employment in vain; incendiary fires in many localities took place without their authors being detected; and everywhere poor-rates were steadily on the increase. Certain retrenchments had been effected by the Duke of Wellington's administration in the subordinate ranks of the public service; but the emoluments of higher office were still untouched. The expenditure of 1829 amounted to £51,835,137; and this, though somewhat less than that of previous years, seemed to languid industry and political discontent an intolerable sum to pay in taxes on the comforts and necessaries of life.

Motion for reduction of salaries. On going into Committee of Supply, Sir James brought forward a motion for the reduction of official salaries, grounded on the prevalence of distress, the

* Debate on Address, February, 1830. Huskisson's Speeches, p. 475.

increased value of money, and the reduced cost of living. 1830.

"He never rose in that House," he said, "without embarrassment; and imperfect recovery from recent illness aggravated that feeling on the present occasion. The task he was about to undertake was an ungracious one, for though all liked economy and reform in the abstract, they very seldom relished it when it came to be acted upon with respect to themselves. He felt this; but his sympathies were not confined to those who derived their incomes from the public purse. His compassion was rather directed to those from whom the taxes were drawn, and he could not turn a deaf ear to the distresses of the country. That distress was general; for notwithstanding that the speech from the Throne said that distress was confined merely to some parts of the country, yet the whole efforts of ministers to fritter down our misfortunes have produced nothing but the greatest possible disappointment; and, changing hope into despair, they had gone nearly to convert patient endurance into the angry spirit of resistance. He would assume one or two general propositions:—first, that the Bank Restriction Act of 1797 had produced two leading and striking effects, the first being the depreciation of the value of money; the second, the raising of the price of commodities. The latter was not denied, and it came within the scope of his notice that the rise of prices was coincident with the rise of salaries. Mr Addington, in 1802, when he was forced to ask Parliament for an additional grant to make the Civil List adequate to the necessities of the times, said 'that the causes of that application were unavoidable. Sixteen years had passed since the schedules were fixed, and he left it to the sense of every one to see how great had been the rise

27th Feb.

1830. of prices in the interim.' In 1804, fresh debt had accumulated in the Civil List, and Mr Pitt, then Prime Minister, used the following expressions, the first sentence of which was important, as it showed that the augmentation was only intended to be temporary:—'It would afford relief,' he argued, 'that the Civil List should accommodate itself to circumstances as they varied; for in this case it would be reduced in time of peace. There was no one who reflected on the great increase in prices who could suppose that his Majesty should be able to restrict his expenses within their former limit.' Mr Percival, in 1809, applied for an increase of the salaries of judges; and in the expressions he made use of there was a full opportunity to ascertain his opinions, as to the extent of the depreciation which had taken place in the currency. His object was to have £1000 per annum added to the salaries of the judges, and that was, as he expressed it, merely to make their real equal to their nominal income. Here was an increase of 25 per cent., and from this we might calculate the depression of the currency. In that year, 1809, wheat corn was 84*s*. the quarter, and gold £4 10*s*. 9*d*. the ounce. The calculation therefore, in this instance, was not made on the price of gold alone (the capital error of the Committee of 1819), but on the price of commodities likewise. With regard to the depreciation of the currency, he thought that the fact of the high prices during the war precluded the necessity of any observation on that point. He thought certainly that the fact of the depreciation was equally evident with that of the high prices; but it did happen that they had a resolution on their books negativing that depreciation. This resolution was that at the period when a guinea in gold was selling at 28*s*., Bank of England paper was equal to it in value,—*i. e.* that things unequal in the public estimation were yet equal to one another: a doc-

trine so absurd that within the same year it became necessary 1830.
to pass an act imposing a penalty for passing a guinea for more than 21*s*., or a one-pound note at less than the value it purported to bear; and yet the people are asked to confide in the wisdom of Parliament, and in a Government formed of the mere shreds of the administration of that day. But they are told that it was God, not man, who caused this state of things. At one time the harvests were over-abundant, at another they were scanty. At one time they had too much produce, at another too little. At one time we had too much drought, at another too much rain; while the apprehension never seemed to have occurred to any Chancellor of the Exchequer that every addition to taxation was an addition to the sterility of the soil, and lent a further gloominess to the inclemency of the heavens.

"It was but a few years since salaries of £3000 a year had beeu raised £1000 a year, or 25 per cent., to make up the difference between the two standards of prices. Then followed the restoration of the currency to a metallic standard, and that made a difference of 25 per cent. additional, independent of reduction in taxation. The consequence was that salaries were now raised to a rate of £7000 instead of £3000, at the value of former years. At that former period we did not know of any unfaithful stewards. Mr D. W. Harvey had said it was the duty of landlords to reduce their rents; and he agreed with those who had in reply observed that, since the war, rents *had* been reduced from 25 to 30 per cent. If, however, the landed interest were called on to submit to another reduction of 25 per cent., he would say boldly to nine-tenths of the landed interest,—at once sell your estates. In fact, such a measure would be a secret or silent mode of transferring their estates to their creditors.

1830. It was a thing they could not bear, and it would be absurd if they did. Then consider the effect of low wages. If the labourer had not bread, all property, whether freehold or funded, must be placed in the greatest jeopardy. He had never supported the Corn Laws, but the country gentlemen had been driven to them by necessity. They were as a pebble, but a pebble which in the sling of a stripling might overthrow the giant. Free trade had relieved some articles of secondary necessity, whilst there was a monopoly of the articles of first necessity; and thus there was a transfer of a burthen from the strong to the weak. Until the questions respecting currency and corn were adjusted, free trade would operate with the greatest possible injustice. War taxes entered largely into the prices of articles of necessity, and they could not become cheap. When Government increased the value of money, and did not reduce taxation, they encroached on the comforts of the labouring classes. Taxation prevented the fall of prices. He had heard something of luxuries, but he knew not whence the notions of luxuries were derived. Were they drawn from the gorgeous palaces of kings, or the rival palaces of ministers, or from those of East India Directors, rich with the monopoly of the China trade, or from those of Jew Loan Contractors, who supplied to foreign States the gold from the coffers of the Bank of England?

> 'Ill fares the land, to hastening ills a prey,
> When wealth accumulates and men decay.'

"What was now the boast of this happy country? Where was the furniture that adorned the poor man's cottage?—all was gone—pinching hunger and despair now held their place in the labourer's habitation. The weaver in

the county which he represented earned but 4*s*. 2*d*. a week, 1830.
out of which he had to supply his family. Oatmeal, water, and peas, were his sole food, and for these he had to work fourteen or fifteen hours a day. So extremely low were wages, that even the power-looms were under-worked. The country had now come to the point when something must be done:

'Hic locus est, partes ubi se via findit in ambas.'

It was not becoming in the Treasury Bench to say that the only exception to retrenchment must be among those classes to which its occupants belonged. The next course was to alter taxes and obtain high prices, by returning again to the ancient standard of England. From the Tudors to the Revolution silver alone had been the standard of this country. From that time to 1793, silver and gold conjointly had been the standard; and in 1819 the measure was an anomaly, if not a novelty; but so far from this measure having been in full operation for ten years, as had been so often repeated, it had been in full operation only for a few months. The act did not come into operation till two years after it was passed. The year after it was to have come into effect, such was the distress, that Lord Castlereagh agreed that the repeal of the Small Note Act should not come into operation till the charter of the Bank of England expired. Prices rose and prosperity continued for a short period, and only for a short period. To re-consider the Small Note Bill, the House must re-consider the standard, and the whole system of banking. But Government was inexorable. The Duke of Wellington had said 'You shall not inquire.' If you argue the question keenly in print, the Attorney-General is ready to pounce upon you. He will file *ex-officio* informations for publishing what has a tendency to bring

1830. ministers into contempt. It was only in a moment of distress that useful purposes were effected, and he hoped that the House would not pass to other measures till retrenchment was pushed to the utmost. Two modes presented themselves—to reduce the number employed, or to diminish the salaries. He might speak freely of the act of 1819, for he had voted for that measure. He was then a very young member governed by authorities, and overborne by his friend Mr Ricardo, upon whose faith he pinned his own. Mr Ricardo assured the House that the difference would be only three per cent. in private obligations, as it would be governed by the price of gold, which was then £4 1*s*. per ounce, and he (Sir J. Graham) thought it right to try the experiment. He certainly had his doubts, and he could not help having them after the statement of his friend Mr Baring. However, he was overborne by authorities. He voted for the measure, and thought he had done right. Lord Liverpool had since frankly acknowledged that the difference instead of three was twenty-five per cent., which Mr Baring had always contended it would be. He now saw that the prognostics of Mr Baring were much nearer to the truth. Rents, prices, and wages had all been depreciated by the abrupt enforcement of a gold standard twenty-five per cent. at least. In his opinion, monopoly in banking was theoretically wrong and practically mischievous. To make gold the solitary and exclusive foundation of the currency, was, he thought, absurd: silver and corn, as articles of universal need and appreciation, being as well suited for the purpose, and if combined with gold, capable of affording a much sounder basis of value. But if Parliament was resolved to adhere to what it had done regarding the currency, it was bound to put back the pay of public servants to what it had been at the beginning of the century."

He was listened to with attention throughout, and the debate which ensued betrayed many symptoms of uneasiness on the part of Government. The views he propounded, however, on the subject of the currency found but partial acceptance among the members of Opposition, and a pledge of retrenchment having been given by Government, he did not press his motion to a division. Lord Althorpe would not endorse without reserve his bill of attainder against the monetary legislation of 1819 and 1826; and Mr Huskisson had been a party to the measures of those years. Nevertheless, in the practical object of his motion both heartily concurred; and he may be said to have taken no step at this period in Parliament without their approval. While they still remained independent of each other, their tendencies and ideas daily more and more converged towards a line of policy, conservatively liberal regarding reform, but radically frugal regarding expenditure; and the eager and active member for Cumberland was the confidant of both. 1830. Reception of his speech.

In redemption of the pledge which had been given, various reductions were made in the army and navy estimates for the year, amounting in the whole to a saving of £1,000,000; but no corresponding reduction of taxes was announced. A variety of attempts were made to enforce that object; Mr Hume proposing to cut down the military establishment by one-fifth, and to sweep away

1830. customs and excise duties to the extent of between £8,000,000 and £9,000,000; and Mr Poulet Thompson proposing to refer the whole of the questions connected with the incidence of taxation to a select committee. But Government was able to defeat every proposition with one insignificant exception made by the Opposition. No sign of ministerial sympathy for the malcontent tax-payers appeared, and the cry for retrenchment grew every day more loud.

Lord Althorpe chosen leader.

The Liberals for some time had been without an acknowledged chief. Mr Tierney, the leader of the Opposition during Lord Liverpool's administration, had retired in 1828. Mr Brougham was their foremost debater in the House of Commons, but he did not possess the confidence of the great body of the Whigs, and was never allowed to direct their councils as a party.* The man whose opinion gradually came to be of most weight was Lord Althorpe; but he had never put himself forward, and whenever his friends urged him to assume the ostensible leadership, he invariably declined, and placed other names before his own.

A thoughtless sneer of Mr G. R. Dawson, early in 1830, that the Opposition "were only a loose bundle of sticks and would always be beaten," is said to have piqued Mr Portman into making one more attempt to persuade Lord Althorpe to become

* Roebuck's Hist., vol. i. p. 464.

leader. Accompanied by Sir F. Lawley and Mr Pendarvis he waited upon him to urge the point; and received for answer that if they could get forty-five members to concur with them by the following Saturday, he would be prepared to say finally what he would do. But he made it a preliminary condition that he should himself first communicate with Lord J. Russell, Sir J. Graham, and Mr Brougham, without whose approval he should certainly not take any decisive step. That approval was cordially given, and more than the required number assembled at the appointed time at the Albany to salute him as their chosen chief.* He was asked by one of those present whether any communication had taken place with Mr Huskisson on the subject which had that day drawn them together. He replied with his usual directness and simplicity that there had been nothing of the sort. Upon this, Sir J. Graham stated that, acting only as an individual, he had thought it right to apprize Mr Huskisson of what was in contemplation; and he was glad to be able to give the assurance that the proceeding in which they were then engaged was in no way calculated to diminish the probability of their being able to act on various questions in concert with that gentleman and his friends. Arrangements were subsequently made for the supervision of the Government measures. Lord Althorpe 1830.

* Unpublished Memoir of Lord Spencer, p. 198.

1830. and four other gentlemen engaged to consider the various topics likely to arise in Parliament, at least once a week; and no independent action was to be taken without their cognizance.*

Privy Councillors.

Early in May, Sir James Graham gave notice that he was about to move for a return of all the salaries, pensions, and emoluments, then receivable by members of the Privy Council, setting forth the name in each case, the services rendered, and the length of time for which such emolument had been received. In reply to an intimation from the Chancellor of the Exchequer that he would not consent to give the return as framed, but that the information sought for might be found in a comprehensive enumeration of all civil and military offices and salaries under the Crown, the Hon. Baronet made use of expressions which, being caught up at the time and repeated in the press, became the watchword of party discontent out of doors, and the theme of angry reproaches against their author within the walls of Parliament, though all intention of applying them individually was promptly disclaimed by him. In rejecting the counter-proposal of Mr Goulburn for an indiscriminate return of places and pensions, he declared "that he was not disposed to stoop to ignoble game while flights of voracious birds of prey were floating in the upper regions of the air." Great was the curiosity excited by his

Birds of prey.

* Unpublished Memoir of Lord Spencer, p. 200.

announcement that he meant to persevere with his 1830. motion, and that he would not shrink from specifying in detail the grounds on which he claimed its concession as a matter of public justice from the House. The task he had undertaken was so invidious, and the imputation of unworthy motives was so certain, if he were betrayed into dwelling with particular emphasis on two or three cases only, while the impossibility was so plain of multiplying invidious illustrations without lessening their apparent enormity, and raising an insurmountable host of objections in the House, that his friends were filled with reasonable misgivings as to the effect on his own position of the part he had undertaken to play. Many were the private warnings and cautions—from some, not to be too violent; from others, not to be too vague—with which he was pestered for some days previously. At length the 14th of May arrived, and found him in every way equal to the occasion. The speech he then delivered was, upon the whole, the most telling and important he ever uttered. As a composition it was doubtless inferior to many others; and from the nature of the subject, it was incapable of being made a vehicle for exalted or ennobling thoughts. But it proved that the man was equal to the exigency when the exigency was great; it stirred the blood of the most sluggish reformers to a sense of the urgent need of some restorative action in the state; and it aided potently in producing the belief among the

1830. community at large that there were, after all, in Parliament men of courage and ability enough to say plainly what was wanted, and to denounce those whose private gain was the nation's loss. There never was a speech made in Parliament so full of direct personality; yet there never was a speech more punctiliously free from offensive or discourteous expressions. In this respect it is indeed a masterpiece, containing the weightiest charges in the civilest words, and dealing the heaviest blows with a gloved hand, of which none could fairly complain. Ministers were able to defeat him in the House, but they felt keenly the damage that had been done to their failing reputation, and in private, bitter were their reproaches and complaints. The friends of Sir James exulted in the power and discretion he had shown; and (not without reason, as events soon after testified) declared that his political fortune was made.

Privy Councillors. "I assure you that I very much regret that his Majesty's ministers should think it inconsistent with their duty to grant the returns for which I am about to move. I must confess that I am both sorry and surprised at their resolution. I am sorry because it will entail on me the necessity of exercising your patience for some time; and I am surprised, for I am at a loss to know upon what grounds they can intend to resist my motion. I feel myself so strong in principle, that I think I may safely rest my case on general principles alone, without resorting to any other ground. The general principle is, that the representatives of the people, the guardians of the public purse, are entitled, as of right, to call for statements of what sums of public money have been received by any particular individual, or number of individuals, or class of individuals, and it is for the ministers to show some special reason for the exception to the general rule. If I am right, as to the general rule, it is incumbent upon ministers to produce the returns, and in the shape in which I now ask for them, as similar returns have been asked for before, and have been granted. I asked in 1821 for a return of the places held by members of either House of Parliament under the Crown, stating the income, salaries, and emoluments enjoyed by each officer, and specifying whether they were held for life, or liable to removal on the demise of the Crown, and that return was granted. There was another return for the number of pensions and sinecures enjoyed for offices chiefly executed by deputy, which was also made. The House will observe, that in these returns it is especially stated what members of either House are in the receipt of any income, salary, or emolument under the Crown. It therefore rests with the Right Hon. Gentleman to show the distinction and difference between the two classes — between the members of either House of Parliament and the members of the Privy Council. I allow that it is with the people of England a matter of constitutional jealousy, narrowly to observe what part is pursued by the persons whom they return to represent them in Parliament, and what influence is likely to be exercised over their votes by the Crown. I admit also that the power of electing Privy Councillors makes some difference: it is competent for his Majesty to choose from either House such members as he may please for his Privy Council, and there are in it at this moment many members of both Houses. But, sir, I ask, upon what

1830.

1830. principle is it that there should be less jealousy observed respecting the Privy Council than has been evinced toward this House? It cannot be contended that the Privy Council is not a body recognized by the statute and known to the House? Were it necessary I could cite many authorities in proof of the fact, but I shall content myself with referring to three. I find that by the statute of Henry VII. it is made death, without benefit of clergy, to attempt or compass the life of a Privy Councillor. Secondly, there is another statute, the 12th and 13th William III., which commands that no man born out of the kingdom, except of English parents, shall be a member of the Privy Council. The last is an act of Anne, which provides that the Privy Council shall continue for six months after the demise of the Crown, unless sooner determined by the successor. The Privy Council, therefore, is a body known to the law, and it is known to this House; for I think I have frequently heard it stated by you, sir, from that chair, that an address to his Majesty should be presented by members of the Privy Council. If, then, I am right upon the general principle, that members of this body are liable to public scrutiny as well as members of this House, being fully recognized by the Constitution, the onus of the proof, why, in this instance, there should be any exception to the general rule, lies on the Right Hon. Gentleman. And if he fail in this proof I consider that I have a right to demand the returns for which I move. But then the Right Hon. the Chancellor of the Exchequer objects to my motion, saying that the return I ask for is superfluous, since the return moved for by the Hon. Member for Lincoln will fully answer the purposes I have in view. [Sir James here read the motion alluded to, which was conceived in these terms:—'For a return of the persons in our civil or military establishments, holding two or more commissions, offices, or pensions, pay, or allowances; specifying the date of the office, and the amount received by each person, for the year 1829.'] Now, sir, I think I shall be able to show the Right Hon. Gentleman himself—and I am sure he will have the candour to acknowledge it—that this return would not answer my purpose. The return, be it observed, is for those persons holding two or more commissions, offices, pensions, pay, or allowances, in our civil or military establishments. Now it will be my duty to analyze the Privy Council, and I have to state that there are only thirty of its members who hold two offices, while there are one hundred and thirteen who hold offices under the Crown. If, therefore, I contented myself with the return of the hon. member for Lincoln, I should only have had these thirty pluralists, while the remaining eighty-three would escape unnoticed. In now bringing forward this question, I may be exposed to something like taunts when I allude to the documents on which I propose to ground it. It is one which I have endeavoured, at the expense of much time and labour, to form with all possible accuracy from returns laid before this House; but as they are scattered over an immense space, and appear in the intervals of a long period, I may not always have succeeded in avoiding errors. Besides, for some offices and places there are no returns at all. In these cases, however, I have obtained the best information that could be procured except a Parliamentary Return. But before proceeding further, I think it is well to state that it is not my wish to say anything that may appear unkind or invidious towards any gentleman. My motion is of a peculiarly delicate and painful nature; and notwithstanding the allusions of the Right Hon. Gentleman on a former occasion, I hope I shall forget nothing that is due to the feelings of individuals. The course I shall pursue

1830.

1830. will be to analyze this document. I will divide the Privy Council into classes; and doing so I shall, in the first place, except the Royal Family; they derive their incomes from the votes of this House, and under Acts of Parliament; there is nothing mysterious about them; they have frequently been considered and discussed in the Commons House. There are then, as far as I can ascertain, 169 Privy Councillors, exclusive of the members of the Royal Family; of these 113 are in the receipt of pay, pensions, or allowances to the annual amount of £650,164. The average amount distributed to each individual will be about £5753. Of these emoluments £86,103 is paid for sinecures; £442,000 for active service; and £121,650 for pensions. Of these 113 Privy Councillors, 30 are pluralists, that is to say, they either enjoy sinecures in conjunction with some post of active service, or they at the same time fill civil and military situations. The total amount annually received by them is £221,130. The average amount distributed to each is £7371. The number of Privy Councillors receiving diplomatic pay is 29. The gross amount received by them annnally is £126,176. The average amount distributed to each is £4347. Of the 113 Privy Councillors 69 are members of either House of Parliament. Of these 69, 47 are peers, and they receive £378,840, or on an average each receives £8069. Twenty-two members of the House of Commons are also members of the Privy Council, and they receive £90,849, or the amount distributed to each is about £4130. The House will remember that of the 113 Privy Councillors who are in the receipt of the public money, 69 are members of either House of Parliament; and I can state that 29 others hold offices, or receive money, who did hold seats in the House of Commons when the office or the emolument was obtained. The number of members of the House of Commons who are also Privy Councillors is 31; of these 22 are in the receipt of the public money. Now I have given to the House a complete and entire statement, to the best of my ability and belief, of the question respecting these offices and emoluments, as it fairly stands. I cannot positively take upon me to assert that there are no mistakes; a few errors may have unavoidably crept in; but I am quite sure the statement is as near the truth as a person not official could possibly bring forward. If the Right Hon. Gentleman objects to it, and says it is not accurate, my answer is simply this—Grant me my motion. I call upon the ministers to join issue with me, so that the people of England may be satisfied. And now, sir, I think it my duty to state another fact, which I can bring forward with more certainty, because it is founded on a return from the Treasury, for which I myself moved. It is a return of the number of persons employed in the public offices in the year 1797, and also in the years 1805, 1810, 1815; also specifying the number of persons employed in 1827, and the reduction made since 1819. Now here I may observe, that it is a singular fact, while comparing the number of persons employed in 1797 and 1829, that the price of wheat, which after all is the true standard, was at both periods nearly the same. There was only a couple of shillings difference. Now, comparing the amount of money paid to persons employed in public offices in 1797 and in 1827,—in 1797 the amount paid was £1,374,000, there being then 16,207 persons employed: in 1827 it was £2,788,000, the number of persons employed being 22,912. This is a comparison between the two years, as made upon a former evening. The average 1830.

1830. amount paid to each person in 1797 was £84; in 1827 it was £121, making a difference of nearly 30 per cent.; and as to the numbers, it is a thing extracted from this return to which I have alluded. It may be important also to remark, that in 1810 wheat was 105*s.* a quarter; at present it is 56*s.* Now a point that has been argued is, that fees were paid to certain officers before 1812 which were subsequently abolished; and thus it came to pass that the appointments before this period appeared smaller, while subsequently they appeared larger than they really were. This is published in a book by Mr Dean, the Chairman of the Board of Customs, whose work I look upon as one of the highest value, and always consult as my manual upon questions like the present. But even from this statement, the saving effected appears to be a matter altogether insignificant. The whole amount of fees abolished was £160,000, and now, taking into consideration that wheat is now 56*s.* a quarter and was then about 105*s.* a quarter, let us see what is the difference between the years 1810 and 1827, considering the number of persons employed and the salaries paid to them. In 1810 the number of persons employed was 22,931, and the sum paid to them £2,822,000. In 1827 there were 22,912 persons employed, and the amount paid to them was £2,788,000. Thus it appears there were only 21 persons fewer employed in 1827 than 1810; while the difference in the expense was less than £100,000. In what state then are we unfortunate country gentlemen placed? The price of wheat, as I have stated, differs nearly by one-half; thus we are called upon to receive half-prices and to pay double annuities; while the persons employed receive double annuities and pay but half the price. This presses heavily, not only on the gentry who have large estates, but on the whole community, and they regard it, as the Commons of England well may, with jealousy, and on it they ought not to hesitate to pronounce a strong opinion. Sir, I shall not detain the House long; but there are a few points on which I wish to speak. On a former evening I happened —in terms which were very displeasing to the other side of the House, though they were uttered with entire sincerity and singleness of purpose on my part—to state that I for one could never consent to begin reduction with humble and powerless individuals, while those possessing influence, and power, and property, were suffered to pass scathless. Sir, I cannot suffer these persons to go scot free. This does not fall in with my notion of justice; and I for one will never cease to urge his Majesty's ministers to turn their attention to this most important question without loss of time. I might bring forward many illustrations in proof of the facts I have stated. There is, for instance, Mr Penn, who is superannuated on an allowance of £750 per annum, and who, being unfit for active service, has been made Agent for Ceylon, with a salary of £1200 a year; this I should call an objectionable proceeding; but why should I complain of this, when there is my Lord Cathcart, who with emoluments to the amount of £2000 a year in this country, enjoys the post of Vice-Admiral in Scotland, with a salary of £2013, and all his military allowances as a general officer, and a colonelcy of a regiment. I cannot think, sir, of touching Mr Penn's salary till I have reduced and regulated Lord Cathcart's emoluments. Again, there is Mr Browne enjoying a salary of £1200 for a situation in the civil department of the army, while he at the same time receives half-pay as a commissary. Nothing, it is true can be more improper, or more opposite to all principle and

1830.

1830. justice than this; but when I look at the gallant Admiral opposite—and I am sure he will excuse my frankness, and I might almost say boldness, in thus alluding to him, for these attributes are supposed to belong almost exclusively to his own profession,—I say when I look at him, I could not be dastardly enough to complain of Mr Browne, and pass over the far greater emoluments enjoyed by one much higher in rank and official station. The gallant Admiral, in addition to his salary of £1000 as a Lord of the Admiralty, receives the full pay of Major-General of Marines, and if I am not considerably misinformed, he has lately been paid £3000 as arrears of half-pay. And now, if the House will allow me, I will read the form of oath administered to all Lieutenants in the Navy, and the other subordinate officers, before they can receive their half-pay; here is the oath,—

"'I, ——, do swear that I am not in holy orders, and that I had not, between the —— day of ——— and the —— day of ———, 18—, any place or employment of profit whatsoever under his Majesty, nor in any department of his Majesty's service, nor in the colonies or possessions of his Majesty beyond the seas, nor under any other government.'

"This is the oath the junior officers must take, while their superiors are exempted from any such restriction. Is this just? Is it right that the gallant Vice-Admiral opposite, who is in the enjoyment of his civil emoluments and of his full pay as a Major-General of Marines, should be exempt from taking an oath of this kind, while it is imposed on a poor Lieutenant? I might now mention another case,—that of the Vice-President of the Board of Trade, who, we were informed the other night, was oppressed with such a redundancy of business that he had not a single moment to himself, yet he receives £600 a year as Agent for the Cape of Good Hope. Then there is the First Lord of the Admiralty, who enjoys his salary of £5000 a year, which, be it remarked, was considerably augmented during the war—at the period of high prices,—and who, in addition, has a large sinecure in Scotland of £3150 per annum, as Keeper of the Privy Seal. In like manner, I might complain of the Commissioners of Customs and of Excise, who received large augmentations of their salaries in 1801 and in 1816, on the alleged ground, as stated by a minister in this House, of the diminished value of money and the increased price of provisions, and whose salaries have not been reduced since money has risen in value, and all things have fallen in price; but, sir, there would be no justice, no principle, no honour in this, while my Lord Melville, or my Lord Rosslyn, holding the Privy Seal of England, a sinecurist in Scotland, and the receiver of large military emoluments, can be presented to our notice. I confess that all this might not be sufficient to entitle me to my motion. I accordingly feel bound to state the parliamentary objects I have in view. My first and great object is to see if the service rendered be equivalent to the sum of money which is paid for it. My second object is to inquire if the rule that half-pay should abate on taking civil office should not also apply to full pay; and my third is to ascertain whether retired pensions and allowances of ministers should not abate when they return to office. These are the three substantial grounds on which I move for my return; and if it be granted to me, I pledge myself that I will bring these questions fairly before the House. I hope the House will consider them not unworthy its attention; and if it do not, I must declare that this return is necessary to enable me to bring them fairly

1830. forward. The honourable member for Newcastle has introduced a motion respecting superannuations: it is a question blended with all our civil establishments; but from the mode in which it is treated, one would suppose it was now introduced for the first time—that it had never been mooted—that it had never been discussed before: but what is the fact? That it is most amply and ably discussed by the Finance Committee,—that Committee upon which the Right Hon. Secretary for the Home Department once lavished such high praises, saying it was formed of the most able and experienced men in this House, at least as far as financial matters were concerned. And what does the Finance Report state? First, the alarming fact that £484,000 was paid for persons in a non-effective state, while £4,371,000 was the expenses of the effective, or one-ninth of the whole sum was paid to those in a non-effective state; and the Report went on to say,—'That no half-pay should be payable to any officer holding any other office or employment, civil or military, under the Crown (except in certain staff situations), or in the service of a foreign state.' And, sir, this regulation is acted on with rigour as far as it affects the humble and defenceless classes; and certainly the principle is a sound one, but it should be universally applied. The Report further adds,—'They are far from being disposed to discourage the appointment of individuals who have served their country in the military or naval professions to civil employments; but when those individuals adopt the Civil Service the Committee conceive they should receive the same remuneration for it as civil servants would receive, and no more. The Committee, upon a careful consideration of all the principles and circumstances affecting this part of the case, recommend in the

strongest manner that the payment of all half-pay be forth- 1830.
with replaced upon the footing on which it stood previously to the year 1820, with respect to all military or naval officers hereafter to be appointed to any civil employment or office under the Crown, or under any foreign government.' Now, here a positive recommendation is distinctly given, and why did not the Government, after all their professions of economy, accede to it? The defence of the Government is that they are not to blame—that they did all they could to reduce the superannuations to the standard of 1820; that is to say, to reduce them one-tenth, and the Chancellor of the Exchequer plumes himself on having introduced a bill upon the subject. This he did on the 2nd July, 1828; but, as he stated, the opposition was so strenuous, so insurmountable, that he was compelled to yield. But I beg the House to attend to the very words of the Chancellor of the Exchequer, who so zealously, and faithfully, and enthusiastically brought forward this measure. In proposing the bill he said, 'I feel that this measure is particularly severe, and I particularly regret the necessity of proposing it.' Yet after this strenuous support it was stated that it was the fault of the House that this measure was not carried. The House will, I trust, observe on what the expressions of the Report and the sentiments of this trustworthy Committee bore; it was, as I have stated, in returning to the practice of 1822, to reduce all these allowances one-tenth. Yet the Chancellor of the Exchequer gave up the question, even without a division. Sir, humble and undistinguished a member as I am of this House, I will take upon me to declare that if ministers will only afford me their support, I will undertake to carry this repudiated bill triumphantly through the House in the course of the next week. But what has the

1830. Chancellor of the Exchequer done? He has referred the question to another Committee; and to a Committee how constituted I will tell the House. But in this too I will abstain from all personal allusions, contenting myself with a general description. Let me first state, however, that in the Finance Committee there were six ministers, two ex-ministers, eight members of counties, seven representatives of cities and boroughs. The present Committee on the superannuations consisted originally of eighteen members. My Right Hon. friend the Chairman of the late Finance Committee has been since forced upon them, and to counterbalance him, they have added a ministerial member; there are now consequently twenty members, of which four are ministers, four ex-ministers, six county members, five representatives of cities and boroughs. Thus nearly one half of the Committee consists of ministers or ex-ministers. Before I sit down I beg to refer to the argument with which I know we shall be met upon this occasion, as we have often been met before; I mean by the argument of vested rights. If the House will pardon me, as that argument has been answered in better language than I could possibly use, in terms too most carefully considered by the noble Lord who used them, I will quote them from the last speech delivered in this House by the Marquis of Londonderry. It was upon a motion in which, in opposing the opinion of Mr Canning on this subject, the noble Lord said, 'If this notion of vested interests and freehold rights were to go forth, then there must be an end of legislation: these rights and interests would meet them at every turn, and put a stop to every measure, however beneficial or necessary. Why should the public offices be conducted on a plan different from private concerns? If a banker or private merchant wished to remove a clerk, or lower his salary, he did it at once. Now would any man contend that that clerk would have a right to turn round and say,—I gave up a fellowship at college and a place in Church to accept of your clerkship, and, therefore, you ought not to dismiss me. If any hon. member on the other side were to bring forward a motion of this kind'—[Ay, sir, these were days before we, on this side of the House, had transferred our services to the Crown, and had deserved by our conduct the name of 'His Majesty's Opposition']—'If any hon. member on the other side were to bring forward a motion of this kind, and he (Lord L.) were to meet it by saying that the salaries in the public offices were vested rights, were a kind of freehold and could not be tampered with, the idea would be scouted.' These, sir, were some of the last words of that noble lord in this House. They merit our praise, for they are true,—they deserve to be inscribed in our recollection, and I trust they will not be forgotten in the vote of to-night. It is the higher classes of offices that are the subject of my motion; it is they upon whom I propose to take your vote to-night; it is they who are included in the returns for which I am about to move. I seek to regulate them; and until I see these returns denied me by the vote of this House, I will not believe that even the influence of the minister of the Crown will be sufficient to refuse them. I have read somewhere, and I fully subscribe to the truth of the observation, that the mark of a wise and prudent government, and that which distinguishes it from an unwise and imprudent government, is well to know the time and manner at which no longer to refuse what is demanded of it. Let the Government now show its wisdom and prudence; for if ever there

1830. was a time when the people of this country imperatively demanded a searching scrutiny into the public expenditure, it is at this moment. I will put to public proof the question whether the conduct of the ministers deserves to place them high in public opinion, on the score of the use they make of their patronage. On that subject we have a pledge of theirs most solemnly put forth, that they would voluntarily make every saving required by the public interest, and capable of being carried into execution consistently with the public safety. I will put that pledge of theirs to the test; I will propose a measure of substantive retrenchment, economy, and reform. That is the issue which we are to try to-night. On a former occasion I yielded; I took their pledge. Let them now redeem it, let them give me these returns, and we shall then see whether they have been willing to keep good faith with this House, and with the people of this country. In conclusion, I beg to move for 'Returns of all salaries, pay, profits, fees, and emoluments, civil and military, received between the fifth of January, 1829, and the fifth of January, 1830, by the members of the Privy Council, the amount paid to each individual, the cause for which paid, and the source from whence derived.'"

Debate on the motion.

The Chancellor of the Exchequer complained of the invidious selection of a particular class of public functionaries as the subject of the return; and argued that every legitimate purpose of information would be served by adopting the amendment which he proposed. Lord Milton contended that the object of the motion was to ascertain whether the ministers had meted the same measure of justice to

persons in high stations that they had to individuals 1830.
in subordinate capacities. It was not directed *ad invidiam* against individuals, but to procure valuable information with regard to the influence exercised by the Crown over the whole body of the Privy Council. Sir George Cockburn defended himself from the strictures that had been passed upon him, and declared that were he then to quit political life he would be a poorer man than when he entered it. Sir H. Hardinge entered into some details explanatory of some of the instances of pluralist officials which had been alluded to, and General Grosvenor reproached Sir James with originating a proceeding of "such a vexatious and agitating kind," although but a short time before he had said that there was no essential difference between ministers and himself, except on the question of the currency. Lord Althorpe, on the other hand, observed that the importance of the motion had been raised in his eyes by the promulgated intention of Government to resist it; it looked as if there was something to be concealed. He maintained that the House had a clear right to inquire into the names and duties of all who received the public money, whether belonging to the Privy Council or to any other body. Mr Goulburn had spoken of the motion as if it were a matter of obloquy and disgrace to receive the public money; it would be neither obloquy nor disgrace to receive it if it were earned; and he could not con-

1830. ceive any objection to the motion that did not imply the necessity of not letting the public into the secret how its money was disposed of. Mr Huskisson said that, in his opinion, the information to be gained by the amendment would not be equal to that which was asked by the motion. He entreated the Chancellor of the Exchequer to give way upon this point, and he would tell him upon what ground. The Right Hon. Gentleman had said that the production of the information would expose individuals to public obloquy. Now, if the Hon. Baronet's statement went forth to the world, as go forth it must, without means being afforded of correcting that statement by the production of the correct returns, the Privy Council would, indeed, be held up to public obloquy. Mr Hume, Sir J. Yorke, and Mr Portman likewise supported the motion.

His reply. Sir James Graham in reply said that what he complained of on the part of the ministers was, that they gave too much—more than he required. He asked for one thing and they gave him another. He asked for a list of about 175, and they gave him a list of 1500, or 2000. He asked as if it were for a glass of wine, and they gave him a glass of wine certainly, but diluted with a bottle of water. His motion referred to the great officers of state, and his object was to ascertain what their emoluments were, in such a manner as that they should stand out clearly and distinctly apart from any other class of the public servants. The amendment of Mr Goulburn included them with many others, and would be useless for the purposes he had in view. Suppose he were trustee of an estate, and that he demanded from the steward or agent of that estate a return of a certain class of the upper servants of the establishment, and that, instead of complying with his requisition, the steward should give him a list of the whole establishment, agricultural labourers, grooms, lacqueys, and all, would not such a proceeding fill the mind of the trustee with suspicions? He had been charged with being factious. At the commencement of the Session, ministers gave certain pledges, and upon those pledges, and upon the faith of their being redeemed, he professed his willingness to give them his support, with the single exception, he believed, of their measures regarding the currency. But they had departed from much of what they had led the House to expect, and accordingly the points of difference between them and him were increased. 1830.

Effect on the House.

The House divided,—147* voting against the Government majority of 235. But the impression which had been created was not measurable by the nominal result. It cannot perhaps be more vividly

* In the minority were Mr Huskisson, Lord Palmerston, Mr C. Grant, Mr Stratford Canning, Lord G. Bentinck, Mr E. G. Stanley, Mr Brougham, Mr Labouchere, Sir H. Parnell, Sir C. Wetherell, Mr F. T. Baring, Lord Ebrington, Mr T. B. Macaulay, Mr R. Gordon: Lord Althorpe acted as teller.

1830. conveyed than in the words of one who watched with jealousy and distrust every proceeding of the member for Cumberland.

"Whatever Sir James Graham undertakes he does extremely well. Nothing could exceed the spirit, the talent, the propriety of his speech. Nothing could be better calculated to engage the sympathy of such an assembly, and of all high-minded independent men. The tact with which he selected his instances, his total disregard of all other considerations than the interests of the people, his high tone as a representative of the Commons of England, his carelessness of consequences, and whether his arrows might hit the present or ex-ministers or ministers *in petto*, whether on this or that side of the House, and all, as he well knew, arrayed against him in their hearts, was that of a tribune of the people. His success was immense, and the cheers unbounded. Peel is not yet returned to the House,* and poor Goulburn was more than usually flat. His objections to the return were substantial enough, but he was as unhappy in his defence as Sir James Graham was felicitous in the attack. No question of this nature was ever before taken up in this manner, treated with such talent, and supported by 147 members. It is a sign of the times. What with his industry and talents, his fine manner and person, his aristocratical bear-

* His father died, May 3rd, 1830.

ing and connections, and his factious independence, Sir James Graham may go a great way."* 1830.

Compliments and flatteries now flowed in from all sides. His motion had not been looked on as a party one in the ordinary sense of the term; and many Tories who were ill-affected to the Government felicitated him on his personal success. He was not disposed to put lightly in hazard the reputation he had won, and he prudently abstained during the rest of the session from taking frequent part in debate. But ere it closed he resolved to try his hand once more in the direction where he had already been so fortunate. No branch of the public expenditure was more open to criticism than that for diplomatic services; and having got up his subject with his usual care, he made a statement in Committee of Supply regarding the extravagant cost of the South American Missions, which Government found it impossible satisfactorily to answer. He reviewed the proceedings of the Foreign Office in this respect during the five years preceding. In 1825 Mr Morier had received a sum of £8987 for eight months' service in Mexico; Mr Ward's mission to the same country had in twenty-five months cost £19,862. Mr Cockburn had received £15,975 for thirteen weeks' residence in Colombia; and Lord Strangford had received £6786 for an unexplained, and, it was to be feared, inexplicable embassy to

Diplomatic salaries.

* Mallet's Journal, 15th May, 1830.

1830. Brazil. Many other items of a like description followed; and upon the whole a case of prodigality appeared to be made out which called for the marked interposition of the House. He ended by moving to reduce the vote for the year from £28,000 to £18,809. An animated discussion followed, and the motion was only lost by 19 votes in a House of 217.*

On the same evening we find him making one of the majority which enabled Sir James Mackintosh to carry a clause in the Forgery Bill, abolishing the punishment of death in all cases save that of the forgery of wills.

Death of George IV. George IV. died at Windsor on the 26th June, and Parliament was soon afterwards prorogued and dissolved. The Opposition resolved to make greater efforts than before at the elections. They felt, to use the words of Sir James Graham in one of his retrenchment speeches, that "the time for dallying was past," and that if at the commencement of a new reign the public establishments were renewed on the old footing, all hope of practical economy must be indefinitely adjourned. No great question, however, fixed popular attention, or divided parties out of doors by a broad line of demarcation; and Mr Brougham was thought by many to have committed himself to a rash enterprise when he announced his intention of standing for Yorkshire. In Cumber-

* Hansard, 7th June, 1830.

land there were no signs of opposition to either of the sitting members. The county had begun to feel proud of its junior representative, whose votes and speeches had become the talk of many a fireside, where previously his name only had been known. But the recollections of 1826 were too recent to permit any serious thought of carrying a second Liberal for the county, and Sir James, believing as he did that any attempt of the kind would be hopeless, would have been content to abstain from exciting topics in his addresses to the constituency upon the occasion. 1830.

A number of his supporters in the Brampton district having invited him to a public dinner at Dalston, Sir James, in accepting the compliment, expressed a hope that nothing would be done to deter persons of different opinions from taking part in the demonstration. He had many friends whose opinions on all subjects except those of party politics he valued highly; and if there was this time to be no battle in the county, he should be glad of their presence at the dinner. This reply was followed by the public intimation that several of Sir J. Lowther's friends had signified their intention of being present. In the *Carlisle Journal* the subject was commented on with some severity, and the old apprehension was expressed that an understanding had been come to for the division of the county representation between Blue and Yellow, and The Dalston dinner.

1830. the compromise thereby of its independence.* "A man can only belong to one party, that which means right, or that which means wrong. Let Sir James and his friends make their election between the two; but don't let them hope that they can so trim their sails as to please both." But his constituents in general were more than satisfied with his parliamentary conduct, and the dinner which took place on the 5th of August was attended by 600 freeholders.

French Revolution of July.

Ere the day arrived for the Dalston banquet, events had occurred of which the tidings as they spread far and near stirred the souls of the most apathetic, and kindled in the bosoms of the more sanguine anticipations of coming change, which a week before they would have spoken of but as dreams. A popular insurrection had burst forth at Paris in consequence of the attempt of Charles X. to subvert the constitutional rights of the nation. What the issue might eventually be, none could tell. All that was known for several days was that the streets of the French capital ran deep with blood, that the half-armed people had repeatedly repulsed charges of cavalry, and that many of the Swiss Guard of the King had been cut to pieces in attempting to maintain their posts. The incomplete intelligence arrived in England in the midst of the elections, and it exerted a powerful influence over their result.

* Carlisle Journal, 31st July, 1830.

Every day the popular feeling rose higher; and by 1830.
the time the squires and 'states-men of East Cumberland had assembled at the peaceful and picturesque little village of Dalston, under the presidency of Mr Blamire, to thank their representative for his recent services in Parliament, and to drink his health and success in future, one absorbing solicitude had filled men's minds, and each asked his neighbour eagerly, How goes the fight in France? Intelligence had reached Carlisle of the complete overthrow of the old *régime*, but all was still conjecture as to what form of government would be substituted in its stead. The Duke of Orleans had been named by the Deputies, Lieutenant-General of the Kingdom, and Lafayette had been placed at the head of the spontaneously reorganized National Guards; but the King still lingered at Rambouillet, and had with him it was said 10,000 troops who remained faithful to his cause.

On the temper of the more thoughtful, and on the mind of Sir James himself, prone at all times to take the gloomy side of things, a deep shade of anxiety was cast. There were some, indeed, who had come to meet him there who troubled their heads little about the sins of the Bourbons, or the fate of the Barricades. Low rates and high taxes, cheaper government and a larger share of power for the independent occupiers of the soil, with a good many reminiscences and boasts of the superiority of

1830. the Blue flag above the Yellow, made up their notion of politics. But the prevalent tone was one of feverish excitement. Vehement speeches were uttered by those around him, and, yielding to the contagious influence of the hour, Sir James made a speech the most vehement of all, in favour of party ties and party aims. When his health was proposed he said,—

"I am not about to deliver to you any premeditated address, for in speaking from the heart it is not necessary to do so; but I will at once tell you, with all the frankness of a friend, the matters that press on my mind, and the feelings which play around my heart. First, as to the explanation requisite on this occasion: my hon. friend Mr Blamire has told you all. The first intimation I had of this dinner was from him, and my answer to him respecting it you have just heard read. I confess that I am a party man, because I conceive that by party we are enabled to achieve more than a man can do singly; and because by it we are better qualified to concentrate and strengthen public opinion. It is, perhaps, the infirmity of human nature that we should be required to act thus, but it is necessary, and with this conviction I commenced my career in public life. Disregarding the connections of family, the opinions of private friends, and more than all the prejudices and sentiments of my revered father, I adopted the local political opinions of my grandfather, who fought the good fight of independence in 1768, under the old Blue flag of freedom. I adopted his sentiments—the sentiments of that local party which had always struggled for independence. I became a Blue; Blue I am, Blue I have always been, and Blue I trust I shall always continue to be. I am not ashamed to own it, and God forbid the Blues should ever have cause to be ashamed of me. I admit that new circumstances give new turns to men's ideas, and to their motives of action; and however much I may court and value the support of the men of my own party, it would be little less than an act of insanity to reject the support of those who, though they will not go all lengths with us, are willing to tender their assistance so far on public and general grounds. But it would be pusillanimous—it would be a dereliction from the path of truth—were I to conceal what are my opinions as a party man. It is as difficult to say where the last shade of Yellow ends and the first of Blue begins as it is to say where those of light and darkness mingle; yet no man fails to distinguish between night and morn, nor ought any man to be afraid to avow whether he belongs to the one party or the other,—for there can be no difficulty in ascertaining the distinction. In this country there must always be two great principles to divide public men—two great parties to one of which a public man must attach himself—I mean the Court party and the Country party. The Court party are doubtless Englishmen, and actuated by English feelings; but the object of all their endeavours is the advancement of kingly power—the height of their ambition kingly smiles. The Country party have a different end in view. It is their object to uphold popular rights, to defend popular feelings, and to forward the happiness of the people; and the proudest reward to which their ambition aspires is popular approbation. These are the feelings which actuate our public men; and while England remains England, Englishmen must always continue divided on these great principles. My part is taken in this struggle for principle. I range myself with the Country party—that party which, locally speaking, adopts the bright and unfading Blue for its symbol.

1830.

1830. I adopted it in early life; I have adhered to it ever since; and, if I know myself, I never will forsake it. In saying thus much, I trust I have said nothing to give any man offence; to have said less would have been weak and pusillanimous. And when I see so many of my constituents around me, men of the most enlightened, the most liberal, and the most independent feelings, coming forward to support me so cordially, I think the charge that I have been 'trimming my sails' to catch popularity from another quarter recoils upon the heads of those who have made it. I have been misrepresented on another point—I have been held up as inimical to the liberty of the press. Now if there be one man in the country more attached to the liberty of the press than another, I am that man. I entered Parliament in the year 1819; and one of the first things that I did was to record my protest against the infamous Six Acts. I voted against them, and I spoke against them, with all the little ability I possessed. And notwithstanding the enmity of the Whig Attorney-General—the recreant Whig Attorney-General with whom I, with many other friends of liberty, then acted, and with whom I then fought side by side—notwithstanding, I say, his present deadly enmity to the press, I still consider every one of those acts which restrains the liberty of the press as uncalled for and unnecessary. And one of the last acts I performed in the House of Commons was, to assist Lord Morpeth in resisting the new tyrannical and still more uncalled-for restraint which Sir James Scarlett has had the effrontery to impose upon the press. I will go further, and say that I know of no restraint upon the actions of public men at all to be compared to the free exercise of the liberty of the press; for while it presents the best medium for ascertaining public opinion, and thus becomes invaluable to public men, it affords the best tie between duty and inclination. It cannot work miracles upon our hearts; but it is a check upon the conduct of public men, which they cannot and they ought not to contemn. I say that liberty which it still preserves ought not to be contracted; its ends are good, its designs beneficent. Like every other good which we possess, it has its alloy: yet every true and wise man, knowing the benefit it confers, will refrain as much as possible from complaining of its abuses. It is the touchstone of the character of public men; and we must not examine its action too nicely. I have, however, to complain that I have not had justice from it. I have been hardly dealt with in a journal—not belonging to my opponents, not inimical to the principles I have ever advocated—but from a journal maintaining, and I will say honestly maintaining, similar opinions. Unable to put their finger upon any overt act that could invalidate my claim to the character of an honest and independent man, they have insinuated a suspicion of motives the most unpraiseworthy of any by which a public man can be actuated. Motives are known only to a higher and superior intelligence, by whom they will be judged and requited, and it is not for mortals to fathom the depths of the human heart; but I think if I know myself, by no such unworthy motive as have been insinuated have I ever been actuated. This meeting has fortunately given me the opportunity, and I readily seize it, to contradict the charge. Before you condemn me, I hope you will wait to see whether or not I deserve it. I know it is your duty to watch narrowly the conduct of those to whom you entrust so much power—for I am not ignorant how such power has been abused,—but act the part, at least, 1830.

1839. of kind masters, and if I do well give me the encouragement I may deserve. Gentlemen, the letter from me which your chairman read, fully expresses my idea as to the importance of this meeting. I have there said, and I repeat it here, that when the ministers of the Crown see that my opinions are backed by so large and enlightened a body of my constituents, they must be inclined to listen with more deference to the representations of one who warns them of their danger. The meeting of to-day is a cause of no little pride to me—not merely as a source of personal gratification, but as it will enable me more powerfully to enforce those plans of retrenchment in the public expenditure of which I am the advocate. My power is increased ten-fold by this strong expression of your opinion. I therefore do most warmly exult in it and thank you cordially for it; and I assure you most sincerely that it shall only prove an additional stimulus to renewed exertions for the good of the people. Gentlemen, I am fully aware, that were I to follow the course which prudence would dictate, I could not retire from public life at a better time for my own sake than at this moment, for I could never expect to receive a prouder mark of distinction than this. And to me there is always a tinge of melancholy in scenes like this, for it is all fleeting; and if I were to shut the book of public life at this page, and not open another chapter, it might be to my advantage. But I am in the full vigour of life, and therefore I shall gladly make another attempt to serve you better. Disregarding then the dictates of prudence, I ask you to continue towards me that favour which I have for a short while enjoyed, for a longer period. Vain, indeed, may be all our endeavours to will it so; for as it has been truly and beautifully observed, we see around us too many things to

warn us, 'What shadows we are and what shadows we pursue.' 1830.
But whilst I am permitted to represent you, I shall labour to promote the interests of the people. I entertain a strong conviction that though the sun of constitutional liberty has in a neighbouring country just set stained with blood, it is destined soon to rise again with new refulgence, and that the day-star of Reform is about to visit England also. But to revert to my public life; I would now briefly state what the House of Commons will shortly have to deliberate upon, and what I shall urge and support with all my power,—a further reduction of taxation; moderate but effective reform in the representation, by reducing the expenses of elections, multiplying the number of places for receiving votes for counties, increasing the number of electors by adding copyhold and customary tenures to freehold, transferring the franchise of decayed boroughs to populous towns, and throwing open the franchise of cities and boroughs to the householders rated at £10 or £20 a year. These things I will urgently promote. I see and feel that on the happiness of the people depends the safety of the State, the security of property, and the enjoyment of liberty. I have represented this to the ministers, but my voice has been unattended to. I have told them of their danger, but they have not heeded me; when they see that my representations are backed by the opinions of my constituents; when they find that I but echo the sentiments of a body of men whose opinions are not to be bought, and whose conduct is not to be swayed by any personal consideration—they will surely then be inclined to pay some deference to such representations. But if they are not to be arrested in their career by the earnest warnings of their own countrymen, surely they may

1830. well take heed of what is passing in another country, within sight of our own shores, where if the mad career of an infatuated and bigoted tyrant had not been arrested by the all-subduing voice of freedom, we should have witnessed such scenes as Europe might have shuddered at. If they are not so warned, be the responsibility upon their own heads; I have done my duty, and you have done yours."

The applause with which this speech was received by those assembled in the great tent at Dalston was re-echoed wherever Sir James appeared. His popularity was indeed at its height, and the consciousness he seems to have been unable to repress of its fleeting and fragile nature is eminently characteristic of the man.

7th August. Dinner at Whitehaven.

Two days later another dinner was given to him at Whitehaven, by some of the unlooked-for incidents of which the position he sought to maintain as a "moderate reformer" seemed likely to be compromised in opposite ways. The committee having announced that it was not meant as a party demonstration, several persons who were known as partizans of the Yellow cause attended, and notwithstanding the lengths he had gone in his Dalston speech, a good deal of susceptibility was evinced in some quarters as to the reasons and motives for the repetition of an announcement of this kind. What did it mean? Was a compromising silence to be observed by all who took part in the proceeding, and this at a moment of such exciting interest in politics at home and abroad? Sir James became sufficiently aware of the existence of suspicions and misgivings, and not unskilfully strove to allay them. In responding to the toast of his health, he took care to say that when accepting the invitation of his friends, he had done so as the Blue candidate for the county. He spoke as a party man. To party we owed much of the prosperity and greatness which, as a nation, we enjoyed. To every public measure, and to every public man, party was of advantage. It bound men together by the same hopes and by the same fears, who were actuated by the same friendships and the same aversions; party was the living depository of principle, its assertor and its guardian. As a party man he had entered public life; such he had ever continued, and such he must ever remain. Party was the hoop that bound the disjointed staves of society together. It was the key-stone of the arch that gave compactness, strength, and durability to the whole. 1830.

The toast "Constitutional Liberty and the friends of freedom in France" having been proposed, Mr J. Gibson said he wished to hear the sentiments of their guest on the great and glorious revolution which had just taken place.

Sir James said that when he first read the Ordinances issued by the King for crushing the liberty of the press, and with it the liberty of France, he had but one sensation, that of trembling

1830. anxiety to see whether that great and noble people would rise up at once and vindicate their rights by overthrowing that reckless tyrant, that heartless monarch, that insane man,—or wait the surer but not less certain progress of time, for expelling from their bosom the serpent which they had nourished only to sting them. This anxiety was speedily put an end to by the intelligence which had spread joy throughout the land, and raised one universal feeling of exultation amongst all men who knew and felt what liberty was. Never, he would venture to say, did history record a revolution more necessary in its commencement, more signal in its warning to all tyrants, more just in its vengeance, or more speedy and glorious in its termination. The rights of free men were not to be compromised by, nor held at the will of, despots, and this lesson could not be too strongly impressed upon all men—that the people have an indefeasible right of resistance to kings and to kingly power, whenever that power is exercised against their liberties. Constitutional kings reigned only in virtue of their compact with the people: if they set aside that compact, all allegiance was at an end, and resistance became a virtue. This great lesson France had taught to the domineering and audacious tyrant who sought to raise a despotism on the ruins of her free constitution; and it gladdened his heart that such a lesson had been read. From the depths of his soul he lamented that any blood

Duty of resistance to despotism.

should have been shed; but never was blood shed in a more sacred cause; and he hoped that it was the last that would be required. But if the battle were not yet ended, if the fight must be again renewed, he could have but one wish, he could entertain but one hope, and that hope was, whatever the cost, whatever the sacrifice, that the cause of the people might triumph. He was sincerely desirous of seeing a constitutional monarchy established in France. He trusted that the French people would show with what moderation they could use victory, by sparing the life of the wretched prince who had been their sovereign; and he hoped, on the other hand, that the dethroned monarch would not attempt to protract the struggle which he had provoked; but if he should do so and cause more blood to be shed, on his head must fall the just resentment of an injured people. On principle he was himself attached to kingly government, as the best for securing the happiness of the people; and he hoped the French would follow the example set them by the English people in 1688, introducing such modifications as time and increased knowledge had shown to be necessary. 1830.

Mr Wilfred Lawson, of Brayton Hall, who was to propose him on the hustings the following day, lauded the sentiments which they had just heard from Sir James,—sentiments which he said proved him to be worthy of the confidence of the freeholders

1830. of Cumberland. From one part of his speech, however, he must beg leave to differ, and that difference would be best shown by the toast he was about to propose, "May the heads of Don Miguel, King Ferdinand, and Charles Capet, be severed from their bodies, and rolled in the dust—and the more speedily the better."

The murmurs of some of those present were drowned in the vociferous cheers with which this frantic aspiration was received. The fact of the toast having been drunk, was reported in the London journals without the expressions used by Sir James, so little in accordance with its terms; and many ascribed to him unwittingly participation in sentiments which on the very occasion in question he had deprecated and disclaimed.*

The new Parliament.

The result of the elections was upon the whole very unfavourable to ministers. Mr Brougham, who upon the hustings professed to have no claim founded upon rank, station, or territorial stake in the county, was returned with Lord Morpeth for Yorkshire; and Mr Hume was returned for Middlesex. From the days of Mr Fox the choice of these two wealthy and populous counties has generally been regarded as a sure omen in times of excitement of what is likely to follow elsewhere. Mr Denman was returned for Nottingham, Mr R. Grant for Norwich, and Mr Huskisson retained his seat for Liverpool. The

* Mallet's Journal, 11th August, 1830.

Secretary of the Admiralty, Mr J. W. Croker, and three members of Sir R. Peel's family, lost their seats. 1830.

Although the Government showed in several respects a willingness to yield to popular opinion, their influence manifestly declined, and a sense of conscious weakness betrayed itself in their general conduct. The abolition of the punishment of death for many minor offences indicated no reluctance to pursue the path of law reform. The Beer Act was avowedly passed as a concession to the wants and feelings of the labouring classes; and Mr Hume admitted, towards the close of the session, that Ministers had carried retrenchment further than any of their predecessors. But the proceedings against the proprietor of the *Morning Star*, for libels on the Lord Chancellor and the Duke of Wellington, raised a storm of obloquy not easily allayed. The appointment of Sir James Scarlett as Attorney-General had been received with satisfaction by the Whigs, to whom as a party he had always professed to belong. But his ex-officio prosecutions of the press were considered an obvious dereliction from former principles; and the length to which they were carried would at any time have brought their author into popular disrepute. When not long afterwards the memorable *ordonnances* of Charles X. appeared, suspending the liberty of the press and other fundamental rights of the French people, the fact was deemed

1830. corroborative of the suspicion that the English Government had countenanced Prince Polignac in the fatal policy which led to the overthrow of the Bourbons. The imputation was no doubt unjust; but the course adopted regarding Don Miguel, and still more that which had been pursued at home with reference to the press, gave colour to the charge, and tended greatly to weaken the credit of the administration. Their supporters surveyed the prospect before them with feelings of dismay.* Whether the Duke would have yielded to the suggestions of those who would have had him seek to strengthen his position by a re-union with the Canningites, had circumstances favoured the attempt, it is vain to conjecture. Mr Huskisson had shown himself on more than one occasion but too anxious for office; and though he had recently drifted further in the direction of popular aims than he had ever done before, it may be doubted whether he and his ex-official comrades would have refused to re-unite with their former colleagues, had any moderate programme of concession been proposed to them. But it is certain that no material modification of his policy was ever contemplated by the Duke; and at the very moment when he was first brought into personal communication with Mr Huskisson since their severance in 1828, a terrible fate was to summon the amiable

Death of Mr Huskisson.

* See Letter of Lord Londonderry to the Duke of Buckingham, 28th Aug., 1830: Courts and Cabinets, vol. i. p. 47.

and accomplished, but too complaisant statesman, 1830.
from his dreams of ambition. On the 15th September Mr Huskisson died from the effects of an accident which took place at the opening of the Liverpool and Manchester railway: and with him perished the last chance of renovated popularity or influence for the Wellington Government. The small section of politicians which had thus twice within so short a time been deprived of its head, appears no more as a specific quantity in political calculations. Its elements soon afterwards melted into the opposing masses of Progress and Resistance as their respective affinities determined.

Letter of Lord Grenville.

From his calm retreat at Dropmore, Lord Grenville watched the increasing rapidity of the current of events, with the dispassionate eye of one who ventures no more into the troubled eddies of the stream. He deplored the death of Mr Huskisson, not only because he appreciated highly his personal qualities, and shuddered at the horrors of his fate, but because he seems to have regarded him as the last hope for the Conservative party's retention of power. Writing to a near relative in office, "he grieved to see how very unsuccessfully the elections had turned out; and he knew from but too good authority, that whatever face ministers might put on the matter, they did not disguise the fact among themselves. There was not more want at the beginning of the last French Revolution, to augment and

1830. consolidate the force of all friends of quiet and good order, of whatever description, than existed in the present state of things, looking either at France, Europe, or England. Would to God he could see any symptoms of a similar disposition either to call for such co-operation or to yield it. Yet it would be the true wisdom of both parties so to act. His anticipations were of the most gloomy sort. How much he wished and prayed they might be deceived."*

* Letter to the Duke of Buckingham, 21st Sept., 1830.

CHAPTER IX.

THE ADMINISTRATION OF EARL GREY.

1830.

THE speech from the throne addressed to the new Parliament deplored the revolt of the Belgians as uncalled-for, and denounced the efforts of incendiaries to increase discontent at home; but nothing was said of reform, and the existing frame of Government was declared to be the chief source of the national welfare,—a blessing which it was the duty of all to transmit unimpaired to posterity. When questioned in the Lords as to the intentions of the Government, the Duke of Wellington stated that he was resolved to crush sedition wherever it appeared; but that he had never seen any plan of parliamentary reform which would be an improvement on the existing system of representation; and that so long as he remained in power every proposal of the kind should be resisted. In the Commons Mr Brougham gave notice of his intention to bring forward a comprehensive measure on the subject, and pro-

1830. Fall of the Wellington Ministry.

2nd Nov.

1830. nounced the Government to be the feeblest and least efficient he had ever known. Lord Althorpe said the times required pre-eminent ability and skill in those who had the direction of affairs, and that he looked in vain for such qualities in the existing administration. Sir E. Knatchbull, speaking the sentiments of the alienated section of the Tories, called upon the Radicals to co-operate with them in measures of opposition to ministers,—an appeal to which Mr Hume responded with an assurance that his vote would cheerfully be given for their expulsion from office. Sir Robert Peel encountered the formidable array against him in a manner sufficiently temperate and discreet, and deprecated successfully any amendment to the address. He calculated, not without reason, upon the probability of discord springing up amongst his assailants whenever any definite plan of parliamentary reform should be brought forward; and could he have induced the House to agree to a new civil list, and a bill to provide for a regency in case of the demise of the crown before the Princess Victoria should have come of age, the Session before Christmas might have terminated without the occurrence of any untoward event. But others saw as clearly how the game was to be lost and won; and they prepared to act accordingly. Out-of-doors great disappointment was expressed at the language of the Premier, and a feeling of uneasiness and apprehension spread amongst all classes of the community.

1830. King's visit to the City.

Meanwhile, an incident occurred which contributed more, perhaps, than any other to reveal the weakness of the Government, and to precipitate the coming change. In the morning papers of Monday, the 8th November, a letter appeared with the signature of Sir Robert Peel, informing the Lord Mayor Elect that the King and Queen were compelled to decline visiting the city on the following day. Great excitement was caused by this announcement: the Funds fell three per cent.; and when the House met in the afternoon, Lord Althorpe asked the reason why such advice had been given to their Majesties. The Home Secretary stated that serious grounds existed for apprehending tumult and violence in the streets; that the Metropolitan police were likely to be attacked in the discharge of their duty; and that the Duke of Wellington had been warned by the Lord Mayor not to accompany the King to Guildhall unless attended by a strong escort of troops. Ministers had, under these circumstances, recommended their Majesties to postpone their visit to the city. A desultory debate ensued. Mr Goulburn challenged a vote of want of confidence, and said the Government would willingly give place to other men if it were carried against them. Sir James Graham replied that looking at the way in which the recently-chosen House of Commons was constituted, it was obvious why the Chancellor of the Exchequer suggested such an issue. The Opposition had no intention of taking his advice in

1830. point of form, but they would meet his wishes substantially as the business of the session proceeded, and questions would soon arise, the decisions upon which would put to the test the degree of confidence
8th Nov. reposed in Ministers. "Upon that day se'night the sense of the Commons of England would be taken upon that which he (Sir James Graham) considered the most vital and important of all questions, namely, whether it was expedient or not, that the state of the representation of the people of the United Kingdom should be considered with a view to its amendment. In reference to that question, the Duke of Wellington had declared himself against all reform; and the Right Hon. Baronet (Sir Robert Peel) had declared himself unable to see his way, and that he could give no opinion upon it. His Majesty's ministers, therefore, and the public, had come to an issue upon that great question, whether it was expedient that the state of the representation should be considered with a view to its alteration. That was the point upon which they had come to an issue; and, as far as he could see, the declaration which had been made by the Duke of Wellington against reform, and the sentiments which had been expressed by the Right Hon. Baronet, had, in an incredible short period of time, effected the greatest possible change in the sentiments of the public with regard to the ministry. The Home Secretary, in his letter published that morning, had stated that it

would be dangerous for the King to go in a procession to the city by night. Why, within one short week his Majesty had gone after night-fall to the theatre, and he had encountered no danger or disrespect whatever: he was, on the contrary, received with the most loyal and enthusiastic demonstrations on the part of an attached and devoted people. What had since intervened? That celebrated declaration of his Majesty's Prime Minister, that nothing should induce him to discuss this question of Reform; and that if it should be brought forward by others it should be opposed by him. From coming into contact with a great body of constituents, he was tolerably well acquainted with the opinions of the population of this country; and he would say upon that point, in reference to which the Duke of Wellington had declared that he would concede nothing, that his Grace was at direct issue with the people of England; and when he said the people of England, he meant not merely the lower orders, but the middle classes of society, in conformity with whose sentiments the Government must be conducted, or it could not stand. The Right Hon. Baronet had himself upon a former occasion stated that he rested upon public opinion, and that he was ready to stand or fall by its decision. Now, public opinion demanded a reform of the representation in the Commons House of Parliament, and while the Right Hon. Baronet and his colleagues declared that they would

1830.

Cause of the Duke's unpopularity.

1830. not grant it, the people of England said it must be granted, or that there would be no peace in the realm, and no security for property. That was the point on which the ministers and the people of England had joined issue, and which he hoped would soon be brought to trial. He trusted, therefore, that no premature discussion would be introduced with regard to the confidence of Parliament in ministers; but that upon the great question of Reform the decision of the House would be taken. The declaration of the Duke of Wellington which had rendered him so unpopular had astonished, alarmed, and confounded the people of England. The noble Duke had previously enjoyed a portion of the confidence of the public; but that declaration had made him the most unpopular minister that was ever known in England. At the same time he (Sir J. Graham) must say, and he said so from the bottom of his heart, that any act of personal violence offered to that noble Duke would be a stain upon the annals of this country which years of future glory would not wash away. He did hope, whatever opinion might exist as to the civil conduct of his Grace, that eternal gratitude which he deserved for his splendid military services, for his dauntless valour, and for his glorious achievements, would wait on him, and that his person or his life would never be placed in hazard in this country. He feared that the noble Duke was too fond of ruling alone; and that he was obstinately

attached to that policy which he thought was right; 1830.
but he trusted that the noble Duke would not continue unwisely to pursue a line of conduct which might place the peace and the prosperity of the country in jeopardy; for in his conscience he believed that public opinion had pronounced—decisively pronounced—against the policy of the noble Duke.",*

New symptoms hourly appeared of the ministerial catastrophe that was at hand. Vacant appointments were rapidly filled up, and rumour multiplied the number and value of the consolatory arrangements in favour of old friends, with which every outgoing Government is certain to be charged. Dr Philpotts had shortly before been nominated to the Bishopric of Exeter; but the revenues of that See being less than that of others, he was to be permitted, it was said, to retain the Rectory of Stanhope, in the county of Durham, worth £4000 a year. On being questioned in the House as to the report, Sir Robert Peel admitted its accuracy; whereupon Sir J. Graham instantly gave notice that on that day se'night he would move an address to the King, praying that the petition of the parishioners might be granted, and that they might have the benefit of a resident pastor. Before the day arrived, the Government had been overthrown by whom the promise had been made to the new prelate that he should be suffered to hold Stanhope *in commendam;* and, on an as-

Bishop of Exeter's claim to Stanhope *in commendam*.

* Hansard, Debate in Commons, 8th Nov., 1830.

1830. surance that no actual re-appointment to the Rectory, after it had been vacated by the act of episcopal consecration, should take place without opportunity being given of parliamentary discussion, Sir James consented further to postpone his motion.

Sir H. Parnell's motion.

An opportunity soon arose for trying the strength of parties in the manner he had indicated. The new Parliament had been called together for the specific purpose of settling the Civil List. The arrangements proposed by ministers did not materially differ from those which had subsisted in the previous reign; the amount was somewhat reduced, but many of the personal expenses of royalty were mixed up with official charges with which they had nothing to do. Sir Henry Parnell, who had been Chairman of the Finance Committee, and who had borne a conspicuous part in all the recent efforts made in favour of public retrenchment, moved as an amendment that the subject should be referred to a select committee. The course was an unusual one, and was understood, as indeed it was intended to be, simply a mode of raising the question of want of confidence in ministers. It had, in point of fact, been suggested with that view, as being more likely to combine, in a vote which pledged individuals to nothing further, all the various sections who were discontented with the existing Government. The debate was brief. No speech that could have been made on either side would probably have turned a vote. Men's minds were made up to the necessity of a change; and it seemed to be tacitly agreed that the sooner it came the better. Lord Althorpe succinctly supported the amendment; as did Mr Bankes, Mr Charles Wynn, and Mr Holme Sumner, all of whom were members of the Tory party. On a division, Sir H. Parnell's motion was carried by 233 to 204; and on the following day the Duke informed the House of Lords that he and his colleagues had resigned. 1830. 15th Nov.

Earl Grey Premier.

To Earl Grey the task was confided of forming a new administration. The dream of a long life was at last about to be realized; and King and people were at length to make amends for a quarter of a century of exclusion and neglect. He told the Peers that he was the only man in England who could at the time form a Liberal Government;* and he told William IV. that he would only accept office upon condition of carrying into effect his own principles of Reform. The egotism which had caused him so many mortifications and done his party so much harm, exultantly asked now whether it had not been justified, and it prepared to exact unlimited satisfaction. To form a Government that would have any chance of standing, it was necessary to engage, in the first instance, a certain amount of Tory support. With this view he offered a seat in his new Cabinet to Sir Edward Knatchbull, who declined, and to the Duke of Richmond, Mr C.

* Hansard, Lords, 22nd November, 1830.

1830. Wynn, Lord Palmerston, Lord Goderich, and Mr Charles Grant, who accepted. Lords Lansdowne, Holland, Althorpe, and Carlisle occupied places by his side; Lord Anglesea was appointed Viceroy, Lord Plunket Chancellor, and Mr Stanley Secretary, for Ireland; while the Duke of Devonshire and Lord Wellesley accepted the chief places in the household. Lord J. Russell became Paymaster of the Forces. Of the remaining posts in the Government many were given to the Premier's relatives and connections: his son-in-law was named Privy Seal, and his eldest son Under Secretary for the Colonies; Lord Melbourne was nominated Home Secretary; and Mr Ellice and Mr Ponsonby became the one a Secretary of the Treasury, and the other a junior Lord. But of those who had taken a prominent part in the Commons in the struggle which had ended in the fall of the Wellington Cabinet, Lord Grey took small account. Give him time, and he would provide for them all respectively in their turn. But power was not for the plebeians. Mr Brougham was offered the Attorney-Generalship, which he indignantly spurned, and only obtained the Great Seal from the fears of the King. Sir J. Newport and Sir H. Parnell were never thought of for leading positions; and Sir James Mackintosh was a mere jurist and man of letters, having no pretensions to a seat in the Cabinet.

It was the Premier's boast that the new administration represented a wider extent of broad acres than any that had preceded it for a considerable 1830. time; and when it is recollected that the houses of Cavendish, Russell, Howard, Spencer, Lennox, Petty, Paget, and Stanley contributed to its formation, it cannot be denied that he was justified, in the aristocratic vaunt. It had been a theme indeed of reproach on the part of the Whigs, that the Tory administration of the previous reign consisted, in great part, of men who had raised themselves by their talents to eminent political rank, and who were destitute of great territorial possessions. Mr Canning was notoriously a poor man; Mr Huskisson, Sir George Murray, and Sir Henry Hardinge were not rich; Lords Aberdeen, Bathurst, Sidmouth, and Castlereagh possessed no more than average fortunes; and nobody knew exactly how much Mr Peel would inherit from his manufacturing father. Lord Grey's ambition was to be able to present to the King a list which should outweigh in point of property any other that could be formed. But while doing so he was desirous of propitiating in some degree the Radical supporters, on whose votes after all he must in a great measure rely. Sir James Graham furnished a connecting link between repugnant parties. By his votes and speeches he had become identified with the more advanced section of Reformers; while his family connections were calculated to bring additional strength to Government in both the Upper and the

First Lord of the Admiralty.

1830. Lower House. These considerations, rather than any sympathy or admiration for his rhetorical displays, led to his being offered a seat in the Cabinet as First Lord of the Admiralty; and they probably conduced moreover to his being named soon afterwards one of the committee of four, to whom was

20th Nov. confided the task of framing the Reform Bill.

The Cabinet arrangements having been completed, a new writ for Cumberland was moved for on the 22nd November, by Mr Spring Rice, who had become Financial Secretary of the Treasury. The day after his appointment Sir James wrote to Major Aglionby:—

"*Grosvenor Place, 20th November*, 1830.

"MY DEAR SIR,

"Lord Grey has urged me at this eventful crisis to accept office with him; and, somewhat reluctantly, I have consented to be First Lord of the Admiralty, with a seat in the Cabinet. Althorpe is Chancellor of the Exchequer, and Brougham, Chancellor; Lord Lansdowne, President of the Council; Lord Palmerston, Foreign Affairs; C. Grant, India Board; Duke of Richmond in the Cabinet. With such colleagues, and reform, peace, and retrenchment the avowed principles of the Government, it was difficult to refuse, and I hope you will not object to my acceptance. My seat is vacated. I hope to be re-elected, and it would delight me if you would consent to second my nomination, as a proof that my conduct on this occasion has not diminished your confidence.

"I shall be ready and anxious on the hustings to declare the motives of my conduct, and to state the principles on which the new ministers found their claim to public support. I shall hope to be in Cumberland a day or two before the election. I trust that you will send me a favourable answer, and believe me, 1830.

"Your faithful and obliged,

"J. G. GRAHAM."

Major Aglionby readily assented to his request; and for the third time he was returned for the county without opposition. With the exception of Mr Stanley, who was ousted from the representation of Preston by Mr Henry Hunt, all his colleagues resumed their seats before Christmas; and the Regency Bill having been passed without difficulty, Parliament was adjourned until the 4th February.

Grillon's club.

On the 1st December he was admitted a member of Grillon's club, to which, since its formation in 1805, many of the distinguished persons who have taken part in public affairs have belonged. Every Wednesday during the Session the members of the club dine together, and the feuds of the previous day are forgotten, or made the theme of pleasantry and genial humour at a table where all opinions have their representatives. When he entered this society, he found among its members the gifted but eccentric Earl of Dudley and Ward, whom Canning had thought worthy of succeeding him in the Secretaryship of Foreign Affairs, and whom the Duke of Wellington had insisted on retaining in office, but over whose infirm brain the gloom of aberration was already

1831. settling down. There he found Sir R. H. Inglis, Oxford's recent choice, and Sir R. Wilmot Horton, pre-occupied with ideas and plans of general emigration. There he met Lord F. L. Gower and Mr Agar Ellis, both fonder of letters than politics; Lords Harrowby and Wharncliffe, Mr Robert Grant, the Bishop of Rochester, Sir T. Acland, and Lord Clare, with many more long since passed away.

Residence at the Admiralty.

Early in the new year he took up his residence at the Admiralty. Between the two-fold duties of his office, and of the Committee appointed to prepare the Reform Bill, his time was wholly absorbed; and the zest with which he took to official work he was at no pains to conceal. In the prime of life, possessing a fair inheritance, member for his native county, his ambition gratified beyond his expectations, blessed with a happy home—there was nothing left him to desire, save the distinction of success in the unaccustomed part he had undertaken to perform. Great was his exultation, and great the energy with which he set himself to master the unfamiliar details of his office, and to comprehend thoroughly the principles and maxims on which its traditional policy was based. He laboured incessantly during the day, and often far into the night, to conquer the technical ignorance that besets and blinds every man who for the first time essays to guide and govern a great department. He had studied agricultural and economic science carefully; his reading had been deep and various in history and public law; but about ship-building, naval drill, contracts, gunnery, store-keeping, and the manning of the navy, he knew, as he himself confessed, absolutely nothing. He had it all to learn, and that quickly and well, at the peril of humiliating exposure by the "old hands," who, ejected from Whitehall, were still powerful at Westminster. There was one indeed from whom he had nothing to fear. Lord Melville, upon quitting office, frankly communicated to his successor information the most minute and valuable, as to the defects which existed in the department, and the remedies which it was most advisable should be applied. When the proper time came Sir James did not hesitate to acknowledge that he had availed himself of that experience, and had been guided by that advice. When first assailed with party asperity for the changes he deemed it his duty to introduce, he disdained to throw any share of the responsibility upon Lord Melville. But when the wisdom of those changes had come to be admitted by many who had originally opposed them, he took a fitting opportunity for acknowledging the obligation he felt himself under for the timely and useful advice.* Meanwhile, how was he to accomplish all that was thus suddenly required of him? and while

1831

Lord Melville.

* See speech on Navy Estimates, Hansard, 16th March, 1835.

1831. learning his business, how was he to parry the searching and sinister questionings of angry opponents acquainted by long habit with every difficulty, and eager for an opportunity to expose the fancied incompetence of the new First Lord? Nobody indeed could tell him how, nor was it for some time clear to himself. But ere many weeks had passed, he began to feel the ground growing firm beneath his feet.

The new Chancellor of the Exchequer.

Lord Althorpe was at this time his most intimate friend,* and scarcely a morning passed without a call from Sir James, to consult about something new, or to confer as to how some apprehended difficulty might be overcome. His great mental activity and inexhaustible power of pleasant and useful talk gave him for the time a sort of ascendancy over the matter-of-fact and easy-tempered Leader of the Commons. In opinions they never entirely agreed; and there remained, notwithstanding all their close intimacy and unreserved interchange of views, some questions of moment on which they were never in accord. But these were few, and at the juncture of affairs which had then arrived, the two men were peculiarly well fitted to work together for their mutual benefit and that of their party. The one slow, forbearing, and politically inert, with a highly-merited reputation to sustain, was wholly free from personal aims, resent-

* Evidence of Sir J. Graham, before Committee on Naval Administration; May, 1861.

ments, or pretensions to cloud his judgment or beguile him into party errors;—the other quick, active, subtle, and ambitious, eager for work, covetous of distinction, and anxious to secure the ascendancy of his party, was full of suggestions and devices, shrewd guesses at the unavowed motives of adversaries, and anticipations of the possible estrangement of loosely-linked friends. Plunged suddenly into the perplexities and complications of aggressive leadership, Lord Althorpe had gladly availed himself of aid, which the giver was only too delighted to render. So long as they remained in Opposition and were free to choose the topics of occasional debate, the toil of making up for a general statement of facts did not seem excessive; but when the case was reversed and a variety of subjects required to be mastered and dealt with as it pleased angry opponents to raise them, or as the exigencies of the public service might demand, the amateur grazier felt himself often weary of his task, and turned longingly to the thought how he might make his escape to his woods and breeding farms in Northamptonshire. Colleagues like Lord Grey, Lord Holland, or Lord Melbourne, could do little to appease his disquietude at his conscious unfitness for the trying position he was placed in. It needed all the fearless energy of the Chancellor, and all the indefatigable aid in fiscal and financial calculation of the Secretary of the Treasury, to induce him to front the well-disciplined 1831.

1831. array of ex-officials, who knew far better than he did all he did not know of usage, precedent, and detail. But Lord Brougham was no longer in the Commons; and though all the requisite facts and figures were furnished him by Mr Spring Rice, Lord Althorpe found himself unable without previous practice to turn rapidly and with the ardour of the advocate from one mass of details to another. Sir James did not wait to be asked to help him, but, privileged by the terms of confidence on which they lived, frequently offered to relieve him of a portion of his burden. Thus we find him frequently taking charge of matters in Parliament, and acting as the representative of the Government there, when the matters had no connection with his own department. His willingness to save trouble to his friend and colleague was as great as his willingness to take it upon himself. Their opposite natures seemed adapted for each other's wants; and their party gained thereby.

Debate on the altered Civil List.

On the 4th February, the new Chancellor of the Exchequer brought forward the remodelled Civil List, which he proposed to refer for examination to a Select Committee. It gave £510,000 to the King for life instead of £970,000, as the late ministers had proposed: the difference, so far as its items should be kept up, was to be placed on the Consolidated Fund, and thereby brought under the direct control of Parliament. No real saving was effected. The Pension List was to be divided into two parts. The one of £82,000 was to be placed on the Consolidated Fund, and the residue only retained at the disposal of the Crown. When items in the former fell in, Parliament might recommend their re-disposal or not at its pleasure. When vacancies in the Royal Bounty occurred, the King might fill them up at his discretion. Lord Althorpe stated that on looking more closely into the charges for the royal household he had changed the opinion in some respects which he had expressed in Opposition. To the King moreover was given the credit of saving the country the expense of an outfit for the Queen, for which there were precedents in the case of the consort of George III., and in that of the Princess Charlotte. Another version of the story, however, assigned to Mr Charles Grant the real merit of this economy, which, many of the other members of the Cabinet thought ill-advised and inopportune.* The Whigs hoped to obliterate their frugality in this instance by subsequently recommending Parliament to settle £100,000 a-year on Queen Adelaide; and the Tories had no scruple in seeking to propitiate royal favour by upbraiding them with democratic parsimony. 1831.

Mr Hunt and Mr Guest thought too little had been relinquished by the Crown, and Mr Goulburn thought too much. Sir James Graham frankly dealt

* Roebuck, Hist. of Whigs, vol. ii. p. 46 (*note*).

1831. with both classes of critics. He was as incapable as the ex-Chancellor of the Exchequer boasted himself to be of truckling to popular clamour, or seeking out-of-door applause at the sacrifice of "the decent splendour of the Sovereign," whose comfort and whose means of suitable hospitality ought not to be abridged. But the Court was not held in seclusion. The King lived in sight of his people, and he did not believe that they wished to see his fitting magnificence reduced. His Majesty had offered to surrender his hereditary revenue from the Duchy of Lancaster, which Henry IV., Henry VII., and the Protector Cromwell had successively severed from the ordinary income of royalty. They had to make an equitable bargain for the future with the sovereign, and their duty was to be just.

The first Whig Budget.

Lord Althorpe's first budget was a failure. He would have been true to himself had he possessed the power to keep the promises of reduced taxation which he had made, leaving the co-relative work of retrenchment to follow, for which there had not yet been time. But a Cabinet constituted like that of Earl Grey could not easily be persuaded to adopt sweeping reductions. The majority of them were pledged to nothing of the kind; four-fifths of the existing House of Commons regarded economy as the arithmetic of Jacobinism; and pressure from without was a thing in which they did not yet believe. Sir James would indeed have gone any lengths in retrenchment with the new Chancellor of the Exchequer, and Lord Goderich and Mr Charles Grant had not forgotten the principles of Mr Huskisson. But the utmost they could persuade the rest of the Government to sanction was an abolition of the duties on cotton manufactures, glass, and sea-borne coals, and a reduction of those on tallow, tobacco, and newspaper stamps. A charge of a half per cent. was proposed on the transfer of funded property. Lord Althorpe's statement was made on the 11th February. The estimated revenue for the year was £47,150,000, and the expenditure £46,850,000, upon the estimates bequeathed by the late ministry. Painfully conscious how short his proposals would fall of what was expected of him, he seems to have lost his usual clearness of perception; for in no other way can the singular error be accounted for of miscalculating the sum of £350,000, the amount of the beer duties. The omission did not long escape notice; and it threw discredit upon the whole of his statement. The new tax on public securities was fastened on eagerly by the Opposition, and held up as a proof of the subversive ideas imputed to the new Government. Lord Althorpe, who would fain have had Sir Henry Parnell among his colleagues, ingenuously paid him the compliment of declaring that his measures had been framed in accordance with the views expounded in the work on "Financial Policy," recently published by the Hon. Baronet. But Sir Henry dis- 1831.

1831. claimed the budget as being practically irreconcilable with the views and recommendations put forward therein. Mr Praed, the rival at Cambridge of Mr Macaulay as a debater, made his *début* on the occasion, in a speech which fully realized the high expectations of his party, and on which he was felicitated warmly by the First Lord of the Admiralty, who immediately followed him. He proceeded to reiterate the views he had so often expressed in Opposition, as to the injustice of the fiscal and financial measures of the two last reigns, no part of which he would shrink from, now that he was in office. He defended the new tax of one half per cent. on the transfer of property in the funds, as being no more a substantial breach of faith with the public creditor than the omission to keep up a Sinking Fund, a special guarantee for which had been inserted in every borrowing Act of Parliament by Mr Pitt and his successors, or than the reduction of interest from five to three per cent. The principle which he and his friends had always contended for in Opposition was, that relief should be given by a commutation of taxes to those classes of the community whose industry was too heavily burthened. They had striven to redeem their pledge by repealing the coal tax, which was a hindrance to manufactures of all kinds, and the duty of threepence-halfpenny a yard on calico, without regard to coarseness or fineness of quality, which amounted to a tax of forty to sixty per cent. on the

Tax upon Transfer of Stock.

humbler consumers. To supply the deficit thus created, they must resort to some new expedient; for their predecessors had left but a surplus of £300,000 in the Treasury. But as the opinion of the House had been pronounced strongly against the change of taxation they had thought it right to propose, it would be withdrawn, as Mr Pitt withdrew the proposal to extend legacy duty to real property in 1796.* In a word, he stood gallantly by the friend with whom he sympathized so deeply, and cheerfully shared with him the burthen of blame he knew he did not deserve. 1831.

But the effect was depressing on the spirit of their friends, and proportionately stimulating to that of their opponents. In the discussion on the Army Estimates, Sir R. Peel commented sarcastically on the abandonment of the promise of non-intervention in the case of Belgium, and of the promise of retrenchment as exemplified in the unreduced strength of the army. Sir J. Graham replied, but ineffectively. His speech elicited no responsive cheer, and was coldly received until towards the close, when adverting to some taunts that had been thrown out regarding administrative inefficiency in suppressing sedition in Ireland, he reiterated in strong language a determination previously expressed by Lord Althorpe to maintain the Union at all hazards. He wished the House to recollect that, without employing any military force, ministers had succeeded in

Speech on the Army Estimates. 18th Feb.

* Hansard, Debate, 14 Feb. 1831.

1831. vindicating the law—that without shedding even a drop of blood by the hand of a soldier (except in a solitary instance) the insurrectionary spirit that prevailed in the country had been subdued. "Was there nothing, too, in the state of Ireland to justify some caution, when, in that country, with loud, and he might say shameless, assertions, Great Britain had been threatened that the Union should be repealed by physical force? Yes, he said threatened, for the use of physical force was threatened. What had been done? The Government had vindicated the supremacy of the law, and by the courts of law. Such threats had been met by the civil power, and when made had only induced the Government to exert the powers the constitution had placed in their hands. He adopted to the fullest extent every word of what his noble friend (Lord Althorpe) had said on a former evening; and though he considered civil war as the greatest of all possible evils, short only of dismembering the empire, he, for one, would fight for Ireland, as he would fight for Kent—*toto certandum est corpore regni*. He was not blind to the perils of such a contest; but as far as it depended on him, the country should never cease to resist the separation; and he was sure the whole people of England, who had never been conquered, would not allow themselves to be overcome by the people of Ireland. He corrected himself: he did not say the people of the two countries were opposed; it was not the people of Ireland who threatened, it was only some demagogues" [O'Gorman Mahon exclaimed, "Name, name!"] "It was only one or two demagogues, who knew not in what the interest of the country consisted, who sought for the repeal of the Union. There never was a country which had derived more benefit from another than Ireland had from England since the Union. That country derived wealth from this, and found here the market for her produce. It was not the Irish people, and it was not the Irish patriots—they never would; it was only demagogues who desired the separation." [O'Gorman Mahon repeated his call for names.] 1831.

Mr O'Connell did not happen to be present; but O'Gorman Mahon, who had succeeded him in the representation of Clare, demanded whether in using the term "demagogues" allusion had not been made to that learned gentleman and himself, as they were the only members of the House who could be said to have taken any part in promoting the agitation for repeal. He vehemently denied the justice of the imputation that incentives to physical violence had been held out to the Irish people, and complained that threats of civil war should have been resorted to by members of the Government as a means of stifling agitation for the restoration of a local legislature in Ireland. He ended by repeating the question he had already put, as to the intended O'Gorman Mahon.

1831. application of the offensive epithet which had been used.*

Sir James repudiated any special application of the phrase to the hon. member for Clare, but this explanation not being deemed by him satisfactory, he sent his colleague, Major Macnamara, early the following day to the First Lord. The substance of what took place is authentically given in the following statement, which appeared in the *Times*, dated the 21st February :—

"Lord Althorpe, on the part of Sir James Graham, and Major Macnamara, on the part of O'Gorman Mahon, meet and agree to the following statement :—

"Major Macnamara called yesterday on Sir James Graham, when he told Sir James that he came in courtesy to ask whether in using the word 'demagogues' he had intended to allude to O'Gorman Mahon? Sir James in answer said, that at the moment he used the word, O'Gorman Mahon was not in his contemplation: he was sitting behind him, and he did not see him or think of him at all.

"Upon Major Macnamara asking Sir James if he would make this declaration in the House of Commons, Sir James said, before he agreed to that, he must consult a friend, to whom he would refer Major Macnamara.

"He accordingly consulted Lord Althorpe, and it

* Hansard, Debate on Army Estimates, 18th Feb., 1831.

is the opinion of Lord Althorpe that he ought to make it. 1831.

"It is the opinion of Major Macnamara that such a declaration in the House of Commons ought to be satisfactory to O'Gorman Mahon.

"Althorpe,

"W. N. Macnamara.

"*London, Feb.* 20."

Explanations in the House.

When the House met that afternoon, Sir J. Graham, on the motion that the Speaker do leave the chair, rose and said, he felt extremely unwilling to obtrude upon the time and attention of the House, respecting a matter of a private and personal nature; but he threw himself on its indulgence and good feeling. The matter to which he was about to advert had reference to what had taken place on a recent occasion, when it might be recollected that in the heat of extemporaneous debate, he had made use of the term "demagogues." It appeared that his having used that term had given offence to an hon. member of that House, who had subsequently asked him whether he had meant to include him (the hon. gentleman) within his application of it. His answer he would then state to the House. "Consistently with the truth, he was able to state that when he used the phrase 'one or two demagogues,' he had meant no reference to the hon. member for

1831. Clare, for he it was who had called on him for an explanation. It so happened, that while he was addressing the House, the hon. member was sitting behind his back, so that he could not see him; and, indeed, he was not at the time aware of the hon. gentleman being in the House." He had made this statement in justice to the hon. member, at the suggestion of his noble friend (Lord Althorpe) near him. What he had now to add was the dictate of his own feelings. He had used the phrase "demagogue" with reference to the hon. member for Waterford (Mr O'Connell), whom he now saw in his place, and he therefore felt himself, considering the declarations which that hon. and learned gentleman had made in that House and elsewhere, in relation to the atonement of personal offences—declarations which, he must say, should make him extremely cautious in the use of intemperate language, and other hon. members equally cautious in their expressions of opinion regarding his conduct,—and recollecting, besides, the peculiar situation in which the hon. member stood just then towards the Government,—recollecting all this, he said, he felt himself bound frankly to tell the hon. member that he was sorry he had applied to him the term.

Mr H. Davis considered the explanation of the First Lord of the Admiralty quite unnecessary, the rather, as the Right Hon. Baronet had, on the evening in which he used the term "demagogue," explained his regret at having used a term so likely to be offensive. 1831.

Mr O'Connell expressed his surprise that under the semblance of an apology which he had not called for, the First Lord of the Admiralty should have thought fit to allude, in the manner he had done, to what he called his (Mr O'Connell's) declaration of atonement for personal offences. He thought such observations had been better omitted. As to the position in point of law in which he stood to the Government, they would have ample opportunity of discussing that matter on an early day.*

Agitation for Repeal of the Union.

The agitation for the Repeal of the Union was one of the greatest difficulties with which Government had to contend. The Marquis of Anglesea, who had forfeited his post as Viceroy in 1828 by the avowal of his conversion on the Catholic question, had become, on his re-appointment by the Whigs, the object of unsparing attack by Mr O'Connell, because he declared his resolution to put down the public demonstrations in favour of Repeal; and before the new Chief Secretary had set foot in Ireland he had received the nick-name of "Shave-beggar," as descriptive of his want of administrative experience, from the great master of vituperation and ridicule. Irritated by the daily attacks upon him, Mr Stanley had sent a hostile message to Mr O'Connell

* Hansard. Proceedings in the Commons, 21st Feb., 1831.

1831. a few weeks after his acceptance of office; but the challenge was declined by the learned gentleman, on the ground that "already there was blood upon his hand, and that he had registered a vow in heaven never to risk human life again." Various meetings and societies, formed for the purpose of procuring the restoration of a separate legislature for Ireland, were dissolved by successive proclamations under a special statute which had force in Ireland only, and which was popularly known as the Algerine Act. The language of the "great agitator" rose in violence with each new measure taken to thwart him; and he was finally made the subject of a prosecution in the Court of King's Bench for sedition. After filing a demurrer and then withdrawing it, he was induced to plead guilty, with the expectation, if not upon the understanding, that no more than a nominal sentence would be inflicted upon him. Such was his position when the altercation took place in the House of Commons to which reference has been made. Ministers believed that in the coming struggle for Reform the agitation for Repeal would be forgotten; and they were conscious that they would stand in need of all the aid which the popular party in Ireland and its eloquent chief could afford; and he was content, on his part, to allow a formal conviction to be recorded against him in order to get rid of the consequences which would have attended a vindictive demand for judgment.

Several members of the Government, however, doubtingly acquiesced in this method of eluding for the moment the "Irish difficulty." As a means of consolidating the strength of the entire popular party in Parliament and throughout the kingdom, its success was complete. To carry Reform without resort to absolute force, as the event proved, was no easy matter; and its advocates had certainly no strength to spare. But Lord Grey and several of his colleagues feared the cry for Repeal, and hated its author. They knew not how to do without his aid, yet they shrunk with apprehension from the idea of increasing the popular power which, when won, he openly told them he would turn against their maintenance of the old system of exclusive and sectarian rule. It is, indeed, inconceivable how men like Sir James Graham and Lord Althorpe should have been blind to the fact that by the very composition of the Government of 1830, they furnished the great leader and liberator of the Catholics with unanswerable arguments against themselves. They boasted of the part they had borne in annulling religious disabilities; yet they practically justified the reproach that emancipation had been meant as a cheat and not as a reality, by deliberately excluding from office every man of the no longer contraband creed. There was no reason why the professional promotion he was pre-eminently entitled to, should not have been offered to Mr O'Connell upon

1831.

Anti-Catholic system of Government.

1831. the change of ministry; there was as little excuse for the unconstitutional and unwise neglect of Mr Sheil, Lord Killeen, Mr M. O'Ferrall, and Mr Wyse. Unhappily for the cause of good Government in both countries, Lord Grey's contempt for everything Irish, and resentment towards everything Catholic, because he was not singled out for gratitude in the triumph of toleration in 1829, was suffered to overrule all considerations of national justice and national policy so long as he remained in power; and the only excuse for the acquiescence of his younger colleagues in his selfish and sinister system, must be sought for in their belief that any schism in their party would be fatal to all chance of Liberal progress.

Retrenchment.

The times, indeed, were rife with trouble, and the complication of foreign affairs at the commencement of 1831 was such, that notwithstanding all the vows of non-intervention made by the new Government, it was impossible for them to discard the contingency of England being entangled in continental struggles, or being compelled to rely on her isolated strength for defence and safety. But ministers had given pledges of retrenchment too circumstantial and specific to be eluded; and in the management of the navy it was universally believed that a large saving of public money might, and therefore must be effected. The new First Lord was heartily desirous of making good in office all he had said in opposition: and if he could not as yet venture to cut down the greater items of naval expenditure, he was resolved to prove his sincerity as a practical reformer by plucking up many of the sinecures and superfluous charges, that had so long cumbered the ground. He was still more anxious to establish in the department, the great constitutional practice of strict appropriation of public moneys, to the specific purposes for which they were asked from and granted by the House of Commons. Strange as it may now appear, it is nevertheless true, that up to 1831 no serious attempt had ever been made to apply this essential principle of administrative responsibility to the Navy; and the consequences of the opposite system were strikingly set forth by Sir James, when bringing forward for the first time the estimates for the year. Their form was not new in any material respect; but while the sums required for the different branches of the service were kept apart, the rule was laid down, that no surplus which might accrue in one should be applicable to the wants of another. The financial principle thus applied had been first established by Lord Somers in the annual Appropriation Act of 1689; but it was supposed to be difficult to apply it strictly to the conjoint though separate needs of the Victualling Board and the Navy Board: and Admiral Russell, who was then First Lord, was not a man who liked the limitation of his administrative power. 1831.

1831. In 1798 the Appropriation Act was nominally extended to the Navy. But as a gross sum continued to be devoted to the whole of the service, without strictly ascertaining what was required for the use of each of the principal sub-departments, the aim was to that extent missed, and the effectiveness of administrative responsibility lessened. In the opinion of Sir James, "the time had arrived for giving full effect to the change which was contemplated rather than effected in 1798, and for enforcing the authority of Parliament in the relegation of the supplies for the naval service, in the same manner as in the other services. Holding strongly this opinion, it was his duty to bring before the House a few facts to show the great and growing departure from the rule laid down in 1798. Works of great extent in the naval department had been begun, completed, and paid for, without the sanction or even the knowledge of Parliament. These works had been paid for out of the surplus on votes, which were greater than was needed for the purposes to which it was intended they should be applied:" the difference having been made up by the Navy Board out of surplus moneys in their hands. A greater number of men were employed—in one recent year no fewer than 3000—at the public cost, more than were sanctioned by the vote of the House of Commons. In this way £1,243,100 had been paid in wages since 1820 over and above the amounts

Specific votes to be specifically applied.

specified in the annual estimates. The amount had 1831. been chiefly taken from the sums voted for ship-building materials and provisions, the contracts for which had been reduced. He had been told by the subordinate officers of the department that, owing to the peculiarities of the service, it was impracticable to avoid estimates in the gross, and the application of balances in excess under one head to deficits under another. But in his opinion the practice was inherently vicious, and he was determined to try whether it could not be brought to an end. He would endeavour that henceforth each branch and sub-branch of expenditure should be clearly kept distinct in the estimates; and no transfers of surplus funds during the year would be allowed. A larger vote than usual would be asked for 1831, for timber and the other materials of ship-building, in consequence of the misappropriation in the few preceding years from that species of outlay to other purposes. He could have wished to retrench, he said, in this costly item: "but he could not consistently with his duty—feeling that these were not the times when short-sighted economy should be studied in our arsenals, and applied to our means of providing for the maintenance of the honour and safety of the country." Nominally he would ask for a few hundred men more than last year, 22,000 seamen and 10,000 marines: not that he meant to keep the whole of this force afloat, but to keep up the avail-

1831. able strength already existing under the express sanction of Parliament. The total estimates for the Navy in 1830 were £5,594,955; those for 1831 would be £5,875,386, being an increase of £280,431. The naval strength of the country could not under existing circumstances be diminished. All he could do, therefore, with a view to immediate retrenchment, was to cut down superfluous places and excessive pay in the civil branches of the department. Two commissioners of the Victualling Board, and as many of the Navy Board with certain minor officers, would be discontinued; and the salaries of the Treasurer of the Navy and the Paymaster of Marines would be saved. In the dock-yards he had made reductions in the pay of superintendents, clerks, &c., of £16,674, after allowing for superannuations. In all, the reductions in his office would amount to £27,238 a year.*

Greenwich Hospital. Exception was taken by Mr Warburton and Mr Hume to the retention of Royal yachts in the service for the year, while an extra floating hospital in the river had been refused on the score of expense. No little complaint likewise was made at the continued deduction of sixpence a month from the wages of seamen in the mercantile marine for the support of Greenwich Hospital, to which in age or infirmity they were not eligible. The First Lord defended the vote for the yachts, which was incon-

* Hansard, 1831, vol. ii. pp. 947, 958.

siderable in amount, on the ground that since the days of William III. such vessels had been kept up as part of the paraphernalia of Royalty (at which the House seemed disposed to laugh), and for the better reason that they afforded an opportunity for rewarding cheaply officers who had seen service, but who might not be qualified for hard duty. The question of the additional hospital was under the consideration of the Treasury; and a bill had been prepared for introduction after Easter to open the great National Asylum of Greenwich to deserving seamen of the commercial as well as the royal Navy.* The latter announcement was received with cordial thanks by the representatives of seaport towns who happened to be present; and the entire of the votes for the Navy were carried in committee without a division.† 1831.

Accounts by double entry.

His love of clearness and precision in all that related to the public expenditure, and his singular capacity for dealing with the most complicated details of business, was remarkably displayed in the complete reform of the naval system of accounts, to which he applied himself immediately after his accession to office. The great extension of naval operations during the protracted period of hostilities which terminated in 1815, and the com-

* This was not done, but the naval sixpences were abolished, and the charge placed on the Consolidated Fund.

† 28th March, 1831; Hansard, vol. iii. p. 947.

1831. plications which arose in the accounts during that period, from the exceptional modes of meeting the accumulating demands for naval expenditure and debt during years of great financial pressure, had involved the accounts of the department in great confusion. There was little disposition on the part of Governments in those days to lay before the House of Commons and the country more information respecting their financial proceedings than they were obliged to furnish; and public opinion was not sufficiently strong to create an earnest determination in Parliament to require it. Sir James stimulated public opinion on this question, and initiated a beneficial reform in the national accounts, which is still in progress. In the fifteen years of peace which preceded his accession to office, little had been done to place the naval accounts on a better system. "Figures," as he once said, "were generally supposed to throw some light upon a subject; but in this case all was mystification and error."* He became convinced that every effort to establish greater faithfulness and frugality in the expenditure of the votes of Parliament would be futile until he succeeded in applying the constitutional control of the House of Commons; and he felt that to accomplish this object it was necessary to introduce a system of accounts capable of reducing to order the vast

* Evidence given before Select Committee on Board of Admiralty, 30th April, 1861.

and complicated details of naval finance. His first step was to prepare his estimates of the annual sums required to be voted to meet the expenses of the navy, in a simple form, intelligible to the House and the country. His next step was to take measures for securing to the public, satisfactory proof that the moneys granted were expended in conformity with the votes of Parliament; and with that view he ordered that the whole of the naval accounts should be kept upon a system (which was then partially under trial) similar in principle to that which was universally applied to the varied operations of commerce. His opinion was, that accounts which concerned all should be intelligible to all. 1831.

Old method of Navy Book-keeping.

But how was this to be done? Not only had the Victualling Board and Transport Board their separate moneys received and expended, their tallies under the heads of stores, wages, balances, and borrowings, which they stoutly resisted every attempt to bring within one comprehensive view, but the old fashion of reckoning had from time immemorial been kept up in them all, which excluded the very idea of striking a balance on foot of each distinct branch of outlay, to say nothing of a general balance on foot of the total outlay of the department. Lord Melville had been induced to authorize, some time before, the trial of an experiment (which most of the "old hands" about him told him would prove utterly

1831. chimerical), for keeping certain portions of the accounts by way of double entry. Upon taking his seat at the Board, the new First Lord was made aware of the fact of this experiment being in progress under the direction of Sir J. D. Thomson and the Hon. R. Dundas, members of the Committee of Accounts of the Navy Board; while the old system continued to be the only one practically recognized throughout the department. He found upon enquiry that the attempt to apply the new system had been entrusted mainly to Mr W. G. Anderson, then a very young man occupying a subordinate position in the Account Department under Sir John Briggs, who brought to the execution of his task those qualities of intellect and temperament which have since rendered him one of the most eminently useful members of the Civil Service. Sir James communicated personally with both these gentlemen, and after carefully examining all the impediments and hindrances wherewith the proposed change was beset, he was satisfied by them that beyond a great amount of time and trouble which must necessarily be expended in the first instance in framing and building up a proper system of reckoning by way of debit and credit, no real difficulty lay in their way. The decision was forthwith taken that the old imperfect method should be set aside; and Sir John Briggs, assisted by Mr Anderson, with ample powers for the purpose, was eventually entrusted with the introduction of the system of double entry into every branch of the naval service. 1831.

This system has now been thirty years in operation. During that period the naval force has been more than doubled, and there has been a corresponding addition to the magnitude of the naval accounts. The improvements of which Sir James laid the solid foundation have stood the test of war, and with such success that few departments of the State can account with greater clearness and accuracy for the expenditure of the public money entrusted to their charge. When the complicated details of our naval expenditure, conducted in every part of the globe, in every description of currency, and through a multitude of subordinate agents, are considered, too much praise cannot be given to the author of these practical reforms for the energy with which he pursued them, and the early period at which he brought them to a successful issue. Nor was the benefit of these measures confined to the department in which he introduced them. They have been extended to other departments of the State with equally beneficial results.

CHAPTER X.

THE FIRST REFORM BILL.

1831.

The Reform Committee of Four.

WHEN Lord J. Russell waived his claim to a seat in the Cabinet at its first formation, he stipulated that the introduction and conduct of the promised Reform Bill should be intrusted to him. Lord Durham, Sir J. Graham, and Lord Duncannon were associated with him in a Committee of Four, who were to investigate the whole subject and report the result of their consultations to the Cabinet.

Mr Brougham's plan of Reform.

The scheme of Reform prepared by Mr Brougham early in November, and which he had only been prevented from bringing forward by his elevation to the Woolsack, was especially referred to them for consideration. It was based upon the enfranchisement of all householders in towns, and all copyholders and leaseholders in counties ; upon the gift of representation to all the seats of modern industry, and the curtailment in a corresponding degree of the power of nomination to seats in the Commons, by individuals of rank or fortune.* Whatever Mr Brougham's wishes might have been, he was too conscious of the strength of the nomination and rotten borough influences in the existing House of Commons to hazard the success of his project by any sweeping measure of disfranchisement. With all the power of Government and all the selfish interests of a corrupt system arrayed together against him, he knew that it would have been vain to do so. He could hardly have expected in any event to carry a Reform Bill, no matter how framed, by the independent votes of Opposition; but with a view to eventual success, he was bound in prudence not to provoke such an amount of hostility, as would have stifled the proposal ere it had been thoroughly discussed. The case was now essentially altered, and the new Chancellor was willing that the Committee should modify his plan so as to render it more generally acceptable. 1831.

General objects.

Early in January they had made some progress in their labours. Three great objects were to be if possible attained,—the extinction of rotten boroughs, and the transfer of seats to populous counties and towns,—a diminution of the length and cost of elections,—and the extension of the suffrage to such numbers of the people as would satisfy the com-

* Roebuck's History of the Whigs, vol. i. p. 420.

1831. munity at large that all its interests would be henceforth efficiently represented in the House of Commons. The members of the Committee were all of them too much in earnest in support of their respective views, and differed too widely from one another in their habits of thought and ways of looking at the complex workings of society, to come easily to a complete agreement in matters of detail. But after frequent deliberations and a close study of the territorial map of political power, they came to the conclusion, that the close borough system could not be materially curtailed in its influence, unless a line of demarcation were drawn, which should disfranchise all towns not containing at least 2000 inhabitants: and they further agreed that no place should return more than one representative, which had not a population of 4000.

Principal features of the plan.

The consequence of adopting these rules was to put an end to sixty nomination boroughs, and partially to disfranchise forty-eight others. Of the 116 seats thus alienated, fifty-five were given to counties, and forty-two to towns: five were transferred to Scotland, three to Ireland, and one to Wales, and the remaining sixteen were to be extinguished. The time of elections ought to be reduced, they thought, to one day in boroughs and two days in counties. In the latter, polling districts were to be created, and some minor provisions made regarding elections which would tend to diminish their expense. The great points of difficulty were the franchise and the mode of voting. Lord Durham had always advocated household suffrage and the ballot; and he now proposed the latter with the £10 qualification in towns, as the least which could be offered to the people with any chance of their accepting it. Lord J. Russell was not opposed to this measure of pecuniary fitness, provided open voting were retained; but, as he afterwards stated in public, he feared the increase of corruption if the means of inquiry into its use among so numerous a class were rendered impracticable. If they must have the ballot, he would prefer to try the experiment with a £15 or £20 constituency. 1831.

Influence of Lord Duncannon.

Lord Duncannon, who had a greater knowledge of the existing constituencies of the kingdom, and a clearer insight into the probable working of those which it was intended to create, attached less importance to the point in dispute between his colleagues; and was ready to adopt whichever course might seem most likely to conciliate public opinion, without needlessly alarming the Court. He was one of the few men connected with the administration whom the King really trusted; and this was the more remarkable as his votes in Opposition had generally been more Radical than Whig. But without any of the superficial qualities of a courtier, he had the rare faculty of attracting and keeping the personal confi-

1831. dence of men the most opposite in character and temper. He was a man of few words either in public or private, and seldom indulged in professions or promises; but every one felt who came in contact with him that he was not merely a man of honour, who would do all he said, but a man of settled purpose and sagacity, who was bent on accomplishing what he undertook, and who knew how it was to be done. He lived on good terms with men of all opinions; and when there was a misunderstanding between two of his own party, he was oftener trusted than any other individual with the confidence of both. No violence or folly could disconcert him, and no enthusiasm or eloquence beguile him into going further than he saw his way. He never dissembled his disapproval of the course taken on many occasions by Mr O'Connell; yet he preserved in a degree perhaps unexampled his uninterrupted confidence and respect. Lord Grey had named him one of the committee, not only on account of the practical information he was capable of affording, with respect to counties and boroughs in England and Ireland, but as a sort of counterpoise to the petulant and wayward Lord Privy Seal. This he understood thoroughly, although no hint of the kind ever fell from him in look or gesture. But he had far more regard for the interests of his party, and it may be fairly added for the interests of the country at large, than for the humour of the Premier; and as each element of the contemplated scheme came to be analyzed and dealt with, the main consideration in his mind was,—will it promote the success of the measure, or put it in jeopardy? When Lord Durham proposed the adoption of the ballot, he avoided pronouncing any opinion until he had consulted Lord Althorpe, whose directness of purpose, dispassionate earnestness, and shrewdness of perception, he was peculiarly fitted to appreciate. The Chancellor of the Exchequer had by this time probably begun to understand, how little dependence could be placed on William IV.'s assurance, that he was "quite in favour of Reform:" and seeing that the sole chance of carrying the measure lay in making it such as would, from the outset, command an irresistible amount of popular support, he told Lord Duncannon by all means to make the ballot a part of the plan. 1831.

Opinions of Sir James.

Not very dissimilar was the course pursued by Sir J. Graham, with whom Lord Althorpe's counsel went for more than that of any other man. He was wedded to no book theory of the constitution, and as little to any philosophic formula of change. His first and last thoughts on the subject were,—what improved mechanism would work best for the common weal; and what could be got without violence, with which the people at large would be content. His horror of civil commotion was extreme. He looked on the interposition of physical force in the solution

1831. of political controversies, as the evil of evils, for sake of averting which there was no sacrifice of personal or party self-love that ought not to be made, reserving always to individuals the liberty to stand aside if they would, sooner than actively further measures they could not thoroughly approve. Things in the abstract right or wrong, formed in his mind but a very limited category. Legislation was with him essentially an experimental science; and no law was in his comprehensive view worth enacting or worth retaining, whose practical benefits did not demonstrably outweigh its real or supposed drawbacks. Half his life was spent in comparing and pondering opposite results, and determining judicially in the silence and solitude of his study, on which side the balance lay. "Upon the whole" again and again recurs, throughout his private correspondence and public judgments (for judgments they frequently were),—a phrase which a statesman of a constitutional country may well employ, as eminently expressive of the true candour and humility of wisdom.

What was best "upon the whole."

At a county meeting held at Wigton in the previous year, he had stated his views respecting the suffrage at considerable length. He objected to the establishment of any one uniform franchise for counties and towns. Occupancy, he thought, should constitute the basis in the latter, and he was willing that the pecuniary limit should be wide. He deprecated, however, sweeping measures founded on untried theories. He would not agree to deprive the freeholders of their distinctive franchise, upon the chance of "finding more honest electors in a wider range of people." He was for trying the effect of alteratives to restore the constitution to vigour, much fearing to use the knife upon any vital part. He cited the opinion of Lord Chatham, a reformer and a politician whom none would accuse of want of firmness, that into those parts of the constitution which through time or circumstances had decayed, it would be wiser to infuse new vigour than to lop them off, in order to give new health and vitality to the body. He looked forward to strengthening and consolidating popular independence in the towns by municipal reform, the breaking up of the old corrupt and exclusive bodies, and the throwing open of corporate as well as parliamentary franchises to all persons rated at a certain amount. In counties he would enfranchise copyholders and leaseholders; but beyond that he was not then prepared to go.* These were his notions of Reform as declared while as yet the prospect of their realization appeared to be distant; and by these he was disposed to abide in the main, now that events had unexpectedly brought men to the verge of a great and decisive struggle. He had not much faith in the efficacy of the ballot; but he was content to acquiesce in its being submit- 1831.

* Speech at county meeting held at Wigton, January, 1830.

1831. ted to the Cabinet for approval as a portion of the general scheme. His views respecting the county franchise were substantially adopted. A majority of the Cabinet ratified most of the recommendations of the Committee as presented to them in a report by Lord Durham. They struck out, however, the provision respecting the ballot, and fixed the borough franchise at a rent of £10 a year.

The King desirous of delay.

On the 30th of January Lord Grey waited upon the King at Brighton, and submitted to him the reasons in support of each part of the proposed bill. No material objection was raised by his Majesty; but the Premier was urged to defer any premature announcement of ministerial intentions on the subject, upon the ground that it was very desirable to avoid, if possible, any legislation of the kind during the Session. Lord Grey's self-love did him good service on the occasion. His susceptibility on the score of his own reputation for consistency and courage was awakened; and he gave the Sovereign to understand that it would be impossible for him to retain the government, failing to redeem the pledge on which he had undertaken it. William IV. well knew that it was too soon to think of another change of ministers, and did not press the point further at that time. A few days afterwards Parliament re-assembled, and Lord Althorpe announced that a measure of reform was in course of preparation, and that it would be introduced on the first of March. Upon that day, so memorable in parliamentary annals, Lord J. Russell laid before the House of Commons the ministerial design for its reconstruction. Great as were the anticipations formed of the project, it confessedly exceeded those alike of friends and foes. In the House itself, a fourth of whose members were to be deprived of their seats, for which they had paid prices so high, the prevalent feeling was one of mingled indignation and dismay. Out-of-doors there arose a shout of exultation, hushed for a moment by misgivings as to the persistency of Government in the course thus indicated, and then renewed again and again in a louder tone, as the conviction spread that the scheme was a reality, and would neither be compromised nor abandoned by its authors. Public meetings voted by acclamation thanks to the ministers for having proposed such a measure; and petitions in its favour daily covered the tables of both Houses. 1831.

Opinions of Sir R. Peel.

Within the walls of Parliament meanwhile the great controversy had begun. For seven nights the first reading of the bill was deferred,—threescore and ten speakers being animated by an irrepressible desire to expose the anomalies, or demonstrate the merits, of the plan. On the third night of the debate, Sir R. Peel explained the course which he meant to pursue. He disclaimed all objection in point of principle to the fair consideration of the question of Reform, and contented himself with

1831. taking exception to the specific provisions of the bill. Discarding alike the notion that the state of the representation then existing was better than any that could be devised, and the dogmatic assertion of any theory within whose inflexible limits constitutional changes ought to be made, he grappled courageously with the great difficulties of the measure, and sought to show the unsatisfactory results he believed it would practically entail. Great allowance must, in historic equity, be made for his position at the time. Four months had scarce elapsed since the pre-eminent chief of the party of resistance had staked and lost his hold of power, upon the principle of opposition to any substantial alteration in the electoral system. Sir Robert, indeed, had warily avoided endorsing that unwise declaration; but the bulk of his party had made it their watchword; and we now have the best evidence (that of the private letters of the Duke of Wellington himself) with what passionate earnestness he adhered to his memorable text.

The Duke inflexible.

Time had been fully given for re-considering the impracticability of resisting all concession; yet we find him declaring in March, 1831, his unaltered "conviction that the system of government, or rather no government, which the Whig Bill would establish, would, by due course of law, destroy the country; and he was therefore for opposing it without compromise of any description. He confessed he had never been able to see his way to the call of representatives from Birmingham, &c., without the infringement of some great principle by which the government of the country had hitherto been carried on. To disfranchise Old Sarum and Gatton would be equally inconsistent with the principle on which every charter, every property in the kingdom, was held." * A few days later the Duke wrote, "That there was no course open to him excepting to persevere in his opposition to the bill. He could see no reform, however moderate, that would not violate some principle; and he could not for the life of him see that any reform was necessary, excepting for the gratification of certain individuals. In his opinion the fault of which those were guilty who opposed the measure, was the admission that any reform was necessary. . . . He certainly never would enter the House of Lords from the time the bill passed. . . . He would not be degraded even with the House of Lords." † 1831.

Of these opinions Sir Robert Peel was not ignorant; and he had to choose between tacit acquiescence in them, when challenged in debate, or the enunciation of an independent policy of his own, the first effect of which must inevitably be to distract and weaken the Conservative party, who still looked

* Letter, 19th March, 1831. Memoirs of the Courts and Cabinets, &c., by the Duke of Buckingham: vol. i. p. 250.

† Ibid. p. 260.

1831. to the Duke as its head. But the right hon. baronet felt that the legitimate term of his subordinate service was past. Secondary office no longer had any charm for him, and he resolved to be premier or nothing. With the Ultras who had driven him from Oxford in 1829, because he would no longer thwart Catholic Emancipation, and who, in further vengeance, had driven him from Downing Street in 1830, he had broken for ever. His aim thenceforth was to re-constitute a great and powerful party upon principles of cautious concession. He saw it was vain to oppose the movement then in progress; but he knew that reaction would sooner or later set in, and that then his time would come. He had been seventeen years Secretary for Ireland and Secretary of State, and he was not unwilling to be relieved for a season from the cares of office, and to have more leisure for study and reflection than he had theretofore enjoyed. It was in this frame of mind that he proceeded to lay down the bases of his future policy; and though in many particulars he seemed still to cling to waifs and spars of the recent wreck, which he was soon content to let go, it cannot be denied, that in other respects, he chose well the materials for the raft on which he meant to float through the surge of the impending storm.

Moderate Conservatives. There were many influential members of Opposition who viewed an obstinate adherence to the policy of the Duke with despair. A majority of the people were certainly for Reform; and if a majority in the House of Commons should not be found in its favour on the second reading, a dissolution would inevitably furnish ministers with one in a new Parliament. The interposition of obstacles certain to be overborne could tend but to inflame popular passion, and to render a compromise more hopeless than ever. But if by wise and timely interposition, a counter-project could be placed before the eyes of the nation, dealing with many acknowledged abuses, and satisfying the claims of the great unrepresented towns, without altering generally the old franchises of the kingdom, many timid people of all classes would willingly accept the compromise, and the Court, which was already vacillating, would eagerly throw its weight into the Conservative scale. 1831.

Middle class constituencies.

The weightiest objection urged by Sir Robert Peel throughout the practical discussions on the bill, and that whose force more than one of the authors of the bill subsequently felt constrained to acknowledge, was the arbitrary concentration of electoral power in the hands of £10 householders in towns, and the disfranchisement to a great extent of those who belonged to the working classes. It was unhappily too true that the freemen of many boroughs had been convicted of habitual venality; and it was only right that some effort should be made to check the spread of corruption. But there was neither justice nor policy in legislating against whole classes of

1831. the community, not one man in twenty of whom had ever touched the unclean thing, on the plea that purity was indispensable to the well-working of a reformed representative system, and that by giving a virtual monopoly of power to the middle ranks of society, increased virtue would be attained. A very few years sufficed to prove how empty was the speculation in point of fact when the experiment was practically tried; and the ultimate relinquishment of the clauses disfranchising freemen indiscriminately, is a confession that the proposal was not regarded as really indispensable by its authors. Too many instances might be pointed out of new constituencies created by the Reform Bill exclusively of £10 householders, which have proved themselves as accessible to the arts of corruption as any of the old constituencies in which freemen predominated; and not a few of those who refused in 1831 to give heed to the expostulations of Sir R. Peel, have since been obliged to admit that if a remedy for electoral venality was the object of the invidious partiality shown to the £10 householder class, the cure ought to have been sought in another direction.

Disfranchisement of working classes.

Sir Robert Peel contended for the preservation in towns of a suffrage founded on the old principle, that whoever kept house and paid rates for a given time, ought to have a voice at elections, whether his scot and lot were great or small. There was in this a definite and intelligible principle, not theoretically unassailable, perhaps, but one that all could appreciate, as based on the acknowledged relation between liability to public burthens, and a constituent voice in the selection of those who imposed them. Lord J. Russell had told them that he found the ancient constitution of the country in 25 Edward I., and in the statute *De tallagio non concedendo*. But what did these statutes express? Simply that "taxes should not be levied without the consent of the commonalty of the realm." And then, argued the noble Lord, if reform be a question of right, which he held it to be, here was the right anciently established. If this were the right principle of the case, how far had the authors of this bill consulted it when they proposed to disfranchise so many thousands upon whom taxes were levied? The law justified no such distinction; yet they would at once disfranchise all tax-payers rated under £10. How could they justify this their distinction, particularly upon their own premises? Where was there here any regard to consistency or right? Great force lay in the argument urged by other constitutional reasoners in favour of retaining the principle of continuous residency, as a basis of the suffrage, more comprehensive and just than the payment for a few months of an arbitrary amount of rent. Rents and rates varied immensely in different places, and must always do so; whatever the nominal sum therefore might be, it would as a test be blundering and blind; as a mark of social 1831.

1831. discrimination partial and unjust. Such arguments were overborne at the time by the all-absorbing consideration, that as there was but one bidding for Reform, the country could not afford to refuse it. Sir Robert Peel, Lord Wharncliffe, and Mr Baring might have produced a better and more lasting scheme of franchise; but they could not have persuaded the bulk of their party at the time to agree to the general re-distribution of seats which ministers had proposed, and without which, once it was proposed, public feeling would not have been contented. No practical alternative was thus presented; it was the bill as drawn by the Committee of Four or nothing; and no bill meant revolution.

Speech of Sir James.

Sir James Graham denied that "ministers had laid themselves open to the charge implied by the language of the right hon. baronet (Sir Robert Peel) of cowering to taunts from the Opposition side of the House. They had never shrunk from the responsibility of bringing forward the measure, and still less had they ever wished to throw any of the responsibility on, or share any of the honour which he believed would accrue from the measure, with the members of the late ministry. He might entertain a private opinion as to the policy of the late ministers respecting that partial Parliamentary Reform, adopted by the House of Commons as fit and proper in the cases of Penrhyn and East Retford; but conceiving that reform to be inadequate, and that the country now needed a searching, substantial change, he, for one, could not regret

the course which had then been pursued. But this charge of 1831.
a disposition to avoid responsibility came with an ill grace from the right hon. gentleman, who had now abandoned the high ground taken up by the Duke of Wellington, the head of the administration of which Sir R. Peel formed a part: and who, admitting that some change was necessary, had not only not proposed any measure of his own, but had acted with the noble Duke, who had denied the utility of all reform. The Duke of Wellington contended that it was not the universal wish of the people to have reform, and that to suppose so was a vulgar error. The noble Duke also laid it down, that our present system of representation was so perfect, that the wit of man could not conceive anything more so, and that he could not fancy anything more excellent. But the right hon. baronet had departed from this principle; he had relinquished this high ground, and stated that to some measure for modifying the representation, not brought in on the responsibility of ministers, but on that of some other person—on the responsibility of some member in his individual capacity—to such a measure he would give a reluctant consent. The right hon. baronet must regret, he thought, that he brought forward such a charge, when he himself could not deny that there was a necessity for reform, and that there was no difference between them as to principle, but only as to degree. The only discussion could be, whether the step the ministers had taken was too great; for it being admitted that some change was necessary, their measure could only be blamed as too sweeping and extensive. So far from shrinking from responsibility, there was no responsibility connected with the measure which he, as an individual, had not incurred, and which the Cabinet had not taken on themselves. Considering it necessary, they had shrunk, indeed,

1831. from the responsibility of delaying the measure one day or one hour longer than was required to prepare it; and they thought it would have been unwise and unfair not to bring the measure under consideration, at their own risk, with the least possible delay. As far as he was concerned, he could say, both for himself and his colleagues, that they had not lost a single hour in bringing forward the measure. He was anxious to state, that they conceived it was not consistent with their duty to the public to bring forward any shifts, or temporizing schemes, or what Mr Burke emphatically called those miserable expedients — half measures; neither had they taken any indirect course for encouraging or for exciting the honest and just expression of the people's demand for reform. It was not consistent with the pledges they had given on accepting office, that they should nicely balance the means of redeeming the pledges they had made to the nation, or that they should devise plans barely and legally to redeem those pledges, cheating the people by the name of reform, but carrying no real reform into execution. Neither did they think that any justification could be found for delay. They had before them the example of Catholic emancipation — they saw the benefit of early concession — that delaying to concede just claims when resistance was possible, only led to more extensive demands, and ultimately to the necessity of making sweeping and unconditional concessions. It was inherent in the nature of things, that the refusal of just claims led to granting claims that at first no man dreamed of making. The reason too was obvious; when justice was denied, men became convinced that the authority that was capable of denying it was itself an injustice, and ought to be abated. Sir Robert Peel had argued that the measure was one which tended to deprive the lower classes

Danger of deferring concession.

of the people of the franchise which they had exercised, he said, much to the advantage of the country. He would venture to oppose to the assertion of the right hon. gentleman the broad principle laid down by a statesman who was deservedly considered as the very highest authority on constitutional law. Mr Fox asserted, 'that that was the best system of representation which secured to a country the largest number of persons whose circumstances were independent; and that system, on the contrary, was the worst, which embraced the largest number of voters, who, from being in dependant circumstances, were incapable of deliberation, and must act as they were commanded.' He might refer to opinions given by Sir R. Peel himself in 1828 in the case of Penrhyn. The right hon. baronet then laid down a doctrine to which he gave his cordial assent. He said, 'I agree that these privileges are not to be treated as the property of the electors; they involve considerations of public trust; and if they are abused by the majority of the electors the innocent parties must take the consequence of their association with the guilty.' He understood the distinction drawn between the present case and that of the violation of a trust; and if there were such a violation in the case of Penrhyn, there was none in the case of the 40*s*. freeholders. There had been no disposition even to refer to any former misconduct on their part. One honourable gentleman, indeed, said, that it had been given in evidence before a committee of that House, that they had been driven up to the hustings like oxen, and that they did not know for whom they were to vote. But between 1821 and 1829 an election had taken place, that of Clare, which proved emphatically that the 40*s*. freeholders had emancipated themselves from this thraldom, and

1831.

Middle class constituencies.

1831. that they were capable of exercising a deliberate judgment. The right hon. gentleman, in the able speech he made on the occasion, quoted a passage from Nathaniel Bacon, in which he cordially agreed. Bacon was speaking of the effect of the statute of Henry VI., by which the right of election, that before was vested in the whole commonalty, was restricted to the possessors of freeholds of 40*s*. value. 'This change was no less good than great. For, first, those times were no times for any great measure of civility. The meanest held himself as good a man as the greatest in the country, and this tended to parties, tumults, and bloodshed. Secondly, where the multitude prevail the meaner sort are on the upper hand, and these, generally ignorant, cannot judge of persons nor times; but being led by faction and affection, made their elections, and thereby the general council of the nation, less generous and noble,' etc. But if this example were thought too ancient, he contended, that a clear precedent for what was now proposed regarding the franchise of English towns, had been set by Sir R. Peel only two years before, in the act framed and carried by him for disfranchising great numbers of persons in Irish counties, and limiting electoral rights to persons possessing tenements worth £10 a year.

Nathaniel Bacon.

"Referring to the glowing eulogium of Sir R. Peel upon the dignity and reputation which the existing constitution enjoyed throughout the world, as the best practical means ever known for preserving the happiness and developing the strength of a nation, he (Sir James) would argue that so far from furnishing a reason against improvement and repair, such considerations furnished an additional ground for attempting to make them while there was yet time. The *Royal George* floated in harbour with all her sails set, every rope in

The Royal George.

its place, and every flag and streamer fluttering in the wind, every gun ready for use, and every disciplined mariner at his post, when in the midst of sunshine she had capsized and foundered. The right being clear, a glance at the actual state of the representation would, he thought, satisfy every reasonable man, that it was such as now required the efficient application of that right. It would be found that twenty-eight boroughs, the population of which were under 1000, sent 56 members to Parliament. There were ninety-seven boroughs where the electors did not exceed 100; nine where they were under 10; and twenty-seven where the number was between 10 and 25: these returned a great proportion of the representatives. Of all the boroughs enjoying the franchise there were 115, in none of which did the number of electors exceed 200. Although, therefore, all the borough electors were pure and independent men, the system brought into play a mere miserable fraction of the community. But how stood the fact as to their independence? Out of 221 borough members more than one-half, viz. 127, were nominated by 111 peers and commoners; 143 peers and commoners returned, in one way or other, 193 members; and it was capable of proof that there were 16 peers who filled, by their mere nomination, 76 seats in that House. Such was the cause of complaint on the part of the people; and no man who fairly considered the subject could come to any satisfactory conclusion but this,—that it was necessary to make a strenuous effort for the redress of so great a grievance. In applying himself to the remarks of Mr Croker upon the manner in which the line of disfranchisement had been drawn, he would admit that if ministers in drawing that line had been influenced by such feelings as appeared to be insinuated against them, then would they not only be un-

1831.

Statistics of Borough representation.

1831. worthy of the situation in which they were placed, but they would be unfit to associate with any body of private gentlemen. Ministers had acted, not from sinister views, but had proceeded on the principles of men of honour. He should surprise the House if he read the list of boroughs which must have been interfered with if ministers had drawn the line so as to affect Knaresborough, Tavistock, and Calne. Ministers had no other document to refer to than the statistical returns of the year 1821. He did not mean to say that it was a perfect document; he knew that it contained errors; but there was one advantage connected with it, namely, that its details were evidently favourable to the extension of the franchise. Now if the line had been drawn with reference to the population of Calne, they would have been obliged to disfranchise 11 other boroughs, namely, Malton, Newport, Andover, Grantham, Devizes, Hertford, St Albans, Dartmouth, Bridgewater, Pomfret, and Chippenham, each of which was smaller than Calne. If they had taken as the line of distinction the population of the borough of Knaresborough, they would have had to disfranchise, wholly or partially, 23 other boroughs, including Calne, Tavistock, Ripon, Chichester, Peterborough, Shrewsbury, Tewkesbury, and Barnstaple, which were inferior in extent to Knaresborough. Therefore it was that Calne, Tavistock, and Knaresborough were not interfered with; since, if ministers had included them in their plan they must have disfranchised a far greater number of boroughs than they thought it expedient to interfere with. He, however, was quite sure that, let ministers have drawn the line where they would, objections of a similar nature would have been advanced by those who were unfriendly to Reform. He founded himself in supporting the present proposition on the principle of justice, which was the groundwork of all good policy, and adhering to that at the same time that he did not overlook the signs of the times, he was thoroughly disposed to make this large concession. That it was calculated to remove the crown from the brow of the Sovereign, and shake the stability of the House of Peers, was contrary to all reason; for he could not understand how monarchy could be endangered by making it rest on the affections of a loyal people. On the contrary, all experience showed that the throne of England never ran the risk of invasion, much less of subversion, except when attempts were made forcibly to overbear the just wishes of the people, and to stifle their aspirations after liberty. That this reform would be a cure for all the evils which afflicted the country, he did not believe. But when Parliament should be freely chosen by the people, though it might not work for them all the benefits which they expected, yet they would know that all would be done for them that was possible; and they would then be more tranquil, more contented, and more peaceable; the government of the country would be put on a safer basis, for he knew none so safe as the extension of the suffrage to the most intelligent and industrious classes of the community." 1831.

This speech, though full of matter, and prepared with considerable care, was on all hands regarded as a failure. Great expectations had been formed of the strength the First Lord would bring to his friends in debate upon the question of questions; and proportionably great was their disappointment. His tone at the outset was as usual grave and imposing, and though the prefatory observations seemed needlessly diffuse, Impression made on the House

1831. he was supposed to be only clearing the ground for what was to follow, and that, his hearers did not doubt, would be striking and pointed, if not conclusive or original. In that crowded and excited House there were many whose convictions were still agitated by conflicting doubts as to the true policy to be pursued. There were Tories who could not make up their minds to refuse all Reform, and Whigs who trembled at the fearful consequences they heard daily predicted from what they had promised to concede. On both sides there were numerous waverers, and continually there proved to be not a few who shrunk from the responsibility of voting at all. It was emphatically an occasion, when a wise and eloquent speech might produce great effect; and no man assuredly had stronger incentives to do his best than Sir James. Yet he failed signally to impress either friends or foes in the manner he desired. His arguments in reply to Sir Robert Peel on the most important points, had in many respects been anticipated by Mr Stanley, whose vivacity and vigour contrasted favourably with his more ponderous and less telling replies. A great rhetorical effort was required to efface the impression made by the member for Tamworth on the fears and susceptibilities of the House: but the House listened for it in vain. As a retort in debate, the reiteration of Bacon's words was well enough in its way; but the legislative wisdom

of the sixteenth century seemed, after all, a dry 1831.
rotten beam to prop the new edifice, which, if it was to be reared for lasting use, must rest on more solid foundations. The one irresistible plea for some representative reconstruction was total change of circumstances and times. Since the period referred to, there was no blunder in social or political science which the Parliament of the Plantagenets had not committed with all the care of minute enactment and all the cruelty of penal law-making. They strove to settle by statute what every workman should have for his hire, and what every noble should spend on his dress; how the farmer should till his land, and the tradesman should buy his wares; handicraft, husbandry, commerce, and conscience, were each in turn made the subject of elaborate laws; and if the statute now relied on which concerned popular franchises must be read by the same discolouring light of feudal prejudice and passion, as that whereby other acts of the period were to be interpreted, the anomalous fact that while the freemen of the counties were thus summarily disfranchised, those of the towns were left undisturbed in the exercise of their privileges, might well have caused misgiving as to the reality of the philosophic motives assigned for so partial a change: if indeed the negative pregnant did not furnish an argument quite as good of precisely the opposite tenour. Still less to any practical purpose was it to quote

1831. the plausible generalities of Mr Fox about personal independence as the test of electoral eligibility. In an infinitely varied state of society no rule can be more superficial or unsound than one based on the assumed dependency or independency of certain great masses of men. A few links at opposite ends of the chain may be confidently referred to the antithetical conditions; but for the imperceptibly graduated links that lie between, who shall undertake to speak? It is not the social rank of a man's calling that affords a security against the pressure of pecuniary influence, nor the simplicity of a man's way of living or habits that renders him presumably servile or base. There is not a more helpless or pliant tool of improper influence at elections than the struggling tradesman, the young surgeon, the clerk at a hundred a year, or the decayed merchant whose trembling hold on the position of a gentleman in his native town depends on the humour of his banker. Talk of the dependency of the skilled artizan, with more work than he can do, and a choice of employers at thirty shillings a week: compared with any of these, he is both positively and relatively far better able to repel dictation or to resist menace; and, to his honour be it said, he frequently and unostentatiously does so. No one who has fought a contested election in a country town can fail to recollect instances illustrative of this truth. The question is not whether pecuniary independence be or be not desirable in the voter, but whether any form of law which can be devised will furnish a test of the fact. Calmness of judgment, habits of sobriety, and honesty of disposition are obviously desirable; but who pretends that any of these can be even inquired into under the provisions of a statute? Equally vain would be the attempt to fix by law who are and who are not liable to be swayed by the influence of others to vote contrary to their sense of what is right; and few will probably be found gravely to argue, that the occupancy of a £10 house or shop furnishes the much-desired dividing line between sturdy consistency and subserviency of soul. 1831

Working-class claims and interests, however, awakened little genuine sympathy in the House; and there were other topics by the skilful handling of which Sir James might have retrieved the failure of the first half-hour. But the consciousness that somehow or other he was not in the vein, had begun to creep over him. Abruptly, and as it would seem, without any very clear conception of what he wished to express, he betook himself to the high-flown language of imagery, evoked the spectre of the ill-fated man-of-war to which he likened the constitution; and after tediously dwelling on details until trope had been drawn into allegory, he seems to have lost the clue to extricate his obscure meaning, and, as was said by Sir Joseph Yorke, "when he let his ship go down, he capsized both his argument and his metaphor." After this unlucky passage, there was no apparent

Claims of the working classes.

1831. effort at recovery. He continued for some time to specify a number of details, some of them capable of being interwoven with effect in a well-composed and animated train of reasoning, but which, read from official papers in a low and dispirited tone, could not serve any other purpose at such a time and in such a place, than to betray how paralysing was his own consciousness that he had failed. There was, indeed, but one opinion on the subject among those present; and one of his colleagues is said to have declared that he wondered "how he could ever again have the face to look at the ivory ship in the hall of the Admiralty."

Second reading of the bill.

The Opposition were not yet sufficiently re-organized to venture on a division; but on the second reading it was resolved that the strength of parties should be tried; and after two nights' debate in a House of 608 members, ministers found themselves in a majority of only one.

General Gascoigne's motion.

Great was the exultation manifested by the Conservatives at this result, which virtually decided the defeat of the measure in the existing Parliament. The re-action so anxiously expected was said to have begun; and, in contemplation of its approaching triumph, certain of his former colleagues pressed Sir R. Peel to say whether he was ready to take part in a new administration. No definite answer could, however, be extracted from him, and his subsequent conduct showed that he read the signs of the times more discerningly than his sanguine friends. He was determined to prolong the contest in every form 1831. and to the latest moment; but he refused to abandon a defensive attitude, and rightly believed that any attempt at regaining power by the help of the Court, would only prove a signal for convulsion, by which the ministry and the Church would be put in imminent peril. To the majority of his party these views were not indeed revealed; and they confidently reckoned on his being borne willingly back to office as soon as a decisive vote of want of confidence should justify the King in getting rid of his Whig advisers. It was accordingly determined that upon going into Committee on the Reform Bill, a resolution should be moved declaring that the total number of members for England and Wales ought not to be reduced; and when accordingly an amendment to that effect was pressed to a division by General Gascoigne, Government were left in a minority of eight.

The question did not involve any of the fundamental principles of the Bill; and some of its sincerest supporters were in fact of opinion that the proportions settled by the acts of Union with Scotland and Ireland respectively, had better not be materially altered. Sir Robert Wilson, who had for years been a staunch friend of Reform, felt so strongly on the point that he promised to vote for the amendment; and though warned that he should thereby put in jeopardy his seat for Southwark, he

1831. kept his word, and was accordingly ousted a few weeks afterwards by Mr William Brougham. In the debate, however, of the 18th of April, Lord J. Russell stated that Government opposed the amendment, not only because they thought it intrinsically wrong, but because they knew that it was the first of a series intended to prevent the progress of the measure. An angry discussion ensued, in which reproaches and insinuations were more freely than ever interchanged; and at its conclusion the Reformers were beaten by 299 to 291. The public did not at first apprehend the full significance of this vote. Several popular journals even tried to convince their readers that it was rather a gain than a loss, inasmuch as the number of constituencies was in consequence certain to be greater than had been proposed. But a few hours' reflection served to convince nearly all that a decisive check had been given to the progress of the bill, and that the administrative existence of its authors was in danger. A dissolution as the only alternative became the one absorbing thought. Public meetings were hastily summoned to petition for it; and denunciations of the obstructive majority in Parliament waxed fiercer and more unqualified from hour to hour. General Gascoigne's motion was carried on Monday night; and on Wednesday morning the *Times* contained an article, showing by an analysis of the division, that it had only been carried by the votes of members for the rotten boroughs which the bill would have swept away. 1831.

"The unanimous enthusiasm of the people of England in defence of the national rights and liberties, was never so manifest within our recollection as on the present question of the Reform Bill: nor have we found recorded a single instance of rich and poor, high and low, men of all conditions, professions, and fortunes, feeling an equal sympathy in any cause, except, indeed, that of war against some hated public enemy. That enemy is now the usurper of the people's franchises, the cut-purse of the people's money,—the robber of the public treasury under the forms of law—of law enacted by the plunderer himself to favour his own extortion, his own systematic conversion of the fruits of other men's industry to selfish or criminal uses. When, night after night, borough nominees rise to infest the proceedings of the House of Commons with arguments to justify their own intrusion into it, and their continuance there, thus impudently maintaining what the lawyers call 'an adverse possession,' in spite of judgment against them, we really feel inclined to ask why the rightful owners of the House should be longer insulted by the presence of such unwelcome inmates? It is beyond question, a piece of the broadest and coolest effrontery in the world, for

Articles in the *Times*.

1831. these hired lacqueys of public delinquents to stand up as advocates of the disgraceful service they have embarked in."

Sir Robert Inglis brought this article under the notice of the House as a breach of privilege on the following day, and moved that the printer be summoned to the bar. It was palpable, he said, that the object of the press was to overawe the freedom of debate, and to degrade the existing legislature in the judgment of the community.

Question of privilege.

Sir J. Graham said, "In his opinion, when great questions were agitated in that House, much latitude ought to be allowed to the press in discussing them on both sides. And he would ask, was the public expression of feeling and opinion on this occasion confined to one side only? He made no complaint individually on that score; yet, week after week, Sunday after Sunday, some good-natured friend of his, who he supposed had recently left the warm precincts of office, not without casting 'a longing, lingering look behind,' assailed him with the interrogatories,—What will they say to this at Cockermouth? What could he (the member for Cumberland) say to his constituents on such and such a point? * He had been constantly vilified, his motives misrepresented, and his public conduct

* The allusion was understood to be to articles in the *John Bull*, over which Lord Lowther was said to exercise particular influence.

passed in unfair and unjust review; but did he complain? Far from it. Such strictures operated only as a stimulus to make him the more sedulously attend to the duties of his office. They only impelled him to discharge those duties fairly and fearlessly, in the manner which appeared to him most likely to prove beneficial to the country. If a course of severity were adopted with reference to one side, it would be wholly impossible in common justice not to visit with like penalties those who stigmatized the measure introduced by ministers as revolutionary, and who abused, in the foulest manner, those who supported it, as individuals who wished to overturn the Constitution. There was, he admitted, a strong feeling on this subject out of doors, but he maintained that language equally violent and pointed had been used within the walls of the House. If, however, these attacks were to be taken as questions of privilege on one side, they were equally so on the other; and those who would punish the newspapers for what they might consider libels, would be bound themselves to abstain from many of those observations which had been used but too freely in the course of the debates on Reform. It would then be their bounden duty to suppress all those passages in the speeches of members which stigmatized the measure of Reform now proposed by the ministers, under the sanction of the Sovereign, as tending to bring about a revolution. Why, it was but the

1831.

1831. other evening in the course of the discussion, that the late Secretary at War (Sir H. Hardinge) declared that the Reform Bill would, if carried, shake the Crown from the head of the Sovereign. That sentiment had been since repeated in the House, and echoed in the newspapers, and yet no one on that side of the House had thought of treating it as a breach of privilege, or an invasion of the right of free discussion. Better at once shut up the gallery of that House, and proclaim to the world by a rigid enforcement of the standing orders that no strangers should be admitted, and that no account of their proceedings should go forth to the public. They might as well put an end at once to all free discussion as attempt by a proceeding like that recommended by the hon. baronet (Sir R. Inglis) to endeavour to prescribe the limits within which it was to be carried on. If he were himself called on to express an opinion on the subject of the article in the *Times*, he would say that he could not defend it; but he called on them, at the same time, before dealing with this question in the manner proposed, to consider that they were a deliberative assembly, and that they could not as parties exercise a sound discretion in the capacity of judges." *

The crisis. A similar motion was made the same day in the Peers by Lord Wyndford, in which the right was claimed for both Houses by Lord Tenterden to visit with

* Hansard, vol. iii. p. 619.

fine and imprisonment at their discretion all who should publish libels on the honour and dignity of Parliament. The Chancellor warmly protested against a doctrine so unconstitutional; and in neither House did the threatened proceedings against the press come to anything. They contributed nevertheless to inflame in no slight degree the popular feeling; and thus injured the cause they were designed to serve. 1831.

Defeat of Ministers.

Matters were brought to a crisis on the night of the 21st, in a manner which neither party probably had foreseen. The greater part of the evening had been wasted in the Commons, in desultory wrangling about privilege, election petitions, and what not; and towards its close Mr Bankes moved that the House, not the debate, should be adjourned. The object of this was to prevent the House going into Committee of Supply, and thus to defer the report being taken on the Ordnance estimates. Lord Althorpe declared plainly that by taking this step all public business would be brought to a stand, and he remonstrated earnestly against a course so unusual and uncalled-for. The adjournment notwithstanding was carried by a majority of 22; and ministers were then left no choice but to insist on a dissolution, or to resign. A Cabinet was held early on Friday morning, and Lords Grey and Brougham waited on the King to submit the unanimous result of their deliberations. Notice had been 22nd April.

1831. given in the Upper House by Lord Wharncliffe of an address praying his Majesty not to dissolve Parliament; and as it was certain to be carried by a large majority, the wavering mind of William IV. would, in all likelihood, see in it a reason for not exercising the royal prerogative. A few hours therefore would make all the difference; and the Premier and the

Interview with the King.

Chancellor told the King that if they were to remain his servants, Parliament must be prorogued that day with a view to its immediate dissolution. His Majesty raised numerous objections, and said the necessary preparations had not been made. Lord Brougham assured him that every requisite arrangement was in progress, and that no difficulty on that head would arise. "But the Guards," said the King, "they have not had notice, and I cannot go down to Westminster without them." "Pardon me, Sire," replied the Chancellor, "we know how bold the step is, that, presuming on your great goodness and your anxious desire for the safety of your kingdom and happiness of your people, we have presumed to take,—I have given orders, and the troops are ready." * The Sovereign, startled at this announcement, asked how they had dared so to act; and whether the Chancellor was not well aware that this was treason? The Keeper of the Great Seal frankly owned that in ordinary circumstances it might be so considered; but he and his colleagues felt that upon that day's pro-

* Roebuck's History of the Whigs, vol. ii. p. 151.

ceedings hung the peace of the realm and the security of the Crown. He was willing to bear individually all the blame of what had been done; but he conjured the King to listen to and follow the counsel that had been given him. Lord Grey assured him that with the existing Parliament he could not go on; and William IV. was well aware that a Tory administration could not at that moment be formed, capable of carrying on the government. He yielded, therefore, a reluctant assent, and the same afternoon Parliament was dissolved. 1831.

CHAPTER XI.

THE SECOND AND THIRD REFORM BILL.

1831.

1831.

Contest for Cumberland.

PREPARATIONS were now made throughout all parts of the kingdom to take advantage of the opportunity thus afforded, of securing a majority in the House of Commons favourable to Reform. The instincts of self-preservation would, of course, impel the many constituencies that were menaced with total or partial disfranchisement to return men who would defend their privileges; and the vast preponderance of territorial influence was arrayed on the same side. It was necessary therefore that every nerve should be strained, and every seat contested, that there seemed to be a chance of winning by means of the extraordinary excitement that prevailed, if the object of popular wishes were to be secured by constitutional means. Places that hitherto had been regarded as incontestable, were accordingly made the scenes of unaccustomed conflict; and wherever the tradition lingered of a friend of Fox having been formerly returned, it was resolved to try whether a disciple of his political school might not again head the poll. 1831.

In Westmoreland, Yorkshire, Durham, and Northumberland, the presage of electoral conflict was loud: and all Cumberland was astir. More than ten years dah passed since the representation had been disputed, and the recollection of what had then occurred did not encourage the idea that Lord Lonsdale's influence could be successfully encountered by a second Liberal. But it was not a day of nice calculation. Men's blood was running at fever pace, and they were no longer capable of weighing difficulties or counting cost, or of explaining to one another how what they wanted was to be done. All they could tell was, that nine out of every ten men were bent on accomplishing it, the surest, if not the only, talisman for the accomplishment of logically demonstrable impossibilities. The return of a second Whig for Cumberland had hitherto been accounted such; and such it unquestionably still looked to Sir James Graham, who for the fourth time addressed the constituency. Before he could leave London, news arrived that the "Blues" meant to try whether they could not carry two Reformers for Cumberland, and that they meditated putting up Mr Blamire of Thackwood Nook as the second candidate. On being referred to, Sir James expressed great doubts

1831. as to the possibility of success, knowing as he did the vast territorial influence of the family of Lowther, and believing, as he was justified in doing, that that influence would be strained to the utmost to resist their entire exclusion from the representation. Some apprehension naturally suggested itself to his friends in London, that in the attempt to carry both seats his might be put in jeopardy, and the question was repeatedly asked, who was Mr Blamire, and what was his position and calling? "He is a very good fellow," was the reply, "who farms a small estate of his own; beyond that, I know of no other pursuit he has except horse-dealing; but don't be alarmed," he added laughingly, "he is not going to ride over me." It was nevertheless no laughing matter. Though in jest he might thus speak of him, Mr Blamire was not a man whom Sir James was disposed to make little of, either publicly or in private. His property was indeed not large, but his personal energy and worth had long given him a position of influence in the county. In 1828, his nomination to the Shrievalty had been made the occasion of a display of feeling on the part of the squirearchy and yeomanry almost without precedent. The fact was dwelt upon by Sir James in a speech made at a public dinner given him at the time. His support, on the other hand, had been at both the former elections cordially rendered to the master of Netherby, and he had been specially chosen to occupy the chair at the Dalston

Character of Mr Blamire.

dinner. In proposing his health on that occasion, Sir James had declared that "there was no one who possessed more entirely his confidence, or to whom he was under greater obligations. Fears had sometimes been expressed of disunion between the gentry and yeomanry of the county; but this seemed impossible whilst such a connecting link between these two classes was formed by his hon. friend, who lived on terms of intimacy with both, and was the friend of both,—a gentleman who had innumerable claims upon their consideration and regard." It would have been as ungracious as impolitic, therefore, to alienate such a man; and while the First Lord of the Admiralty could not help thinking it rash to bring forward Mr Blamire as a candidate, he had certainly no wish to offend him. 1831.

Conference at Carlisle.

On arriving at Carlisle, he met the heads of the Liberal party in the county, most of whom were already pledged "to go for Blamire." A long and exciting discussion took place, Sir James wrestling in argument with one after another of his best supporters, whose enthusiasm in the cause had blinded them, he thought, to the electoral strength of the outworks of Lowther Castle. "It will never surrender," he said, "to mere shouts or threats: and where are your resources should it resist? Won or lost, a contest must be a very expensive affair; and, if Mr Blamire or his friends are not prepared to meet it, on whom is it to fall? Am I to carry Blamire on

1831. my back?" The question was answered by Mr John Graham, a well known and worthy resident of Carlisle, who exclaimed, "Take care, Sir James, that Blamire hasn't to carry thee on his back." A laugh and a cheer followed this sally. The dignity of the First Lord was ruffled for the moment; but his good sense quickly pointed out the expediency of giving way to the course his party was obviously bent on pursuing, and once he gave his assent, he had too much tact not to do so thoroughly. Cordial union and a joint canvass was speedily agreed on. The Tories had first despised and then defied the effort to bring in Blamire; but they deemed it wise not to start a second candidate on their side, persuaded that many would split their votes with Lord Lowther and one of the Liberals, and that thereby jealousy and division would be sown between them.

County Requisition.

Meanwhile an address signed by several hundred electors called on the constituency to support Mr Blamire, the nephew of John Christian Curwen, who had spent £100,000 in sustaining local independence, and the grand-nephew of Mr Henry Curwen, who had fought the memorable county battle of 1768. The requisitionists declared that Sir James Graham had fully redeemed the pledges he had formerly given them, and asserted their unabated confidence in him. But they expressed their earnest hope and expectation that he would cordially coalesce with Mr Blamire, remembering that he owed his own return to the independent yeomanry and middle class, who were now determined to place by his side in Parliament a man worthy to be his colleague, and one who would faithfully act upon the same principles. They further declared that they would disregard any disclaimer on the part of Mr Blamire, and that they were resolved to carry his election free of expense. 1831.

A subscription was forthwith opened, and a considerable sum was raised. But the main contributions which the 'statesmen and small freeholders were able and willing to give, consisted in their refusal to put their new candidate to any needless outlay for travelling charges or refreshment. Individual assurances to this effect were hardly perhaps believed, and old electioneerers smiled incredulously when they were made. But in the multitude of simultaneous promises there is safety; and the pledges which scores would have broken, many hundreds kept.

Popularity of Mr Blamire.

Throughout the entire county intense excitement prevailed. Long before the day of election arrived, the one engrossing topic was the coming struggle. "As soon as the packman arrived in the village he was surrounded by an eager group of politicians, to whom he retailed, with his blue ribbons and neck-ties, the news of the efforts making elsewhere for the return of the champions of Reform." Every scrap of information was seized on with avidity and earnestly discussed on all opportunities. The personal popularity of the

1831. new candidate was great among the 'statesmen. "Those who perchance had seen Blamire at their 'ingle-nooks,' or wooden settle, partaking of their homely fare of milk and barley-bannock, used to say 'he was a born farmer, aye, and every inch a gentleman.'"* In the prevalent enthusiasm, yeomen and tradesmen seemed alike to feel that the success of the popular cause rested solely on their individual exertions. The women were all for the "Blues," and even the children learnt to cry "Graham and Blamire." The only polling place in those days was Cockermouth: and many still remember the stirring scenes of turmoil and triumph that marked those bright days of May. From the hill-girt lakes, from the sea-port towns, from the moors, from the mines, gay and motley parties in quaint attire thronged the roads. Every horse and vehicle, every gig and "drosky," every market-cart and jaunting-car, was pressed into the service, and the eyes of many an humble freeholder, who wended his way on foot from sequestered valley or hill-side, were raised in wonder at the varied forms of "trundling-kist"† in which their wealthier neighbours passed them by. The journey to the county-town was one continuous ovation. Every village had its May-pole with its garlands and flying streamers. Grey coat and broad cloth mingled in the throng. Here was seen "the gaudy neck-tie and

* Dr Lonsdale's Biographical Sketch of W. Blamire, Esq., p. 20.

† Carriage or post-chaise.

the gaudier vest, coat of skirt immense, and pockets unfathomable, the knee breeches, and brown tops and spurs and ponderous whip; and there the aspiring youth (Young Cumberland of that day) with blue surtout and gilt buttons. All rode together and fraternized at the well-known hostelries on the road, and there formed pictures worthy of the pencil of Hogarth and the pen of Defoe." * Some came from the confines of Durham, and others from the neighbourhood of the Border, forty miles distant and upwards. Large numbers of colliers were brought from Whitehaven to vote for the Tories. But the utmost efforts of the party, backed by all the influence of the proprietory and clergy, were unable to secure the promises of more than one-fifth of the constituency. 1831.

Result of the canvass.

The results of the Liberal canvass made it clear that a decided majority of the electors might be relied on to vote for both candidates. In such cases, there are always overwise persons perplexed with misgivings, and prone to torment others with their groundless fears. Mr Blamire, it was whispered, might head Sir James on the poll. The moment he did so the Tories would give him their split votes, and thus secure the defeat of the First Lord of the Admiralty. The cause of Reform was bound up in the sustainment of the ministers who proposed it; and if the second seat could not be secured, care

* Memoirs of Blamire, p. 22.

1831. ought, at least, to be taken that the first should be filled by the right hon. baronet. Mr Blamire himself suggested the adoption of means for quenching these doubts; and with a feeling that did him honour, he suggested that the joint committee should take care that if, at the poll, the numbers were not the same for both, the preference at the close of each day should be secured for Sir James. He sought, moreover, an interview with Lady Graham, and told her that if through any cause her husband's return should seem to be in danger, he had made up his own mind to retire from the contest in time to prevent an adverse result.

The hustings at Cockermouth.

The election took place on the 5th of May. Early in the day Sir James and Mr Blamire, accompanied by a large concourse of mounted freeholders, entered Cockermouth, which had never been so full before. In his address from the hustings, the First Lord directed attention to the vague and indefinite nature of the promises put forth by his rival, Lord Lowther; and counselled them to draw from his Lordship a more certain and particular statement of his political principles, especially with regard to Reform. Was he for schedule A or schedule B, and what measure of extended franchise was he prepared to yield? The show of hands was declared to be in favour of the Liberals; and the friends of Lord Lowther forthwith demanded a poll. At the end of the day the numbers were respectively, for Sir J.

Graham, 218; for Mr Blamire, 215; and for Lord Lowther, 71. Upon the announcement, Lord Lowther declared that he was not discouraged; "he had had adverse winds to contend with, but he hoped on the morrow he should be able to bring up lee-way." The morrow came, but the weather had not changed. The popular candidates started at an early hour for the Whitehaven district, and after canvassing there all day, returned in the evening, to be hailed with the announcement that the triumph of their cause was all but complete. The numbers then stood, for Sir J. Graham, 542; Mr Blamire, 532; Lord Lowther, 236. When the cheering had subsided, the right hon. baronet said, "I appear before you as a culprit, and I am ready to acknowledge my offence. I have committed a wilful trespass to-day; I have been on a poaching excursion among the Yellow preserves,—I have been at Whitehaven this morning. But I went not alone; I took a comrade with me; we sported with a double-barrelled gun, and at every rise we brought down a brace." With a passing joke about what had been said of lee-way, and the heavy sailing qualities of the *Lowther Castle*, he adverted to the rumoured indecision of Lord Lowther, up to the last moment, as to which county he really meant to stand for. "Let me say a word or two about Westmoreland. You all know that the noble lord is a great gallant amongst the ladies; but I have found out that he is a libertine

1831. 6th May.

1831. in his way; for I find that he has been courting two sisters at once. Not content with the possession of one, he turns her off, and courts another sister. On the 27th of April he makes love to the younger sister in Westmoreland, pours out with unmeasured ardour professions of unalterable attachment to his affianced bride; but, ah! false swain, within three days he abandons her, and makes love to the Blue-eyed Maiden of Cumberland. But, if I mistake not, neither his gold nor his professions will win her. I, as a married man, may be deemed a fair umpire in the case. There are two bachelors contending for this charming buxom lass—this Blue-eyed Maid of Cumberland; the one with all the glittering attractions that gold can purchase, to dazzle the eye and to ensnare the heart,—the other with but a disinterested affection, and an anxious disposition to minister to her comforts and her wishes, but unaccompanied with the appendages of wealth. He is the one to whom she will give her hand; he is the one in whom she will confide; she will scorn the heart that offers wealth as a pledge of its sincerity, and tell the noble lord that gold is of no avail. He must return to the forsaken sister in Westmoreland, whom he would have turned over to some ready friend."

The Blue-eyed Maid of Cumberland.

7th May. On the third day (Saturday), the Conservatives put forth their most strenuous efforts; but the scale was not to be turned. The aggregate numbers on that evening proved to be, for Sir James Graham,

942; Mr Blamire, 917; Lord Lowther, 453. Further contest was now clearly useless; and Mr W. Holmes, the Tory whipper-in, advised Lord Lowther to withdraw. His Lordship had taken no little offence at some of the observations regarding him upon the hustings which had fallen from Sir James; and appeared to have been particularly annoyed at the way in which his name was associated with certain paragraphs in the *John Bull* newspaper. By his desire Mr Holmes waited on Sir James, at Brayton, the residence of his brother-in-law, Sir Wilfred Lawson, to demand an explanation. The words complained of were in point of fact generally understood to have been used in the spirit of banter, for which license has always been given and taken by opponents at elections; and the successful candidate did not hesitate to give an assurance upon this head which Mr Holmes accepted as satisfactory. Curiously enough, the sort of connection with which the right hon. baronet had twitted Lord Lowther, existed at the time between himself and another public journal. The *Carlisle Patriot* had been established by means of a joint-stock fund in 1815; Dean Milner had written the prospectus, and the former possessor of Netherby being one of the original proprietors, his shares had devoled at his death to his son. While he occupied an independent station in public life, the discrepancy between his opinions and those of

1831.

Retirement of Lord Lowther.

1831. the journal gave him little concern; but upon his taking office the case was altered. The circumstance of his holding a nominal share in the paper was locally well known; and although he neither had the power nor the wish to influence its political tone, he did not conceal his annoyance at the frankness with which many acts of the Government had been criticized in its columns. He willingly availed himself therefore of an offer made by the editor, Mr Ramsay, to purchase his shares: and thus he relieved himself from a position that on both sides was felt to be embarrassing.

Majority of Reformers in new House.

In Carlisle two Reformers were returned as well as in the county; and throughout the kingdom the expression of opinion was decisive in favour of the bill. Four members pledged to its support were returned for Yorkshire, and as many for the city of London. Sir T. Acland, Mr Bankes, and Sir E. Knatchbull lost their seats; and in nearly all the counties Liberals were returned. At Liverpool General Gascoigne was defeated; and at Newark the Duke of Newcastle was unable "to do what he would with his own." In Ireland and Scotland the results were similar; and ministers could boast of more than one hundred majority in the new House of Commons. A great opportunity presented itself on the reconstruction of the Reform Bill, not only of amending its original faults, but of initiating, in the true and comprehensive sense of the term, a system of imperial legislation. The inherent defects of the first bill were suffered unhappily to remain uncorrected in the second. Instead of one general measure for the United Kingdom, three separate measures had been framed in January, and were now re-produced in June; and instead of an attempt being made to provide for the representative claims of all classes of the people, the former sharp line of distinction was still retained. Ireland and Scotland were dealt with as if they did not form parts of one united realm; and four-fifths of the population of all three countries were as wholly excluded from the benefit of electoral rights, as the middle classes of the manufacturing towns had previously been. The prejudices of race and the prejudices of class conspired to render imperfect and inconclusive the scheme of 1831; and they effectually prevented its becoming what it might have certainly been made, a permanent bond of union between the three constituent elements of the empire, and a symbol of reciprocal confidence and trust between the three great sections of society,—that which subsists on realized property, that which subsists on the profits of industry, and that which subsists on the wages of labour. The owners of property had heretofore enjoyed a virtual monopoly of representation. The industrious middle classes were now offered a share of the great privileges of freedom; but the working classes were not merely left out of

1831.

Fundamental defects in the Reform Bill.

1831. the pale of the new franchise about to be created by the £10 clause, but they were, to no inconsiderable extent, thrust out of their old and imperfect rights as residents and rate-payers. Lord Brougham and Lord Durham were fully conscious of the shortcomings of the plan in this respect; and they would willingly have obviated them had they possessed the power. Sir J. Graham and Lord Duncannon were equally alive to the mischief likely to ensue, from keeping up the anomalous distinctions between the three portions of the empire. They reasoned unanswerably that the true way to quench ideas of legislative secession, was to obliterate from the statute book in all essentials of right and privilege, the invidious distinctions which practically rendered legislative union an elaborate lie.

Three bills instead of one.

The demand for Repeal had for the moment been hushed in Ireland, by the desire for Reform; and no one lent his influence and eloquence more unreservedly than Mr O'Connell, to secure its triumph. Then was the time to have proved the sincerity of the oft-repeated pledge that the two countries were to be governed by the same laws and in the same spirit; and no method would have been so easy or certain of success, as the enactment of one measure of Reform for the United Kingdom. It was on all hands admitted that the relative proportions, fixed by the Acts of Union with Scotland and Ireland respectively, required revision. They had been founded on estimates of relative population and revenue, which in the lapse of years had ceased to be true; and by the three bills introduced by ministers, the actual and relative number of representatives to be sent by each country to Parliament, were thenceforth to be changed. All this might have easily been set forth and enacted, in one or two introductory clauses of a single comprehensive measure: and the general provisions conferring the right of suffrage would (with certain adaptations to local circumstances,) have naturally followed. But the majority of the Cabinet would listen to no suggestion of the kind. They looked with undisguised apprehension and aversion on the dissemination of political rights, among even the educated portions of the operative class; and though they had made much ado two years before, about the disfranchisement of the forty-shilling freeholders of Ireland, they inflexibly persisted in limiting Reform for that country within pecuniary conditions, which in the course of a few years reduced the constituencies to numbers, which Mr Pitt and Lord Castlereagh would have been ashamed to defend.

1831.

Exclusion of working classes.

It may no doubt be said that those whose interests were neglected or compromised in the manner referred to made no attempt to exact terms, or to frustrate the second Reform Bill. This is indeed most true, but it touches not the point of the argument in either case. It was not the policy

1831. of Mr O'Connell to urge the adoption of legislative forms which would have constituted new impediments in his way, whenever he should revert to his proposal of Repeal; and the working classes were beguiled into the belief, that the measure then pending was but the opening of one half of a folding door, and that those who should enter thereby, would be certain from within to open for them the other. Without stipulation or bargain of any sort, the great bulk of the people zealously joined in obtaining for the £10 householders what they required; and the popular feeling in favour of the bill, which was reintroduced on the 23rd June by Lord J. Russell, was unchilled by disunion or distrust. The details of its progress belong to history rather than biography, and need not even in outline be recapitulated here.

Conduct of Opposition. Had the Opposition, instead of resorting to vain and vexatious delays, endeavoured by wise and generous amendments to shadow forth another scheme of Reform, less partial in its character, they might have possibly divided the strength of the majority; * and they would, in all probability, have given a different direction to the course of public affairs. But after the decisive vote on the second reading, which was carried by 367 to 231, their sole purpose

* The majority of 232 to 148, by which Lord Chandos carried the £50 tenant-at-will clause against ministers, shows what might have been done.

appears to have been to protract indefinitely, the discussion of each subordinate provision, in the hope that the tide of opinion out of doors might turn, and that their prophecies of the flood-gates of anarchy and ruin about to be opened by the measure, would come at last to be believed. Not only Sir C. Wetherell and Mr Croker, but Sir R. Peel himself, continually indulged in such anticipations. The common sense of the community rightly discerned how groundless and unreasonable they were, but it erred in supposing them therefore to be false or feigned. There cannot be a doubt that the great bulk of the Conservative party had suffered themselves to be talked into a dread at this time, that the foundations of society were about to be disturbed, and that the existence of all the established institutions of the country would be placed in imminent peril by the reduction of the number of rotten boroughs, and the concession of a £10 franchise. It is very hard now to realize the fact, or to understand how a man like Sir R. Peel should have devoted his best energies to diffuse and inflame such fears. But the records of Parliament tell us, that after many a summer evening and autumn night had been consumed, in futile efforts to delay its progress through the Commons, the second Reform Bill was sent up to the Lords.

1831. 22nd Sept.

What will the Lords do?

"What will the Lords do?" was now the question put by every man to his neighbour. A certain

1831. section, of whom Lords Harrowby and Wharncliffe were the chief spokesmen, had from the first, professed themselves to be in favour of some concession. They had reckoned perhaps on material changes being made by the Commons in committee, and they hoped that upon these they should be able to build up a scheme of compromise. But as the measure stood substantially unmodified, they shrunk from the reproach of deserting the bulk of their party; and as those who sympathized with them in the other House had voted there, so they made up their minds to aid the Duke in throwing out the bill.

Proposal to create new Peers.

In the interval which took place between the first and second reading of the bill in the Lords, the Cabinet discussed more than once the project of the Chancellor, for the creation of peers. The Duke of Wellington was said to calculate upon having a majority of sixty against the bill: less than that number, therefore, would not do. For this, Lord Durham avowed himself prepared; but few of his colleagues were of his mind, and many of them clung to the belief that without resorting to such an alternative, the Upper House would yield. To quicken their conversion, the First Lord of the Admiralty suggested a middle course. He proposed that the King should be asked to create a "small batch at first, in order to convince the Peers that ministers had the power and were prepared to exercise it." *

* Roebuck, Hist. of Whigs, vol. ii. p. 224.

But even from this tentative expedient the Premier shrunk, and nothing was decided on. 1831.

While things remained in suspense, a letter was addressed to Major Aglionby by Sir James, which, though it has immediate reference to subjects of local interest in Cumberland, betrays the deep anxiety with which he awaited the decision of the Peers.

"*Private.*

"*Admiralty,*
October 1st, 1831.

"MY DEAR SIR,

"I am very much obliged by your kind and friendly letter. I should have indeed rejoiced if I could visit Cumberland at the time of the sessions; and having laboured hard with you to reduce the debt and expenditure of the county, I should have been proud to reap the fruit of that labour, and of our unflinching economy, by the attainment of the object ever in view, which has been a large reduction of the county rate. The right measure, however, will be taken; and comparatively, it matters little with whom the credit of it may rest. I only hope that the reduction will be sufficiently large to make a sensible difference to the rate-payer, and greatly to diminish the income of the county; since, if public money be raised, it is always spent, and the only sure mode of diminishing expenditure is stopping the supplies. When the county hereafter engages in new and extravagant works, let the burthen be felt at once in the shape of an additional rate, and not [eased] by contracting debt; and the advocates for prodigal outlay will soon become few, and be easily overborne by the weight of public opinion. It is impossible for me to leave

1831. town for a single day. If the Lords reject the bill, which I fear is probable, we have arrived at the crisis of our fate, and the country is on the verge of portentous events. I cannot quit my post at such a moment, and every personal consideration must give way to what is due to my colleagues and my country.

"With sincere regard, and a grateful recollection of your constant friendship,

"I ever am very truly yours,

"J. R. G. GRAHAM."

On the 8th October, the Lords, after a long and memorable debate, by 199 to 158, rejected the ministerial measure; and thus ended the second Reform Bill.

Popular outbreaks. In London next day many of the shops were closed, and the public securities fell. The event came upon few persons by surprise; yet the effect produced throughout the country, was one of panic and excitement without a parallel in our day. To forebodings of political change of a revolutionary character, were added grave misgivings as to tumult and disorder: and when the intelligence that Nottingham Castle had been sacked and burnt was quickly followed by the tidings that Bristol was the scene of disorder, and that it had with difficulty been saved from destruction by fire, the best and wisest for a moment felt their confidence shaken. But nothing is more certain than that the mass of the community never sympathized in these acts of turbulence and brigandage. Had an anarchic spirit really prevailed at the time, there existed no armed force at the disposal of Government adequate to suppress it. The number of troops in the realm, scattered as they were in remote stations, would have been wholly insufficient to protect the capital and the great towns. Projects were put forward for the enrolment without delay of a general civic guard. 1831.

Fears of the King.

The terror of the Court was intense; and it was aggravated by the fear that Lord Grey and his colleagues would either resign or keep Parliament sitting. A vote of confidence, moved by Lord Ebrington and carried by 329 to 198 in the Commons, three days after the hostile vote of the Lords, exonerated them from adopting the former course; and their genuine reluctance to feed the rising flame of popular commotion, deterred them from pursuing the latter. Had they been animated by the feelings or purposes of the leaders of 1641, they would probably have acted otherwise; and virtually, if not in terms, have declared the sittings of that assembly permanent, which, recently returned by the enthusiasm of the nation, vibrated with every change in the feverish pulse of opinion. But the Cabinet of 1831 were wholly different men; and though their party antagonists would not, or could not, be brought to believe it, they were at heart quite as anxious as themselves to preserve intact the old institutions of the State. They ventured indeed, as Sir James

1831. Graham said, "to drive nearer the brink than any had ever done before; but they did so because if they let go the reins, the horses would be maddened into plunging headlong into the abyss whence extrication would be impossible."

William IV. assured ministers that he should regard it as a great misfortune if they abandoned their posts; or relinquished the hope of modifying their measure so as to obviate in part the objections of their opponents. Parliament was prorogued on the 22nd October, to be re-assembled before Christmas; and in the interim the Cabinet had to consider how much should be yielded for sake of effecting a speedy settlement, and what expedients should be resorted to in case all efforts at compromise failed. Because the middle classes were thoroughly averse from threats of violence or tumult, they heard with uneasiness the resolves of the political unions not to pay taxes, should the Peers again throw out the bill; and they consequently looked to the Government to devise some means whereby matters should be prevented from coming to extremities.

A creation of Peers resolved on.

From every side the suggestion came that to carry the bill there should be a creation of Peers. The King had early foreseen that to this alternative things might drift; and long before it ever was proposed to him, he took pains to convince his ministerial advisers that he never would agree to it. His repugnance was shared by the Premier and the

Duke of Richmond, by Lords Melbourne, Goderich, and Palmerston. Of the opposite opinion were Lords Althorpe and Durham, the Chancellor and Sir J. Graham. When first the question was mooted, there seemed to be no chance of arriving at any agreement. Less than forty would not suffice to turn the adverse scale, and there was the hazard that some lukewarm adherents would take offence at so arbitrary a use of the prerogative, and consequently withdraw their support. The expedient was confessedly one irreconcilably at variance with Whig principles, and one which, once sanctioned by success, would in periods of crisis, render the power of the Crown superior to the constitutional will of Parliament. Yet something must be done; and if not this, then what? In a paper laid before the Cabinet, the Lord Privy Seal discussed at length the probable consequences of making a large addition to the peerage, and sought to prove that no important defection need be apprehended from the ministerial ranks, provided the step were taken only in the last resort, and palpably for the sake of saving from destruction the hereditary chamber. His arguments satisfied some, and staggered the resolve of others; and finally, Lord Grey was authorized to ask his Majesty at once to make a limited number of Peers, as had been originally recommended by Sir J. Graham. The idea pleased the King, who was rather surprised at its apparent moderation; and upon the condition 1831.

1832. that eldest sons only should be called up to sit during the lifetime of their fathers, he intimated that he would not object to the plan. He wished however, that it should be kept in reserve, and that further time should be afforded for ascertaining what changes might have been wrought in the minds of Opposition Peers, by the modifications of the original measure, which had been made in the third edition of the Reform Bill. The Duke indeed remained inflexible,* and the great body of the Peers would certainly adhere to him. But through his private secretary, Sir Herbert Taylor, William IV. was at the time actually trying to bring about an understanding with the moderate Conservatives; and Lords Wharncliffe and Harrowby encouraged the hope that provided the Upper House "was not swamped" (to use the language of the time), an accommodation might be come to.†

The third Reform Bill.

The third Reform Bill differed materially from the two which had preceded it. The total number of the House, 658, was to be retained. Schedule A contained but 56 boroughs; and Schedule B but 30 instead of 41; and the basis now taken for both was one compounded of property and population, instead of the latter alone. The occupier

* Letter to the Duke of Buckingham, Jan. 1832; Courts and Cabinets, vol. ii.

† Correspondence referred to in Gleig's Life of the Duke of Wellington, vol. iv. chap. 2.

of a £10 house would have been entitled to vote under the first bill in whatever instalments he paid the requisite rent; he was now excluded unless the payments were at least quarterly. Upon the whole, all the changes made were in a Conservative sense; and ministers deprecated popular exaggerations of the benefit the measure would confer, in order that they might seem justified in the use of language calculated to allay the excessive alarm of their opponents. Sir R. Peel bitterly taunted them with having been driven to yield at last, concessions they had previously refused; and asked, if the advantages likely to ensue were really so much less than the community out of doors had for a season been led to believe, where was the urgency which had been pleaded as justifying the hazard of national convulsion? Nevertheless he intimated his determination to persevere in resisting to the end, a measure which he still thought uncalled for, and which he did not believe could be permanent. 1832.

The Lords induced to yield.

When the bill went up to the Lords, the Bishop of London, the Earls of Harrowby and Haddington, and Lord Wharncliffe announced their intention to vote for the second reading. The Duke did not conceal his anger; and reproached them with having been for months trying to bring about a compromise. For his part he would have none of it, and he meant to abide by his former decision. The Duke of Buckingham gave notice that upon the defeat of the minis-

1832. terial scheme, he was prepared to submit a qualified measure, which many of his party would be ready to support. In point of fact it was clear, that by alternately siding with the Whigs and with the ultra-Tories, the moderate minority believed that they could ensure the passing of a half measure, and their own elevation
May 9th. to power for the purpose. The second reading was carried by a majority of nine; but on going into committee, an amendment by Lord Lyndhurst to postpone the consideration of Schedules A and B was carried by a majority of 35. The Premier and the Chancellor, by the unanimous desire of the Cabinet, on the next day called on the King to fulfil his promise of making a sufficient number of Peers; and upon receiving a peremptory refusal, the whole administration resigned. William IV. sent for Lord Lyndhurst, then Chief Baron of the Exchequer, and requested his advice, regarding the construction of a new administration. Sir Robert Peel declared that nothing would induce him under the circumstances to undertake the government; and the Duke once more was named Prime Minister, while Mr A. Baring reluctantly consented to be Chancellor of the Exchequer and leader of the House of Commons. With high character, long experience, great possessions, and excellent parts, the "first merchant in the city" was still unequal to the position. He was too clear-sighted a man not to perceive the necessity of large concessions to popular feeling, and

too candid and courageous to deny it. The Whigs believed that they were to be supplanted, while something like their bill was to be passed; they thought they had been duped, alike by the moderate Conservatives and by the King; and many of them gave way to vehement expressions of chagrin and anger. In the press the conduct of the sovereign and of those immediately about his person, by whom he had been swayed, was held up to the utmost odium; and Lord Lyndhurst and the Duke were denounced daily for the part they had shown themselves willing to play. But all this would have availed little, had it not been for the unexampled outburst of popular passion which marked the eventful days immediately following the resignation of Lord Grey. Within a week every district of the metropolis, and nearly every great town in England, in unanimous and enthusiastic public meetings, had petitioned the House of Commons to grant no more supplies until the Reform Bill had become law. Resolutions to refuse payment of taxes were widely adopted, and Lord Milton, when questioned in Parliament, avowed that he had told the collector to call again, as for the present he was not sure whether he would pay any contributions to the State under existing circumstances. The King and Queen, on their return from Windsor, were hooted and insulted by the populace, without intermission, from the verge of the suburbs until they reached the palace; and huge placards on every 1832.

1832. vacant wall bade the people, "Go for gold, and stop the Duke." The country, habitually so grave in its decisions and so slow to move, in a paroxysm of sudden passion reeled on the brink of civil war. At the last moment the Duke of Wellington gave up his perilous attempt, and the humiliated monarch was forced to recall the Whigs.

Interview with the King.

William IV. received Lords Grey and Brougham under the influence of mortification, which he did not affect to disguise; and throughout the entire interview he kept them standing. The discourtesy was the more marked as Sir Herbert Taylor was present. They refused to resume office without a positive assurance that they should have full power to carry the bill. And when this was verbally conceded, the Chancellor required that they should have it in writing. The royal surrender at discretion was thereupon committed to paper in the following words:—

"The King grants permission to Earl Grey, and to his Chancellor, Lord Brougham, to create such a number of Peers as will be sufficient to ensure the passing of the Reform Bill—first calling up Peers' eldest sons.

"William R.

"Windsor, May 17th, 1832." *

Even this singular document failed to re-assure the Cabinet; for beyond the influence that might be

* Roebuck, History of Whigs, vol. ii. p. 331.

exercised by the belief that they possessed the power to overwhelm resistance in the Lords, they did not yet see their way. As a threat, the wholesale creation of peers sounded very effective and formidable; but when the hour seemed to have come for its fulfilment, there were few of those responsible for the step who were thoroughly prepared to take it.* What they would have ultimately done, or whether they could have eventually agreed as to the mode of putting into execution the extraordinary power conceded to them, must ever remain conjectural. Rough lists were drawn out of the individuals to be thus ennobled; and Sir James was pressed to allow his name to be included. "They want me to go with the rest," he said to a friend; "and say that as the title of Preston was formerly in my family, I must take it as that of a revived peerage. But I have no fancy for figuring in the unwelcome list; and all my ideas of political life are centred in the House of Commons." He was not, however, required to decide on the occasion in question what he would do. 1832.

The Bill carried.

While the Cabinet hesitated, means had been devised to relieve the sovereign from the painful necessity of keeping his pledge, and his ministers from requiring him to do so. In compliance with a confidential circular written by Sir H. Taylor in the

* Lord Brougham is understood to have subsequently declared that the power never would have been used. Roebuck, Hist. of Whigs, vol. ii. p. 336.

1832. name of the sovereign, seventy peers, including the Duke of Wellington and Lord Lyndhurst, consented to withdraw from the House, and thus to permit the dreaded bill to become law.

Division of Cumberland.

In Committee on the bill, Mr W. Bankes had objected that while Dorsetshire was given but one additional member, Cumberland was to have two. Though courteously put, the objection was pointedly aimed at the First Lord of the Admiralty, as one of the draughtsmen of the bill. Cumberland, it was true, had a population of 156,194, while Dorsetshire had but 144,000; but in point of wealth, as tested by the comparative numbers of £10 houses, and of those at and over £40 a year, the latter had superior claims. In the boroughs of Cumberland there would be under the bill 40,000 inhabitants: in those of Dorsetshire but 24,000. The number of £10 houses in Cumberland was 2,400; in Dorset 3,050: houses rated at £20, and under £40, were in the former 536; in the latter 828: above £40, in Cumberland 114; in Dorset 216. The existing freeholders of the former were 1,527: of the latter, 2,002.

Sir James replied that the whole of the case had not been fairly stated. Dorset was the largest county that was to have three, and Cumberland the smallest that was to have four representatives. Yet a fair comparison would show that there was a considerable disparity between their electoral claims. Even after the addition of two seats, Cumberland would return in all but eight members, while Dorsetshire and its included boroughs would return eleven; in other words, one member would under the bill be given to every 19,000 persons in Cumberland, and one to every 13,000 in Dorset. The plain and simple rule adopted by the framers of the measure was, that every county which, by the census of 1821, contained 150,000 inhabitants, should have four members. Dorset fell short of that mark, and consequently would have but three. He confidently challenged any answer to this plain statement, which furnished ground for any imputation of partiality on the part of ministers. 1832.

It was finally determined that the county should be divided. The sitting members naturally agreed in their preference for the eastern division, which was that in which their influence principally lay. No one thought of opposing either of them, and the day of their return to the first reformed Parliament was one of unbroken satisfaction and joy.

CHAPTER XII.

ADMINISTRATION OF THE NAVY.

1832.

1832. Retrenchment in the Navy.

WHILE public attention was absorbed by the struggle for Reform, Sir James was steadily pursuing those investigations into the practical working of his own department, which enabled him to amend many portions of its mechanism, and in a considerable degree to economize its cost. He and his colleagues had come into office on a pledge of retrenchment, and he at least had not forgotten, nor was he disposed to elude, the binding efficacy of that pledge. He observed indeed with disappointment, a lurking tendency early betrayed by some who had formerly professed a creed as thrifty as his own, to fall into the old ways of waste and jobbing. Lord Althorpe shared his feelings on this subject as on so many others, and cordially assisted in the maturing of every project which he or Sir H. Parnell could devise for lessening the expenditure; and those who preferred in their departments the preservation of places for the sake of patronage, and the perpetuation of needless outlay in the hope of mollifying the antipathy of the subordinates left them by their predecessors, rejoiced in the adoption of an opposite course in the administration of the navy: for this entailed no sacrifices on their part, while it held out the prospect of reduction in the total amount of the estimates in future years. Already some important reductions had indeed been made. The salaries had been reduced of the Secretary of the Treasury, the Home Secretary, the Colonial Secretary, the Lord Privy Seal, the President of the Board of Control, the Master of the Mint, and the First Lord of the Admiralty, ten per cent.: the salary of the First Secretary of that department had been reduced twenty per cent.; and the salary of the Deputy Controller of the Navy had been reduced twenty-five per cent. Ministers, said Sir James, had not begun with reducing the salaries of inferior officers; they had begun with the salaries of the Cabinet; and having had their own salaries fixed by Parliament, they had proceeded to administer strict justice between the public and the officers below them. Two commissioners of customs had been abolished, and the salaries of the remaining commissioners had been reduced from £1400 to £1200 a year. Four commissionerships in the Victualling department had been abolished, with salaries from £800 to £1000

1832. per annum; three other offices with smaller salaries; and altogether he had abolished nine salaries, varying from £800 to £1000 a year,—besides reducing forty or fifty unnecessary offices.

Department as described by Sir James.

The constitution of the department as it existed in 1830, formed as it had been by gradual deviations from the original ground plan of the time of the Restoration, appeared to him full of anomalies and defects. The Board of Admiralty, reconstructed by patent on every change of administration, was held responsible to Parliament for the due application of all sums voted annually for the service, for its maintenance in efficiency in time of peace, and for its preparedness for employment in the event of war. Nominally the Board was supreme, and the authority of the First Lord, if he chose to exercise the powers which traditionally devolved to him, was paramount at the Board. As a member of the Cabinet he was presumed to know, and yet forbidden to disclose, those reasons of State which even in times of peace must govern the administration of the great department to which the nation has always looked mainly for security and defence. The Junior Lords, whether civilians or naval men, held office by the same tenure as their chief; and being, as well as the Secretary, members of the House of Commons, they were liable to be called in question for any act, whether of omission or commission, afloat or ashore, done at home or abroad, by any person wearing the uniform or enjoying the pay of the navy. Yet neither individually 1832. nor in their collective capacity with the First Lord at their head, were they able to exact such an account of the conduct pursued in two of the main branches of the department, as would have enabled them to exercise an effective control or superintendence over them. The Navy Board and the Victualling Board, although theoretically speaking sub-departments, were so distinct and separate in their constitution and practice, that though not assuming the form of independency, they had practically come to be, in many essential respects, independent. The one had charge of the dock-yards, and exercised an almost absolute discretion in all matters connected with ship-building. To the other was entrusted the care of provisioning the navy. The Navy Board consisted of five members, of whom, at the time, Sir Byam Martin was the chief. It fulfilled the principal if not the whole of the duties afterwards performed by the Surveyor of the Navy. "It had the control of the dock-yards, very much as the Controller now has, with this difference, that the Controller now-a-days is subject to control, (which as head of the Navy Board he then was not,) and acts under the direct orders of the Admiralty. The Navy Board acted as an independent board, save only that with most voluminous correspondence it conducted its business with the knowledge and the imperfect control of the Admiralty, but based upon correspondence as between two independent boards, very

1832. voluminous, and sometimes very tedious. The communications with the Admiralty personally were confined to the First Lord and the Controller. The Controller was a permanent officer during pleasure, but really during good behaviour. The Admiralty notified the number of ships for which there was a pressing call to the Navy Board, and the Navy Board either built or contracted for building. In 1831 party feeling ran very high; Sir Byam Martin was in the House of Commons, and honestly much opposed to the Whig Government; and though, from a sense of duty, he would not allow his private feelings and opinions to influence his public conduct more than he could avoid, yet the communications were not exactly pleasant between the First Lord and him. Although Sir Byam Martin was holding a permanent position in the Admiralty, under the First Lord, he continued to act as a public man in the House of Commons upon his own political views. The system of business by which the affairs of the Admiralty were carried on as between the First Lord and the head of the Navy Board, was carried on very much as between independent bodies. "Lord Grey warned me," said Sir James, "when I went to the Admiralty, that he had found the inconvenience of such independent action; and he told me that he thought I should find, as I did find, that the control of the Admiralty was imperfect, that the machinery was cumbrous, and that concentration was necessary; and that concentration would be found to expedite the 1832. transaction of business. I came to the conclusion that the Controller was then rightly designated the Controller of the Navy, that really he exercised, with regard to a great portion of the expenditure, a great deal more control than the Board of Admiralty or the First Lord. I thought the arrangements altogether amounted to an inconvenient division of authority; but I should not have trusted my own judgment upon short experience, had I not had the authority directly of Lord Grey, the head of the Government under whom I served. Lord Althorpe, the son of Lord Spencer, was my most intimate friend; he was, I believe, born at the Admiralty and trained at the Admiralty, and through Lord Althorpe I had ready access to the opinion of Lord Spencer: and backed by the opinion of Lord Spencer, and by the authority of Lord Grey, and exercising my own judgment, however imperfect, I came to the conclusion which led me to propound to Parliament that concentration. The Navy Board sat at Somerset House; the Board of Admiralty at Whitehall: the functions and the duties of the Junior Lords of the Admiralty, under that system, were very much what Mr Canning described to be the duties of Junior Lords of the Treasury,—to make a House, to keep a House, and to cheer the minister. In the business of the Admiralty they had very little to do. They had no departmental

1832. duties assigned to them, no subdivision whatever; they made a board; the quorum at that time consisted of three. The correspondence was carried on by the Navy Board and the Victualling Board with the Admiralty, very much as the correspondence is carried on at the Horse Guards with the War Office; it was very similar in form, and very voluminous. I paid great attention to the Finance Committee, which preceded the fall of the Duke's Government, illustrating the operation even of imperfect systems with superior talent and administrative power in the hands of the heads of departments. The Board of Ordnance, just before he became Prime Minister, had had the advantage of the Duke of Wellington, as Master-General, and Sir Henry Hardinge, as Clerk of the Ordnance; and under their administrative direction at that time, the department was considered a model, when it passed under the review of the Finance Committee. It was admitted on that investigation that it was the best conducted of the public departments; and I thought that the Duke, in a very concise manner, there laid down the principle of the management of the Board and of its success: and *mutatis mutandis*, without varying the Admiralty patent, I thought that some sub-division such as he effected might be followed; and the scheme I introduced is founded very much upon that model,—sub-division of departments among the members of the Board; the supreme control of every matter of importance, involving new principles, being referable to the head." * 1832.

Such were the ideas he sought to embody in the bill introduced by him early in the session of 1832, for the general reconstruction and consolidation of the civil departments of the navy. His speech on the occasion was an elaborate and lucid exposition of the whole subject, comprehending a retrospective view of the growth of the separate powers he sought to concentrate and combine.

"The House was aware that the Civil Service of the navy was conducted by three Boards,—the Board of Admiralty, the Navy Board, and the Victualling Board. These Boards derived their existence from patents under the Crown; they thus derived their command, authority, and jurisdiction from the same source: but there was this difference between them in practice,—the Commissioners for executing the office of Lord High Admiral went out with the administration; but the others never did. He felt that nothing would be a greater departure from the principles which ought to govern the advisers of the Crown than any proposition which would endanger the efficiency, diminish the strength, or risk the superiority of that branch of the public service. In a discussion which had taken place in the preceding year relating to the appropriation of the votes of Parliament, Sir George Clerk had said:—'The individual who brings forward the estimates is, I am well aware, responsible for their correctness; yet when

* Evidence given before Select Committee on Admiralty, 3rd May, 1861.

1832. they have been once voted, the Admiralty has no control over the expenditure of those sums; they are issued by the Treasury on the requisition of the Navy and Victualling Boards; and it was not until very lately that the Admiralty had an opportunity of knowing how the money was expended; for even the books of the Navy Office would not show under what heads the money was laid out.'" * * *

Civil departments of the navy.

Referring to the period previous to the Revolution, he cited several passages from Pepys's Memoirs, in which it was stated "that James II., when Duke of York, on his appointment to the office of Lord High Admiral, found himself compelled to dismiss the subordinate boards; and that with the assistance of four commissioners, he united the whole control of the civil administration of the navy in his own hands. The effects of this alteration were almost immediately visible; it was the first dawning of that brighter era which was followed by the splendour which had since encompassed the navy of Great Britain, and had at length raised it to that pinnacle of glory where it had since remained, the envy and wonder of surrounding nations. It was a singular fact, that during the temporary absence of the Duke of York from this country, the power of the subordinate boards was restored, and it was subsequently found necessary, with a view to the improvement of the navy, to pursue the same course once more, and to abolish these subordinate boards. The evils of such a system might be classified under two heads,—those connected with the want of a direct and concentrated control over the various branches of the service; and those connected with the irregular application of the monies voted by Parliament for its support. * * *

"The statement he was about to make was founded on official documents, and he was perfectly satisfied of their accuracy. The Government thought it necessary to erect some works in the year 1826; the works were commenced before an application was made to Parliament, at an estimated expense of £44,000 and upwards. The estimate laid on the table in 1827 amounted to £30,000, and the sum voted by Parliament was £8000. The next case was that of the Melville Hospital. No estimate was laid on the table of the House till 1827. The estimate given by the Victualling Board to the Admiralty was £35,027: the estimate laid on the table of the House by the Admiralty was £25,000: the sum expended was £61,655, and the whole of the sum voted by Parliament on account of that establishment was £7000. The next case related to the considerable outlay at Cremil Point. No estimate was presented to the House in this case. The estimate originally given in by the Victualling Board to the Admiralty amounted to £291,512. The expenditure began in 1824; that was one year before an estimate was presented. The total expenditure until 1830 was £249,441; and the whole of the sum voted by Parliament between 1825 and 1830, that is, from the commencement of the work until the period of his coming into office, was £74,000. There was no general plan or estimate submitted to the Admiralty or laid before Parliament. A sketch was made, but it was not drawn up in the regular form of a plan of estimate. No general vote was passed by the House—not one shilling more than he had stated was voted. Yet the work was all but completed, and an additional sum of £155,334 had actually been paid. Including the bake-house at Deptford, the sum expended from 1825 to 1830 for these works amounted to £835,400, while all that Parliament had voted was £270,000, leaving £565,400 to be provided for from other sources. This surplus, it appeared, might be applied to any other purpose 1832.

1832. than that for which it had been voted, without the intervention of Parliament—a proceeding which was highly objectionable. The House would naturally imagine that all this could not have taken place without the authority of the Admiralty, that Board being responsible for the arrangements connected with the public service. Having stated to the House the excess of the outlay under the head of building, from the year 1825 to the year 1830, beyond the votes of Parliament, he would state to the House how that outlay was met during these four years. In the year 1827 the sum voted by Parliament for the purchase of timber and stores was £1,060,000, the sum expended was £876,000, leaving a balance of £184,000 unaccounted for. In the year 1828 the sum expended less than that voted was £42,000; in 1829 it was £230,000; in 1830, £195,000. Under the head of timber and of materials there was expended in four years £1,029,000 less than Parliament had voted. Out of that surplus the expense of the buildings was provided for. He would next offer a few illustrations of the disobedience on the part of the subordinate boards to the directors of the Admiralty. Two regulations which, had they been strictly followed up, would have been found extremely useful, were introduced by Sir George Cockburn when he was at the Admiralty. The first of these regulations had reference to the establishment of a check on the issue and receipt of public stores in the dockyards: and it was supposed that, by keeping a ledger at each of the out-posts, and a counter-ledger at the Navy Board, no fraud could be committed as long as the two books corresponded in their items. A more judicious regulation, if carried into effect, could hardly be devised; but it unfortunately happened that, up to the present moment, it was impossible to obtain any information whatever from the ledger kept at the Navy Office. Another circumstance that he might mention, was the subtraction of the public property from the dock-yards, which, under the present system, it was impossible to prevent; in illustration of which, he might state that in the course of seven weeks five and a half tons of copper, with the King's mark, had found its way from Chatham to Birmingham, and the fraud had only been discovered by a mere accident. He felt that he had gone to some length in his statement of these abuses, but he hoped that the House would excuse him, because he had done it from the feeling that, as he was about to propose a great change, he was bound to show that there was ample reason requiring that change. It would hardly be credited, that although the most accurate accounts were kept in the King's yards of the stores which had been expended in building any particular ship, and of the quantity of labour employed upon it, yet if the House were to call for a return of the money any particular ship cost, it would be impossible to obtain it without its being a compound of the most extraordinary errors that could be imagined. A sort of cabalistic system has been adopted, in lieu of the ordinary figures, which produced very singular consequences. Besides which, the old war prices had, till within the last months, been almost universally kept up--prices that were in many instances 25, 30, and 40 per cent. above the present prices current. He would mention one or two instances as illustrative of this fact, which appeared in the course of an inquiry held during the last three months. Up to the period of last November, lead, which was now contracted for at 14*s*. 6*d*. per cwt., was entered as costing 21*s*. 6*d*. Iron, which, at the present price, was from £8 10*s*. to £9 14*s*. per ton, was charged 1832.

1832. at from £13 14*s*. 8*d*. to £13 19*s*. 1*d*.; and copper, the actual price of which was 8*d*. per pound, was charged at 1*s*. 3*d*. The use of figures was generally introduced for the elucidation of a subject, but in this case it only led to confuse and entangle the question, so as to produce one complete tissue of delusion. He trusted that he had now shown that the present system was defective both in theory and practice, and that a remedy was highly desirable. The measure which he had to submit to the House, was a measure which might be executed by the prerogative of the Crown, without the intervention of Parliament; for it chiefly depended on a recall of the patents of the Victualling and Navy Boards. There were, however, some minor points which would come within the province of Parliament, and he was therefore glad that an opportunity was thereby afforded of taking the sense of the Legislature on the subject, as it was far from his intention to counsel the revocation of those patents without the approbation of Parliament. What he intended to propose, subject to the consent of the House, was the total abolition of the Navy and Victualling Boards, so that there should be but one board for the management of the whole naval affairs of the country; by which arrangement every department—the building of ships, their repairs, the outlay for stores, the application to Parliament for money, the distribution of the money when voted, the necessary attention to the Appropriation Act—would all be under the control of one board, which would be responsible to Parliament for the public service of the country.

"What he proposed was to divide the whole of the naval service into five great departments, with an officer at the head of each. The first of those officers would be the Surveyor-General, whose duty would be pretty much the same as now. He would have to superintend the dock-yards, to look to the building of the ships, the care of ships in ordinary, and be responsible for their proper repair. The second would be the Accountant-General; he would have to superintend the accounts of the Victualling and Navy Boards,—accounts which at the present time were not kept on the same principle, the double-entry having been advantageously resorted to by the Navy Board, while the same practice in the Victualling Department had been prohibited by an order from the Board of Admiralty. This order, however, would be no longer continued; and he thought that from the same system being adopted in every department, the Accountant-General would be found competent to the whole of the labour. The third officer would be the Storekeeper-General, whose duty would be very much the same as at present. He would have to see to the supply of the principal articles necessary for the consumption of the fleet. The fourth officer would be the Superintendent of the Victualling Department, whose duty would be very similar to that of the present Victualling Board, except that some of those duties would be transferred to the other departments. The fifth officer would be the Superintendent of the Medical Department, and of the hospitals at home and abroad. These, then, were the five divisions under which he proposed to place all the business connected with the management of the civil affairs of the navy in all its branches. He should propose that the officers at the head of those departments should not be commissioners, holding their situations by patent and possessing co-ordinate authority with other boards, even with the Commissioners of the Admiralty itself, as was the case at 1832.

1832. present; but that they should be appointed under warrants from the Board of Admiralty, and that they should retain their situations during the time they performed their duties properly. The arrangement which he thus proposed would, he thought, be found superior even to the plan lately adopted in the Board of Ordnance, because the chief officers connected with it were liable to be changed with the administration of the day. Thus when they had acquired a competent knowledge of their duties, they might, by the change of administration, be deprived of office, which would be handed over to others, who perhaps were wholly unacquainted with the business they were called on to perform. Therefore it was that he wished those five officers to hold their situations by warrant from the Admiralty during good behaviour. Instead of four commissioners with the First Lord, he proposed that there should be five commissioners,—one to preside over each of the departments he had enumerated. This system had all the advantage of the arrangement of the Board of Ordnance. It gave the regular cognizance of each department to its own proper head, while the whole would be brought under the consideration of the General Board, and everything that demanded investigation would be decided before the Board, and the proceedings would be regularly noted by the Secretary. There would thus be a just division of labour; an undivided control and a due responsibility on the one hand, and on the other that unity and simplicity which he held to be the very essence and life of public business. He might now perhaps without vanity be allowed to state the number of officers that had been reduced in the previous year, and the number which he would be able to reduce hereafter if the House acceded to his proposition. Mr Croker had talked of the 'gleanings' of the present ministry. He would give him a specimen of those gleanings; and he hoped the right hon. gentleman would not impede the labour of the gleaners. In the course of the previous year he (Sir James) had been able to reduce four commissioners, producing a saving to the amount of £4000 a year; thirty-seven superior officers, effecting a saving of £9470; twenty-five inferior officers, a saving of £1285; and eight clerks, a saving of £1970. If the plan which he now proposed met with the approbation of the House, he should be able in the next three months to reduce five commissioners, to the amount of £6000; three secretaries, £2600; twenty-nine superior officers, £10,280; six inferior officers, £1440; and fifty-four clerks, £11,950, making altogether a total saving of £49,059 a year. He should imperfectly discharge his duty if, after dwelling so much upon the misappropriation, in defiance of Parliament, of money voted for particular service, he did not propose to the House a plan to prevent it in future. This would be done by a more efficient system of audit. There was no difficulty in the proposal for making the financial year terminate on the 31st March instead of the 31st December. There was no such difference between the transactions of the merchant and the statesman, and the merchant closed his banker's book at the end of the year, although his own books might be kept open to complete his mercantile transactions. He proposed that the Admiralty should audit their Treasurer's account at the close of the financial year. The accounts themselves might be kept open till the 30th November, which would be adopting so much of the French system of accounts as appeared applicable to the naval service of this country. The great advantage of the present measure undoubtedly would

1832.

New system of naval accounts.

1832. be, that it would convert a nominal into a real responsibility. It would make a large reduction in the number of public officers, and a large reduction in the public expenditure; it would redeem all the pledges he had ever given when on the other side of the House, and it would exemplify all the principles for which he and his friends had ever contended. Notwithstanding, if he thought in his conscience that it was not calculated to benefit the public service, and to improve the efficiency of the British navy, none of these considerations should induce him to bring it forward. But entertaining an opinion that it would promote the public service, he was anxious that the House should allow him to bring in the bill."

Attack of Mr Croker.

Mr Croker, in a speech of great bitterness, assailed the positions taken up by the First Lord, which he undertook to show were wholly indefensible.

He disputed all the facts, historical and recent, which had been stated as the ground-work of the proposed plan; and he denied the force or fitness of the reasoning which had been reared upon them. Mr Pepys had been cited as an authority for the abolition of the Navy Board by James II.; and he asked from what work the passage to that effect had been quoted. Receiving no answer to this inquiry at the moment, he proceeded in a strain of increased asperity to expose what he deemed the ignorance and superficiality of Sir James in quoting, as he said, at second hand, from the Memoirs of Mr Pepys, an assertion which was not in reality to be found in any part of them. "If the right hon. baronet referred to the small volume of Memoirs of the Navy, he would tell him at once that no such occurrence was or could be described in that work, which did not mention any event antecedent to the year 1673, and therefore it could mention nothing relative to what had passed at the Restoration in 1660, or on the Duke of York's going abroad in 1668; and he would take upon himself to state, in the broadest terms, that there was not in that book the slightest foundation for the right hon. baronet's assertion relative to the dismissal or re-establishment of the subordinate boards at those periods. But if the right hon. baronet should turn round and say, that he founded his statement on some passage in Mr Pepys's voluminous Diary, commonly called his Memoirs, he would be equally unfortunate; for the assertion of the right hon. gentleman was not only that the Duke of York abolished the boards at the time of the Restoration, but that the boards having been restored upon that Prince's going abroad, they were again abolished upon his return. Now unluckily for the right hon. baronet, as the first events were previous to the commencement of the Memoirs, so the latter events happened to be subsequent to the last date of the Diary of Pepys, which contained no occurrence of a later date than 1668. So that here was chronological certainty that the First Lord's reference to either of Mr Pepys's Memoirs was entirely unfounded. From the Restoration to the present hour the Navy Board had never been abolished. He therefore gave as direct a contradiction to the fact stated by the right hon. baronet as he had done to the allegation of his authority for that statement. Perhaps the right hon. gentleman might have fallen into the same error as Pepys's editor, by mistaking the Admiralty Board for the Navy Board; though that even would not account for the right hon. baronet's having stated that the Navy Board was abolished at the Restoration. He had himself had the honour

1832. to fill the office of Secretary to the Admiralty for twenty-two years. During that period he conducted of course all the public correspondence, and much of what was considered private communication; and he declared, upon his honour and conscience, that in the course of all that time he never knew one instance of what could be considered disobedience, nor any conduct which could be fairly considered a thwarting of the views of the superior board. Never did he witness anything like the opposition of which so much had been said on the part of the Navy and Victualling Boards. If there were any such, he must say that he never heard of it; and he must further declare his full persuasion that, if it had existed, it could not have escaped his notice. He, therefore, was enabled to give that part of the statement of the First Lord of the Admiralty as complete a denial as he had given to the other portions of it. They had been told that it originated in the circumstance of all the boards, whether superior or subordinate, being created by patent; and that, consequently, the inferior boards presumed on their equality, and refused obedience. Now this argument struck him as being absolutely ridiculous. A lieutenant in the army was a commissioned officer; so was the Duke of Wellington; but he believed that no lieutenant had ever been found to disregard the commands of his superior officer on the ground of his holding, as it were, under the same tenure. By a strange fatality, every fact which the right hon. baronet advanced, failed him; and every height which he climbed only made his fall more deep and heavy. As to the alleged misapplication of funds to the building of a hospital at Chatham, a mill at Deptford, and a Victualling establishment at Portsmouth, all this was beside the real question at issue: for the principle

of expending parliamentary grants for purposes other than 1832.
those for which they were voted might be right or wrong; but it was with the Admiralty, and not with the Navy Board, that the responsibility of this appropriation lay. In the course of five years £560,000 were said to have been applied, in ways not especially voted by Parliament. This was perfectly true; but as a charge against the Navy Board the same answer was ready, that it was so applied on the authority of the Admiralty itself; and the application could not, therefore, be used as an argument for the dismissal of the Navy Board. He was prepared to prove that not one item of the expenditure had been appropriated without the full knowledge and sanction of the Admiralty.

"The right honourable baronet seemed to him not to have sufficiently distinguished between estimates and accounts; though certainly no two things could be more different. An estimate was in its nature uncertain—we estimated what we could not ascertain, and all the naval monies were voted on estimate; an account, on the contrary, which related to the actual expenditure, might be given with perfect accuracy, and, accordingly, we might have at the end of any year an accurate and minute account of the actual expenditure of all those sums which were estimated at the commencement of the year. The estimate was, to a certain degree, a vote of confidence; the account afforded the check, and the control, and the proof, that the confidence was not abused. Accounts must tally to a farthing; but estimates must have, as every gentleman in his private affairs knew, a latitude of allowance; an estimate included not only all foreseen expenses, but it always provided a certain surplus for unforeseen contingencies. The portion of naval expenditure which could be reduced to a certainty was very small; the part which must be subject to

1832. the uncertainty of an estimate was very large. Now the naval votes for the five years alluded to amounted to about £6,000,000 a year; and he would ask, was it to be expected that on so large a sum, less than £110,000 or £120,000, that was about two per cent., should be allowed for contingencies, and to insure a surplus at the end of the year? The charge of misappropriation was absolutely unfounded—the money had been voted, and the service to which it was applied was also voted; although the exact amount to be spent on each head of service within a given time was not, and could not be, estimated. The time which it was contemplated by the original estimate, sanctioned by Parliament, that this work would require, was fourteen or fifteen years; but in consequence of a surplus of £320,000 having, in the course of two or three years, accumulated in the naval Treasury, it was determined to apply it to this object, and the result was, that the work, a most useful and necessary work, and expressly voted by Parliament, was completed in six years instead of sixteen. Here, then, was the explanation of the right hon. baronet's most formidable case of misappropriation."

With reference to the non-reduction of labourers in the dock-yards, Mr Croker said that "in direct and positive contradiction to every syllable of this charge, he would take upon himself unequivocally to assert, in the face of the right honourable baronet, that there was no disobedience on the part of the Navy Board; and the First Lord of the Admiralty was, he must presume, misinformed, and therefore had misstated every one of the facts. It was not the case that a positive order was given; the order was contingent, and to this effect,—that it being necessary to reduce the public expenditure as much as possible, with as little inconvenience to the public service as could be, and their Lordships having determined to reduce the number of workmen in the yard, not, as stated by the right hon. baronet, to 6000, but to a number which should be stated at a future time. So that these positive directions of the Admiralty to the Navy Board amounted to nothing more than this, "we intend to reduce the number of workmen, but to what extent we have not yet determined." The reduction was not to be immediate, nor by discharge, nor by any other means within the control of the Navy Board; but was to take place by the hand of God, and the course of time. Was it upon such evidence, so misapprehended, so misstated, so misapplied by the right hon. baronet, that the ancient constitution of the navy was to be overthrown, and the whole duties of the Navy Board transferred to the special responsibility of the right hon. baronet, who had shown himself to be so entirely unacquainted, not merely with the course of business, but with the clearest facts of the cases which he had attempted to state?" 1832.

Rejoinder of Sir James.

Sir J. Graham, in reply to Mr Croker, said "he thought he had good reason to congratulate himself that throughout the whole of his long and premeditated speech the right hon. gentleman had busied himself with replying, not so much to the speech with which he (Sir J. Graham) had introduced the present measure to the House, as to the speeches which he had made on naval affairs, not only in that but also in former sessions of Parliament. He could not help being surprised that there should be so strong a lurking suspicion in the mind of Mr. Croker, that he (Sir J. Graham) had misquoted the authorities which he had produced on a recent occasion, in support of the provisions of the present bill. He would not enter into any investigation of the reasons

1832. which induced the right hon. gentleman to entertain such a suspicion—he would only say that he believed he was not more likely to make a misquotation, to gain a temporary advantage in debate, than the right hon. gentleman, and therefore he was surprised to hear himself accused of falsifying, though not intentionally, the authority of Mr Pepys. In the first instance, Mr Croker had endeavoured to make the House believe that he (Sir James) had addressed it without any authority; but then, seeing that he held in his hand his authority, namely, the first report of the Commissioners of Inquiry into the civil affairs of the navy, which Mr Croker said he knew by heart, he boldly stated that he (Sir James) had not read it correctly to the House. He would therefore apply himself to the refutation of that charge, and as the best mode of doing it would be by producing the authority itself, he would read that of Mr Pepys in the first report. In that report the history of our navy was traced with great minuteness from the earliest times down to the present. It stated that on the Restoration, the Duke of York was appointed Lord High Admiral, that the Navy Board was dismissed, and that a plan was devised for the restoration of the navy. Mr Croker had said that this report must be inaccurate, as the small memoir of Mr Pepys on the state of the navy was the only document of his that was then known to be in existence. But the Commissioners who drew up that report were as accurate in their statements as Mr Croker, and perhaps a little more so. They proceeded as follows:—'All the proceedings of the Duke of York in the management of the navy, either when he was Lord High Admiral, or after he came to the throne, are minutely detailed in a great number of manuscript volumes in the Pepysian library at Cambridge, of which thirteen volumes have at our desire been sent for our perusal.' They then proceeded to state the contents of those volumes. The right hon. gentleman had asserted that the Duke of York did not set aside or abolish the powers of the Navy Board. The Report proceeded:—'The powers which had been granted to the Commissioners of the Admiralty and Navy Boards were recalled, and the entire management was put into the hands of the Duke, as Lord High Admiral, to whom three new Commissioners were appointed, to act with the Treasurer of the Navy, the Comptroller, the Surveyor, and the Clerk of the Acts, as principal officers and commissioners of the navy.' This was a new Board of Admiralty, constructed by the Lord High Admiral; and what were the results? 'Great progress,' said the Report, 'was made in the preparation of the fleet, owing to the skilful management of the Duke of York and Mr Pepys.' The Duke then went to take the command of the British fleet during the Dutch war. He controlled the Navy Board: but the same careful management which prevailed while he was present to superintend it did not prevail during his absence. A sudden change took place in the management for the worse, which on resuming his management at home the Duke instantly checked. He went abroad again for five years; in his absence new men were appointed to the Navy Board, without either experience or industry; the effect of which was that all became again supineness at head quarters, that waste prevailed, and that the navy became inefficient. At the end of five years the Duke returned, suspended all the members of the Navy Board, and confined their duties merely to the accounts. Mr Croker asserted that the modern practice never accorded with the law. Why,

1832. that was the very charge he had brought against the hon. gentleman and his colleagues. He (Sir James) said that the practice which they had followed was a vicious practice, for which nothing like a satisfactory defence could be offered. But, said Mr Croker, no loss was ever sustained by this practice. No, but loss might have been sustained by it; and if it had been suffered to continue, loss would have been sustained by it. This practice was gradually increasing, and during the last four years that the colleagues of Mr Croker were in power, this practice had been carried to a more dangerous extent than it ever had been at any previous period. Mr Croker had stated that the surplus of the different grants voted was regularly carried to the general service of the year. He (Sir James) admitted that such was the fact; and it was owing to his having found a very large surplus under the head of timber, on coming into office, that he had been enabled to carry on the naval service so long without applying to Parliament for fresh funds. But what was Mr Croker's explanation respecting the existence of this surplus? Most jejune and unsatisfactory. He said that under the head of wages they would find that a deficiency of money was voted; but in reply to this he (Sir J. Graham) was prepared to contend that nothing could be more unconstitutional than the keeping a larger number of men than that which was voted by Parliament, and paying their wages out of the surplus belonging to other grants. He assured the House that during the last year there had not in any part of the world been one boy borne on the books of the navy more than the maximum for which he had asked wages during the previous year. When he came into office, however, he found 1500 men more employed in the navy than had been voted by Parliament.

The right hon. gentleman considered that the total amount of estimates voted for the naval service of the year was applicable to any particular estimate, and that the money granted was not restricted to the professed purpose for which it was granted. That was a doctrine conformable certainly to the practice, but he looked upon the practice as the primary cause of all the evils which pervaded these departments. If the present bill were sanctioned, it would convert a nominal into a real and efficient control. It was his intention to re-enact the audit, which was sanctioned by the Act of the 2nd of William III. As the audit at the end of the year could not be either a perfect or a final audit until all the accounts were furnished, he proposed to keep the accounts open until all the other accounts were received, even from the most distant parts of the world. He would keep the audit also open until two months after all the accounts were closed, with their vouchers, and then the expenditure on each head, whether it was a surplus or a deficiency, was to be fairly stated to Parliament. That was the best answer that could be offered to the objection which Mr Croker had urged against the measure which he had introduced; for it proved the utter absurdity of his having introduced it with a view of giving irresponsible power to the board over which he presided. He had submitted his plan to Mr Barrow, one of the present Secretaries to the Admiralty, whose experience was, at least, as great as that of Mr Croker; and from him he had received every assistance, which he felt proud to avow, and should ever remember with the most grateful feelings. Mr Barrow not only thought the present measure practicable, but salutary, and that it would have the effect of correcting many of those grievances which he well knew had existed. 1832.

1833. He was also supported by the opinion of the present Board of Admiralty, which he trusted he might say contained as much naval knowledge as any previous board. He had no personal interest in the change; he gained no advantage or patronage by the measure; indeed, he sought none, but he implored the House for the sake of the service over which he had the honour to preside, he entreated the House for the sake of that service, to allow the bill to be read a second time." *

Sir Byam Martin, whose presidency of the Navy Board the bill was to bring to an end, could not be expected to approve of the contemplated change. He pronounced the scheme to be wholly impracticable; and by reference to details endeavoured to prove the perfect efficiency of the old system, and the certain failure of the new, if it should ever be tried. Mr Keith Douglas, Sir George Clerk, and Sir George Cockburn, expressed similar opinions. But the House grew thinner and thinner as the vaticinations of coming evil grew more angry and more dull; and Mr Croker, seeing himself deserted by the bulk of his party, declined to call for a division.

Power of impressment.

Among the changes called for in the press and in the new House of Commons in 1833, was the formal abrogation of the power of impressment. The country, long at peace, had seen this as well as other usages of war practically abandoned. An annul act suspended the ballot for the militia, and seamen no more feared being taken out of merchant ships against

* Hansard, Debate in Commons, 27th Feb., 1832.

their will, and being compelled to serve in a man-of-war. Why should not the sailor have at least an equal security for the permanence of his exemption from compulsory service as the farm labourer? Was the principle less sound on the sea-coast than on the village green? And as Parliament saw fit to interpose its veto between the shepherd and artizan and the arbitrary prerogative of the Crown, why should it not do the same for the hard-toiling and venturous mariner who belonged to the mercantile marine? Popular opinion made little of the distinction which veteran officials drew between the right to enact from time to time a parliamentary exemption from a liability to serve in a force which existed by parliamentary title, —and an interference without precedent, on the part of the House of Commons, with a right which time immemorial had been exercised without dispute, in virtue of the royal prerogative. The executive, it was said, had substantially become not only responsible ministerially for all its acts to Parliament; but there was no branch of its authority which could or ought to be recognized as above the advice, and, if need were, the direction of the legislature. Discretion in the use of administrative powers there must always be; but the definition and limitation of such powers belong to the representatives of the people, and who could form a better judgment of what was truly requisite for national defence as distinguished from the retention of old, clumsy, and vexatious

1833.

1833. powers, the very mention of whose exercise had grown hateful to the community, and the attempt to revive which, in practice, in a time of perturbation or peril, might be attended with ill effects? A season of profound peace was that in which the national armoury might most fitly be over-hauled, the old and obsolete weapons finally removed, and others more safe and more efficacious, as being more adapted to modern usages, substituted for them.

Views of First Lord on impressment.

The First Lord of the Admiralty was not insensible to the force of reasonings of this kind. He saw that the days of reliance on impressment as an ordinary resource for manning the fleet were gone never to return; and he certainly did not regret that they were so. With characteristic foresight he strove to prepare the way for the practical discontinuance altogether of the system; and with this view he had for some time been engaged in elaborating a plan for the registration of seamen, among whom, upon the sudden outbreak of war, a ballot should take place, with permission to find substitutes as in the militia. The original idea of the scheme he had found in a letter of Lord Nelson, addressed to Earl St Vincent, when at the head of the Admiralty; and he spared no pains to collect opinions and suggestions of experienced naval officers as to the best method for its development and application. But he had good reason to know what difficulty would be made in the highest quarter to the statutable adoption of the plan, if a sweeping renunciation of the prerogative were insisted on by way of preamble. The Sailor-King, as he deemed it a compliment, when he was in good humour, to be called, was especially susceptible on every point that related to the navy. "All his predilections," said Sir James, "were in favour of the profession; and when he wore the crown of England he still considered it an honour to be a member of it. At my first interview on my acceptance of the office of First Lord of the Admiralty, his Majesty addressed me, and said it was right that I should bear in mind two great examples in the administration of naval affairs. He told me that in his opinion the two great examples were the Earl of Sandwich, and Earl Spencer, both civilians."* The King had served afloat in his youth, and had been flattered by Mr Canning with the appointment of Lord High Admiral,—of whose too great powers it was found necessary to deprive him after a few months' experience of his incapacity to use them. The suspicions with which he had been filled by the irresponsible advisers who had his ear, as to the subversive tendencies of the Reform Bill, had not fallen asleep. He continued to remember with unallayed mortification and resentment, the compulsion put upon him to acquiesce in that measure; and he only waited

1833.

Professional predilections of the King.

* Evidence given before Select Committee on the Admiralty, May, 1861.

1833. a convenient opportunity for manifesting his feelings towards the ministers who had over-ruled and humbled him. Sir James was perhaps one of those whom he disliked and distrusted least; although he could hardly have been ignorant of the part he had taken in the Cabinet, on more than one critical occasion, when the advice given by him was little in accordance with the views entertained by his Majesty. But he liked the manner in which the affairs of the Admiralty had generally been conducted since 1830, when the "old hands" were displaced, to a combination amongst whom he ascribed, though erroneously, his own summary eviction from the department a few years before. The First Lord understood too clearly the infirmity of a mind, which never strong, was now disturbed and weakened by the continued excitement caused by the exceptional circumstances of the time. Strange stories had already begun to be told of his confused notions * and eccentric manners, and

* When the King entertained, as he not unfrequently did, officers of both services, he loved to give their united healths as a toast, and sometimes indulged in brief but energetic comments on the excellence of naval and military organization, and its suitableness to the wants and feelings of the country. "The courage and talent of every class," he observed on one occasion, "is enlisted in the national defence. There is a striking proof of the fact at this very table. Here on my right is my noble friend Lord ———, who traces a proud pedigree back to the Normans; and here on my left is my gallant friend Admiral ———, sprung from the very dregs of the people!"

every day it became more and more an object of real importance upon public grounds to avoid the necessity of discussing in the royal closet topics of an irritating nature. 1833.

Motion to abolish impressment.

Sir James was satisfied that if any good was to be effected regarding the practical abolition of impressment, he must be allowed to introduce his contemplated Registration Bill, without any formal disclaimer of the ancient prerogative; and when, therefore, Mr Buckingham moved a resolution declaring "that the forcible impressment of seamen for his Majesty's navy was unjust, cruel, inefficient, and unnecessary,"—he deemed it his duty to oppose it. It was one thing to seek a substantial relief of the mercantile marine from a liability in future, which in past times had proved a source of great and grievous hardship to individuals, and it was another to ask Parliament to assert without qualification that the practice of times past had been vicious and criminal because wanton and unnecessary. This was not the way to deal with a difficult and important subject. It had been discussed on grounds of constitutional analogy and right. But the question resolved itself into this,—was there any difference between the power which the Crown had of enforcing that assistance in defending the nation as respected the land and the sea service? The statute of Charles II. had been alluded to, which pronounced unregulated and indiscriminate impressment of men as soldiers illegal, and

15th Aug.

1833. it had thence been inferred that the silence of the law on the subject of impressment of sailors from the merchant service was a proof that it also was illegal. Now his mode of drawing the inference would be wholly different. The true legal inference was just the reverse, and he would infer from the fact of impressment having been for so many ages constant and notorious, and from the law having forbidden the practice of impressing soldiers, that the silence of the law respecting sailors was proof almost positive, that the Legislature acknowledged the necessity regarding the latter, and recognized the right in the executive. But not only was it the practice for ages, and as such acknowledged by the common law, but the uniform usage had been confirmed by the statute law. It was acknowledged to be by the common law part of the rights of the Crown, and to stand in that respect on just as strong ground as the liberties of the subject. He cited the able argument of Mr Justice Foster, in his work on Crown Law, in support of this view, an argument which had never been answered, and which he believed to be unanswerable. He trusted the House would not for a moment imagine that he was supporting in the abstract the system of impressment, which could only be regarded with any permissive indulgence, as one of the evils consequent upon a state of war; and which it was the duty of every British statesman to attempt to modify, if not altogether avert. But he could not consent to abandon the right to resort to this means of defence in seasons of emergency; and he would not seek popularity at the expense of the honour, dignity, and safety of the nation. The true way to get rid of impressment was to obviate its necessity by rendering the Navy more popular among seamen. He had anxiously sought to accomplish this object, and he trusted not altogether ineffectually. But on the question of political right he was content to rely on the authority of Lord Chatham, whose recorded opinion he quoted at some length; and on the question of practical necessity he could not disregard the opinion of Lord Nelson, which was against any absolute prohibition by enactment. He would however undertake that a measure calculated to obviate the necessity for resorting again to the practice in seasons of exigency, should be carefully prepared, and when matured he should submit it for the consideration of the House.* 1833.

Mr Hume and Sir Edward Codrington supported the motion, which Mr Labouchere and Captain Elliott opposed. Colonel Torrens moved, as an amendment, "That it is the opinion of this House that it is just and expedient to mitigate the system of forcibly impressing seamen into the navy, in every way not in- Amendment of Colonel Torrens.

* Hansard, Debate on Impressment, 13th August, 1833.

1833. consistent with the power of the Crown in cases of emergency;" and the wording of the original motion having been abandoned, the question was put in this form, and defeated only by fifty-nine votes to fifty-four.

Bill for Registration of Seamen.

Mr Buckingham subsequently renewed his proposal absolutely to do away with impressment for the navy, and moved for a committee to inquire into the best substitute that could be found for the same.

Sir James recapitulated the arguments he had formerly used on the subject. "He would not argue the abstract question of the propriety of impressment. He confessed that he thought that impressment was amongst the greatest evils of a state of war; and that it ought never to be resorted to but on the greatest emergencies. Since 1815 it had in no instance been used; and he avowed that he was convinced of the soundness of the principle, if it could be carried into effect, of avoiding altogether having recourse to compulsory enlistment." He himself contemplated several changes with respect to prize-money and pay, favourable to the seaman. He offered as an alternative a bill which he had spent many months in preparing, to secure a complete registration of seamen in the United Kingdom. When duly registered, the men would, in case of war, be liable to be balloted for, as in the militia; and by this means he hoped to be able to get rid of the chief hardships attendant upon the abuse of the power of impressment. He moved as an amendment for leave to bring in his bill, which was carried on a division by 218 to 130.* 1833.

In bringing forward the navy estimates, the following session, Sir James reviewed the general course of retrenchment which had taken place in recent years. The navy estimates for 1830 were £5,594,955; in 1832 they were reduced to £4,878,634; and those for 1833 had been still further reduced to £4,658,134; in other words, the current expenditure for the navy would be found less than that of 1830 by a sum of £946,821, of which £220,500 had been effected during the current year. He had been accused of effecting retrenchment by sacrificing the efficiency of the service. Captain Yorke had stated that Portsmouth dockyard was swept clear of timber, cordage, sails, and stores of all kinds; so that if a man-of-war was unexpectedly to put in there to refit, the thing could not be done. The First Lord read a return of the actual contents of that dockyard at the time when it had been described as thus left bare, and showed how greatly the fact had been mis-stated. Referring to similar imputations cast upon his administration of the department by the Duke of Wellington, he showed that the ship-loads of timber in our yards were in 1832, 64,023, against 56,633 in 1830, the last year of his Grace's administration; while the expenditure of timber was 12,406 against 15,401;

Navy Estimates of 1833.

* Hansard, Debate on Impressment, 4th March, 1834.

1833. and so on through all the principal items of naval stores there appeared to be a larger stock in hand than there had previously been. Comparing the total outlay of the last three years with that of the three preceding, it appeared that £147,790 more had been expended in the former than the latter. Comparing our available strength at sea with that of France, Russia, and America, there was no cause for disquietude or misgiving. "No maritime state had a navy equal to that of Great Britain, and with that superiority we ought to be content." He could not for sake of economy, however, consent to reduce our armaments further; and he therefore asked for 18,000 seamen and 9000 marines for the service of the year.

Mr Hume complained that retrenchment had not been carried further; while Sir E. Codrington objected that the pay of the men and the half-pay of officers of the navy was too low. The House however was satisfied with what had been done. Mr Croker had not been returned to the new Parliament; and none of his former colleagues sought to revive the discussion of the preceding year. The votes for the service of the navy were consequently agreed to without a division.

Navy Estimates of 1834.

In moving the estimates for the department in 1834, Sir James reverted to the pledges of retrenchment given in 1830, and challenged the judgment of the House upon the question, whether or not they had been redeemed. Reduction of expenditure had been indeed begun before the change of government. Under the Duke of Wellington's administration £2,000,000 of taxes had been repealed, and a corresponding retrenchment had been effected in the public expenditure. He and his friends had said when in opposition that economy ought to be pursued still further; and when they came into power they were fairly held accountable for the realization of the hopes they had thus held out; but, justice to themselves as well as to their predecessors, required that what had been done up to 1830 should be borne in mind. Manifestly what had been previously accomplished left less to be achieved, and diminished the means of achieving it. Notwithstanding what had been effected however, in the way of reduction, in the three years 1828, 1829, and 1830, quite as much and more had since been taken off the burthens of the people. Taxes amounting to a sum of £3,200,000 had since then been repealed; and the national expenditure had been proportionably reduced. This saving and relief had been effected by temperate and gradual reforms. They could only be temperate by being gradual, only effectual by being systematic; for unless they were systematic they could not be permanent; and if not permanent they could not possess that principle which was of vital importance, that of progressive decrease, by which the efficiency of the public service was main- 1834.

1834. tained; and without that, economic reform would be a curse rather than a blessing. This year they were prepared with a further saving of half a million. In this reduction the Admiralty bore its share. In his department the reductions in the estimates in the course of three years had been £1,200,000 and he had this year to propose a further reduction of £180,000, as compared with the estimates of the year preceding. This retrenchment had been effected chiefly in the dockyards, where the number of men employed had been brought at length within the limit of 6000, prescribed by the Duke of Wellington's administration. Another item of economy was in the price paid for provisions, to the extent of £42,000. He had likewise sought to effect a reduction of charges in the pay and support of seamen, by substituting for 500 men, 1000 boys: a measure which if successful would have the additional recommendation, that by early training these latter to the discipline of the service, and attracting them to it, an additional facility would be created for dispensing in time of war with the practice of impressment.

Mr Hume's objections.

Mr Hume found fault with Government for keeping up so large an establishment as 27,000 men, which he moved to reduce to 25,000, the number which had been deemed sufficient in 1823. He broadly accused the First Lord of abusing his patronage by promoting aristocratic youngsters over the heads of experienced and deserving officers, and said that Sir James had, since he had been in office, taken care of his Tory friends just as his predecessor had done with respect to the Whigs. 1834.

Sir James repelled warmly the imputation of having shown class preference in his distribution of patronage. He had fairly recognized the claims of men of merit, regardless of family or birth. But as to distinction of party, "he took it as a high compliment, though an unintentional one, that he had not prostituted the influence of which the office he held gave him the command."

The amendment was negatived by 196 to 20; and other attempts to cut down important items met a similar fate.

If in some particulars economy was practised by the New Board of Admiralty with a too unsparing hand, in others it was commended by the judgment of all disinterested observers. Mr Croker, the astute and expert ex-secretary of the department, watched with lynx-eyed vigilance every administrative change; and from time to time he was said to inspire those forebodings of the demolition of our naval ascendancy, which came from influential quarters in Parliament and in the press. But the public faith in the "old hands" was worn out; and the King, who had his own reasons for disliking and distrusting them, gave his personal support to Sir James. Upon the whole, his success was great; and during his administration of the navy, he fairly

1834. earned the character for official ability, which in all the changes and conflicts of after years none ever thought of questioning. He used himself to say, that he ascribed not a little of his success to the circumstance of his having been thrown into deep water at once, instead of having his blood chilled and his faculties benumbed by wading long through the shallows of subordinate office. A great responsibility was laid upon him, and he was able to bear it. New measures founded on new ideas were needed, and it was essential that they should be designed and executed with a breadth and freedom not easily obtainable amongst men secluded by official habit from communion and sympathy with the doubts, and hopes, and fears of society around them.

CHAPTER XIII.

BREAK UP OF THE GREY GOVERNMENT.

1834.

The first fruits of reform were in every way notable. The remodelled constituencies, full of good humour and gratitude, sent 450 members to Westminster pledged to support ministers. Every blockhead exclaimed, — what unprecedented strength! Every sagacious observer of the signs of the times thought within himself, what a source of division and weakness! Parliamentary government is indeed too finely-balanced a machine to be with impunity overdriven by the friendliest hands, and with the best intentions. A reliable majority in the House of Commons is on all hands admitted to be the first postulate of administrative power: yet we have seen governments carry great measures and bring the country through great difficulties with an indescribably small majority; and we have seen governments

1834. First fruits of Reform.

1834. contrive to exist without any majority at all. What we have never seen is, a government that could long endure the support of an unusually great majority. While the lassitude of recent victory lasts, associates in triumph may peacefully slumber together; and if the country happens to be weary of conflict, the murmurs of schism may not speedily interrupt their repose. But when the party battle has been fought in the fervent belief that great changes hang upon the issue, and when from the down-hill steep the victors look impatiently over a promised land, to be occupied and appropriated, the task is no easy or enviable one which devolves upon their leaders. They have never yet gone far under such circumstances before mutiny and desertion have begun to appear in their ranks; and they have seldom made a Sabbath day's journey, without beginning to dispute by the way.

The use to be made of Reform.

At the beginning of 1833, the members of the administration were assured by their flatterers, that having fairly won an unlimited lease of power, they had only henceforth to enjoy it. Certain pledges which they had given must indeed be redeemed; but they might take their own time, it was said, about the order and rate of redemption. The Tories had resisted the Reform Bill on the express ground, that if passed it would overthrow all equipoise of parties, and give the Whigs a permanent monopoly of power.

Lord Lyndhurst had said so * on the memorable night when the last stand was made against the measure in the Peers: and his exultant opponents were weak enough to construe literally what the great rhetorician had said. Not all of them; for already Sir J. Graham entertained an opposite belief, and began to warn such of his colleagues as would listen to him, that if they attempted suddenly to blow off the steam, they would blow the concern to pieces. He believed that the impetus which had been acquired was too great not to carry them yet a long way; and his whole anxiety was that by wise and watchful foresight they should vindicate their claim, and show their power to guide, and thus to govern opinion. We have already seen how energetically he laboured in his own department to prove his fidelity to the promises given of economy; and how cheerfully he flung overboard the resources of personal patronage and power. With a high sea of popular expectation running, he regarded such things as worse than lumber; and he sometimes looked aghast when he saw others clinging to and insisting upon keeping what they could of them, as the most valuable part of the ship's freight. When the Chancellor of the Exchequer was at length able to show a respectable surplus of income over expenditure, it was clear that the chief part of it had accrued through the savings 1834.

* Hansard, Debate in the Lords, May, 1832.

1834. of the First Lord: and it was not the fault of either if a like disposition to ecomony was not manifested in other departments. Lord Althorpe was indeed able to show that salaries had been abolished to the extent of £192,000. £57,000 had been likewise saved in diplomatic salaries. The income of the year 1833 was £46,853,000, and the expenditure £45,366,000: for the army, £7,006,496; for the navy, £4,505,000; for the ordnance, £1,634,817; and for the civil establishments, £2,138,953. Reductions were consequently made in taxation to the extent of upwards of one million sterling. The charter of the East India Company having expired, the trade with the East was thrown open; and Negro Slavery was finally abolished in our Colonial Possessions. Of both measures Sir James had been for years the earnest advocate; and their legislative realization he always regarded as among the best public acts in which he had the good fortune to participate.

Lord Grey's policy in Ireland.

Had the Government used the augmented power which the passing of the Reform Act gave them, to inaugurate a policy of justice and conciliation in Ireland, the deplorable condition to which things were tending there, might have been averted, and the ten years ensuing, instead of being consumed in an intermittent struggle for the repeal of the Union, might have been devoted to objects of political and social improvement. There were some members of the Cabinet well disposed to adopt such a course. They could not justify the adherence to a system which excluded every Irishman from posts of power in the imperial as well as the local administration. Two-thirds of the representatives of Ireland had from the first voted for Retrenchment and Reform; yet no Irish peer or Irish commoner had a seat in the Cabinet; while the offices of Viceroy, Chief Secretary, Under Secretary, and the Command of the Forces in Ireland were still monopolized by English Whigs. As little could Lord Lansdowne, Lord Melbourne, or Mr C. Grant, defend the perpetuation of sectàrian preference in every branch of the provincial executive. Every judge of law or equity in the supreme courts was a Protestant; with two exceptions, every assistant barrister; and without exception, every stipendiary magistrate; and nineteen out of every twenty persons holding the commission of the peace were of the favoured creed. More than one member of the Cabinet had in opposition voted for a redistribution of Church property, in the sense of equalizing the ecclesiastical condition of the different persuasions, or for the direct endowment of the Catholic clergy, in order to effect that object. Yet now that they were in office, no attempt was made to do either, and no expectation of the kind was even held forth. Throughout many counties, resistance was organized among the Catholic peasantry to the payment of tithes; and the ineffectual efforts made to enforce their collection by aid of the police and military

1833.

1833. added fuel to the flame of prædial disturbance and crime.

O'Connell-ism. O'Connell's mind oscillated between two aims, in themselves incompatible, but neither of which he could be induced to forego. As a Catholic he demanded religious equality: as an Irishman he desired the restoration of a domestic legislature. He was too impulsive and enthusiastic to relinquish either purpose, and he therefore failed in both. In 1831, and even later, there were many Protestants of intelligence and property, who remembered the days of the old local Parliament with pride, and the means whereby it had been made away with, not without emotions of bitterness and humiliation. They saw absenteeism and mendicancy increasing,—enterprise, literature, and art languishing. The promise of security, wealth, and peace held forth at the Union had not been realized. For this they knew that in some degree agrarian outrages were to blame; but these in their turn were, they believed, in a great measure referable to neglect and misrule. It is not easy to define with precision the depth of these sentiments, or to say how far a man gifted with O'Connell's marvellous power of suasion, might have turned them to account, had he refrained from embarking in the struggle against tithes. He was, indeed, not wholly unconscious of the effect such a movement was calculated to produce; and at first he had held aloof from the attack upon the Established

Church, which, left to himself, he would probably have postponed as a hindrance to the success of his favourite project. But in this he was opposed by the Catholic Bishop of Kildare and Leighlin, Dr Doyle, a man of singular sagacity, talent, and influence, who had contributed in no slight degree to the success of the movement for emancipation; and who, regarding Repeal as a phantom, sought to concentrate the popular mind upon the attainment of sectarian equality. In favour of this principle Dr Doyle knew that the Catholic party could command the sympathy and aid of a large section of English Liberals, some of whom were opposed altogether to the maintenance of an establishment; and some of whom, like Sir J. Graham, had avowed their conviction that a Protestant endowment could best be sustained by the creation of a Catholic endowment by its side. Mr O'Connell regarded with suspicion and distrust the idea of connecting by a pecuniary tie the priesthood with the State. He would have been willing, however, that a glebe and manse should be set apart for the parish priest; and if this were done out of the surplus revenues of the Anglican Establishment, so much the better.

1833.

Two-fold objects of O'Connell.

Lord Anglesea thought with Dr Doyle, that the surest antidote to Repeal would be the reduction of the Establishment to congregational limits; and he told the Cabinet that if they would save the Union they must sacrifice the Church. But no proposition

1833. of the kind would be entertained by Lord Grey. Creeds were indeed equal in his eyes; but the Establishment was sacred. Its bishoprics and benefices had, since the Revolution, been systematically used as an auxiliary means of providing for the younger branches of noble families, and for their creatures and dependents. The Tories had made this use of them; why should not the Whigs? The crozier of Derry had passed in due succession from the profligate clutch of Harvey * to the feeble grasp of Knox; † and Lord Grey now recklessly flung it, with its appendant purse of £12,000 a year, to the Honourable and Reverend Dr Ponsonby,‡ whose only claim consisted in being his brother-in-law.

Lord Grey's notion of an Establishment.

Meanwhile the personal sufferings of the parochial clergy, whom resistance to tithes had suddenly reduced from comfort and affluence to absolute want, the deep sense of individual wrong thus engendered, and the fierce passions, on the other hand, aroused when the mechanism of the law and military force were resorted to, rent asunder the frail ties by which the modern Rienzi strove to knit together opposing factions; and the war of creeds burst forth anew.

No prospect was held out of a change of sys-

* Afterwards Earl of Bristol.

† Brother of the Earl of Ranfurly.

‡ Brother of Viscount Ponsonby of Imokilly.

tem in Ireland consonant with the vaunted principles of Emancipation or Reform; and it became but too evident that without the renewal of organized agitation, these boasted measures would remain but a dead letter. It certainly was no part of Mr O'Connell's design that incendiarism and outrage should prevail; but his admonitions to observance of the law were unheeded by the peasantry, and ridiculed as insincere by the Government, who looked upon his political threats as more formidable than the worst excesses of obscure marauders and assassins. Mr Stanley, who had recently entered the Cabinet, undertook to crush both by the provisions of a single enactment; and the first measure of importance submitted to a reformed Parliament was the memorable Coercion Bill. The local executive was thereby empowered to suppress by proclamation any political meeting or society whatever which might be deemed injurious to the public good; and for the trial of offenders, courts-martial were substituted for the ordinary tribunals; the writ of Habeas Corpus was suspended, and the right of appeal to the verdict of a jury set aside. The Premier introduced the measure in the Lords, where it was adopted without a division. In the Commons it led to hot and harassing debate: a minority of eighty, which included Mr Abercrombie, Mr Grote, Mr J. Romilly,* Mr Bulwer,†

1833.

Coercion Act.

* The present Master of the Rolls.

† Now Sir Edward Lytton.

1833. Mr Roebuck, Mr Hume, and Mr C. Buller, contested line by line its more important provisions.

Irish Church Temporalities.

A bill was introduced by Lord Althorpe for diminishing the number of bishops, suppressing certain sinecures, and augmenting small livings, in Ireland. This did not touch the question as between different persuasions. But by its provisions a tax was imposed on all sees and benefices, in lieu of church rate (or cess), which was thenceforth abolished. All episcopal and chapter lands were vested in a Board of Ecclesiastical Commissioners; and the occupying tenants were empowered on certain conditions to convert their leases of twenty-one years into perpetuities. The increased value which the act would confer upon Church property, might, it was said, be fairly dealt with as belonging to the State; and by the 147th clause, it was declared that it should be lawful to appropriate any portion of such accruing increase to purposes of secular utility, without regard to the religious belief of those who should participate in the benefit. Mr F. Shaw moved the rejection

6th May. of the bill, on the second reading, upon various grounds, but especially because it infringed the inviolability of Church property, and established a principle which might one day lead to its total alienation. Sir R. Peel, Mr Estcourt, and Sir R. Inglis, took the same view; and many Whigs, who declined to vote with them then, declared that if the obnoxious provision were not expunged in Committee, they would do so on the third reading. Mr Stanley, Mr C. Grant, and others argued, that admitting it was not desirable that Church property should be diverted to purposes not ecclesiastical, the question was whether the property which the present bill would divert was Church property or not. It was from an Act of Parliament that the Church derived its power over leases, and that Act of Parliament enacted that it should not be lawful for any bishop to grant a lease for more than twenty-one years. The bill proposed to give the Church the power of granting leases in perpetuity, instead of confining them to twenty-one years, renewable at any period of that term. This would be a great advantage to the tenant, as it would enable him to sell his lease in perpetuity; and it was this property, which was neither the property of the Church nor of the tenant, which the Government were now preparing to deal with under this Act of Parliament. The Church would receive and the tenant would pay the same as now; and yet, though the advantage to the tenant was obvious, they were told that the tenant ought not to make any pecuniary remuneration for the pecuniary advantage which he would receive from this change in the existing law. It might as well be argued that when a copyhold tenant enfranchised himself from the lord of the manor, he ought to pay no fine for his enfranchisement. In the case of the Church of Ireland, the bishops were the lords of the manor, and the Church

1833. tenants were the copyholders; but as the bishops had no power beyond twenty-one years, it was only the State that could enfranchise the tenantry, and for that enfranchisement the State was entitled to demand a remuneration. Inasmuch as this was not either the property of the Church or the property of the tenant, and inasmuch as the State had the right to confer upon the tenant the perpetuity of his lease, there was nothing unjust in calling upon the tenant to pay for the advantage which he thus derived from the State.*

Withdrawal of the 147th Clause.

The Radical party contended that the measure did not go far enough, and that provision ought to be made for further reducing superfluous sees and benefices; but for the sake of the principle of appropriation to general uses of even a contingent surplus, Mr O'Connell and Mr Hume concurred in supporting the measure. Towards the end of the session it became known that, as originally framed, the Lords would certainly refuse their assent; and as ministers when proposing the Coercion Bill had pledged themselves to carry both measures or to resign, a question arose amongst them whether the appropriation clause had not better be withdrawn. After much discussion, they decided in favour of this course; and on the 21st June Mr Stanley moved in Committee that the 147th clause should be expunged.

* Hansard, Debate in Commons on Church Temporalities Bill, 6th May, 1833.

The scene which ensued is thus described by one who, having from the first regarded the proposition as objectionable, could not but perceive the damage ministers had done themselves, by first introducing and then abandoning it:—"No one who was present on that memorable occasion can forget the excitement which the discussion of this proposal caused. Reformers then, for the first time, discovered how wide a difference separated those who seemed to be united. I can remember that among the Scotch members, of whom I then was one, the feeling against the Church of Ireland was strong; and how surprised most of my colleagues were to find that any Scotch Reformer should venture to think that the Irish Church was even defensible. Political feeling ran high. Lord Althorpe escaped the discussion,—a happy fit of gout came, like the cloud on Æneas, to save him from the conflict. Mr Stanley conducted the debate on behalf of the Irish Church; and Mr O'Connell, fortified by a large support on the side of Reformers, spoke, unlike his usual oratory, a short condensed speech, which concentrated in half an hour eloquence worthy of Demosthenes, and rained flakes of fire upon the ministerial bench. I need not trace what followed; there was little doubt in the minds of most of us, that from that time the Cabinet as well as the party was split; and within the Cabinet, the most conspicuous leaders on the side of the Establishment were Sir J. Graham and

1833.

Scene as described by Mr Colquhoun.

1833. Mr Stanley. The final separation between the two sections of the Reform party is a matter of history."*

Vainly did those who belonged to the really dissentient sections of the Government seek to defend the position they had in common agreed to take up, by endeavouring to throw doubts on the probable extent of the surplus fund. Equally unavailing were their protestations that a collision between the two Houses would have been the result of adhering to the terms they had first recommended as the basis of legislation. "The country could not afford a revolution once a year,"† and many practical advantages would be sacrificed in the attempt to coerce the other branch of the legislature. But in point of fact no power to coerce any longer existed. Out of doors there was no popular feeling to which ministers could now appeal. In the new House of Commons they had lost influence perceptibly; and the Court would not a second time have listened to advice like that which it had been compelled to follow a year before. With the aid of a portion of the Conservatives, the bill with many alterations finally became law; but the consequences of its discussion were destined ere long to prove fatal to the existence of the administration.

Result of discussion. It was in the course of these debates that Sir

* Letter from Mr J. C. Colquhoun, then M. P. for Dumbartonshire.

† Speech of Lord J. Russell, 21st June, 1833.

James became convinced how untenable was the position of compromise on the question. He had not without misgiving assented to the offer to devote the new ecclesiastical fund to civil uses, accompanying his assent with the explicit declaration that nothing could have induced him to do so, if he imagined that he should thereby be held willing to secularize any portion of the acknowledged property of the Church. Other members of the Cabinet made the like reservations at the time; and when a contrary implication was put upon the language of the bill, they insisted in debate upon disclaiming it. But their disclaimers were equally disregarded by both sides. Tories and Radicals, who concurred in nothing else, agreed in this, that if Parliament once sanctioned the alienation of the improved value of Church lands to objects of general utility, because the Establishment had more than enough for its legitimate wants, it might fairly be called on to reconsider from time to time the actual amount of those requirements, and it would no longer be possible to contend for the indefeasibility of ecclesiastical revenues. Ministers had failed to vindicate the distinction with which they had satisfied themselves in the judgment of either the legislature or the country; and the bitter experience of the session of 1833 taught them the folly and futility of trying to find common terms of agreement on great and critical questions, when the meaning and aim of those 1833.

1834. who thus endeavoured to preserve concord were really irreconcileable. Whatever others might hereafter do, Sir James made up his mind never again to expose himself to the reproach, which in common with his colleagues he had incurred on this subject; and he made no secret of his resolution, whenever the appropriation question should again be revived, to take his stand upon the only ground that he saw was open to him as a public man, because the only ground that to the public would be intelligible or defensible,—that of direct and unconditional resistance. It did not become necessary to re-discuss the point in the Cabinet once the bill had passed. All were sick and weary of the subject, and all were willing to hope that some time would be suffered to elapse before it was forced again on their consideration. But no expectation could have been more illusory. The Anti-tithe war in Ireland did not abate in consesequence of the passing of the Temporalities Act. A million sterling was set apart under a special statute, to be advanced to the Protestant clergy by way of loan, to relieve their pressing needs. There appeared however no likelihood of their being able to recover the arrears outstanding, or to obtain their incomes in future; and at the commencement of 1834, Lord Wellesley, who had replaced Lord Anglesea as Viceroy, urged the necessity of making some legislative attempt to settle the tithe question. This it was clear would present an irresistible temptation for the re-opening of the appropriation controversy, but there seemed to be no help for it. 1834.

Popular discontent in Ireland had continued without abatement during the autumn and winter. The warfare carried on by the peasantry against the payment of tithes was accompanied with many outrages against life and property. A general sense of insecurity prevailed; and Government, unable to suppress crime or to conciliate the confidence of the community in general, cast the blame of all upon the agitation for the Repeal of the Union. In the King's speech at the opening of Parliament in February, 1834, regret and indignation was expressed at the continuance of such excitement, to which the prevalence of illegal and criminal practices was directly attributed. Nothing was said about the causes of social or sectarian discontent, out of which the demand for a separate legislature had sprung; but the King was advised to denounce from the throne all discussion of the question, as seditious and disloyal, and to point without disguise to its authors as enemies to the peace and welfare of the State. Had ministers been agreed among themselves upon a course of policy towards Ireland at once remedial and repressive, this initiatory invective which they put into the mouth of their master might have been less indefensible. But the majority they still supposed they could command in the Commons, and the success of their general measures during the pre- Want of a consistent policy.

1834. vious session, had rendered them careless as to Irish opinion and feeling; and at the commencement of the memorable session of 1834 they were, as soon appeared, without any consistent purpose or policy.

Views of the Marquis Wellesley.

Lord Wellesley, though certainly not wanting in dignity or courage, was all against high-handed reliance upon extra-constitutional law, or the employment of mere force. With the experience of a veteran he distrusted, and with the true pride of a statesman he despised, the transient submission that could be obtained by terror. He felt that the condition of things in Ireland was irreconcileable with any principle or theory of representative rule. Three-fourths of the people of that country were still practically banned, as unworthy of the honours or distinctions of citizenship, though clothed with electoral privileges, and invited to exercise them.* The Viceroy would have put an end to this injustice, and harnessed local ambition to the Imperial car. He would have dealt comprehensively with the question of endowments, for he had been trained in the school, and he still cherished the maxims, of Mr Pitt. But his counsel was left too long unheeded. Many of the Cabinet suffered their resentment against the vituperative language of Mr O'Connell and his friends, to warp their judgment as legislators and ministers; while others, who perhaps deplored the use of such terms even more deeply, saw no hopes of peace or progress

* Memoirs of the Marquis Wellesley, vol. iii. p. 406.

in Ireland, until a more conciliatory tone was taken 1834.
in Parliament in the discussion of her grievances, and until substantial changes were effected both in law and administration. To the latter view no man became more thoroughly a convert eventually than Sir James Graham; and, as will be seen, no man more cheerfully or continuously proved himself ready to make personal sacrifices in the cause of sectarian justice and national conciliation. But in 1834 the Established Church was in danger, and its clergy were reduced to sudden want by the popular refusal to pay tithes; and with him the spectacle of this subversion of public law and private right created a stronger feeling of aversion to the great Catholic demagogue, than he would perhaps have owned: and it swayed perceptibly his acts and words. As long as ministers held together in their course of legislation, the public could know little of the differences of sentiment that existed among them. But from the commencement of the luckless Session of 1834, the bonds of party cohesion seemed to be loosed, and before its close the Reform Administration, recently so triumphant and so powerful, had crumbled into ruin.

Case of Baron Smith.

The first occasion upon which a want of unanimity among the members of the Government betrayed itself, was Mr O'Connell's motion for a Committee to inquire into the conduct of Baron Smith, when presiding as a judge in criminal cases, and espe-

1834. cially with reference to a charge addressed by him to the grand jury of Dublin. The venerable Baron was one of the most upright and accomplished men upon the Bench. In early life he had been the advocate of Catholic claims, and his abilities and attainments were such, that Mr Burke had publicly addressed to him the arguments by which he hoped to influence the opinions of Protestant adversaries of Emancipation. In the Irish Parliament of 1799, he was one of the few independent men of probity and talent who supported the Union; and it is possible that some recollection of the bitterness of that memorable struggle, stimulated unconsciously the anger of his later years at finding the controversy revived. Be this as it may, the learned Baron was led, on more than one occasion, when addressing grand juries in disturbed districts of the country, in his capacity of going Judge of Assize, to comment on the nature of the criminal combinations against property which brought so many offenders before him for trial, and to pour forth the vials of judicial wrath on the leaders of the political agitation, which he believed to be at the root of the mischief. These charges attracted no little attention at the time. They were extolled as master-pieces by the alarmed friends of social order, and quoted in Parliament (on one occasion by Mr Secretary Stanley) in justification of extraordinary measures of coercion. The questionable practice of delivering quasi-political

harangues from the bench, threatened to become 1834.
habitual with the learned judge; and when presiding at the Commission in the city of Dublin for the trial of ordinary offenders, in October, 1833, he addressed the grand jury in terms more pointedly and pungently rebuking the political agitation of the day, than any he had previously used. "For the last two years," he said, "I have seldom lost an opportunity for making some monitory observations from the bench. When the critical and lawless situation of the country did not seem to be generally and fully understood, I sounded the tocsin and pointed out the ambuscade. Subsequent events deplorably proved that I had given no false alarm. The audacity of factious leaders increased from the seeming impunity which was allowed them; the progress of that sedition which they encouraged augmented in the same proportion, till on this state of things came at length the Coercion Bill, at once to arrest the mischief and consummate the proof of its existence and extent. * * * I consider the epidemic of our day to be a turbulent abuse of the right of petition, making it a channel for the conveyance, not of submissive prayer, but of refractory invective and insolent dictation. This abuse seeks to turn that which it so distorts (as was done about two centuries ago) into the means of demolition, and that which Shakspeare I think has called 'hurlyburly innovation.' An appetite for this latter seems the

Charge to Grand Jury of Dublin.

1834. main-spring of insurrectionary movement at the present time; while those who instigate it may be turning the restless impulse to purposes more regular and systematic, and more their own. * * * I abominate the misleader, while I pity the misled."

There was no mistaking who was aimed at here. Mr O'Connell took the accusation to himself, and called on the House of Commons to say whether language of this kind, unprovoked by any political case in the calendar before him, was justifiable in the judge. There was besides another and a different ground of complaint against Sir William Smith. Among other eccentricities, he was in the habit of sitting up during the greater portion of the night, and rising late in the day. In term he seldom entered Court until long after his brethren on the bench; and upon circuit he frequently did not begin business until past noon. A return had been moved for by Mr Sergeant Perrin in the preceding Session, from which it appeared that at the summer assizes of Armagh, Baron Smith had sat with brief intermission, from 11 o'clock of the forenoon of one day, until six o'clock the following morning; and that in the course of that time he had disposed of a considerable number of the gravest criminal cases, several prisoners not having been put upon their trial until after midnight. Nobody was found, in the warm and protracted debate which arose, to defend such an abuse of judicial discretion; yet nobody, on the other hand, insinuated a doubt as to the integrity and humanity of the judge. He was, in point of fact, well known for his patience during inquiry, and his leniency in pronouncing judgment. But he was a very old man, and he was wayward and vain. He piqued himself upon being able to keep his attention alive for seventeen hours without flagging, while witnesses grew stupid, and jurors dozed. It was not alleged that any of his midnight decisions were partial or wrong; but the scandal of the scene as described to the House was irresistible, and the Secretary for Ireland, Mr Lyttleton, declared it impossible for him to refuse his consent to the motion. Mr Stanley, Lord Althorpe, and Lord John Russell, expressed a similar view. Sir James Graham briefly but warmly dissented from his colleagues. He had come down to the House with the understanding that they meant to oppose the motion. He, for one, still retained his opinion, and had seen no reason to change it. As one who valued the independence of the judges, and his own character, he must declare that if the motion were carried, and if, as its result, an address were presented to the Crown for the removal of Baron Smith, it would be a highly inexpedient, nay more, a most unjust proceeding. The present would be the most painful vote he had ever given, since he felt it incumbent upon him to sever himself from those friends with whom, during a public life of some duration, he had had the honour

1834.

Sir James differs from his colleagues.

1834. of acting; but feeling as he did the proposition to be one dangerous in itself, he conceived he should be betraying the trust committed to him by his constituents, if he did not declare against it. Baron Smith was ably defended by Mr Shaw (whose speech was pronounced by Mr Sheil to be one of the most telling he had ever listened to), by Sir J. Scarlett, and Sir R. Peel. On a division the Committee of Inquiry was carried by 167 to 74; Sir J. Graham and Mr S. Rice voting in the minority. Next morning the First Lord tendered his resignation, which was declined; and in the following week the vote was rescinded by a majority of six.

Progress of schism. This beginning of ministerial schism gave rise naturally to many bitter comments, calculated, as such observations usually are, to widen the breach that otherwise might perchance have closed. The vote, and still more the speech, of the First Lord of the Admiralty was characterized as being not merely an open desertion of his colleagues, but an unnecessarily pointed condemnation of them. He might, it was said, have gone away, as others did, or have given a silent vote in the minority. But his protest was stigmatized as an ostentatious and self-opinionated act of independence, which would have warranted Lord Grey in treating him as he had treated Sir Henry Parnell under similar but less irritating circumstances. But the value of the two men to the Government was very different; and the

Premier was not disposed to quarrel with his First 1834.
Lord of the Admiralty. At heart he sympathized instinctively with the sarcastic retort of Sir James, that he was not aware of the rumoured intention of the Irish department of the Administration to come to a truce with Mr O'Connell; and that he could not be justly blamed if he had unknowingly seemed to thwart such a design on the part of those who had so often and so recently denounced the Irish leader, as the arch-enemy of order and of law. Taunts of this kind, however, did not affect those who, in and out of Parliament, were loudest in their censures; and when, three days later, in bringing forward the Navy Estimates, the dissentient minister volunteered a brief but emphatic acknowledgment of the economy effected by his predecessors in the department, which about equalled in amount what he had himself done, the anger of Mr Hume and Mr Cobbett broke forth in open imputations of tergiversation and Toryism. How well calculated these reproaches were to pique a sensitive and haughty temper, into doing or saying more than might have been otherwise said or done, those can best judge who have watched the operation of this species of annoyance in a popular assembly. It is certain that many a man has been driven faster and further than he meant to go, by provocation of the kind; and it is unfortunately certain that the efficiency of the irritant is too often in proportion to the wanton-

1834. ness with which it is applied. In the instance immediately before us, few will now hesitate to own that the attacks made were unjust,—in what degree, if any, they unconsciously swayed his judgment or his subsequent course, who can tell?

Debate on the Corn Laws.

Early in March the discussion raised by Mr Hume and Colonel Torrens on the question of the Corn Laws, further revealed the disunion prevailing among the members of the administration. The Chancellor, Lord Althorpe, and Lord Holland, had always advocated modifications more or less sweeping, of the protective scale of duties; while Mr Poulett Thomson, Lord Howick, and other holders of subordinate office, were in favour of substituting a fixed duty. The Premier, the Duke of Richmond, Lord Melbourne, and a decided majority of the Government, regarded the proposed change as chimerical; and knowing that for good or evil it could not then be carried in either House of Parliament, the Cabinet determined that the proposition should be met with a direct negative, and that the First Lord of the Admiralty should undertake the task of leading the ministerial resistance thereto: those members of the administration who were not of the Cabinet being left free to vote as they pleased. Any other course would undoubtedly have led to defeat, and probably to the disruption of the party. Not a fourth of the Lower House were then, nor for ten years after, prepared to vote for free-trade in corn; and in the Upper House, not 1834. half a dozen voices would have been raised in its favour. The proposition brought forward on the 6th March was ostensibly to get rid of the Sliding Scale, in order to substitute a ten shilling fixed duty. But Mr Hume avowed that he only meant this as a step towards complete freedom of importation; and that if the ten shilling duty were carried, he should then propose that it should be lessened every year one shilling, until it wholly ceased. Two distinct and incompatible projects of change were thus launched at the same time,—that of a moderate fixed duty, of which Mr Ricardo had been the early advocate, and of which Mr P. Thomson and Colonel Torrens were on this occasion the chief defenders; and that for unlimited competition with all the countries in the world in the production of human food—in support of which not one speech was uttered worthy of the cause at stake, or calculated to make proselytes to the great principle contended for. The discussion turned throughout on the practical question—is a fixed duty more likely than a sliding scale to steady the price of corn? The promise of "cheap bread" was on all hands repudiated as an imposture. Increased employment for the many, and enhanced profits for the few,—higher wages and larger exports,—were the true objects to aim at, not the mere depreciation of the value of agricultural produce, already ruinously low.

1834.

Speech of Colonel Torrens.

Colonel Torrens argued that, "If the abolition of all restrictions upon the importation of human food and raw materials for manufacture, should have the effect of greatly increasing the domestic market, and adding to the numbers of the manufacturing population, there would arise for agricultural produce a more extensive demand; and, on the other hand, if restrictions upon the importation of human food and raw materials had the effect, as they must certainly have, of diminishing profits, lowering wages, and driving our manufacturing and commercial capital to countries more wisely governed than our own, the agriculturists would lose the domestic market, the only one which they now enjoyed, and which they were seeking by unjust and impolitic means to monopolize. What, let him ask, would be the effect upon the rents of land if the manufacturing population of the country were doubled? What would be the effect of such a state of things upon the value and rent of land? What would be the increased rent of houses? What would be the increased rent of land for building, and of garden and pleasure grounds? What, again, would be the increased rent of meadow and pasture land? He believed that if the manufacturing population were thus increased, the rental of the kingdom would be thereby doubled. This would be the means of giving to the agriculturists a vastly increased value for their property, which they now sought to obtain by restriction and monopoly." 1834.

It was to the existing depression and distress in most of the corn-growing districts of the kingdom that Sir James appealed most effectively, in resisting the motion. "He admitted that the prohibitive scale of 1815 had worked ill, and that it had been right to abrogate it. But they had in 1828, by Mr Huskisson's advice, substituted a protective scale of more moderate duties, and they ought fairly to try how the experiment would work. If, in the long run, it failed to secure a reasonable steadiness of price, it could not be maintained. But if during the last five years wheat had been generally purchasable at a moderate cost, there was no sufficient cause for a total and immediate change. The interests of commerce were not suffering from depression; while those of agriculture were. The exports of the country had never been so large, while the profits on farming and the wages of rural labour had seldom been so small. At such a time it would seem to be a harsh and wanton act to abolish the inconsiderable duty which, at existing prices, was chargeable on foreign grain,—an amount of protection too small, he argued, perceptibly to weight manufacturing enterprise in the race with foreign competitors; yet an amount of protection which farmers everywhere regarded as the last remnant of that legislative guar- Speech of Sir James.

1834. antee upon which, after the war, they had entered into leasehold contracts for their land.

"What had been the average price of wheat during the last century? It had been 50*s*. From the restoration of the standard in the reign of William III. down to the year 1792, there was no quinquennial period in which it exceeded 49*s*. 11*d*. During the last six weeks, with a regulated duty, it had actually been 48*s*. 11*d*.—1*s*. less. That fact was conclusive of this point—that an exorbitant price of corn was at present impossible. A scarcity indeed might arise from the vicissitudes of seasons, under the existing law, and the price might be raised at home; yet, in that case, importation was not only not prohibited, but it was even favoured. But in years of average production it was his belief, judging from both theory and experience, that the price could seldom exceed 50*s*. per quarter. He was not disposed to weary the House by recapitulating the evidence taken before the Agricultural Committee of last year. Its tendency was to this effect,—that rent and all prices were rapidly accommodating themselves to the existing standard. The opinion expressed by the Committee was, that no sudden or hasty interference should take place; that much individual suffering indeed must occur, but that the general tendency of things was to settle down to a steadiness of price. Were it necessary to push these arguments further, he was in a condition

to extend them so as to prove, to incontestable 1834.
demonstration, the superiority of our present law as regarded steadiness of price to even a free importation of corn. He would compare our prices to those of Rotterdam; and he appealed to the hon. member for Essex to say whether he could take a fairer market for this purpose than that of Rotterdam, where there existed a perfect free trade in corn. In the five years to which he had just alluded, the variation in the English market being 49 per cent., the variation in that of Rotterdam was 91 per cent. He hoped then that, as a deliberative assembly, the House would pause and consider seriously before it deranged a matter of such importance; involving in that confusion which must attend all rash experiments, the price of agricultural produce."

And had he limited himself to the defensive and deprecatory line of argument here indicated, his speech would hardly have provoked the keenly-pointed and well-aimed reply of the Vice-president of the Board of Trade. But on this as on many other occasions, the rhetorician carried the statesman further than he would have gone, had he not had to make a speech about which there were great expectations. Government was in a difficulty. Their prestige had already been shaken, and their popularity, late so high, was perceptibly upon the wane. Here was a proposal that, if carried in the Commons, would have either driven them to resign

1834. without accomplishing any other immediate end, or have placed them in the humiliating position of having the direction of public policy taken out of their hands, by the reformed House of Commons they had so recently called into being.

Change of property.

"Mr Hume had asserted that his proposal would reduce rents 30 per cent. If it did so he spoke advisedly when he said that two-thirds of the landed property of England would at once change hands. It could not possibly be any benefit to the State that a great change of proprietors should thus suddenly and universally take place; it would be attended with great individual suffering — with much individual injustice. How far soever great evils might eventually attend such an extensive change, brought about under any circumstances, yet if it took place gradually, if an immense mass of land were not thrown at once into the market, those necessary evils would be greatly mitigated, and the suffering occasioned by such a gradual transmutation would be comparatively slight. But if the House were in one night to change the existing system of the Corn Laws, the injustice thereby produced would be immense, and the danger beyond calculation. However unjust such a change in the property of the country might be under any circumstances, it might be safe, if gradual and not sudden. But in the present instance the change would be at once dangerous and overwhelming. It would be equivalent to an agrarian law—it would be a complete change in the existing frame of society. These were the considerations which weighed with him principally in opposing the motion—considerations which could never be dissociated from such a measure as that now proposed. It was a measure that would not be beneficial to the community at large; for no measure could possibly be productive of general benefit which was calculated, like the present, to bring about a great change of property, to cause great individual misery, and to produce the total destruction of an entire class of the community. It would be no small evil that such a change should produce the destruction of any class of the community, and when such a class was the agricultural interest—the most important class of all—his solemn opinion was, that its destruction would be the destruction of the State itself." 1834.

Reply of Mr P. Thomson.

The debate having been adjourned to the following day, Mr Poulett Thomson, the Vice-president of the Board of Trade, undertook to answer the speech of the First Lord of the Admiralty, which he confessed was the ablest he had yet heard on that side of the question. It was an open question in the Government; and were it not so, he should not, as member for Manchester, be found occupying an official position therein. The law of 1815 had held out to the farmers a promise of 80*s*. a quarter, but so ill had that promise been kept, that when intro-

1834. ducing the bill of 1827, Mr Canning assured them that instead of fluctuating from 28*s*. to 112*s*., the variations of price would thenceforth be circumscribed within the narrower limits of from 55*s*. to 65*s*. How had that hope been realized? On the 25th January, 1831, the price of wheat was 75*s*. 11*d*., and at the time he was speaking, it had gone down to 48*s*. and a fraction. The farmers, therefore, who had been induced to take leases on the faith of legislative promises, had most cause to complain of the existing laws. He had no belief in cheap bread. He believed that reducing existing duties on imports would not materially reduce the price of corn. What was really to be anticipated from such a change was the steadying of prices. There would be a more regular and various demand for labour; and in that way the working classes would substantially gain. The practical controversy was not between some duty and none, but between a fixed and a fluctuating duty, with a view to the steadying of prices. Mr Huskisson had been quoted by Sir J. Graham against a free importation of wheat; but his latest opinion in 1830 had been decidedly the other way. Mr P. Thomson would reply to the argument of Mr Huskisson against total repeal by reading a few passages from a work entitled "Free Trade in Corn; the Real Interest of the Landlord, and the True Policy of the State: by a Cumberland Landowner."

"To propose to enrich a nation by enforcing a permanent scarcity of corn, and by obstructing the natural course of trade, is, indeed, at variance with common sense. The consequences cannot be mistaken; the embarrassment of our shipping, mercantile, and manufacturing interests; want of employment, and desperate poverty among the labouring population; an increase of crime, and a tendency to emigration; a loss of our currency, and a fall of the prices of labour and of corn; a diminution of the public revenue, and a derangement of the public finances; and, more than all, the certain eventual ruin of the agricultural interest itself;—these are the bitter fruits of a blind and selfish policy, rapaciously grasping at undue gain, and losing hold of advantages placed within its power." 1834.

In another passage the writer contrasted the state of Poland with that of England in these terms:—

"When England, the land of marine affairs and of commerce, and the best workshop of manufactures in the world, attempted to sell corn in opposition to Poland, a country in want of these advantages, she perverted the natural order of trade; she sold that which it was most profitable for her to buy; and, destroying the means of her natural customers to buy what it was most profitable for her to sell, she artificially lowered the prices of every description of merchandise throughout the long period of sixty-four years. So much for the crusade against the natural order of commerce. No sooner, however, was a sound system of trade in corn adopted, and large importations made, than the medium price of middling corn again rose most rapidly. As a proof how remarkably the freedom of the corn trade had a happy re-action on the

1834. general commerce and manufactures of the kingdom, Dr Adam Smith had observed, 'that the Yorkshire manufacture declined, and its produce did not rise to what it had been in 1755 till 1766.'"

But the author of the pamphlet did not stop here; he was not satisfied with Dr Adam Smith's observations, and he proceeded to say,—

"So far Dr Smith simply notices the fact, but he appears to have overlooked the cause. He points out the revival of our trade, and fixes the date of this amendment; but he has failed to recognize its precise coincidence with the change in our Corn Laws, and with the commencement of the free importation of foreign grain into this country. Till 1815 the corn trade was free, and commerce prospered. In that ill-fated year the prohibitory system became operative; and as in 1766 trade and manufactures revived precisely at the moment when the restrictions on the import of foreign corn were removed, so, in 1815, when these restrictions were again imposed, commerce languished, manufactures failed, and universal distress overspread the land."

Before he laid down the pamphlet, he would say it contained the most satisfactory answer, both to the quotation from Mr Huskisson's letter, and to the speech delivered last night by his right hon. friend.*

Cumberland Landowner. A scornful and exultant cheer followed the reading of these passages. More than once the supposed self-confutation of the First Lord, by the Cumberland landowner, was referred to by subsequent speakers in

* Hansard, March 7th, 1834.

debate; and many a small paragraph-writer clutched at the topic to turn a spiteful sentence by recurring to the capital show-up of his "manifest inconsistency." Sir James maintained a sardonic if not imperturbable demeanour throughout, content with having given forcible expression to the resolution of his colleagues in the Cabinet, and to the feeling of a great majority of the House. He was not insensible to the attack made upon him without reproof, by an official subordinate; and he could not be indifferent to the depreciating effect upon him personally it was calculated to produce. The absence on his part of all attempt to turn the edge of obloquy, or to mitigate the force of the charge of tergiversation, furnished to every thoughtless listener conclusive proof that he had nothing to say by way of rejoinder, from which, though precluded for the moment by the orders of the House, he could not have been debarred on a formal question of adjournment, or by the lips of some of his friends on the Treasury Bench, had he been inclined to explain or deny the applicability of the passages cited against him. And yet, strange to say, it was in his power to put aside the entire of Mr P. Thomson's imputation, by the utterance of half a dozen simple words. In point of fact, the crushing passages were not written by him, nor was he in any way responsible for the publication whence they were taken. It was the production of his friend, Mr 1834.

1834. Rooke of Akehead; and it contained sentiments on various points differing from, if not irreconcilable with, those in "Corn and Currency." But it did so happen that the manuscript had been brought by Sir James, at his friend's request, to Mr Ridgway, in 1828, and that he had interested himself in various ways regarding it. These latter facts only being known, and the pamphlet having been published anonymously, the world of political gossip made up its astute mind that the author could be no other than the laird of Netherby. Passing words of disclaimer in private went for nought at the time; and when he suffered the paragraphs above given to be cited triumphantly against him in the House of Commons, nobody could entertain any doubt on the matter. Four years afterwards, when personal interest in the subject had passed away, Mr Rooke published a work on geology, in the title-page of which is the avowal of his authorship of "Free Trade in Corn; the Real Interest of the Landlord, and the True Policy of the State, by a Cumberland Landowner:" and then, but not till then, did Sir James incidentally deny that he was the writer.

The motion negatived. Lord Althorpe informed the House that he would meet the motion with a direct negative, although his opinions were favourable to an alteration of the existing system. But such a change might be accompanied by other measures, of which nothing at present had been said. The question was not merely a theoretical one, and he did not see that there was any present exigency which demanded an immediate change; nor any near prospect of such an exigency; while, on the other hand, it was well known that great distress existed among the agricultural portion of the population, and that distress would certainly be aggravated by any such measure as that now proposed, if it were only by the great alarm which it would occasion. Though friendly therefore to the principle of a fixed duty, he must oppose the suggestion of Colonel Torrens, and still more that of Mr Hume. Every member of the Cabinet concurred in the propriety of this course. There were certainly some members of the Government whose opinions on the subject were so well known, that it was felt impossible to ask them to vote against the motion; but they would vote as individual members of that House, and not as members of the Government. The motion was negatived by a majority of 312 to 155. 1834.

Exchequer Office Bill.

Having been one of the commission appointed to inquire into the duties and emoluments of the Exchequer Office, Sir James was entrusted with the task of introducing a bill for its reform, founded on the Commissioners' report. The offices of Auditor, of Clerk of the Pells, of the four Tellers, with many subordinate clerkships, were swept away, and in their stead, the posts of comptroller, deputy comptroller, and chief clerk, with a much more limited staff, were substituted: the cost of the old establish-

1834. ment was £41,000, that of the new one £11,000 a year. The antiquated mode of reckoning by tallies, the practice of keeping the books in Norman Latin, and the whole cumbrous and complicated system of forms which had had their origin in mediæval times, were got rid of by the bill; and a simpler and more effectual machinery of account and control was provided. Care was taken to preserve the independent tenure of office on the part of the Comptroller of the Exchequer, in order that he might exercise an efficient check upon illegality or oversight in the issue of warrants by the Treasury. General approbation was expressed of the changes made by the plan; and the resolutions on which the bill was founded passed through committee without objection.
12th May. When the bill itself was brought in, Sir James explained that the measure had grown out of the report of a committee, of which Mr Bankes was chairman. The report recommended the abolition of all those sinecures, or the immediate modification of them, by which political service had formerly been rewarded. In consideration of that sacrifice on the part of the Crown, by which it was deprived of the means of rewarding persons who might have rendered efficient services, the report recommended that superannuations should under certain circumstances be granted. A number of offices were suppressed, such as those enumerated in the present measure, the emoluments of which amounted to

£100,000. In lieu of these means of rewarding 1834.
persons who might have rendered services to the State, the House recommended that pensions to the amount of £42,000 a year should be placed at the disposal of Government. By that measure, then, £58,000 a year was saved. Out of the pensions, the predecessors of the present Government only granted in pensions £16,000 a year, although entitled to grant £42,000. A reduction of the pensions from £3000 to £2000 was proposed in the bill before the House; and in his opinion the relative value of money now, compared with 1817, fully justified such a reduction. With respect to the principle of rewarding persons for public services, without reference to their personal circumstances, he (Sir J. Graham) thought it absolutely necessary to invest the Crown with such a power. As to the length of service which entitled any person to receive a pension, he thought the House would agree with him that a pension ought to be bestowed after two years' service. Suppose a young man, after passing through his collegiate course with honours and academic distinction, when just about entering upon professional pursuits, accepted a situation under Government. By devoting two years to the service of his country he injured his professional prospects just as effectually as if he retained the situation for five years, and in common justice he should be entitled to a pension. He would illustrate

1834. the proposition by a reference to the case of Mr Perceval. Would it be said that, when he left the King's Bench, and gave his services to the Government of his country, he did not by retaining his situation for two years blight his professional prospects as completely as though he had remained in office for five years? Upon these considerations he (Sir J. Graham) was disposed to adhere to the clause as it stood in the bill. The committee divided on an amendment adverse to the principle of the measure, which was negatived by a majority of 63.* And here ends the series of those economic reforms with which his name had hitherto been identified. The current of events was already hurrying the administration towards its fall; and his brief but useful statement regarding the reconstruction of the Exchequer Office was the last made by him as a colleague of Lord Grey.

Differences on appropriation question.

The bill prepared by Lord Wellesley for the conversion of Irish tithes into a permanent rent charge of four-fifths of their amount, had been introduced before Easter; and although objected to in certain particulars by some friends of the Church, and by not a few of her enemies for opposite reasons, it seemed likely on the whole to secure the sanction of the legislature. Before the House went into Committee, however, Mr Sheil, reverting to what had occurred in the preceding session, asked Lord

* Hansard, Debate in Commons, 12th May, 1834.

John Russell, in terms too pointed to be mistaken, whether ministers were finally agreed upon any definite line of policy with regard to the Irish Church, and whether the pledge of conciliation recently given by the Government, when resisting Mr O'Connell's motion for a committee to inquire into the expediency of dissolving the Union, was in sectarian matters, about to be redeemed. Was nothing contemplated beyond the conversion of tithe into rent charge? Or was the inequality of creeds in regard to ecclesiastical endowment to be suffered to continue? 1834.

Declaration of Lord John Russell.

The Paymaster of the Forces replied that while he could not undertake to state what measures might be in contemplation hereafter by the Government, he felt it due to himself to declare that the opinion he had formerly expressed on the subject of the Establishment in Ireland had undergone no change. The present was a bill to secure a certain amount of property and revenue destined by the State to religious and charitable purposes; and if the State should find that it was not appropriated justly to the purposes of religious and moral instruction, it would then be the duty of Parliament to consider of a different appropriation. His opinion upon that subject was that the revenues of the Church of Ireland were larger than necessary for the religious and moral instruction of the persons belonging to that communion, and for the stability of the Church itself. The more he had seen and reflected since, the more had that opinion been confirmed. He did not think it would be advisable or wise to mix the question of appropriation with that of the amount of the revenues; but when Parliament had vindicated property in tithes, he should

1834. then be prepared to assert his opinion with regard to their appropriation; and if, when the revenue was once secured, the assertion of that opinion should lead him to differ and separate from those with whom he was united by political connection, and for whom he entertained the deepest private affection, he should feel much regret: yet considering himself pledged, not only by his general duty as a member of that House, but by the resolution which had been passed to attend to the just complaints of the people of Ireland, while at the same time maintaining his opposition to all projects for the repeal of the Union, he should, at whatever cost and sacrifice, do what he should consider his bounden duty, namely, do justice to Ireland.*

It was upon hearing these expressions, that Mr Stanley is said to have observed to one who sat beside him, "Johnny has upset the coach;" and it was not without cause that Mr Sheil, when looking back to the proceedings of the evening in question, "took credit to himself for having sown the seeds of salutary discord;" for from the answer to his interrogatory undoubtedly sprung the severance that soon afterwards followed.

Mr Ward's Resolution. Mr H. G. Ward, a few days afterwards, gave notice of his intention to move as a substantive resolution, "That the Protestant Episcopal Establishment in Ireland exceeds the spiritual wants of the Protestant population; and that it being the right of the State to regulate the distribution of Church property, in such manner as Parliament may deter-

* Hansard, Debate in Commons, 6th May, 1834.

mine, it is the opinion of this House that the temporal possessions of the Church of Ireland, as now established by law, ought to be reduced." 1834.

When next the Cabinet met, it became necessary to decide how Mr Ward's motion was to be dealt with. The previous question would as an amendment be the least irritating to the Radical section of their supporters, and would leave most freedom of opinion to those whom it was desirable to induce to concur in supporting it. But it obviously implied that the Government was not prepared to negative the principle of parliamentary control over the property of the Church, or the declaration that the Establishment might with propriety and advantage be reduced within smaller dimensions. To get rid of the question for the present session, certain members of the Cabinet were willing, indeed, to adopt this alternative, without caring to anticipate too nicely its logical or legislative consequences. But Sir J. Graham declared that the time had come when it was right to ask, and indispensable to know, whither they were legislatively bound?

Secession of Sir James Graham and Mr Stanley.

A wide difference of sentiment regarding the maintenance of the Anglican Church in Ireland had always existed amongst the members of the administration. One of the first speeches by which Mr Stanley had distinguished himself in debate, was made in resisting a proposal of Mr Hume's, that the revenues of the Irish Establishment should be re-

1834. duced: but for that very motion Lord J. Russell had voted. On many occasions Sir James Graham had declared his resolution to defend to the uttermost the inviolability of what he deemed a fundamental institution of the empire; and the Duke of Richmond and Lord Ripon agreed with him. Lord Althorpe, Lord Brougham, and other members of the Cabinet were supposed to entertain different opinions; but until the discussion of the Appropriation Clause in the House of Commons publicly arrayed these opposite views in contrast, the question did not become a practical difficulty in council. As the day fixed for Mr Ward's motion drew near, it became generally known that a majority of the Liberal party were inclined to support it. The Cabinet had to consider what was to be done. If met by a direct negative, the resolution of the member for Sheffield could only be defeated by the aid of the Conservative Opposition. It was certain likewise to cause the defection of several of the most valued members of Government, who felt too strongly on the subject to hold their offices at the price of their opinions. Lord Althorpe declared that he could not undertake to advise such a course. His own feelings and those of a majority of the Cabinet were in favour of the principle involved in Mr Ward's resolution. The dissentients eventually proved to be but four; and finding themselves so far outnumbered, they intimated to Lord Grey their intention to resign. Long and earnest were the expostulations used to dissuade them from their purpose, and many the suggestions made to obviate the necessity. That which seemed at first the most likely to defer the threatened breach, if not to prevent its occurrence, was the proposal of a commission to inquire into the actual number of persons belonging to each religious denomination in the various parishes of Ireland, in order that evidence might be thereby accurately obtained as to whether the Establishment really exceeded the wants of its members; and Lord Ripon was disposed to acquiesce in that course. But Sir J. Graham clearly saw, that if they remained in the Government, and agreed to the issue of such a commission, they would in good faith be precluded from subsequently objecting to its report as a basis for legislation. It was not, however, until the afternoon of Tuesday, the 27th of April, that he and Mr Stanley finally resolved to place their resignations in the hands of the Premier; and Mr Ward had risen to address the House in support of his motion before Lord Althorpe became aware of their having actually resigned. As soon as the seconder, Mr Grote, had concluded, he rose and stated that circumstances had just come to his knowledge which compelled him to ask for an immediate adjournment of the House until the Monday following, No explanation was offered or required, Lord Althorpe pledging his character that a course so unusual would not have been recommended by him if it had not been unavoidable. The

1834.

1834. crowded House broke up amid a scene of extraordinary excitement; and the morning papers of the following day revealed the cause.

Address of the Irish clergy to the King.

It was the King's birthday, and the Primate of Ireland, accompanied by several of the suffragan bishops and other dignitaries of the Church, waited upon his Majesty to present an address signed by 1400 ministers of the Establishment, praying that he would, as its temporal head, defend it against dangerous and hostile innovations. The King replied, with unrestrained emotion, that he was mindful of the solemn obligations he owed to the Church established by law in England and Ireland, as a man ought to be who was in his sixty-ninth year, and that he was resolved to act in such a manner as that he might quit the world with a clear conscience.

Further resignations.

On the following day the Earl of Ripon, who had shared unreservedly the confidence of Sir James throughout all the recent deliberations, resigned the Privy Seal. The Duke of Richmond happened to be then at Paris, and upon his return, he told Lord J. Russell that he was sorry he had been absent when the final breach occurred, as he thought it possible that he might have been able to avert it. But having throughout their differences advised and acted with those who had gone out, he felt he could not hesitate to do as they had done. On what grounds his Grace imagined that he should have been able to prevent the schism which was in truth the natural 1834. and inevitable result of fundamental differences of opinion long entertained, but which circumstances had not till then shown to be irreconcilable, we know not. The Duke had always been looked upon, previous to 1830, as strongly Conservative. He had voted against the repeal of the Test Act, and the Catholic Relief Bill; and upon questions of commercial protection he had been the steady opponent of all relaxation. Like many of the class to which he belonged, he viewed with anger and disgust the sudden renunciation of their old opinions by the Duke of Wellington and Sir R. Peel; and, believing that had the House of Commons been a more faithful representation of national sentiment, the changes he deprecated could not have been brought about, he reverted to the principles professed by his father in the early days of Mr Pitt, and told Lord Grey that in future he meant to vote for Reform. Hence his nomination to the office of Post-master-General by the Whig Premier, an office which he accepted only upon the understanding that nothing hostile to the Church or the landed interest was in contemplation. The promise he had received had hitherto been rigorously kept; for the Duke did not object to the bill for the removal of Jewish disabilities carried by ministers through the Commons, or to that for the admission of Dissenters to share the

Opinions of the Duke of Richmond.

1834. honours of the Universities which had their support. He concurred readily in the measure of abolishing church rates in Ireland, and diminishing the number of bishoprics there: nor did the first form in which the question of appropriation was raised, namely, with regard to a contingent improved value to be given to ecclesiastical property, give birth to any conscientious scruple in his mind. He demurred, indeed, to the admission of that principle, when subsequently it was sought to be applied generally to the revenues of the Irish Church; but he took less note than others were accustomed to do of the fluctuations of opinion among the masses of the community, and looked on unmoved at the signs of a general hostility to the whole system of establishments, with which the time was rife.

Connection of Church and State.

In all parts of the United Kingdom, and in every class of society, questions more or less directly involving the fundamental one of the connection between Church and State had begun to be eagerly discussed, as for generations they had not been before. The difficulty which appeared insuperable in the way of obtaining a removal of practical grievances, like those relating to Dissenters' marriages and their admission to the Universities, stimulated the zeal of those who wished to raise in all its entirety the question of a Church establishment. In Ireland the assaults upon the Church might be said to have originated in social and political feelings, rather than in speculative convictions or religious scruples. Catholicism was not averse from endowment, and the Catholic leaders had only adopted the theory of Voluntaryism in despair of attaining sectarian equality on any other terms. But in England and Scotland the case was very different. Vast numbers of the wealthy and educated community had been taught from infancy to look upon the Church with jealousy and aversion, not merely on political, but on theological grounds. Their strength lay mainly amongst those classes in the towns on whom great additional power had been lately conferred by the creation of the £10 franchise; and it would have been strange if in its first enjoyment they had not sought to exercise it in a manner consonant with those convictions, to which hitherto they had had no means of giving political effect. Petitions couched in every form of expostulation, argument, entreaty, and warning were presented by the representatives of the remodelled constituencies during the sessions of 1833 and 1834, praying for various modifications of the existing laws regarding non-conformity, but all of them pointing in the same direction,—an abatement of the power and a diminution of the privileges of the Established Church. Many petitions specifically called for a separation of Church and State. A minority of 64, in which the City, Southwark, Birmingham, Sheffield, Bath, Middlesex, Liverpool, Oldham, Carlisle, Gateshead, North and South Dur- 1834.

1834. ham, Tavistock,* and Bridport, were represented, supported a motion to "relieve the bishops from their attendance in the House of Lords."

Anti-religious opposition to the Church.

Sir James attached less importance to proposals of this kind than to the proofs which began to multiply of an active and versatile spirit of antagonism to all ecclesiastical institutions, not merely because they were old or exclusive, but because they fostered the inculcation of religious belief, which was pronounced to be synonymous with obsolete superstition. The views of the earnest and devout Dissenters were as unlike as possible those of the sceptics and materialists of the day; they bivouacked together in committee-rooms and at hustings, and many a layman as well as bishop of the Church suffered himself to be persuaded that their aims and purposes were indistinguishable. Religion itself was said to be menaced, when the temporal pre-eminence of the Church was attacked; and Conservatism, on the very morrow of that great parliamentary discomfiture which its chiefs had pronounced to be irremediable, began to recruit its ranks at the sound of the church bell, and ceased not until it had enlisted under its banners many of those, who in the hey-day of Reform had called themselves Whigs and something more.

* Represented at the time by Lord Russell, now Duke of Bedford.

Lord Grey's first impulse on finding himself abandoned by four of the colleagues in whom he had placed his chief reliance, was to tender their resignations with his own to the King. His pride however was easily piqued by the suggestion that the world would say he was unable to maintain his position when forsaken by men, three of whom, as he said, he had made Cabinet Ministers; and in compliance therefore with the wish of his colleagues and a large number of the members of the House of Commons, he was induced somewhat longer to remain at the head of affairs.* The Cabinet re-assembled, resolved that the vacant offices should forthwith be filled up, and that a draft of the contemplated Commission of Public Instruction should, without delay, be submitted to the King. William IV., who was highly incensed at the attacks recently made on the Church, upbraided Lord Grey in no measured terms for entertaining such a proposition; and he could only be persuaded to sanction the Commission upon the assurance that its inquiries should be conducted *boná fide*, and that no foregone conclusion had been formed as to their result. He made no difficulty, however, about the new appointments. Lord Carlisle became Privy Seal; Mr Spring Rice was made Colonial Secretary; the Marquis of Conyngham became Post-Master-General; and Lord Auckland was transferred

1834.

The vacant offices filled up.

* Speech of Earl Grey, 9th July, 1834.

1834. to the Admiralty as the successor of Sir James Graham.

When the House again met on the 2nd June, the ex-Ministers took their seats on the second bench below the gangway, and several of those who were understood to share their sentiments occupied places near them. Appeals were made to the member for Sheffield to withdraw his motion, and to await the report of the Commission of Inquiry, to which it was announced that the Great Seal had already been affixed. Upon his refusal the debate proceeded. Ministers spoke in terms of deep regret of the severance from their late colleagues, to whose services and talents they paid the warmest tribute of respect. They professed themselves unshaken in their resolution to maintain the stability of the Church, but reasserted the right of Parliament to deal with any superfluity that might be found in its revenues. Mr Stanley on behalf of himself and his friends replied, "that it was impossible to have quitted without the deepest regret, colleagues with whom he had acted in one uniform spirit of kindly feeling,—colleagues among whom, during the whole time that they had sat together in the Cabinet, there had never been heard an angry word or an unpleasant expression towards one another,—colleagues with whom on all great principles connected with domestic and foreign policy it had been equally a pleasure to act and a duty to co-operate. Deeply did he regret when he could no

Cause of resignation stated by Mr Stanley.

longer conceal from himself, that the time was come 1834. which left no alternative for an honest and honourable man, when a difference of no personal nature, mixed with no feeling of unkindness, or want of affectionate regard, but an important and vital difference in principle, compelled the separation of a Cabinet who entertained for each other feelings of political attachment and of private friendship; and whose private friendship he would say with confidence had not been broken in upon by their present political difference. The nature and extent of that difference, however, could not be disguised. If the principle of numerical proportion between the inhabitants of each parish who belonged to the Church and those who dissented therefrom, were to be substituted for universal parochial endowment, there was an end to its pre-eminence and supremacy as an Establishment. The new principle once sanctioned by statute, means would not be wanting to hasten its practical application; and if once applied to Ireland, none could tell how soon an attempt might be made to apply it to England also. He would tell the House boldly and distinctly that the people of England were not ripe for that. He would call upon them to pause before they assented to a resolution which they could not, which they ought not, which the people of England would not let them, carry into effect. He had not thought that he should have ever lived to hear a minister of the Crown propose such a reso-

1834. lution; he did not think that he saw the Legislature that would pass it; and he was not certain that he knew the Sovereign who would assent to it." Sir James did not speak; the debate closed; and Mr Ward was left in a minority of 120 against 390.

Retirement of Earl Grey.

Scarce a month elapsed before new differences arose in the Cabinet, leading to further resignations, and ending in the final abandonment of office by Earl Grey. The Coercion Bill for Ireland had been passed for one year only, and a bill for its continuance with some modifications was introduced in the House of Lords about the middle of June. A majority of the Irish members, and a numerous section of English and Scotch Liberals, required the further omission of the clauses enabling the Lord-Lieutenant to suppress public meetings by proclamation. Lord Wellesley himself considered them unnecessary, and on the 18th May, wrote to the Premier, "that he would undertake to govern the country without them." Lord Grey expressed in reply an opposite view, and urged the Viceroy to reconsider the matter, without regard to what might be the effect upon the position of the Government or the state of parliamentary parties. Lord Wellesley confidently reiterated his opinion; and in the Cabinet Lord Althorpe, Mr C. Grant, Mr Spring Rice, Mr Ellice, and Mr Abercromby, were in favour of acting on his advice. Their opinion, however, was over-ruled, and they agreed to support the bill as it stood. By an act of indiscretion on the part of Mr Littleton, the fact of the division of opinion became known to Mr O'Connell, whose reproaches in debate were felt by Lord Althorpe to be intolerable. He had originally consented to these extra-constitutional provisions with regret, and only from a belief of their necessity. That necessity was now denied by the Lord-Lieutenant and Chief Secretary for Ireland, and disbelieved in, not only by a majority of his own Cabinet colleagues in the Commons, but by Lord Brougham and Lord Duncannon, the latter of whom possessed, perhaps, the greatest amount of personal knowledge and judgment in Irish affairs of any member of the Whig party. It was not without many doubts and misgivings, as he afterwards avowed, that the Chancellor of the Exchequer had made up his mind to surrender his individual opinion, and once more to propose the obnoxious clauses for re-enactment. But beneath the withering invective of Mr O'Connell, whom he knew to be aware of his real opinion, his mind became troubled, and his anxiety to keep the ministry together yielded to his fear lest he should compromise his own political honour. On quitting the House after a long and harassing discussion, on the 7th July, he wrote to Lord Grey, declaring that his position had become no longer tenable. Next morning a conference took place, which terminated in the Premier transmitting to the King Lord Althorpe's resignation and his own. It was upon

1834. An end of the Whigs. learning this event that Sir James exclaimed,—"Then there is an end of the Whigs," an expression which gave great offence at the time, probably on account rather of the tone in which it was uttered than of any meaning with which it could be fairly charged. It was in fact no more than a strange misreading of events. Shattered as the Government was by the loss of so many of the distinguished men who originally composed it, a considerable majority of the House of Commons still preferred it to any other that could be framed.

Lord Grey's resolution had been finally taken. His pride of power and place had been gratified above his utmost expectations. He had had his fill of triumph over the Court and the political party who once believed him banished for life from power. He had seen his early dream of Reform realized; peace with all the world had been maintained; the pledge of retrenchment had been substantially redeemed, and he had been told, by himself and others, until he thoroughly believed it, that but for him none of these things could have been done. Disquieted by the symptoms of mutiny that had early shown themselves in the ministerial ranks of the new Parliament, he had talked of retiring at the close of the preceding session; and now that the spell of his leadership was palpably broken, why should he any longer remain? One of the favourite illusions of his life had been that he was not fit for political pursuits, and that he was not fond of them. The asseveration was habitually on his lips, that nothing but a sense of public duty could overcome his repugnance to the labours of ambition. Even in the days of his mental and physical prime, he was apparently under the impression that he had no appetite for distinction, and no lust of power: and now that these had been satiated, and advancing years had begun to render the toils of public life really irksome, he reverted instinctively to his imaginary indisposition to office, and salved therewith his chagrin at finding himself after all allowed to retire from his own Cabinet alone. His last ministerial act bespoke most characteristically the ruling passion of his life. When William IV. inquired whom he would recommend as his successor, he did not hesitate. The same feeling that in 1808 impelled him, on quitting the Commons, to impose upon his party his relative, Mr George Ponsonby, as leader, now prompted him, as he could no longer govern himself, to hand over the reins to another connection of the family: he therefore named Lord Melbourne as the fittest person to be Premier. The Home Office thus vacated was filled by the appointment of Lord Duncannon; and Lord Althorpe, relieved from his unwelcome obligation as to the Coercion Bill, consented to resume his former position. By many at the time, as well as by the subject of these memoirs, the ministry so recon-

1834.

1834. structed was regarded only as one of transition. The Court was fully impressed with this idea, and was taught to believe that the Conservative reaction which had undoubtedly set in, had made more rapid progress than in the nature of things it was reasonable to expect it should have done.

END OF VOL. I.

CPSIA information can be obtained
at www.ICGtesting.com
Printed in the USA
LVHW110758120522
718525LV00003B/17

9 783375 002350